PENGUIN BOOKS

My Husband the Stranger

Rebecca Done is a copywriter and lives near Norwich. Her debut novel, *This Secret We're Keeping*, was published in 2016. *My Husband the Stranger* is her second novel.

My Husband the Stranger

REBECCA DONE

PENGUIN BOOKS

PENGUIN BOOKS

UK | USA | Canada | Ireland | Australia
India | New Zealand | South Africa

Penguin Books is part of the Penguin Random House group of companies
whose addresses can be found at global.penguinrandomhouse.com

First published in 2017
002

Set in 12.5/14.75 pt Garamond MT Std
Typeset by Jouve (UK), Milton Keynes
Printed in Great Britain by Clays Ltd, St Ives plc

A CIP catalogue record for this book is available from the British Library

ISBN: 978–1–405–92396–5

www.greenpenguin.co.uk

MIX
Paper from
responsible sources
FSC® C018179

I

Molly – present day

And today I lie awake for a moment, as I do every morning, waiting and hoping for the smallest of signs that my husband has come back to me. The empty space on his side of the bed is my first clue that he has not; but so long as I stay here, I can hope. It's a game I play – that I've just woken up from a horribly vivid nightmare he's about to soothe me out of with whispers and kisses. Perhaps he's downstairs in the kitchen flipping pancakes just like he used to, humming along to some obscure radio station, handsome and bare-chested, fair hair clustered up by sleep. And when he turns to look at me, his smile will strike me all over again. His is a double-take smile, the kind it takes a moment to recover from.

But I never recovered from it. Which is why it's my coffee I'm sure he's making right now, my pancakes he's lovingly dousing in maple syrup and butter. And when I finally take a breath and push open the kitchen door, I know – I *know* – everything will be just as it was.

Everything will be beautifully, perfectly ordinary.

Today's the day. I can *feel* it.

*

Through the window the air carries the first warm breath of a summer's day. I open the bedroom door, but I can't smell coffee or pancakes. That's okay — maybe we'll go out for breakfast, to the cafe in the village that stencils stars into the cappuccino froth. And Alex will exchange pleasantries with the couple at the next table and crack jokes with the waitress because he's just that sort of guy, and over eggs Benedict and coffee we'll plan our day, both knowing how lucky we are to have the small things.

My heart races in anticipation as I head down the stripped stairs to the door of the living room, dodging dust and dirt as I go. It is there that I pause; and it is there that both my heart and hope deflate. He is hunched up across the room, back against the sofa, in T-shirt and tracksuit bottoms like always, temporarily transfixed by blank space. His hair is messy, long and unattended to, because no one has been able to persuade him to a barber's.

He has been awake a while: I can tell by the cereal bowl on the ageing carpet next to him, the dried-up dregs of his sugar-laden breakfast now clinging to its contours.

And then he turns to look at me, my handsome husband. But his face does not light up, and he doesn't knock me over with his whole-face smile. He simply takes me in, and it is the neutrality of his expression that is once again unbearable. I swallow my tears, turn round and head back upstairs, disappointment complete for one more day.

*

2

I wash quickly, my customary beginning to each exhausting morning. The flow of our shower is weak, and the water sputters and spits. Still, today I've been organized for once – pressed my favourite polka-dot shirt and black skirt ahead of time. (This is more of an achievement than it sounds, since ironing comes about as high on my priority list these days as sorting my sock drawer or steam-cleaning my curtains.)

I'm trying to impress them at work – mainly because they've finally snapped and issued me with a verbal warning. Constantly teetering on the edge of being fired is something of a problem, so trying to look groomed and at least turning up on time seems like a reasonable way to begin trying to solve it.

From beyond the bedroom window, the sound of a tractor grinding along the back road leading out of the village instils me with urgency, reminds me that country life moves too slowly for me to be idle first thing in the morning. As swiftly as possible I blow-dry my hair, apply make-up and perfume, fasten jewellery.

Ready.

I make my own coffee these days. Back downstairs in the kitchen, I find a clean cereal bowl on the draining board and decant some muesli before opening the fridge for the four pints of milk I bought a couple of nights ago. But it is not there.

I frown. 'Alex?'

Pause.

An eventual monotone. 'Yep?'

'Where's the milk?'

Another pause. 'Don't know.'

'Well, what did you have on your cereal?'

Longer pause.

'Milk.' *What a stupid question*, his tone implies.

I sigh, but it takes me less time to make breakfast at work than it does to play fifteen rounds of guessing games with Alex, so I open the cupboard to replace my empty bowl. And there is the milk, squatting quite audaciously between our his 'n' hers Sydney Harbour BridgeClimb mugs, relics from our last-ever holiday.

I put my hand against the carton and it's warm.

'Brilliant, Alex. Well done.'

I would have said it under my breath if I'd known he was standing right behind me.

'Well done for what?' he asks, because I have, after all, just said his name.

'Nothing,' I tell him, wrenching the top off the milk and pouring it down the sink.

And the reality is, it is nothing. Or at least, it's four pints of milk. It cost me a quid at the corner shop, and I can replace it within minutes. If I was to stop and think rationally, I would know that it's a mistake anyone could have made – I could have made the same one myself, if I was knackered enough. But my instinct, of course, especially when I'm tired, is to always put it down to his brain.

Because I *am* tired – it's the last day of a long week. I am exhausted, in need of coffee and fuel, and nervous about work.

In the end, it's the little things that get to you. It's the insults he levels at strangers that come out of nowhere. It's our favourite joke in our favourite film, missed for the umpteenth time. It's being handed black tea with the tea bag still in. It's not holding hands any more, because – for reasons my compassion can't comprehend – holding hands no longer feels natural to the man who's been by my side for almost seven years. And yes – it's the sour carton of milk on a Friday morning.

So when I say *nothing*, I mean *something* – but Alex is rarely up for wordplay, and especially not this early in the morning. So as the milk glugs from the upturned carton into the sink, he reaches out and tries to grab it. 'Hey!'

It's milk, and it's sour, so instinctively I tighten my grip. For a couple of ridiculous seconds, we try to wrestle it from one another, before his strength wins out as it always does. The milk, predictably, is flung upwards with force. It lands in my hair, all over my shirt, my face, my skirt. Some of it goes up my nose. A lot of it goes in my eyes. I gasp, inhaling the foul smell, the sourness.

Momentarily blinded and short of breath, I grope for a tea towel and smear it across my face to clear my eyes. I'm furious: another avoidable fight, another avoidable mess. The milk carton is on its side at my feet, soaking into the soles of my tights. Stinking fluid is leaching across the concrete floor – the exposed innards of this cottage a constant reminder of our half-finished dream renovation project – snaking under the fridge and ancient kitchen units like something toxic. We might as well have just stuffed rotting mackerel into the wall cavity.

'What the hell did you do that for?'

Alex's hair may be long now – grown out like a surfer's – but his temperament could not be less mellow.

'Forget it,' I tell him, quickly swallowing away my hurt and frustration. 'I'll clean this up.'

'You're an idiot, Molly,' he says, wrenching open the back door and steaming out into the garden. 'That was your fault.'

This makes me well up, and I know it *is* partly my fault – pretending each day when I open my eyes that the old Alex is back. That game can never be a fun one, and I'm always going to lose.

My chest is heaving, my eyes damp with frustration, but *don't cry, don't cry, don't cry* echoes in my brain. I can't show up at work with red eyes on top of everything else.

I see Alex pacing outside in the tangled undergrowth of our garden, so I take the opportunity to slip back upstairs, trying not to panic about the fact that I'm going to be late.

The sour stench in my nostrils is already unbearable. I bend down and roughly pull off my tights, discarding them in a sopping, stinking ball into the sink. Then I remove the rest of my clothes and climb back under the shower, where a frustrating dribble of lukewarm water makes a half-hearted attempt to dilute the milk in my hair. We've had the plumbing redone here, but for some reason the shower still carries no pressure, and Alex is no longer interested in being handy around the home. So property defects remain just that until I beg his brother for yet another favour.

A couple of tears escape, along with a thought that blindsides me where I stand, a pathetic picture as the shower sputters over my naked frame. It strikes me with such force that I virtually keel over.

I can't live like this any more.

By the time I make it back downstairs, it is nine o'clock and I am supposed to be at my desk, conducting a telephone interview for this month's lead feature on the magazine I work at.

Alex is in front of the TV once again, sports news on a rolling loop as it so often is. He is fixated these days with watching sports as opposed to partaking, and he hasn't worked – or at least, held down a job – since his accident just over three years ago.

I hesitate before I speak. 'Alex, could you please clear up the milk in the kitchen? I don't have time.'

He shakes his head and tuts, like that is just about the most unreasonable thing anyone has ever said to him. 'Why should I? You spilt it. It was *your* fault. I'm not clearing up your mess.'

My tears threaten to fall, but I push them back. '*Please*, Alex. If you don't it's going to smell terrible . . .'

His hair has flopped over his eyes; he pushes it back. 'Is that supposed to be a joke?'

I exhale. 'Of course not . . .'

'You're taking the piss?'

'I just want you to clear it up so it doesn't –'

'I can't smell it, *can* I?' It is a challenge, an accusation.

Alex hasn't been able to taste or smell anything since the accident, which is basically like having a permanent head cold. He can tell the difference between sweet and sour, and he knows when something's spicy – which is why he's always got a bottle of hot sauce appended to his palm – but we don't go to restaurants any more, and he no longer shows any interest in cooking. Because he loved to cook and eat, before. That was part of his soul.

No wonder it gets him down.

I make a single, shallow breath. 'I know you can't. But –'

He is on his feet now. 'You clear it up! You're always doing this – leaving me jobs to do while you swan off to work! How do you think that makes me feel, Molly? Everything's all right for you, at least you get to leave the house!'

'You could leave the house! You could, but you don't! You just need to try . . .'

'Just go to work, Molly. Earn all that money, feel superior. Go on – go.'

He couldn't make it any clearer, so that's exactly what I do.

I arrive at work an hour late, a thick slick of sweat across my back. The air con no longer works in my car, I can't afford to get it fixed, and the weather is stifling. The sprint up the stairs in my building doesn't exactly help either.

As I enter the open-plan office at Spark (ironic, because

I've never worked anywhere more depressing), I see him straight away. Sebastian, standing next to my desk, laughing about something with my colleagues. Then he spots me and his face slackens slightly, like the jaw of a dog before it goes in for the kill.

We're facing one another in the meeting room (despite his efforts to convince us otherwise, Seb isn't enough of a big shot yet to have an office he can call his own). It's hot and airless because the windows are jammed shut from an ongoing lack of maintenance, and there is peeling paint and carpet tiles so scuffed they could no longer accurately be described as carpet. I am personally of the opinion that a public toilet would engender more creativity than this room.

'So, Molly, why exactly are you an hour late?'

I am not about to confide in Seb, primarily because he's a duplicitous snake.

'There was an . . . incident at home.'

Seb leans back in his chair and throws me a sarcastic smile that tells me if I'm not about to be cooperative, then two can play at that game.

'And the jeans?'

Paul, our CEO, hates his employees wearing jeans in the same way as most employers would hate them making out across desk partitions. He doesn't normally work Fridays, being the sort of company director who sees four-day weekends as non-negotiable, but it would be just my luck today if he swanned back in because he'd forgotten his sunglasses.

As Paul's right-hand man, Seb enforces his rules with a vigour that borders on sociopathic.

'I couldn't find anything else,' I tell him. (Subtext – nothing else was clean.)

But he's already moved on. 'Your interview was at nine. There were three senior executives at a blue chip company ready and waiting to take your call.'

I nod. 'I know. Look, I can call them back . . .'

Seb laughs like a cartoon villain. 'Yes, okay, Molly. Because I'm sure they're hanging around in their board-room just *waiting* for you to dial in.'

The way he's mocking me reminds me a bit of Alex, only Alex has a slightly better excuse for it than simply being a bell-end. I fantasize for a moment about the day I will quit this soul-destroying job and as part of my resignation speech run through my back catalogue of Sebastian's various character defects in very slow and painstaking detail.

'Dave stepped in, luckily for you,' Seb informs me. 'So what you need to do right now is go back to your desk, plug in your headphones and speak to that com-pany in Brussels. Ten thirty.'

I work as a writer on a magazine that interviews companies from around the world, then charges them to publish PR pieces that make them look fantastic. We sit on a bank of desks, calling the companies, inter-viewing executives (in English, fortunately), writing the articles, filing them. Then we do it all over again.

The work is robotic and feels soulless, but I had to take the first job I could after Alex's accident. I could no longer commute to London, where I was a copy-writer at a large advertising agency. It was a job and a company I loved – the sort of place where people wore sandals and drank espresso, did the odd impromptu yoga pose on the stripped walnut floorboards. The decor was all exposed brickwork and exotic pot plants – some of which even bore miniature fruit that no one dared to eat – and (get this) there was even the luxury of climate-controlled air. We got free lattes, macchiatos and mochas, filtered water, snacks. And to top it all off they indulged our highly strung creative brains with a pool table and video games and mini trampolines, as well as a roof terrace with spectacular views of London. Plus the variety of shops, bars and restaurants on our doorstep was mind-boggling. It was the kind of creative haven that people like to mock, but I loved it.

I was desperate not to quit, but I could no longer justify the time away from Alex. So after three months of compassionate leave then six months of back and forth, with the company trying their best to be accommodating, I reluctantly resigned. I considered freelancing, but doing so from our ramshackle cottage or shelling out for office rental were not options, and we needed money fast. So I took the first job that came up in order to keep paying the bills (thank you, Seb). Which is why I'm now working at Spark, on an out-of-town industrial estate between a used-car dealership and a discount furniture warehouse, where we have only a furred-up kettle and undisclosed asbestos issues to keep us amused.

'Oh, and Molly?' Seb takes his final shot as I stand

up to head back to my desk. 'Consider this your second verbal warning. The next one we put in writing and the one after that . . .' He spreads his hands and gives me a self-satisfied little shrug, like he's just cheated at poker and stolen all my chips.

I swallow, think about Alex, and do my best to fold my face into a serene smile, though it probably looks more as if I'm passing wind.

There are about twenty of us in the main office, with all the staff writers sitting on a bank of desks, headphones in like we're in a call centre (which I guess, in a way, we are). I inhale the scent of coffee I didn't have time for this morning and realize I am craving it as I stare at my darkened computer screen, trying to remember where my notes are for the interview.

My deskmate, Dave, is a bit like the new Alex in that he doesn't really go in for observing social etiquette, which is why he regularly ends up falling out with Seb. I suppose it's because Dave's spent most of his working life in a newsroom being a hack (until he was made redundant and had to take the next job that came along, which unfortunately for him was this). He's constantly pushing his luck, turning up unshaven and in fabrics resembling denim. I suspect that if he was any less than brilliant at his job, Seb would have fired him by now. But he knows Dave's his best writer: as an ex-journalist he's a fantastic interviewer and can churn out articles at double the speed the rest of us can. He even knows shorthand, for God's sake.

Dave's been a complete marvel ever since I told him about Alex's accident, making me laugh when I didn't think I could, forcing me to eat when I had no energy left (he's set an apple on my keyboard this morning, and I've lost count of the number of times I've discovered a snack pack of nuts or raisins in my drawer, or a duo of doughnuts in my bag). He's recently divorced – at the time it was messy but now he's very much back on the dating scene and having the time of his life, quite frankly. My favourite part of my week is usually – weirdly enough – Monday morning, when he entertains me with tales of his single escapades from the weekend.

'Everything all right?'

I nod gently. 'Thanks for doing my interview.'

'Oh, it was no bother. Actually, it was quite fun. I'm sure they suspected I knew sweet FA about them, but they couldn't be *quite* sure.' He pats himself on the back. 'Journo skills.'

'Getting up to speed within five minutes is definitely a skill,' I agree.

'I didn't get up to speed at all – bluffed my way through the whole thing.' He sighs in satisfaction. 'I think I've earned my pittance this morning.'

'Didn't Seb give you my notes?'

'Oh yes, he did. With about three minutes to spare. Can't keep these chief execs waiting, can we?'

I smile. 'Tell me you've got an exciting weekend planned.'

He shakes his head. 'Tame by my standards.'

'Just the one date, then?'

'Actually, this weekend's a date-free zone. Pub tonight, cinema with my nieces tomorrow, footie Sunday. Perfect.'

I smile and try not to envy Dave's ordinary weekend, doing ordinary things. Then I feel Seb glaring at me and jump to attention. Working here is like constantly playing one of those wire-loop games, where if you lose concentration for one moment you live to regret it.

'I've got to ring Brussels in exactly four minutes,' I mumble, feeling a surge of panic as my computer finally fires up. What did the company say they want to focus on? Continuous improvement? Organic growth? 'Where the hell are my notes?' I mutter, flicking nervously through the file.

Dave slips his headphones back on. 'Remember, Molly. If in doubt – bluff.'

I smile to myself as I start dialling Brussels. Dave's a big reason I hang on here at all, and is thus partly responsible for the fact that Alex and I aren't homeless and living in a box. Dave doesn't do soppy, so I've never told him that, but sometimes I've felt as if he's quite literally holding me back from the brink.

The brink of what, I'm not quite sure.

Dave's meeting a friend for lunch, so I head alone to my favourite park, where I can sit and stare at the greenery and pretend to feel calm. The interview was actually quite interesting in the end, but at the same time it made me crave to be somewhere far away again with the Alex I used to know. Together, and anywhere but here.

I had no time to make lunch this morning, so I buy

the cheapest cheese sandwich I can find, savouring every mouthful as I try to breathe out my stress. I feel a familiar stab of jealousy as couples walk past me arm in arm on their lunch breaks, laughing and chatting about ordinary things, living a totally ordinary life. The same life I used to live.

My phone rings then, and it's Alex's brother, Graeme.

Graeme was there on the night of the accident just over three years ago. Later, at the hospital, he told us what happened. Alex was staying with him for the weekend in London, where Graeme was renting a swanky flat from an acquaintance. Getting up in the night for a glass of water, Alex became disorientated in the dark and fell down half a staircase, hitting his head on the cast-iron coffee table at the foot of it. Graeme was at his side within seconds. I'll never forget the hysterical phone call I received from him that night just after it happened, Alex unconscious beside him, the ambulance on the way. I jumped in my car, red-lined it all the way down the motorway to the hospital, stared wordlessly at Graeme's colourless face as the news dripped in, torturously slow, like drops of blood from a badly stemmed wound. *Coma. Life-changing injuries. Brain damage.*

Since Alex's accident, Graeme and I have become quite close – he's been an absolute rock, possessing a can-do attitude I suspect is inextricably linked to the trauma of that night. (None of us blamed him, of course, but Graeme blamed himself. He's told me as much – that because it happened while Alex was staying with him, he felt at fault somehow.) And now the Alex he had known for thirty years has been replaced by a stranger; all the memories and experiences they shared for ever altered, their colour and significance subtly changed. My seven years with Alex sometimes feels paltry in comparison.

'Hey. So what's the plan for later? I'm on a half-day.'

Graeme still lives in London but tries to visit as often as he can. It's ironic, really, that he was in Norfolk for so many years, while we were in London – and now we've switched. Sometimes he stays with us when he visits, sometimes he gets a hotel. Occasionally, when Alex is in the right frame of mind, we head to London for a weekend and stay with Graeme instead, depending on where he's living at the time. But all that ever really does is make me wish I was living in the capital again.

'I forgot you were coming,' I confess to Graeme. A sudden change in plans is a bigger deal to me and Alex than it would be to most people, since Alex's equilibrium now depends on structure and routine. If I happen to be late home from work, or Graeme turns up unannounced, it makes him really agitated. And then his mind always leaps to the worst-case scenario: he won't be able to eat what he wants, do the activities he wants, get enough sleep. And then he'll feel ill, will miss seeing the boys on Tuesday, be ditched by his friends, have no mates for the rest of time, etc., etc. He has lost the ability for middle-ground thinking since the accident. Everything's always black and white – either the best thing ever, or the worst-case scenario.

'Oh.' Graeme sounds a little deflated. 'Were you doing something else?'

'No, of course not,' I say quickly, because the thought of Graeme coming for the weekend is quite a relief, actually, if we can get over the hump of Alex being thrown out of sync. Maybe I can use the time to catch up with Eve tomorrow, pop out for a coffee, perhaps even go for a run.

Graeme laughs lightly. 'You can have other plans, Molly. It's not a crime, you know.'

Unlikely: I start most weekends trying to convince Alex to come out and do something, to put his phone down, to eat something other than fast food (it's easy and quick, and though he can't taste it, gives him a satisfying salt-fat-sugar hit). But when Graeme comes up, we sometimes head out for dinner at the pub, or go for a walk, or do anything else that isn't just sitting in front of the television. Though it takes some persuasion, Alex does still want to socialize, and it's important for his recovery to keep doing all the things he did with his friends before (easier said than done, of course – he's less confident than he used to be – but when we do manage to get out and about, more often than not Alex does benefit from catching up with people). Graeme being around generally rescues me from two days of listening to Alex informing me he's bored as he flicks through the news channels, of fighting over the house-work, of staring in despair at all the things that need doing to the house. God, Alex isn't the only one who's bored.

'So, shall I come still?' Graeme presses. 'I can always get a hotel.'

'No, don't be silly. Stay with us. I'll just text Alex to let him know.'

'Great. See you later then.'

'Actually,' I say, 'if you're coming, I might nip into Eve's after work.' I normally like to get home to Alex as soon as possible – I'm acutely aware of him being home alone all day, bored out of his mind. But if Graeme's there, it won't matter tonight, and I want to make the most of the opportunity to socialize, worry-free.

'Great. See you when I see you, then.'

'Oh, Graeme? We had an argument this morning.'

'You and Alex?'

I sigh, nod to nobody. 'I asked him to clean up, but . . .'

'I'm not even going to ask, but don't worry, I'll sort it.' I picture Graeme's sympathetic smile down the line. 'Leave everything to me. Go out tonight, enjoy yourself.'

'Thanks, Graeme. You're a lifesaver.'

2

Molly – present day

Eve's place, as always, is rammed to the rafters with kids. Eve's only got two herself – an eleven-year-old daughter and nine-year-old son – but she always seems to be cooking tea for swarms of their friends. At Eve's, it's always open house, which is great, because that includes me too. She's my closest friend in Norfolk – when we met, we just clicked. She's known Graeme and Alex since primary school and has lived in this village her entire life, only moving out of her mum's house to set up home three doors down with Tom. She's the most fulfilled person I know, which is why I'm always able to rely on her for a balanced perspective. Plus, having known Alex for a long time before the accident, she has some sense of what I'm going through, the profound change he's undergone.

I find her in the large kitchen at the rear of her Victorian villa, one of my favourite places to be. The range cooker means it's always warm, and there are two comfortable sofas looking out through floor-to-ceiling glass on to her perfect English garden. There are about eight kids crammed on to one of the sofas playing a video game in typically boisterous fashion.

Eve is observing it all with a kind of glazed calm, cup of tea in hand, and the smell of a bubbling lasagne blooms from the oven. Her shirt sleeves are rolled up to the elbows, her hair's gone a bit frizzy and she's got a kids-related glow of exertion across her cheeks, but she looks so happy.

I exhale; already I am starting to relax. For the next couple of hours, at least, I know Eve will take care of everything. It feels good when people take care of me for a change.

'How was work?' Eve asks me, probably expecting me to say *okay*, given I'm smiling. But I'm smiling because I love being around the kids. Their happiness is infectious.

I shake my head. 'Awful. I got a second verbal warning.'

Eve's face drops. 'For what?'

'I was late. Me and Alex had a fight.'

'About what?' She comes and sits next to me, passes me a cup of tea and grabs my other hand.

I sip gratefully, shut my eyes. If I could just stay here, drinking tea with Eve, listening to the clamour of children . . .

'Moll?'

I open my eyes again. 'Spilt milk, would you believe it.'

That's the thing about the way Alex is these days – normal daily gripes that would usually go unnoticed (or, at the very most, be registered then forgiven), all too often turn into something they shouldn't. Because we both spend our lives exhausted, battling the constant challenge of it all, some days living on a virtual knife-edge. Explosions over trivialities are inevitable from time to time.

It came as a shock at first, his temper. I think we'd all convinced ourselves that he was angry in hospital and rehab because he was in hospital and rehab – that once we got home, everything would be okay. But of course it wasn't. In fact, it ramped up as he adjusted to being home again, in familiar surroundings but feeling absolutely nothing like himself.

'He left it out of the fridge, then couldn't taste it had gone off, obviously, and then . . . oh God, never mind. I'm boring myself.'

'You're not boring *me*,' Eve says reassuringly, squeezing my hand.

'It wasn't his fault,' I sigh. 'He was tired today, because he went out yesterday. You know what he's like when he's tired.'

'Yep,' Eve says, because she does: everything shuts down and Alex gets irritable, liable to make mistakes that frustrate him later. He does this – has days of burnout where he simply forgets to stop, which then has a knock-on effect for all the days that follow.

Perhaps if Alex had been someone else when I met him – someone less affectionate and tactile, someone less utterly *romantic* – then I wouldn't have felt the weight of his personality change as heavily as I do now. Before, he was into flowers and holding hands and chocolates and romantic meals; yet now he more closely resembles my ex, the first boy I met at university – detached, allergic to PDAs, prone to long periods of inattention and a bit of a temper; the man I clung on to for too long to my own detriment.

It's so hard to accept that my future now is destined to be a slightly repackaged version of my past. Eve would assure me that it's not, but she never knew my ex – so she can't fully understand that my new husband carries many of the same depressing personality hallmarks.

She tries to understand – and perhaps she does, better than anyone – but she still doesn't know how it truly feels to have Alex almost look through me some days, as if he's wondering who I am and why I am there. The spark in his green eyes, the connection between us, is gone. That unspoken something has left the room, and I know it will never return.

'So where's Alex now? Why don't you stay for supper? Ask him to come round too, if you like, there's plenty. I made heaps.'

I smile. 'Alex and a room full of screaming children?'

Eve laughs. 'Sorry. Forgot.'

'We're not screaming, Molly!' Isla informs me in a high-pitched hyperactive giggle as she shoots past us to retrieve the biscuit tin from the counter.

'Er, I don't think so,' Eve says swiftly. 'Dinner's in ten minutes.'

'Mum, I'm *star*ving!'

'That's why dinner's in ten minutes,' Eve replies firmly.

'Where's Alex?' Isla asks me as she skates on the soles of her tights back over to her friends, knowing better than to argue with Eve about biscuits before dinner.

It breaks my heart, that note of nervousness in Isla's voice that Alex might be about to show up and spoil her evening.

Alex used to be great with kids, and Isla and George absolutely adored him. He just had that way with them, a gift for making them squeal with delight, for talking to them, entertaining them. They'd usually be hanging off his legs for the entire duration of our visits here. Eve has explained everything to them, that Alex will never be quite the same since his accident. She even bought them a picture book to help them understand, but they still don't, not fully. Isla asked me only the other day, 'Why doesn't Alex like me any more?' and I had no idea how to answer her. What I wanted to say was that, some days, that's exactly how I feel too.

'He's at home with Graeme,' I tell her with a reassuring smile.

She beams back at me from the sofa, pleased. In much the same way as the man who now sometimes scares her, Isla is rarely able to hide how she feels. I swallow the lump in my throat.

'She doesn't mean —' Eve begins softly as Isla turns her attention back to the video game.

'I know,' I say quickly. 'It's fine.'

Probably sensing the need to change the subject, Eve exhales and says, 'So exactly what does a second verbal warning mean anyway?' She stands up and heads back over to the oven, setting a garlic baguette inside it to warm.

'It means I'm on borrowed time.' I shake my head. 'I

need that job, Eve. I can't risk being out of work.' It is the thought that terrifies me most. Alex is highly unlikely to find work in the foreseeable future, so if I lose my job – especially if I'm fired – our main source of income aside from Alex's meagre benefits is gone, just like that.

'You should really try looking for something else, Moll,' Eve suggests gently.

'With a disciplinary record and an appalling reference?' I ask her with a sigh of frustration. 'I'm trapped there now.'

'You'd just need to find an understanding employer . . .'

'Employers don't want people with baggage, Eve. Would you?'

'Anything's got to be better than working for Seb, surely?'

I shrug. 'Awful as he is, at least Seb knows my situation – that I have to leave at five on the dot every night, that my head's usually elsewhere . . .'

'Why don't you think about freelancing again? At least then you'd be in control of your own hours.'

'And alone at home with Alex every day.' I shoot her a resigned grimace. Not an option – we'd both be climbing the walls.

Eve falls silent and we lock eyes for a moment. We both know the conundrum of Molly and Alex is not one that can easily be solved.

'Well, at least Graeme's up for the weekend,' Eve says brightly, reaching over for a stack of melamine kids' plates from the cupboard. 'You'll get a bit of a break. Stay for supper, Moll. Maybe Alex will have calmed down by the time you get back.'

'Oh, he'll be fine by now.' And the frustrating reality is that he will: our fight will be long-forgotten when I get in tonight. Arguments are dismissed these days as quickly as they are started, which isn't always easy to accept when you've been on the receiving end of his rage.

The timer on the worktop goes off. Isla glances up hopefully from her video game.

'But you'll stay?' Eve asks me.

I glance down to check my phone, the lock screen still my favourite monochrome photograph from mine and Alex's wedding day. The two of us running hand in hand away from the camera down a tree-lined path, laughing uncontrollably.

There's no further communication from Graeme, so I'm guessing everything's okay.

I smile and nod. 'Yes, I will. Thanks, Eve.'

Right on cue, we hear the front door slam – Eve's husband, Tom, home from work. A few moments later he appears, drops his bag on the floor and ambles over to his wife for a hug. He looks almost as exhausted as I feel. Isla squeals and runs over to him for her own cuddle, George right behind her.

'Hey, Moll,' he says to me, squatting down to let Isla clamber on to his back while he lifts George up, a familiar routine. The two children giggle and brush noses over his shoulder as he kisses them hello.

'Hi, Tom.' I smile, trying not to envy this picture of

familial bliss: the bliss I always assumed Alex and I would get to experience for ourselves.

I catch Eve's eye without meaning to. She knows Alex and I were trying, in the months before his accident. It just didn't happen for us in time, and to this day I don't know if that's a good thing or a bad thing. On the one hand, our unborn children have been protected from everything that's happened and everything that's to come. On the other, we might well have missed our only chance, because any talk of starting a family with Alex is on hold now – not to mention the fact we're barely intimate enough to be in with a shot, were we even to decide to go for it.

There's no physical or medical reason why we can't have children. The huge impediments, for me, are entirely emotional.

'Good day? You're just on time, sweetheart. Right, kiddiewinks!' Eve claps her hands, removes the food from the oven and divides it between the plates without so much as blinking. Tom stirs into action too, sorting hand-washing, orange squash, paper napkins. I simply stand there observing, like a useless maiden aunt pressing her nose up against the glass, desperate to be let in.

3

Alex – 18 December 2010

It's less than a week before Christmas, and Graeme's visiting me in London for what's meant to be my final farewell to the city. I'm moving back to Norfolk in February, to help look after our dad, who's ill. I've got a job offer in Norwich, someone lined up to take over the tenancy on my flat and a reassuring series of welcome-back benders lined up with Graeme and all my friends at home.

I'm with Graeme in Soho. Well, I say *with*. I've been sitting solo at our (highly coveted) table for about twenty minutes now while Graeme stands motionless in the crowd at the bar waiting to get served. Quite honestly, it's not my sort of place – there are too many backlit water features and hip young kids slapping brightly coloured cocktails and bottles of champagne on to their credit cards. At heart I'm a country boy – I prefer pies and pints to cocktails and canapés, country lanes to city streets, fields to gated parks with byelaws. But Graeme wanted to check this place out, and as everybody never tires of telling us, we're like chalk and cheese, even though we're twins.

Just as I think I might have to pop down the road for

a swift half while I'm waiting, I see Graeme dip his head next to a beautiful long-limbed, dark-haired girl. She has impressively tanned skin for the time of year, and is wearing a playsuit in pink chiffon with a grey leather jacket and heels. Exactly his type. My brother looks particularly sharp himself tonight, in his favourite black shirt and grey trousers. Graeme, unlike me, is what you might call smooth.

Possessing a confidence and charm I consider myself to lack entirely, Graeme has had no shortage of women to help him forget the fact he's been single for about six months. Objectively speaking, his success rate is pretty impressive, and as I watch the girl throw her head back and laugh at something he's said, I have no doubt he's already got plans to end the night in the same way he usually does. Which means I'll end the night in the same way I usually do too – watching the sports channel with my headphones on, volume up high, not daring to venture from my bedroom.

Graeme's flirtatiousness around women was one of the reasons he was ditched by his ex, Rhiannon, who today called him for the fifth time this week to insist he return all the stuff she left in his flat – though I suspect really she's trying to catch him in the act with one of these beautiful women who seem to constantly crop up with him on social media since they went their separate ways.

Graeme carries on chatting to the dark-haired girl for about five minutes while I carry on flicking through my phone, occasionally glancing up to see if he's made his move yet. At one point he has his hand on the small of her back – classic Graeme – but the next time I look up I catch him disappearing through the front door, talking angrily and gesticulating into his phone.

They've got their drinks at this point but the girl's been left stranded at the edge of the bar, looking a bit embarrassed. She's clearly here with friends – her tray is holding three cocktails – but she's also been left in charge of my pint and Graeme's Pisco Sour, and she's evidently not sure what to do. Stay or go?

Moments later, I am at her side. 'Um, excuse me . . .'

'I thought you'd abandoned me!' She breaks into a smile, then meets my eye and hesitates.

'I'm his brother,' I say quickly, smiling at her and simultaneously registering the sweet scent of her perfume, her glossy hair, her hazel eyes. She is undeniably beautiful. 'I'm who the pint's for.'

She covers her mouth. 'Oh my God. I'm so sorry. That's embarrassing.'

'We look quite similar,' I reassure her.

'You have the same face.'

'Well . . .' I say, with a loose shrug and a smile, 'twins.'

'Of course.' Then her eyes catch mine and widen. 'Oh God, please ignore me! What a stupid thing to say.'

'So,' I say, clearing my throat, because I really am quite terrible at chatting to beautiful women, 'where's he gone, my errant twin?'

'He had to take a phone call.'

'I can take our drinks if you want to . . .' I nod at her own tray of drinks, not wanting her to feel obliged to keep me company. Nothing worse than someone hanging out with you because they think they should.

Looking slightly crestfallen, she smiles sadly. 'Oh, right. Well, thanks. It was nice to meet you . . .'

'Alex,' I supply quickly. 'Alex Frazer.'

'Molly Meadows,' she says, probably just to be polite.

'Sorry,' I say then, feeling like I've been really unkind – both to her and my brother. 'You can wait for him if you like.'

'Er, no,' she says awkwardly. 'That's okay.'

Subliminally, she seems to understand exactly what I didn't really intend to imply: *don't waste your time on my brother.* I feel my cheeks heat up and look at the floor. Finally, she moves off, so I head back to our table, long-since swooped on by a group of lads. I end up standing awkwardly at the foot of the staircase, waiting – as always, it seems – for Graeme.

Eventually, he finds me staring dejectedly into my half-finished pint, his untouched Pisco Sour on the ledge next to my shoulder. 'Hey,' he says breathlessly, 'what happened to our table?'

'I had to go to the loo,' I lie smoothly, without really meaning to.

'Bloody hell. What about the girl?'

You mean Molly? 'You left her waiting for, like, twenty minutes, while you were on the phone to your ex,' I say incredulously, feeling slightly riled on Molly's behalf. Or maybe I'm just a bit sick of him abandoning me all the time for one girl or another.

Graeme shrugs smugly, like he can normally rely on his good looks to override his shoddy behaviour.

'You're such a tosser,' I inform him, lifting my pint to my lips and taking a long draw from it.

'Sucker more like,' he harrumphs. 'I paid for her drinks.'

'Well, here's a tip then – don't leave her waiting at the bar like a lemon.'

Graeme snorts. 'Er, sorry, but when was the last time you even spoke to a girl, let alone chatted one up, Alex? You'll forgive me if I don't take any dating tips from you.'

'Yeah, yeah, all right,' I grumble at him, because although I know he's joking, I've heard all this goading about me not being confident enough around women before, and to be honest it's quite annoying.

'I'm serious, mate! I worry about you. It's not natural, going that long without a shag.'

I think but don't say that the way Graeme approaches his love life is hardly normal either. Never mind that it's only been eight months that I've been shag-free, not eight sodding years.

'We're going to find you a girl tonight, Golden Boy,' he says, surveying the room. 'I am going to Sort You Out, once and for all.'

'You're all right, thanks,' I mutter. It annoys me, his nickname for me, a reference to his longstanding idea that I was always our dad's favourite son.

'You want to go somewhere else, don't you?' he says with an eye roll, misinterpreting my reluctance for disapproval of his choice of bar. 'Fine – but so long as it's not back to yours. It's nearly bloody Christmas. The most romantic time of the year.'

As I wonder if it's really possible that Graeme can have forgotten about Molly already, I consider asking him precisely what he thinks he knows about romance, but then his phone rings. It's Rhiannon again, and once more he gets to his feet. Knowing them as I do, they'll probably be hooking up again before the weekend's out. They've been doing this strange little dance of combining post-split rows with passionate make-up sex for a while now, and I don't see why this time should be any different.

In the end we decide to stay put, and I head to the toilets twenty minutes or so later while Graeme's fetching in more drinks.

As I'm exiting the gents' I run into Molly exiting the ladies'. She smiles uncertainly at me for a moment.

'I'm the nice one,' I say quickly, as a joke.

Her smile spreads, and she shakes her head. 'Again – sorry. You have better hair,' she adds, like she wants to make up for her error.

'Ha. Thanks,' I say. If she's examining my appearance then it's quite a good job that Graeme and I are just emerging from a particularly dedicated period of pre-Christmas gym attendance. He trains in Norfolk and I train in London, then whenever we get together we have one of those sad little ego competitions to see who's fitter.

'Does that ever get confusing?' she asks me. 'The twin thing?'

I laugh. 'Not for me.'

Molly's eyes widen with embarrassment. 'Sorry, I have no idea what I'm talking about! Again.'

I expect her to smile and walk away at that point but she doesn't. 'Well,' she says, lingering on the word without moving.

I realize it's my turn to say something. It always handicaps me slightly, Graeme telling me how awkward I am around girls, because his opinion usually comes to mind at just the point I'm trying to talk to one.

Molly smoothly saves it. 'So, how's it going?' she asks me. 'Boys' night?'

'Well, it would be okay if Graeme wasn't constantly on the phone to his . . .' I trail off at the last moment.

'Dealer?' she jokes.

I shrug with a what-can-you-do smile. 'I've tried telling him.'

'What is it with –' she starts, then stops herself.

'With . . . ?' I prompt her.

She shakes her head, smiles apologetically. 'Never mind. You're brothers.'

'If it helps, it was his ex on the phone,' I tell her sheepishly, before realizing I've probably just made things worse. I scrabble to clarify. 'Not . . . I mean, he's not currently with . . .'

'Guys in bars,' she says then, finishing her original sentence, admonishing herself with a tut. 'What did I expect, really?'

'I'm a guy in a bar,' I say, wide-eyed, 'and I promise I'm nice.'

'Not to be cynical,' she says, though she's still smiling, 'but it's normally the ones who assure you they're nice that really aren't.'

'Actually, I'm pretty sure this is a moot point anyway,' I tell her then. 'Since this isn't technically a bar.'

She smiles, glances around the little toilet-lobby we've found ourselves in. 'Mmm. More like a substandard cloakroom.'

'So how about you?' I say. 'Girls' night?'

'Well, it was until our table was hijacked.'

'Sounds painful.'

She grimaces. 'You don't even *know*. Some lads from the VIP area thought it would be fun to persuade us into drinking games.'

'Can I take it they're not actual VIPs?'

She smiles. 'They're no A-listers playing truth or dare over there, let me tell you.'

'Could be fun?' I suggest.

'I'm a lightweight,' she confesses, 'and they've already got blue tongues.'

I wince a little. 'Ouch.'

'They kept trying to make me join in, so I ran to the loos.' She laughs. 'Oh, I am *so* pathetic.'

'I can keep you company if you like.'

She hesitates for a moment, upon which I smile. 'You're still thinking about me being a guy in a bar, aren't you?'

She laughs. 'Sorry.'

'What can I say to convince you?'

'All right,' she says, like I've thrown down some kind of personality gauntlet. 'Give me your best chat-up line.'

I hesitate, struck dumb for a moment by my distinct lack of talent for seducing girls, especially ones I've only just met. So I decide to come clean. 'I literally have nothing. Sorry. I don't normally –'

She smiles like I've just delivered the most winning line she's ever heard. 'Wow. Okay. You passed.' Then she looks right into my eyes.

As I look right back into hers I think of my brother waiting for me out in the bar and feel a twinge of guilt. 'You see,' I say softly, 'I don't really do the whole chat-up thing.'

'That's good,' she whispers, 'because neither do I.'

At this point the door leading back into the main bar swings open behind us. It's not (thankfully) Molly's friends or Graeme, but it does inject an imaginary sense of urgency into the air.

As Molly shoots me a wide-eyed look that I choose to interpret as a plea for chivalrous assistance, I think of Graeme taunting me, always berating me for not being forward enough with girls. 'Well then,' I say, tilting my head to the left of us, where a fire exit door is slightly ajar.

She looks at the door, then back at me, then grins. 'We can't – can we?'

'It's me or the VIP drinking games, I'm afraid.'

She pretends to sigh, then grabs my hand. 'Well, if I'm going down, you're coming with me.'

It's the sort of joke Graeme would be unable to resist making some crass guffawing remark about – and my ability to let it slide is how I am temporarily able to justify sneaking out of a bar hand in hand with the girl he saw first.

We quickly find a far less pretentious place where Molly insists on buying the Long Island Iced Teas before we squeeze into a dimly lit corner together. Around us the music is oozing, grinding, which makes me want to shuffle closer to her, but I resist. *Play it cool, Alex, you nerd*. I can just hear Graeme saying it.

'You're sure your brother won't mind being ditched? What's his name again?' Molly's sipping on her straw, long hair draped over one olive-toned shoulder in a loose ponytail.

'Graeme.'

'Graeme won't mind? Really?'

'He's done it to me plenty of times before,' I assure her. And he has, especially after splitting with Rhiannon – always texting me to say he's met a girl and will see me back at the flat. Which is precisely the text I've just sent him (my first one ever, I hasten to add).

Between us, with dipped heads and held gazes, we condense our lives. I tell her about my job as a graphic designer, my flat in Balham, the bands I like, some gigs I've been to recently, the sketchbook I carry with me everywhere. I tell her about doing the festival circuit this summer (a distinct and welcome lack of mud), my travel ideas for next year (Iceland and Morocco the top contenders). But what I definitely don't tell her is that in February I'm moving back to the country. I've known her for no time at all, and already it's feeling like a hard conversation to start. So I don't – instead I ask her questions, discover she's a Londoner born and bred, that she lives with her parents in Clapham and is still utterly in love with her city. But she wants to travel too, learn French ('Proper French, not guidebook French'), fly up the ranks in her creative agency, work abroad one day, get better at cooking, run a marathon . . .

'. . . except right now I'm maybe the unfittest I've *ever* been,' she concludes wistfully.

I struggle not to voice what I've been thinking since I met her and what Graeme would just come out and say: that she has an unbelievable physique, which in my humble opinion is in no need of any gym work whatsoever.

'But you're in pretty amazing shape,' she tells me with a smile, somehow managing to pull off the exact same compliment without sounding sleazy, as I'm sure I would.

'Oh, thanks,' I say, briefly glancing down bashfully. 'Me and Graeme do have a bit of a gym thing going on.'

Molly's eyes sparkle. They're stunning hazel, the sort of eyes you can't stop looking into. 'Aha. Competitive brothers.'

'Maybe in the gym,' I concede.

'I need to get back into it,' she says, nodding determinedly like I've somehow inspired her. 'I'm lapsed.'

I resist a stalker-like compulsion to say I'll go with her. 'New Year's resolution?'

She smiles. 'It'll have to be. Tragic, isn't it? But work just takes over. You know what it's like when there's a big pitch on. You get in at seven a.m., drink coffee all day and end up eating pizza at midnight.'

I smile. 'Then lose the pitch.'

'Cue more pizza, then an all-night bender . . .'

'. . . which is exactly why Graeme's in better shape than I am.'

As Molly shakes her head to disagree, a smile sneaks across her face. 'So, Alex,' she says. 'I sort of forgot to check before I kidnapped you.'

I smile back, thinking I'm more than happy to play hostage.

'Do you have a girlfriend?'

I shake my head. 'Nope. Fully available for kidnappings.'

She laughs. 'I was hoping you'd say that.' Pause. 'So . . .'

'Two years ago,' I supply with a smile.

'Two years ago what?'

'My last girlfriend.'

She smiles back, apparently embarrassed. 'Right. I'm not very subtle, am I?'

I shake my head like, *You're perfect*, all the while wondering if there's an elegant way to reassure her that it hasn't, in fact, been two whole years since I've last had sex, but because I'm not Graeme I decide against it.

'You?' I ask her.

'Ah . . . about six months ago. He had a big bust-up with my dad about religion.'

'Religion?'

'Mum and Dad go to church,' she explains, from which I can assume that her ex did not.

'Oh. That sounds awkward.'

'Are your parents?' she asks me, almost hopefully. 'Churchgoers, I mean.' It's a logical enough question, church being something of a generational thing.

I manage not to spit out my drink. 'Not exactly.'

'It's okay,' she says quickly, putting a hand to her chest. 'I mean, I'm not religious myself.'

I smile at her perfectly reasonable assumption that I might be able to sum up my parents using straightfor-ward descriptions like occupation, whereabouts, religious beliefs. But I can't think of anything to say, so I go with the truth. 'Actually, my dad's . . . well, he's . . . a bit ill.'

Her forehead furrows with concern. 'Oh, I'm so sorry. Nothing serious I hope?'

Funny you ask, he's actually an alcoholic with end-stage liver disease. I hesitate – if I enter into the whole story now, there's a good chance it could finish things off before they've even started.

Plus, it's always a particularly excruciating conversa-tion to have when you've got a drink in your hand. I've tried to offset the inevitable raised eyebrow before now by assuring whomever I'm with that I carefully monitor my own alcohol consumption – which I do. The only snag to this is the inherent implication that I do have an underlying drinking problem, albeit one that's under control. So I tend these days to say nothing at all.

'No – nothing serious,' I say, brushing it off.

Unfortunately, like most people, Molly thinks switching the focus to my mum might be a good next move. 'How about your mum?'

I meet her eye and try to smile. 'Actually, my mum died when we were seven.' I elaborate quickly so she doesn't have to ask me to. 'She got run over walking on the verge through our village.'

To her credit, Molly holds my gaze. But her eyes glass over slightly, perhaps because mine have. It's something I've always struggled to control, and I really wish I could.

'Sorry,' I manage. 'My parental situation is a bit . . . unique.'

'No, I'm sorry,' she says eventually. 'I have this really incredible talent for putting my foot in it. You might have noticed.'

I see her swallow back her tears, and almost involuntarily I reach out, grab her free hand and give it a squeeze. 'You definitely don't,' I tell her.

She squeezes me back and we share a look unlike any I've shared with a girl before, and my heart contracts with pleasure.

'Right – another drink?'

I don't know what makes me hesitate before I head back to the bar. 'Don't go anywhere,' I tell her. 'Don't go slipping out of any fire exits, okay?'

It must have come out like a plea, because she smiles the most reassuring smile I've ever seen. 'I definitely won't.'

*

Much later we wander through the streets of London, our shoulders occasionally bumping together, talking about our lives, our dreams, our hopes. The sky is crisp, black and popping with stars. My breath freezes in the frigid air, unfurling in front of me like fog as we walk. Molly's almost as tall as me in heels, and she's striding quickly, keeping pace. I'm trying not to fixate on her figure, which is challenging, because she has just about the most perfect body I've ever seen.

Eventually, I say to her, 'So, Molly. What now?'

'Sorry. I've been waffling on again, haven't I?' Her breath makes a delicate little fog in front of her face.

She hasn't, actually – she's been telling me all about her job and her friends and her parents, and I've been enjoying every minute. I've discovered she's going on holiday to South Africa in January (one of my bucket-list destinations), is a fan of greedy portions in restaurants (big tick) and is in vehement disagreement with the general consensus in advertising at the moment that the headline is dead (*thank* you). Which, given she's a junior in a major agency that more or less sets all the trends, is really quite impressive. I can't stop sneaking glances at her profile. She's stunning.

'Not at all,' I assure her. I'm also liking the way she doesn't seem to have noticed how far we've walked, despite the fact it's freezing, her legs are bare and she's wearing high heels. Not that I particularly want to compare her with my ex Nicola (though for the record – streaks ahead), but if Molly *had* been Nicola we would doubtless still be standing outside the bar, waiting for a taxi, and she'd be crying about her feet and blaming me for the fact they ached.

Molly seems to be made of tough stuff, although it still occurs to me that I want to offer her my jacket, so I do.

She looks across at me, surprised. 'You'll freeze.'

'No, I'll be fine.'

'Don't worry. I can't feel the cold any more,' she says. 'Must be all those Long Island Iced Teas. God, I drank more than *you*. So unladylike.'

'Yeah,' I reply. 'That – or you're already hypothermic.' So despite her protests I take off my jacket and wrap it round her shoulders. It swamps her, but I want her to be warm at least.

'Thank you,' she murmurs. 'You're very sweet.'

'You're welcome,' I say, without telling her I'd quite happily strip down to my boxers if it meant she wasn't going to freeze to death en route home to Clapham.

'So, do you think your brother had a good night? Gary.'

'Graeme,' I say with a smile, imagining Graeme's snort of derision at such an error, before adding with a pang of guilt, 'I hope so.'

'He'll forgive you, won't he? If you're twins. You must be very close.'

I swallow, then mumble doubtfully, 'I'll make it up to him.'

Just as I'm saying this, Molly's hand slips from mine. I look down and in an instant she's fallen in a heap on to the freezing cold pavement.

'Molly?' I squat down, set a hand against her back.

It's quivering uncontrollably, and it takes me a moment or two to realize she's shaking with laughter.

'Oh my God! I'm not drunk, I promise! It's these heels.'

I laugh. 'Are you okay?'

She lifts her face to meet mine. 'I think I've embarrassed myself in every way possible tonight.' And then we pause, faces nearly touching. I exhale against her skin, my heart thumping, and feel her lips brush mine. 'Am I about to do it again?' she breathes.

'No,' I whisper firmly, then lean in to kiss her.

A bitter little breeze is blistering around our noses and ears as her lips find mine. And now we are kissing – a deep, explosive kiss, both of us down on our knees on the icy street.

I have no idea how long it lasts but it's by far the best kiss of my life. *How did I stumble across you in a bar, for God's sake?* Already, I don't want to be parted from her, but it's not long before she starts to shiver again and we draw reluctantly back from one another.

'You're cold,' I whisper as I help her to her feet. 'I'm going to order you a taxi, then call you tomorrow. Once you've warmed up a bit.'

She shivers a little, tucks her chin down into my jacket. 'Okay,' she whispers back. 'Thank you.'

A short while later, as she's climbing into her cab, she says, 'This is deliberate, by the way.'

'What is?'

She shoots me a slightly nervous smile. 'Thieving your jacket.'

I smile back down at her.

'Because at least this way . . . you kind of *have* to see me again. Don't you?'

And that's really it. The story of how I lose my jacket, but find the most incredible girl.

4

Molly – present day

It's a beautiful Saturday morning – the sky is corn-flower blue, the air hot and dry. Graeme, who arrived last night, has gone off to play golf, having failed to persuade Alex to join him. Which is a shame, because golf is pretty much the only physical activity Alex has been interested in since his accident, despite him having abhorred it before.

And conversely the gym, once his greatest passion, no longer appeals – he tells me the machines over-whelm him, and he hates the loud music, the staring and strutting. I get that: the gym can be a pretty macho place, and Alex's lack of pace and strength is humiliating for him. Of course it is – all it does is remind him of who he was before – the guy who could use the machines with his eyes shut, who didn't get confused about which pin goes where, who could lift a certain amount, who didn't get into a fight with someone over the water fountain or forgetting to wipe his sweat off the machine.

So his body is no longer firm from weight training, or lean from cardio. He has filled out and softened, now perhaps the picture of a man who cares about

45

himself less than he did. It's not true really – it's just harder for him to care, when some days it takes all the effort he possesses to dress himself, make his own breakfast, take a shower.

Not that I can talk – I can't afford to be a gym member these days, so my tone too has softened, and I'm squidgy now in places I never was before. The accident has robbed not only Alex of his health and wellbeing. It was once our dream to take on a challenge like a triathlon or a marathon together, but that's well and truly buried now.

Golf is supposed to help Alex improve his planning and concentration, so Graeme gets him to work out the handicaps in his head, remember the route they have to walk, keep score. (Amusingly, Alex has also been advised to visualize himself on the golf course when he feels himself getting angry, but the odds of him pausing to do that when he sees red are about as likely as him stopping to whip me up a champagne supper.)

But at least golf is doing *something*, and he always feels better afterwards, like someone has reached inside his mind to apply some sort of soothing balm. It centres him, balances him, brings back a little equilibrium.

But today he said he was too tired for golf, drained by Graeme showing up last night, taking control of the house and scrubbing down our milk-stained kitchen, all the while talking at Alex about how he was and what he'd done that week and how he was feeling and what he wanted to do tomorrow. By the time I got home from Eve's, fat with lasagne, Alex's face looked sunken and he seemed almost drunk with exhaustion. His eyes were virtually rolling.

Graeme always pushes Alex harder than I do, and sometimes it can be difficult to persuade him that less *is* more, that accepting Alex's limitations is not the same as giving up on him. It can be a tough balance to strike.

So this morning Alex has been pretty much motionless in front of the television, flicking through the sports channels, worn out before the day has even really begun. He slept in longer than usual, so I used the opportunity to catch up on chores – putting on washing, clearing the ironing pile, dusting. I noticed when I got in last night how much tidying up and cleaning Graeme had done in addition to sorting out the milk problem, but we were all fast asleep before I got a chance to thank him properly.

'What do you want to do today?' I ask my husband.

He fails to answer, though I do see him shrug.

'We should go out with Graeme,' I say after a beat. 'He's come all this way.'

'I'm tired,' Alex replies, talking at the television. 'I *told* you I would be, Molly, but you never listen.'

'Well, you can rest this morning and then maybe we could go out somewhere this afternoon. We should go to the beach, Alex, it's gorgeous weather. We could pack a picnic.'

'Yeah,' he says, leaning on the word slightly to let me know exactly how crap he thinks that idea is. But I can't say I blame him – what's the point of a picnic when you can no longer take pleasure in food?

47

'What did you talk about last night?'

'Who?'

'You and Graeme.'

He fills the pause with another shrug. 'Dunno.'

'Boy stuff?'

A lengthy sigh lets me know my questions are start-ing to piss him off, but I can't help myself. Trying to connect with Alex, make him talk to me like he used to, is basically a compulsion. My brain simply won't accept that he's not in there *somewhere*, even after all this time. And if I can achieve it, as I sometimes do – compel him to turn round, make eye contact with me, laugh at something I've said – it's a tiny achievement that will see me through the rest of the weekend.

'Or we could do some gardening. Clear the weeds, make it look a bit nicer.'

Another suggestion for Alex's rehab activity pro-gramme was gardening, so he could feel the soil between his fingers, and because he had a mild interest in it before the accident. But mild interest has now translated into zero interest, and it's much the same with the cottage renovation. I do very occasionally arrive home to a pile of tools arranged on the carpet, or an attempt made at stripping wallpaper, but on these odd times he feels motivated enough to start a job, he rarely sees it through.

The activity programme is intended to draw the two versions of Alex together – the old Alex and the new Alex. To provide a reference point for himself, to be something of a port in the storm. But I have to say, so far the results have been patchy at best.

'I'm *busy*,' he says, finally starting to lose his temper. 'Stop nagging me.'

Still he doesn't look at me. His eyes remain trained on the bright green turf of a football pitch far away, a team he doesn't know, doesn't care about, doesn't follow, had probably never heard of before today. And all the while I'm standing right here behind him, asking as I do every day for him to let me back in. It's exhausting for me too, but in a different way.

So I head outside into the meadow-like garden and sit on the edge of the patio. The mass of long grass is peppered with poppies and cornflowers, so overgrown I have taken to telling people I am cultivating a wild-flower pasture. It's littered too with the remnants of DIY – the trench we dug to sort out our damp problem, the logs of felled trees whose roots were causing structural damage, the semi-permanent skip filled with everything we stripped out that I've yet to get taken away.

Alex inherited this ancient cottage from his father, Kevin, after his death from liver cancer four years ago, and our plan was to renovate it, after which I would quit my job and (hopefully) bring up our family. The perfect plan.

Most of Kevin's stuff is still in storage. We sent some of it to charity and some of it to Mum and Dad's church so they could sell it to raise some money, but Alex was so emotionally attached to much of the clutter that had amassed here over the years that it felt easier to simply rent a unit and tell ourselves we'd sort it out once the cottage was complete. Now, I don't even know if that time will ever come; meanwhile, the storage fees are eating money. And all our style-conscious belongings from our London flat look so awkward and strange in this ancient building that bows and creaks with history, like the removal men got the wrong address on moving day. Slowly they are amassing dust and cobwebs, like they died along with the old Alex on the day of his accident.

When we moved in the cottage virtually needed gutting, since Kevin had barely touched it for twenty-plus years, but the accident came before we could complete the renovation. Fortunately we'd already finished the plumbing and the roof, which largely sorted out our massive damp problem, but there's still so much lingering on unfinished. Electrics, replastering, bricklaying, flooring, carpentry, fittings . . . the list is endless. And we simply don't have the cash or mental grit to finish it off.

I shut my eyes, draw some long breaths, try to hold on to the last time I felt my husband had returned to me.

We were walking through the village together a few weeks ago. It was a good day – Alex had majored on sleep that week, achieved a few odd jobs around the house, seen the lads. We'd avoided arguments. It was one of those weeks where I'd been lulled into thinking that perhaps we'd turned a corner – that he was on the up, would defy all the stats, start making huge strides in his recovery. He'd been laughing more than usual, seeing the funny side of things that might usually make him swear. I remember calling my mum and telling her excitedly, *Something's different, Mum. I can feel it. I need to write down everything we've done this week in case we've changed something without realizing.* Another little daily form of torture – the thought that one innocuous thing, like the food we eat or the water we don't filter or the positive ions we leave to float around the house, might be the key to Alex making a miraculous, science-defying recovery. It's illogical, of course, but there is nothing logical about my life any more.

It was early evening, and we bumped into a neighbour Alex has known since he was a kid. The neighbour was walking his new puppy – a golden retriever he'd named Buddy. We stopped to chat, and Alex squatted down to fondle the puppy's head.

It took me squarely aback. It was as if he'd completely dropped his guard – as if all the warmth he'd lost since the accident had suddenly returned. For so long I'd been questioning his capacity to ever be affectionate again, and now here he was, going all gooey over a puppy the way most girls go gooey over a newborn baby.

'Hey, Buddy,' he kept whispering as he fondled the puppy's ears and got plentifully licked in return. 'Hey.'

I simply stood and watched, trying not to let myself well up as our kindly neighbour smiled and looked on. Eventually I had to gently prise Alex away from them both, though not before Alex had quizzed him fully on where he got the puppy, why, how he decided on a name, how often he walked him and what he did with him at night, as if he was going to be sitting some sort of puppy ownership exam the following morning and wanted to pass with flying colours.

He enthused about little Buddy all the way home, but the best part was when he took my hand and squeezed it the whole time he was talking. Unbelievable for a man who gets animated only occasionally and affectionate hardly at all.

That night it felt as if the old Alex was walking by my side.

I'm still sitting in the garden when I feel someone standing behind me.

'Nearly tripped over you then,' Graeme says, presumably a reference to my jungle of a garden.

To look at, Graeme is simply another version of my husband. He's blond, like Alex, though his hair is short – as Alex's used to be. (I once told Alex he had better hair than Graeme. Now, the exact opposite would be true.) They share virtually identical smiles, green eyes, expressions. Nothing much in the seven years I've known them both has changed that – just the passage of time, perhaps, to scatter a few tiny laughter lines here and there.

'The intention was to come out and tidy the place up a bit.'

'Ah, intentions,' Graeme says mock-wistfully. I feel him plop down next to me.

My eyes remain shut. 'Good game?'

'Bit windy. I beat Luke though, so – every cloud.'

I smile. Luke is an old work colleague of Alex's. I'm always grateful that Graeme gets Alex to socialize as much as possible whenever he's here. His friends, bless them, never the biggest of golfing fans before, have adopted the hobby on Alex's behalf, a gesture for which I am eternally grateful. It's not exactly cheap.

It's not been easy for him, maintaining friendships. Strangely enough, he finds shallow conversations easier to handle, which is why he so often makes small talk with strangers. Strangers didn't know him before – there are no comparisons, no subtext to the conversation, no predefined shorthand in their speech. And because they don't know him, they don't want to discuss things in depth, ask how he's feeling, have meaningful conversations rather than simply bat comments back and forth.

Alex's oldest friends, Charlie and Darren, have dealt with the accident exceptionally well, but so many more of his friendships have fallen away as they realize he's no longer the person he was before. Not just in things like sense of humour, shared interests or taste in music, but in how easily he can handle a conversation, pay attention, tolerate them. He finds group situations tough, and sometimes, especially when he's tired, he makes it clear that he's not interested in talking. Hardly surprising, then, that many of his friendships have collapsed – they didn't want this new, bizarre version of Alex who could offer them nothing in return for their patience.

'Molly, am I right in thinking you're out here counting to ten?'

I smile again. 'That obvious?'

'What's he said?'

'Nothing really. I just annoy him, that's all. He's not in the mood to do anything today.'

'My fault. He's tired. I think I did his head in yesterday with all my bleaching and scrubbing.'

Finally I open my eyes and look across at him for the first time. He smiles hello.

'Thanks so much for cleaning everything up,' I say. 'I meant to say that last night. And the rest of our stuff. The place was a pigsty. I really appreciate it.'

'Oh, that's all right. Hardly the kind of thing you need to come home to on a Friday night, right?'

Or when you're a guest. 'Did Alex help?'

'In his own way.'

'Ah. You mean, he stood and chattered while you cleared it all up.'

'Well, you know. I think it pleases him to watch me work. Revenge for all that dossing about I did when we were younger.'

'When you were . . . younger?' I tease him.

'It's too early in the morning for lols, Molly,' Graeme says drily as we watch a pair of white butterflies flirting amongst the grass stems.

'Only joking.'

Since selling his flat in Norfolk four years ago and heading to London, Graeme has not had a steady job, a home address valid for more than a few months, or any sort of permanence attached to anything (including relationships). He does have a huge circle of friends, an apparent gift for blagging free holidays to Ibiza and many, many so-called 'connections'. If you need someone for anything, Graeme will 'know a guy'. He's dabbled in investments, gambling, nightclub promoting and door work, the latter of which he's been doing with semi-regularity for the past year or so. Some would say that after his dad died he went off the rails; I know it to have happened much earlier in life than that.

Chalk and cheese, people used to say about Graeme and Alex – but what they really meant was that Alex was good and Graeme was bad. Alex was always the one doing his homework, obeying instructions, listening to people; while Graeme was invariably the brother who stayed out late, got into trouble at school and was regularly grounded by an ever-despairing Kevin.

I assumed, somewhat naively, that after Alex's accident Graeme might move back to Norfolk for good, but he never suggested it and I never felt it reasonable to ask. On reflection I think it's probably a good thing there's some distance between him and Alex, who gets so frustrated now when he thinks people are smothering him, in his face, getting in his business. Graeme has never been one to mince his words – even before the accident, he would nag Alex to be more confident, take more risks, be more spontaneous, to essentially be more like him – but instead of smiling and humouring him as he used to, Alex tends to bite back, hard.

'Anyway,' Graeme says now, passing me a takeaway cup, 'I brought coffee.'

I smile broadly. 'Thank you. You can come again.'

'Good to know. So how's everything going at Spark?'

A sip of coffee sends a sorely needed dart of energy through me. 'Oh, fine. I'm on the verge of being fired, but what's new?' My flippancy is entirely fabricated, but only because I don't want to think about work today – or, come to that, Seb. Overpaid and underworked, he's probably enjoying some sort of bottomless brunch at a home counties hotel right now, adjusting his aviators and sucking in his stomach whenever an attractive woman walks past, despite the fact that he's married with kids. He's had the idea for a while that he's some sort of Z-list celebrity, and from what I can work out he hasn't a care in the world most days.

'You know, I've been thinking,' Graeme says.

'Careful,' I say weakly, a poor joke I barely have the energy to crack.

'Still too early.'

'Sorry. You were saying?'

Behind us, from the fence at the boundary of the garden, the call of a blackbird drifts through the warm air.

'I think I should move back to Norfolk. Maybe move in with you guys for a bit.'

I lower my coffee cup. 'What?'

'I'm serious. Work's wrapped up for now . . . I have some time.'

I narrow my eyes. 'You've been fired, haven't you?'

'Ah, that's the beauty of not having a contract, Molly. Nobody can fire you from anything.'

'Oh God, you walked out, didn't you? Are you homeless?'

'Molly!' Graeme smiles. 'This is a nice thing I'm offering to do here. Don't look so . . . stricken.'

'You are,' I conclude. 'You're homeless.' The last time Alex and I went to stay with Graeme in London was a couple of months ago, when he was subletting a spacious ground-floor flat from an acquaintance in Ealing. That arrangement had been due to end the following week-end, and I've assumed he's been sofa-surfing since then.

'Molly, I'm never homeless. I'm actually living with a friend at the moment. Mike. Plus, you know . . . I have cash in the bank.'

I look across at him, the heat of the sun against my face. 'No, you don't.'

He sighs. 'Look, I am genuinely offering to move in with you for a while, help take the load off. You can focus on work, and I'd make sure Alex does more during the day than watch TV. He's always moaning about being bored, right?'

'Y-es,' I say uneasily. 'But –'

'I could free up time for you to have to yourself, you could start going to the gym again, see more of your friends, do stuff for you . . .'

My first, rather ungenerous thought is, *Where was this unfettered offer of help three years ago, Graeme?* Because the past three years – when we were trying to deal with the shock, the trauma, the medical appointments, the not knowing how well Alex would recover if at all, the constant how-long-is-a-piece-of-string response to every question we had, the arguments, the furious rages, the horror as the realization finally sank in that Alex would never be the same again – those were the times when I needed someone by my side. To some extent, he's offering to come in as the dust is beginning to settle, and what is left now is less practicality, more renewed heartbreak as I contemplate spending the rest of my life with a man I definitely didn't marry.

Because he's not Alex any more. He looks like Alex, he talks like Alex and some of the time, he is Alex. But most of the time, he bears little resemblance to the man I used to know.

'In sickness and in health' yes – but this doesn't feel like sickness. At the start it did, with the hospital, and the coma, and the doctors, and the incremental daily victories (*yes – he moved a toe! Yes – he blinked at me! Yes – he said my name! Yes – he went to the toilet unaided!*), but the past year has felt like something else entirely – a long haul of barely perceptible changes and the relentless reality of knowing that this is it. For ever.

Despite what I thought, it turns out I wasn't prepared for that.

I have to ask. 'Where's all this coming from, Graeme?'

'Look, I just . . . last night I realized when I got to yours how hard it must be for you, Moll. Alex was in a filthy mood, the house was . . .'

' . . . filthy,' I supply quickly, so he doesn't have to find a euphemism.

'You're the only one working,' he continues, 'and now that's hanging in the balance. So, I guess it's time for me to step in and do what I should have done three years ago.'

'Why didn't you?' I ask him quietly, since he's brought it up. 'Out of interest?'

He frowns, sips his coffee, stares into the waving grass stems around his legs. 'I guess I wanted to bury my head in the sand a bit, Moll. I've always been like that. If I have a problem, I tend to go for distraction therapy, rather than facing it head-on. It's not an excuse, I know, but . . .'

'It's okay, Graeme,' I tell him. 'Nobody's perfect. The whole thing was traumatic for everyone. And especially you – I can't imagine what it must have been like to . . .' I trail off, overcome for a moment by an image of Graeme bending over Alex's motionless body, screaming his name, quickly becoming smothered in his twin brother's blood.

'Look, Moll,' he says, 'I don't want you to feel obliged, or anything. Because of the house. I mean, just so we're clear.'

The cottage was originally left entirely to Alex in Kevin's will. We offered to sell on more than one occasion and give Graeme half of the money – but for a number of reasons, Graeme always refused. Fortunately, just before his accident, Alex added Graeme's name to the title deeds – so at least he has a share of the place, if only on paper.

Graeme's never made me feel as if he has any claim

on the cottage, but if he needed somewhere to live, perhaps urgently, I'd have no grounds for turning him down, even if I wanted to.

Which, of course, I wouldn't. He's Alex's twin brother after all. I have considered more recently if I should offer to pay him some sort of rent, but my finances being as they are, I don't want to make promises I have no hope of keeping.

'Well,' Graeme says, sounding momentarily uncomfortable, 'how about it?'

I survey the fields surrounding the cottage, brushed gold by the morning sunshine. 'Have you thought this through? Living here, in this house, with Alex – all day every day?'

'Yes, and I've been thinking – I can help try and get him back into work. I can sit down with him, look at applications, make calls for him. And I know people – I could get him something casual. Labouring on a site, bar work or something.'

There was no hope of Alex having the concentration span, patience or attention to detail necessary to go back to his old job in graphic design after the accident. It became painfully obvious very quickly that he would find it far too hard to translate a creative brief on to paper or a screen; nor does he find it easy to think in 3D. It's a lot harder for him these days to even understand that work would have to be presented in a certain way.

But he has attempted three other jobs since the accident – all of which he went on to lose. The first was office assistance work, a mere year later (fired for insubordination). The second, washing dishes in a cafe (sacked for failing to turn up – either on time, or at all). The third, voluntary work in a charity shop (he walked out after getting into a war of words with an elderly customer).

I did feel sorry for him. For a man who finds it exhausting just to make it to midday, the prospect of finding and embarking upon new work is utterly overwhelming. No wonder he couldn't see it through. And those experiences have all bruised him – because he thinks he looks like an idiot when he makes a mistake, that people are laughing at him. It's going to be a task nothing short of monumental to persuade him to try again, unless we can find a boss who really understands.

I remind Graeme that 'casual' is the last thing Alex needs – that in fact he requires rigid structure, short hours and a boss who has the patience of a saint.

'Anyway, I'm not even sure how he'd take it, Graeme,' I conclude. 'You moving in with us. He might think you were trying to control him, baby him.'

'He always says that. It doesn't mean he's right. Plus, you need the help.'

Above our heads, a plane soars. I watch it go, its vapour trail carving a fierce white scar into the smooth blue of the sky.

'Look,' I say eventually, setting down my cooling coffee and knitting my knuckles together, 'I'm not sure I do. Actually, I just want someone to bring Alex back.

And that's never going to happen . . .' Suddenly over-whelmed, I cover my face with my hands, breathe desperately into them for a moment or two.

Because what Graeme doesn't realize is that my exhaustion isn't really physical. I mean it is, to some extent – but what's more tiring is the second-guessing, the constant corrections, the never-ending worry. The thinking about money – how to balance that bill with that expense. The trying-to-be-positive. *That's* the drain-ing bit.

'Exactly, Moll,' he says eventually, softly. 'He's never coming back, so we can only deal with right now. And right now, you need some help. I mean, look at this sod-ding house. It's falling apart. It's a health hazard. Half of the electrical sockets aren't even working.'

'I know, I know, but . . .'

'Why are you so proud? Why won't you let me help you?'

'It's not pride, Graeme. It's just that I'm not sure how much you can really help. All the practical hurdles are passed now.' *And the emotional ones are even harder.*

The improvements Alex has made since the early days have been profound, but what I still can't come to terms with is that permanent peripheral void you can't quite put your finger on – the lack of connec-tion that's hard to define, the small and stupid things you miss. Like companionable Sunday-morning lie-ins; the shared jokes that no one else understands; popping out for dinner without having to faintly panic the whole time you're there, one eye on the clock like you're on a disastrous first date; feeling him play with my hair as we watch TV or fall slowly to sleep in bed.

'I don't agree,' Graeme argues. 'I really think I might be able to make a difference.'

I say nothing further, because there's no other way for me to protest without sounding very ungrateful. And to some extent, property ownership aside, I don't have total say over everything to do with my husband's life. Graeme is Alex's twin brother – he had known him for a full twenty-six years before he met me. When someone has a life-changing accident, cultural boundaries around family become somewhat flexible. Our marriage doesn't just involve me and Alex any more. It involves me, Alex and all the other people who love him.

What's really going on with Graeme crosses my mind again: his job, his living situation. Alex used to worry about him heading down the same dysfunctional path as his alcoholic father, genetically destined to pick up where he left off.

'If you *need* somewhere,' I say carefully, 'then of course you can move in, for as long as you want. Be honest with me.'

'No,' he says, getting to his feet. 'I don't *need* to move in, Molly. I was offering because I thought it might help. But you know best.'

I look up at him, unsure suddenly if this is a prompt for me to deny I know best, to question myself out loud.

'Just think about it,' he says, when I fail to reply. 'I'm not going anywhere.'

He pauses for just a moment to squeeze my shoulder before he disappears inside, leaving me doubting myself all over again as a wife, sister-in-law, friend.

5

Molly – present day

Monday morning a week or so later, and I am deep breathing again outside on Spark's single rickety fire escape. Seb called me out in front of everyone for yawning in our staff meeting, to which I smiled and said something suitably self-deprecating. But the minute the meeting was over I ran out here, leaning over the rusty metal railing, and started heaving air like an OAP attempting a jog round the block.

'Molly?' Dave sticks his head out of the fire escape door.

'Sorry,' I say. 'Be back in a minute.'

He comes out and stands next to me. 'Ignore him,' he says softly. 'You wouldn't have been yawning in the first place if he hadn't been droning on like he was. What a dullard. You saved us all from premature death by boredom. The guy's got about as much charisma as a potato.'

I glance across at Dave and smile gratefully. He looks comfortably unkempt as always, stubble outgrown, salt-and-pepper curls tickling his neck, denim shirt crumpled.

'I'm not upset about Seb,' I say, because I'm not really – these days it's all about Alex. Last night, after a tetchy weekend, we battled over what to eat for supper after he decided that the same chilli I've been cooking for the past three years looked disgusting. He insisted on ordering an Indian takeaway, which turned into a fight about money – namely, that we don't have any – which swiftly became an argument about him not being at work. (I say 'argument'. Most of it was a fairly vicious tirade directed at me by Alex while I pretended to be really absorbed in folding laundry.)

I understand that it gets him down, staying in the cottage all day while I'm here. He's bored, so he starts out most mornings with good intentions, only for motivation simply to fail him. He determines to try a session in the gym, or do some gardening, or the weekly shop, or some DIY, but his brain just won't let him move to the next level. It's frustrating to watch and I know it upsets Alex more than anyone else in the world. He finds it impossible to understand why his mind won't let him do what needs to be done.

But the worst part is, he no longer cares about taking it all out on me. Before the accident, on the rare occasions he'd unwittingly done anything to upset me, he'd have asked me what was wrong, brushed the hair from my face, asked me to talk to him. But he no longer has the patience or the empathy for that.

'This is what it must be like when they get yard time in prison,' Dave says after a few moments. 'Do I wish I was by the river right now with a nice cold pint.' He tilts his face up to the sun and briefly shuts his eyes before glancing over at me. 'You?'

'Swap the pint for a G&T and I'm there.'

We both sigh in unison. In the car park below us, a couple of kids are circling on pushbikes, shouting at each other, laughing. I envy them simply for being kids with a strength that surprises me.

'Oh, how was Friday?' I ask Dave suddenly. 'I never even asked.' He'd been planning a second meeting with a recent blind date, Carole.

'Great,' he says, shaking his head, like he still can't quite believe it after his recent run of disastrous dates. 'We had almost too much in common.'

'Ooh, such as?'

'Well, we both love tapas, hate our jobs, support Everton and know absolutely nothing about wine. That already puts her leagues ahead of anyone else I've met recently.'

'That's great!'

'I know. I'm seeing her tomorrow night. Some sort of nineties indie rock group I've never heard of, but her taste in everything else is pretty damn-near perfect, so . . .' He smiles across at me. 'Let's just say, I'm hopeful.'

I sigh contentedly. 'Oh, Dave. I can live my life vicariously through you now.'

He smiles a little uncertainly. 'Not . . . the being single bit?'

I catch myself, swallow. 'Of course not. I meant . . . being carefree, that's all.'

We are interrupted then by a head appearing round the fire-escape door, which unfortunately belongs to Seb.

'What are you doing out here? This is an emergency fire escape.' He turns his attention to me. 'Did you get that coffee you needed, Molly?'

'Oh, lay off her, Seb,' Dave says. 'Give her a break.'

Seb makes a point of checking his oversized watch. 'Er, it looks as if you've both already had one.'

Dave clears his throat as I slip past Seb back towards the office. 'Seb, I didn't want to bring it up in front of everyone before, mate, but . . . did you know you're flying low?'

Somehow I manage to keep my smile under wraps until I'm back at my desk. Would you believe it, these little exchanges keep me going. Alex used to be quick-witted like Dave. It's one of the things I miss about him most.

I'm home just before six after popping into the shop for bread and orange juice. Evening sunlight dapples the cottage, and I indulge a silent fantasy that I might find Alex in the back garden, ripping up weeds, top off, back glistening with sweat. I imagine for a moment he will turn to look at me, break into his whole-face smile as he heads over to greet me, smearing mud across my cheeks as a joke, before we collapse against the wall laughing. Maybe he'll have picked me a posy of poppies. He hasn't given me flowers since the accident.

But it's also Monday, and Mondays are the day he's supposed to cook, another proposed activity. Nothing complicated – beans on toast would do it – but just something I can eat when I get home. Because he used to love cooking so much.

'Hello?' I head through to the dark cavern of our living room, put my change down on the side. What a contrast to my fantasy — Alex is in front of the television, staring at his phone. I wonder for a stupid moment if perhaps it's one of the apps I'm always trying to get him to use — they're a useful way of recording tasks — but he's yet to be convinced he needs something like that to improve his life.

I hesitate, on the brink of speaking but for a moment afraid. What kind of mood will he be in? Will we have a fight?

It's warm and close in here, but Alex wouldn't think to open our half-rotted windows — he just sheds layers instead. I head into the kitchen to put the groceries away before going back into the living room and throwing the windows open, acting breezy.

I have learned not to go straight in and ask what he's actually done with his day — he interprets this sometimes as a complaint, nagging, the fuse to start an argument. So I rephrase it slightly. 'How was your day?'

'Boring,' he says eventually.

'Oh. Did you see anyone? Did you text Charlie back?' I scribbled it up on the kitchen whiteboard this morning, where he's supposed to check for daily tasks (I eventually figured something physical might be better than an app), but rarely does.

No response.

'It's Monday night. Did you think about cooking

dinner?' I say gently. 'It's on the whiteboard. I texted you when I left the office.'

'Nope,' he says curtly.

'What are you looking at?' I ask, kicking my shoes off and sitting down next to him. I am relieved to almost squash an empty water bottle – his hydration's important, and he doesn't always remember to drink enough.

I lean back into the sofa, reach out, set my hand against his leg, but he doesn't notice. Or if he does, he chooses to ignore me.

'Just clothes.'

'Clothes?'

'Yeah.'

Alex has had this thing recently about polo shirts. He's wearing one right now. Maybe it's something to do with the hotter weather but he simply can't get enough of them. They would not have been his style at all before – in fact I don't think he owned a single one – but now it's all he can think about, and of course, he needs to buy one in every single colour of the rainbow. And in duplicate too, in case they shrink or get stained.

It was watches before, then a particular cut of a particular brand of jean. The obsessions last for a few weeks before he starts fixating on something else. It's a cognitive side effect of his injury, obsessing about certain things, unable to let go. And it's probably quite a neat way of staving off his boredom too.

The particular problem with these shirts is that he likes the designer ones, the ones that cost fifty quid a pop. I try not to panic that he's just emptied his account on something he already has more than enough of.

When Alex first came home from rehab, we'd give him cash to pay for things. But his brain couldn't cope with the mental calculations – he'd simply empty his pockets at the till and tell the cashier to take however much they needed. A debit card was easier for everyone, so I cancelled the overdraft on his current account and gave him a monthly budget, at the same time cancelling my own overdraft and credit card. I just couldn't take the risk of him going on a massive spending spree – it's still one of my biggest fears that he'll apply for a credit card off his own back and do exactly that.

'You don't have enough money in your account to buy those shirts, Alex.'

He pushes the hair back from his eyes where it has flopped forward. 'So put some money in there. I need them.'

'We can't afford it.' I strain to see the screen of his phone but he tilts it away from me like a teenager.

'You're always complaining, Molly. Stop bloody complaining for once in your life.'

Shooting out of nowhere, his comment doesn't so much sting as gently bruise, because I have almost become used to his casual character assassinations. But they are not his fault. He tells things how he sees them.

'I'm not complaining,' I say evenly. 'I'm just telling you the truth.'

'I need them, Molly. It's okay for you to spend money on clothes then?'

Last weekend I bought a summer jacket because my old one fell apart. It's possibly the only item of clothing I've bought in six months.

'I don't buy clothes,' I tell him, my voice heavy. 'You know I don't.'

'What about that jacket, Molly? I know it's new. You're wearing it now! So there's enough money in *your* account then?'

He is staring at me, eyes hot with injustice. I stare back, willing the veil to lift for just one second.

It does, sometimes. I call it *the glimmer*. Sometimes, just sometimes, my old Alex returns to me. The veil in front of his deep-green eyes lifts, and once again he is there, speaking as he used to, looking me right in the eyes, smiling his whole-face smile.

It might only last for a moment, or it might last a little longer, but when it does happen it's as if he's trying to say, *I'm still in here. Don't forget about me, Molly. I still love you.*

But tonight, the glimmer doesn't come. His face remains set, his eyes dark.

'So, what about dinner?' I ask, a way to change the subject, but it's a dangerous question when he's irritated, sure to elicit the response, *Can you just get off my case for two seconds?*

'Can you just put some money in the account please?'

I take a breath. 'Okay, okay. I'll put some money in next week, I promise.'

'Just do it now, Molly. Why do you have to be so awkward all the time?'

'I don't get paid until next week, Alex. You know that.'

'How am I going to pay for these then?' He lifts his phone right up to my face. 'You don't ever want me to have anything nice. Haven't I got enough to deal with?'

'So you didn't play golf today?' I ask him, desperate to change the subject, refusing to look at his screen. 'I thought Darren said he'd go with you.'

He lowers the phone. 'I'm not a baby, Molly. I don't always need someone with me.'

'Okay.' Pause. 'Well, why don't you text Charlie back? You were supposed to let him know about . . .'

'I'm *doing something*,' he growls at me like a teenager. 'Go away.'

I nod, swallow, say nothing for a few moments.

'So what's for tea?' he asks me.

'You were supposed to do it,' I remind him sadly. 'It's Monday, remember?'

'Well, I didn't check the planner.'

I swallow. 'Fine. We'll have curry.'

'I'll order it,' he says, suddenly animated.

'No, Alex . . . we had takeaway last night. I'll cook one.'

'Don't be stupid, Molly, I'm not waiting for you to cook one! I'll order it.' And then he turns his attention back to his phone, navigating clumsily to the food delivery app.

And even though we definitely can't afford it, I don't have the strength to fight with him about it tonight. I've had a bad day, it's hot, I'm exhausted, and all I want to do is sit here together without fighting.

A minute or so later he throws his phone down on to the sofa.

'What did you order for me?' I'd been waiting for him to begrudgingly ask me what I wanted.

He hesitates, and straight away I know he's forgotten me. 'You said you'd cook.'

'I meant . . . I meant I'd cook for both of us.'

He sighs heavily, his face already turned away from mine, bored of my nit-picking. 'Well, you should have said that then.' Conversation over.

The curry is quick to arrive and Alex, unusually proactive, insists on answering the door. I lurk in the background like always, ready to jump in if there is a misunderstanding of any kind. He's already paid online, so simply taking the bag should be reasonably hitch-free.

The delivery person is female and young, and from what I can see at a quick glance, pretty. Alex is laughing, asking her flirtatiously if she found the house okay. His dad always used to ask us that when we turned up, a long-standing family joke, apparently.

'I know where you are!' The girl laughs, like his question is outrageously cheeky. She must have been here before.

'Well, I didn't want you to get lost,' he laughs back.

'Here's your food.'

She passes him the bag, and I see him hand her something in return. 'I got you a tip.'

It's a bloody fiver, my change from the shop earlier. He must have swiped it off the side when I wasn't looking.

'Oh,' she murmurs, her lowered voice a measure of her pleasure, since I doubt she very often gets tipped at thirty per cent. 'Thank you. That's really generous of you.' It's hard to know if she has any idea about Alex, or about me, or about who he really is. Catch him at the right moment and you'd never even know. 'Eating on your own tonight?' she asks him then, and for one horrifying moment I think she's angling to come in.

He sighs. 'Yeah. Unfortunately.'

I swallow a bite of rage, consider stepping out of the shadows to shut this little role play down, but thankfully, she's off.

'Well, enjoy,' she giggles. I can just about see her flirty little wave as she makes her way back to her car.

The words of Alex's first psychologist – also a one-time target for his charm – brood low in my mind like storm clouds. *It's very common for social awareness to be severely impaired in this way, Molly. Don't take it too personally.* But I'd have to be superhuman not to take this personally. He does it with infuriating regularity – with waitresses, ticket conductors on trains, in fact anyone who's obliged to take a temporary interest in him. He's even, on occasion, turned his attention to my friends. He was never like that before, but this strange new overly charming side to my husband is yet another unexpected and unwelcome result of the accident. In fact, I hate to say, he's become much more like Graeme in this respect.

So as Alex enjoys his takeaway I cook myself beans on toast on our ancient hob – a far cry from this afternoon's fantasy of Alex's famous steak fettucine. We eat silently and apart, him on the sofa and me at the table at the opposite end of the living room. Then he puts a box set on – some American action series I've never heard of, presumably a recommendation from Graeme, who's into that sort of thing – and promptly falls asleep.

An hour or so later, having cleared up the dishes and put a load of washing on, I shake him awake, hand him a fresh bottle of water and manage to coax him upstairs to bed. He's grumpy, uncommunicative, tired to the point of delirium.

When I come back downstairs I start robotically clearing things away. As I move a pile of magazines *(Three whole magazines about fishing? Since when have you been into fishing, Alex?)* I discover wedged between them Alex's old work sketchpad and pencil. Absent-mindedly I flick it open, and to my surprise discover several pages of fresh line drawings. They're dated within the last few weeks, and they are spectacular. Alex was a good artist before, but these . . . these are truly special. As impressive as anything you'd find in a gallery, mounted and framed with a price tag of five hundred quid.

The realization that he has not lost his ability to draw, that most precious of skills, strikes me square in the chest, a direct hit to my heart. *He's still in there.*

I examine the drawings, though I feel as if I'm intruding, trespassing on some hidden part of his mind like I'm reading his diary. There's one of the cottage, one of the cafe in the village, even one of Graeme. Is it the drawing of Buddy the puppy that brings tears to my eyes? Or the fact I was hoping, deep down, that in amongst these drawings I would find one of me?

I go outside to sit alone in the long grass of the garden. Around me, the countryside has fallen asleep. The trees have stopped whispering and even the birds are in bed. And it's only so long before the silence and stillness become unbearable. I take a few deep breaths to make sure my voice won't shake before phoning my mum, but we chit-chat for just ten minutes before she has to go off with my dad to a church social (yes, even my parents now have a more interesting life than me). So I decide to dial Phoebe, my oldest friend in the world. I've known her since primary school, and over the years we've always simply slotted into each other's friendship groups as our lives have changed and our social circles have expanded. She still lives only a couple of streets away from Mum and Dad with her parents, she's saving for a flat and has just met a new guy, Craig. I know she found it particularly tough, dealing with the new version of the Alex she thought she knew so well (and the new version of me, who was unable to talk about anything other than how the new Alex was doing). Suddenly, my priority was always Alex, and understandably, she wasn't quite sure where that left her.

But right now, Phoebe's in a pub with a group of friends and can barely hear me. So I find myself calling Graeme.

I actually don't know why I do it. Maybe it's because

in so many ways he is the replica of the Alex I lost, who disappeared without saying goodbye.

'Hello?' Graeme sounds breathless. Probably running for a bus. Or away from someone he owes money to.

'Hey,' I say heavily. 'Sorry, I just . . . I just wanted to talk to someone.'

There is a pause that sounds muffled, like he's put his hand over the mouthpiece. Then, after a moment, he's back. 'Oh yeah? Everything okay?'

'Yeah. It's just been such a long evening, but then I found these –'

And then I hear it. A loose giggle, followed ever so faintly by a *ssshh*.

I hesitate, and then the mortifying realization strikes me. 'Oh my God. Now's not a good time, is it?'

'No, Molly, it's –'

Another soft giggle.

I can feel myself blushing. 'I'm so sorry. You should have said. I'll speak to you another time.'

'Moll, I'll call you later –'

But I have hung up, head already in my hands.

Graeme is so bizarre sometimes. Why the hell would he pick up the phone to me while he's with a girl?

I sigh, switch off my phone and head back inside before I can inflict any more damage on the outside world.

6

Alex — 18 March 2011

'I've got something I need to tell you.'

It's the night before Molly is due to move all her stuff into my flat. We've been dating for a mere twelve weeks, but I know — I just *know* — that she's the one. In my entire six years of dating Nicola, I was never really struck with the idea that she was the girl I would spend the rest of my life with. Looking back, it's hard to see how we made it that far.

But that's not the crazy part. The crazy part is that I still haven't told Graeme about Molly. He's been away on holiday, then she was, and before I knew it several weeks had passed. But it's been three months now, and still I haven't confessed.

It doesn't end there: I persuaded my landlord to let me stay on in my flat (which curiously enough involved him upping the rent), before turning down the job I agreed to accept in Norwich and ripping up the resignation letter I wrote for my current job. Pissed a lot of people off. Graeme knows I've done all that, but he doesn't know why.

I figure it's time to own up.

'Oh yeah?'

We're rewarding ourselves for our earlier workout by sharing a curry in my flat, half watching some entertainment show, talking about work and about Dad. My plan is to tell him about Molly, then for us all to meet up for beers later.

'Yeah . . . it's a bit weird, actually.'

He looks over at me, hair still damp from the shower, mouth full of Balti chicken. 'Weird?'

'Well, you know how I decided not to move back to Norfolk in the end?' It wasn't a hard decision, actually. Yes, I crave the country, and all my friends were ready and waiting for my big return home – but being with Molly has suddenly made the city seem infinitely more bearable. I simply can't risk losing her at this point by moving two hours up the motorway and turning us into a long-distance relationship. I've never met a girl like her before.

Graeme waves his fork around my very-much-London-based living room. 'Er, yeah.'

'Well, I didn't just . . . get cold feet. There was sort of a reason.'

He puts the fork down and beams at me. 'I knew it! I *told* Dad. You met someone, didn't you?'

I beam back at him. 'Yep. I did, as it happens. And . . . I want you to meet her tonight.'

Graeme shakes his head, rarely fazed by impromptu invitations to socialize, and pops a hunk of naan into his mouth. 'Bloody hell, I owe Darren twenty quid now. You sly old bugger.'

Yes, I have been a bit sly, actually.

'So who is she?'

I hesitate. Why is this so hard? Graeme's my brother.

'You remember that girl we met just before Christmas at the bar? The one who you were chatting to and then . . . well, you went off to speak to Rhiannon?'

Graeme's expression darkens slightly. 'Oh yeah. Her. Tray full of cocktails, never to be seen again.'

I say nothing more, just wait for him to catch my eye. '*Her?*'

From outside the window, a train shoots past on the tracks running parallel to my street, the noise roughly on a par with a plane taking off.

I try to smile. 'Yeah, she . . . it was weird, I bumped into her later and we got chatting.'

Graeme's jaw sort of swings. '*That* was the girl you went off with?'

I'd told him it hadn't gone any further with the girl I abandoned him for that night. I'd even invented a name – *Louise*. Lied, essentially. I wish I hadn't done that now.

'Yeah. Her name's Molly.' I shake my head. Funny how it all seemed quite harmless at the time.

'Not Louise, then.'

'Yeah, I know. I thought – I don't know. Maybe I didn't want to jinx it.'

'Well, cheers for that, mate.' He looks more wounded than I was expecting.

'You're always telling me to go for it with girls,' I say hastily, whipping out my only (rather weak) excuse a little too swiftly. 'I mean, you kept saying it, that night.'

'So you thought you'd go for it with her?'

'Gray, it wasn't . . .'

He smiles faintly. 'Go on, say it.'

'Say what?'

'It wasn't like that.'

'Well, it wasn't,' I protest. I can feel myself getting hot and worked up. 'I didn't *intend* to –'

'What did you tell her to put her off me?' he asks me suddenly. 'That I was on the phone to my ex?'

I stare guiltily down at my plate, mumble a lie. 'No, of course not. I only bumped into her later on.'

He raises an eyebrow. 'Maybe you should have told her *I* liked her. How about that?'

'Oh, come on! I bet you're still sleeping with Rhiannon now.'

Graeme petulantly shoves another hunk of naan into his mouth and chews furiously.

'You are, aren't you?'

'Well, maybe I wouldn't be if I'd had my chance with Molly.'

'Don't, Gray,' I mutter. 'She's . . . my girlfriend now.'

'Wow. Don't tell me you're in love?'

I swallow, say nothing and look down at my plate, feeling like a complete and utter tosser. From beyond the window, the pleading wail of a siren calls.

'So are you?' he presses. 'In love?'

'Yes,' I admit. 'I've asked her to move in with me.'

'In here?'

I nod.

He nods back. 'Right. So you're definitely not coming home.'

'Not at the moment. Molly's job's here, and . . .'

'She didn't fancy it? More of a city girl, is she?'

'I haven't even asked her, Graeme. It didn't seem like the sort of thing you do straight off the bat.'

'So how long's it been – three months?'

I nod again, scoop some rice on to my fork and hope we can move on.

'You know what doesn't make sense, mate? That you've taken three sodding months to tell me about her.'

'There didn't seem to be a good time.'

Graeme smiles at me. 'To say *I've got a girlfriend*?'

'There's just been –'

'I get it. You felt guilty.'

'About what?' I say, a little indignantly, though I know full well what.

Graeme shoots me a look I probably deserve, mopping up the rest of his curry with the last piece of his naan. But he remains silent.

'Look, Gray – it's not as if you *said* to me you liked her . . .'

'You knew,' Graeme says lightly, like my own conscience should have done the talking, which of course, it should have. We're twins after all. We do have some level of intuition about what the other's thinking.

'You said you met someone else that night anyway,' I remind him weakly.

'Yeah, which lasted to breakfast. Actually – come to think of it – not even breakfast.'

I can't think of a way to explain that Molly and Graeme having a one-night stand would truly have been a horrible and terrible waste, because Molly is the girl of my dreams. To be honest, even the concept of them hitting it off is a little difficult to get my head around, so I don't want to spend too much time dwelling on it.

'Bumped into her, you said?' Graeme says now.

I nod, lean back against the sofa, pick up my drink.

'Maybe she thought you were me,' he says, goading me in that particular way only he as my twin brother has the knack for.

I don't tell him that for a split second she *had* mistaken me for him. It's irrelevant – I corrected her straight away, for God's sake.

'Graeme – if I'd known you felt that way about her –'

'You *did* know,' he says, cutting me off. 'And you decided to do it anyway.' He shakes his head. 'But look – I'm not going to make a big deal out of it. You're in love, that's great, well done.'

'Come on. Don't be like that.'

He gets up and walks over to the kitchen, puts his curry plate in the sink. 'Don't be like what?'

'Look,' I say, worrying how I'm now going to ask the favour I need from him, 'I haven't explained any of this to Molly. It's all a bit complicated.' *Primarily because I've been a bit of an idiot about the whole thing.* 'Can you just . . . sort of pretend you've known about her all along?'

Graeme smiles at me like he's only just realized what

a fool he has for a twin. 'She doesn't know she was a secret girlfriend?'

I give up trying to explain my bizarre behaviour. 'No, she doesn't.'

'Does she know you were about to move back to Norfolk?'

'No. Look – please, Gray?'

He comes over to me then and takes my face between his palms. 'I will do my very best,' he says, 'not to give you away.'

'Gerroff,' I grunt, upon which he ruffles my hair, so I can only assume we've made up.

The following evening Molly and I carry the last of her boxes from the car up the two flights of stairs to my (our) top-floor flat. Pausing in the living room, she puts a hand to her chest, breathes heavily. 'Wow. I seriously need to go to the gym.'

To me she looks incredible, even in her moving-day T-shirt and jeans. 'Whatever happened to that New Year's resolution?'

'Um, life?'

I draw her into a hug and kiss the top of her head. She's been working long hours recently, leaving precious little time for anything else. 'Believe me, you don't need to worry about it,' I whisper.

'Charmer,' she says, beaming up at me happily.

'So,' I say, as we survey the mound of boxes now taking up all available floor space in the living room, 'what did you make of Graeme?'

She smiles at me. 'Make of him?'

'Yeah.' I smile back. 'What?'

'No, it's just . . . you say it like he's a puzzle that needs solving.'

Oh, Molly. If only you knew.

The three of us went out for beers last night with two of my colleagues, Ryan and Phil. I'd assumed Graeme was coming back to mine afterwards, since I'd invited him to London for the weekend in the first place. But he made his excuses after closing, saying he was going to meet someone he hadn't caught up with for a while, and off he went and we didn't see him again. But then, that's Graeme – ever since I can remember he's had a habit of disappearing without telling anyone where he's going.

'You didn't think it was odd?' I ask her. 'That he went off like that?'

'Not particularly,' she says, shaking her head. 'He strikes me as that kind of guy.'

Ah. Interesting. I suspect deep down I'm still looking for additions to my growing tally of reasons why Molly and Graeme would be the most poorly matched couple in existence.

'What – rude?' I say then, as a sort of joke.

She tips her head at me. 'No, of course not. Just . . . a bit flaky. Anyway,' she says, 'can we stop talking about your brother, and celebrate the fact we just moved in together?'

I smile down at her. 'Yes, please.'

But just as our lips meet, Molly's phone starts to ring.

'Who is it?' I ask her.

She winces. 'Dad. Again.'

I met Molly at her parents' place in Clapham early this morning to load boxes. I get on with them well, but I suspect asking Molly to move in with me less than three months after meeting her in a bar was not exactly the brightest move in their eyes. They're practising Christians – not devout, but they believe in the proper order of things and brought Molly up in the same way. (She stopped accompanying them to church when she turned eighteen, and I swear that sometimes she still gets overexcited on a Sunday morning because she doesn't have anywhere to be.)

But given their beliefs, they do seem pretty cool with our relationship on the whole – maybe because they're pleased I'm at least ready to commit, or maybe because they see it as a fairly low-risk move on balance: Molly moving in two miles down the road with her new boyfriend, who has neither a serious attitude problem nor an allergy to any form of commitment.

Just then, the clouds that have been hanging overhead all day finally burst, and a storm begins to rage beyond the window, loud enough to rattle the glass in the pane.

Molly and I lock eyes, share a smile. 'Just in time,' I whisper.

'Oh, I don't know,' she murmurs, leaning forward to kiss me. 'I think there's something romantic about getting soaked together in the rain . . .'

Her phone buzzes again.

'Sorry, better answer it,' she sighs, pulling away reluctantly and putting her phone to her ear. 'Hello?' She pauses for a few moments while her dad rambles on about something, shooting me a smile to show it's nothing to worry about. 'Yes, Dad. No, they're all in . . . yes. Well, Alex has stuff. Yes. Yes. I'm *fine*, Dad. Yes, I promise. Okay. Love you. Love you. No, I'll speak to her tomorrow. Love you both. Bye.' She hangs up, wincing slightly through her smile. 'Sorry.'

'Don't be. They love you, they care about you.'

She makes a face. 'I think *smother*'s the word you're looking for.'

'Hey, Moll, don't knock it,' I say, but then stop. I don't want to make her feel guilty for being embarrassed by overbearing parents.

'I'm sorry,' she says gently. 'I wasn't thinking.'

'No – I didn't mean it like that. I just mean – you're an only child, their little girl. Of course they're going to worry about you moving in with someone you've only known for a few weeks.'

'It feels longer,' she says, perching on a box.

I smile. 'I'll take that as a compliment.'

She laughs. 'I just mean, I feel like I've known you my entire life.' She sends a little shrug my way. 'Corny, but true.'

'Well, me too.' I deliberate for a moment between going back over to her to finish the kiss we started, or heading into the kitchen to retrieve the bottle of champagne I've had chilling in the fridge since last night.

Another good reason for not yet having divulged the details of

88

Dad's drinking habit to Moll. I can enjoy a bottle of champagne with her and not have to worry that she's wondering quite what she's getting into.

'So, what does your dad think?' she asks me then, taking me a bit by surprise, like I've said something about Dad out loud without realizing. 'About us shacking up together?'

'He's happy for us.'

I haven't yet introduced them, and I haven't yet sat down and told Dad I'm not coming back to Norfolk for the foreseeable future. He thinks my staying on in London is only temporary, that I'm still due to move out of my flat, that my Norfolk job offer comes with a flexible start date. I don't want to upset him, so quite shamefully I told him I've got a big project on at work that I need to wrap up in order to secure my spring bonus. I'll be free to move after that, I told him.

Outside, the rain hammers and the windows shake.

'He's really ill, isn't he?' she asks me gently.

I swallow and nod. 'Quite ill, yes.'

'Are you sure . . . you wouldn't rather move back there? Be with him?'

I can't quite explain why, but there's something about the thought of moving back to Norfolk now that suddenly terrifies me. These past twelve weeks with Molly have felt like everything I've been waiting for my entire life and the idea of heading back to the country without her is a massive punt I'm unwilling to take. I picture myself living back with Graeme in his flat, listening to him jibe me about being single – or if Molly's willing to make it a long-distance thing, his predictable jokes about her meeting new guys with all that free time she has now.

And yet – Dad's so ill. Am I doing the right thing? Is a visit every other weekend really enough?

'Yes, I'm sure,' I tell her firmly. 'I wouldn't have asked you to move in if I wasn't.'

'It's so weird seeing all my boxes here like this,' Molly says, a delicate change of subject.

'Good weird?'

'Yes! It's just . . . I've never lived with a guy before. It's like . . . my whole life's in boxes on the floor of someone else's living room.'

'Well, not your whole life,' I remind her with a smile. 'Most of your stuff is still at your mum's.' Molly has a *lot* of stuff – her bedroom barely looked as if we'd touched it, even as we were leaving.

'Well, all the important stuff's here.'

'Wait there a moment,' I say then, heading back over to my tiny kitchen to grab the champagne and two glasses. (They called it 'open-plan' when I viewed the place, by which they meant it was really just part of the living room.) 'Now's the right time for a toast, I think.'

She smiles. 'You're *so* romantic. Champagne and flowers.' She nods at the posy of wild flowers I bought her this morning, now tucked neatly into an old coffee jar (I'm not *that* organized).

'Oh God. You mean cheesy.' I think guiltily about how many times I've berated my brother for being cheesy around girls.

'Definitely not.' Her eyes are sparkling. 'But just so you know, I do draw the line at teddy bears holding felt hearts.'

'God, we all draw the line at teddy bears.' I pretend to shudder before filling the champagne flutes and handing her one. Our eyes meet. 'I love you,' I tell her.

'I love you too.'

We chink gently, then take a sip. The drink's perfectly chilled, the flat's warm and everything's pretty much perfect. Outside, the wind howls, sending sharp slaps of rain against the window. Tonight all the stars are hiding, tucked safely away behind the storm clouds.

We listen to the storm as we work our way through the champagne, and when Molly gets a little drunker she starts opening boxes and lifting items out to show me, turning them over in her hands, explaining their history. There are the books by Thomas Hardy and George Eliot, her Britpop CDs, photo albums, collection of beer mats, costume jewellery. I'm intrigued by everything; I *want* to know about all the things that make Molly who she is.

'Hey, Moll,' I ask her when it occurs to me, 'did you bring my jacket?'

'Oh, damn, I meant to. It's still in my wardrobe. Wanted to keep it safe.'

'Doesn't matter. Don't worry about it.'

'We can get it tomorrow.'

'No, whenever you're next there.'

'Probably tomorrow then.' She smiles.

I laugh and kiss her. 'Right. Are you ready for our very first supper together as cohabitees?'

'Cohabitees? You make us sound like a tenancy dispute!'

Well, I'm about to make up for the clumsy phraseology by cooking her my famous fillet steak fettucine. The other thing I love about Molly is that, unlike Nicola, she's a real foodie. Nicola saw food as fuel and very rarely attached emotional significance to it – she regularly forgot to eat if she was busy – whereas with Molly, part of the joy of getting to know her has been discovering all the restaurants London has to offer and (even better) annoying our fellow diners by holding hands across the table, staring moonily into each other's eyes and – don't judge me – feeding each other morsels from our plates.

It's the little things I love about Molly, the stuff I know I'm going to value in all the years to come.

Later that night, I am playing with Molly's hair as she snoozes in the crook of my arm, pushing my fingers softly through the strands of it, enjoying the feeling of her breathing deeply against me, when a loud decisive crack from the sky outside shuts everything down in the flat. The fridge rattles swiftly into silence, my speakers cut out and everything goes black.

But there's still an eerie glow emanating from my side of the bed. I roll over carefully, so as not to wake Molly, and pick up my phone.

What I see on the screen sends a little rivet of annoyance shooting through me.

Heard your news. Congratulations. I hope you'll both be very happy together. N x

The next morning I meet Graeme for a coffee before he catches his train back to Norfolk. The day is wet and blustery, the remnants of last night's storm, only it seems far less romantic now I'm walking through it without an umbrella, or come to that, Molly.

I hate this coffee shop — it's the kind of place where you have to choose between seven different varieties of milk with varying percentages of fat content. The cakes it sells are all seed-based, and there are at least four products scribbled illegibly on the chalkboard that I can't even identify, let alone pronounce. Fortunately Graeme's fluent in this weird kind of coffee language, so he translates — but I'm pleased he asks the barista for a croissant too, just to wind him up.

We find a table in the window. I've ordered a distinctly un-hip latte, while Graeme's gone for one of the unpronounceables. They come in glass cups with no handles, the glass allegedly double-walled for heat resistance, and Graeme's milk has a miniature glass bottle all to itself.

He's hungover beneath his beanie, which is pulled right down to his eyebrows, just a few strands of blond hair sneaking out beneath the brim. I try not to picture Dad in his place, first thing in the morning after a heavy drinking session, because right now the two could almost be interchangeable.

I push this somewhat alarming thought away. 'Good night then?'

'Messy.'

The steam spiralling from our coffee makes a little smoke signal between us. 'So what did you think of Molly?'

Graeme pulls a face that implies he thinks this is a strange question. 'I have met her before, Alex. Remember?'

I put the sarcasm down to his hangover. 'Yeah, it's just that you dashed off on Friday night, and –'

'You don't need my approval,' he says, with a hint of a yawn.

'No, but you're my brother, so . . .'

He leans forward, traces the rim of his cup with one index finger. 'Well, look – I'll tell you what. It was a bit awkward seeing her again on Friday, given how we met, but it's obvious how much she bloody loves you.' He lifts his drink to his lips. 'Can't understand what she sees in you myself.'

I feel relief bloom through me. 'Thanks.'

'Does she know how ill Dad is? I got the impression when we were talking about him that she didn't quite understand the seriousness of the situation.'

I hesitate. 'Maybe she doesn't need to. Look – she's not even met Dad yet. Maybe it's our problem to worry about. I mean, yours, mine and Dad's. A family problem.'

Graeme tips his head back like he wants to get a better look at me. 'A "family problem"? That's a bit cryptic. Are you ashamed of him?'

I snort, which has the unfortunate effect of sending a shot of latte through my nasal passage. I grope for my napkin, which predictably is recycled and thus similar in texture to tracing paper. 'No,' I say, blowing my nose. 'Don't be stupid. It's just – I don't know. I don't want Molly to feel guilty that I'm in London when –'

'– you should be at home with him?'

I stare at him. Is that what he thinks?

'I thought that's what *you* were going to say,' Graeme supplies quickly, avoiding my eye.

I set down my cup. 'Look, Gray – we're different, aren't we? You've never had ties, you've always been able to do as you please. But me – well, I've met Molly and . . . decisions like that are just a bit harder now. You know – moving. It's a big thing.'

Graeme half laughs. 'Christ, Alex, you've known the girl five minutes. You were all set to come back until a matter of weeks ago. It's not like you're married with kids.'

'I've never met anyone like her before, Graeme.'

'Well, you've only got one dad. That's all I'm saying.'

I wonder then if Dad has asked Graeme to talk to me, as it's quite unlike my brother to pull emotional blackmail on me. Then I think uncomfortably back to what I did to him with Molly and consider that, possibly, I don't really blame him.

Graeme rolls his eyes. 'You're all he talks about. *Why*

hasn't Alex come back yet? Is his project nearly finished? Do you really think his new job don't mind waiting for him? I mean, I'm there, but you're still the only one that matters, Golden Boy. The prodigal sodding son.'

'Shut up, Graeme,' I say tetchily, because this particular guilt trip is the worst one of all. 'I come up as often as I can.'

'Look,' Graeme says, leaning forward so I can't avoid his eye. 'I do know how it feels, mate. To meet a girl, and suddenly the rest of the world melts away.'

I take a sip of coffee instead of saying what I want to say, which is that for Graeme, this happens every third night or so.

'But Molly's only the second girl –'

'Graeme,' I say sharply, affronted, 'Nicola's not the only other girl I've been with.'

'Fine. But you can count them on one hand.'

'So what?'

'So, I'm just saying – this is bound to feel new and exciting and . . .'

I set my cup down, wipe a small slick of milk foam from my top lip. 'You can really be a patronizing git sometimes, Graeme, you know that?'

There is a silence. A couple with a young baby in a sling sit down at the table next to us and start talking loudly about wine thermometers.

'I'm only going to say this once,' Graeme says quietly then. 'I know London's not *you*, Alex. I know you love your life back home, all your friends, being in the country. Don't abandon who you are for a girl.'

In a way, I'm pleased. Because Graeme's just unwittingly added to my mental list of reasons why he and Molly could never have worked. He has certain ideas he's simply not willing to budge on, but me – I'm willing to compromise. Isn't that what lasting relationships are all about?

Just then my phone buzzes, moving sharply across the table towards Graeme, but I fail to grab it before he catches sight of the screen. '*Nicola?*' A grin spreads rapidly across his face. 'Well, this *is* interesting.'

'Christ. I don't want her texting me.'

I glance down at the screen.

Aren't you talking to me? N x

'Didn't know you kept in touch.'

'We don't. I mean *I* don't.'

'Ah. You're her one-that-got-away.'

'Hardly,' I mumble. 'She dumped me for someone else, remember? Anyway, it's another reason for me not to move back to Norfolk, isn't it? I'd have to see her all the time.'

'Reason, or excuse?' mutters Graeme. 'Right, got a train to catch I'm afraid.'

As he pushes back his chair, a tall brunette with an armful of shopping bags struggles to pass. Taking any opportunity to be chivalrous, Graeme virtually launches himself across our table so he can move the offending chair away from her.

'Thanks,' she smiles, holding his gaze before moving on her way.

'So what are you going to do about Nicola?' Graeme asks me as we exit the coffee shop and head up the street.

'Nothing,' I tell him. 'She'll get the message soon enough.'

'I wouldn't bank on that,' he says darkly, but he doesn't elaborate and I don't ask.

7

Molly – present day

Graeme is down for the weekend again, and he's talking about renovating the cottage. He wants to help us finish everything, or at least make it part-way habitable so we're slightly more comfortable. But the list is expensive, and endless – rewiring the entire house, plastering, bricklaying, flooring, fittings . . .

'Must be quite tempting to sell sometimes,' Graeme remarks as we're running through everything.

His comment pulls me up short – is he testing me, to see how committed I am to staying here? To Alex? Or is he thinking he could do with a lump sum himself?

What I don't bother reminding him is that it's a moot point. Even if I did want to sell, Alex is fiercely resistant to the idea – and if Alex doesn't want to do something, we generally don't. Besides which, I know how much he loves this house and how many of his oldest memories rest within its walls. I'm not sure I could bring myself to tear him away from it.

'You always said –'

He looks surprised. 'I didn't mean you *should* sell. Sorry, Moll – only thinking out loud.' He shakes his head, looks down at his list. 'Right – what are you going to do first out of this lot?'

'I can't afford tradesmen.'

'I know some guys,' Graeme says, his trademark phrase.

I smile. 'Who'll work for free?'

He considers this. 'Mates' rates is basically free. Honestly, Moll – I can hook you up. Just give me the go-ahead.'

'I'm not sure I've got the energy for all this at the moment, Graeme. Plus I don't have any annual leave left. Someone would need to be here with Alex if there are strangers in the house.'

'Er, hello?' Graeme says, turning an index finger in towards his chest.

I hesitate, recalling our previous conversation about him moving in.

'I could just be here for a week or two,' he clarifies quickly, 'if you needed me to be.'

I smile, realize I'm probably being a bit awkward. 'Okay. I mean, if you can.'

'I definitely can. They'll probably need to fit you in around –'

'– paying customers?'

He smiles. 'Look, in the meantime, at least let me buy you some essentials. You know – basic first-world items, like a kettle, vacuum, washing machine.'

He's got a point – our kettle is on its last legs after being started dry by Alex one too many times, the vacuum is suffering from dust overload and so, I suspect, is the barely functioning washing machine.

For the first time, it strikes me that Graeme is of the opinion that I'm possibly a bit incompetent at what I'm supposed to be doing, which is caring for Alex.

'Okay,' I finally relent. 'But only if you're sure.'

'I am,' he says. 'Look, given I do have a stake in this place I feel it's kind of my responsibility too, aside from anything else. So let's go.'

Having been conked out with a headache for most of the morning, Alex is more buoyant on the way to the electrical store. Once or twice, I even catch him humming. Graeme shoots me a smile as the sun breaks out from behind some low cloud, and just like that, everybody's mood seems to lift.

So much so that Graeme sets Alex the challenge of directing us for the last ten minutes of the drive, which goes fine until Graeme says, 'So what if we decided to go to the swimming pool now?'

It should be simple – Alex knows where the pool is. We've been there since his accident, and there's only one on this side of town. He's swum there since he was a little kid, and it's a mere two roads over from the electrical store. But his brain struggles to factor in somewhere new (it's only a simple right turn at the roundabout, as opposed to a left one), and he ends up getting frustrated, swearing at Graeme for ruining his morning, accusing him of trying to make him look stupid, of laughing at him. And I am slightly frustrated myself, because Graeme always feels the need to push it when Alex is feeling upbeat rather than just enjoying the fact he's feeling good.

We only manage to prevent the whole thing from escalating by pulling into the car park and suggesting Alex does a couple of laps on foot to cool off before we head into the store.

But his mood is set now, and when we get inside it only dips further. The shop's busy today; the staff are run off their feet, and we're forced to wait for fifteen minutes in the washing-machine aisle for advice on the best model, disposal and plumbing-in, which Graeme's going to attempt himself. But these days, Alex doesn't really tolerate waiting for anything. Whether it's for waitresses, shop assistants, buses ... waiting makes him agitated, and he never bothers to hide it. The most patient man in the world has now turned into the most impatient. Someone who would never have spoken rudely to anyone – least of all a person he didn't know – now has the capacity to be vicious to strangers, and it makes me nervous.

As we wait, I become slowly fixated by the TVs. The last time Alex and I were in this shop was just a couple of weeks before his accident, and I remember us pausing to watch the screens playing a sweeping drone's-eye view of Sydney Harbour. We gripped each other's hands as we looked on, mesmerized by memories of our holiday the previous year, before he turned to take my face between his palms and kiss me. We ended up making out there in the aisle like teenagers, strangers tutting as they were forced to move round us.

But just like all my best memories, the recollection is bittersweet, because the only person tutting today is Alex. 'How long are we going to wait here for, Molly?'

'She's coming back,' I assure him.

I can sympathize, to some extent. This is exactly the sort of environment Alex hates – there are too many stimuli competing for his attention, and his thoughts are starting to lag as he becomes overloaded, which is when his temper becomes frayed. Pumping background music, way too much going on, bright lights, noise. Plus he's tired from the journey, from having to make conversation with Graeme as well as me, from answering his brother's questions, from the heat.

'Well, what the hell is she doing?' he exclaims loudly, waving his water bottle around in disgust. 'How long does it take?'

'She was helping someone else, mate,' Graeme says calmly. 'We just have to wait. Come and look at the TVs.'

Alex shrugs him off. 'Nah,' he says irritably.

I still find it so hard to believe that the same man who kissed me passionately here three years ago is now stamping about and swearing under his breath, memories of our former life virtually meaningless to him.

'Maybe we should just cut our losses and go,' I say to Graeme.

'No, Moll. We're here now.'

I rub my arms, which are all prickled up with goosebumps, though I'm not sure if they're from the air con or my nostalgia. 'Well, let's find someone else to help then.'

'Oh Jesus, I'm not waiting,' Alex spits. 'I've plumbed in washing machines before. I'm a fucking plumbing *expert*. We don't need these idiots. They won't know what I know. Just *buy it*, Graeme.' And then he walks off.

'Some people are so rude,' I hear a woman near to us mutter.

It's the arguments in public places that are always the worst – especially as they would have mortified the old Alex.

'I should go after him,' I say, my face reddening as I imagine all the other people Alex is probably haranguing and swearing at on his way to . . . where?

'Just leave him,' Graeme says. 'What's the worst that can happen?'

I let out a shot of laughter. 'Did you even just say those words?'

'Well, where's he going to go? We're on an out-of-town industrial estate.'

'That's never stopped him before.' He's been known to try and walk home from the beach before, when we were miles from anywhere.

'Let him go, Moll. Just let him cool off.'

'We shouldn't have pushed him so much in the car. He was in a good mood.'

'You mean I shouldn't have.'

'No, it's just . . . you have to pick your moments with Alex.'

'Yeah, I do – like when he's in a good mood. There's no better time to stretch him than when he's feeling upbeat.'

'I'd rather enjoy the moment.'

'Then he won't ever improve.'

*But the fleeting good moods are what I live for, Graeme.
They're what keep me going on my darkest days.*

And anyway, maybe Alex has his own private ways
of improving. I haven't told Graeme yet about the
drawings I discovered in his sketchpad a couple of
weeks ago; though I have taken to flicking through it
every now and then, idly curious to know if he's been
adding to it. He has, and I've noticed a pattern – if he's
had a good few days, a new drawing will appear (there's
been one of the pub, the plum tree in our garden,
another of Buddy), but if he's not been having a good
time, the pages remain defiantly blank.

Secretly, I am still waiting for the magical day when
a drawing of me appears.

It's almost like having a conversation with him,
looking at his sketchpad, because I'm able to find out
how he's feeling without needing to ask. Of course I'm
desperate to know if it helps, the drawing – how he
feels when he's doing it, where he gets his inspiration
from, whether he knows just how good he really is –
but I can't tell him I've been looking. He'd say I've been
spying on him; and if I brought it up then never saw
another sketch again, I'd never forgive myself.

And telling Graeme would be disastrous – he'd be all
over it, demanding Alex show him, encouraging him to
do more, buying him all sorts of art equipment, psycho-
analysing the hell out of it. All of which can be great when
it's well-timed and carefully judged, but this is Alex's private pastime and I am terrified of scaring him off it.

'I should go and look for him,' I sigh now.

'Molly,' Graeme says, putting a hand on my arm, 'just relax. He's not a toddler.'

I do treat him like one some days – I know I do, and I know I shouldn't, but I can't help it. It's instinct more than anything else.

Our assistant finally arrives to give us the lowdown we need on washing-machine disposal. She's young and pretty, and Graeme flirts with her as he does with all young, pretty girls. He even manages to make her blush at one point, which I assume to be quite an achievement, since I'm sure Graeme isn't the first guy to come in here who's fancied chatting her up.

'What?' he protests, when I shoot him a look after she's gone.

'Nothing!' I laugh, holding up my hands.

'I was just being polite.'

'Politely flirtatious. I was going to leave you both to it at one point.'

Graeme looks strangely bashful then. 'It's not . . . fully intentional.'

I smile and shake my head. 'Ha. I guess you just can't help it if you naturally ooze charm.'

He beams at me. 'Well, thank you, Molly, I'm going to take that as a compliment.'

I laugh. 'Don't, it wasn't one. Right, shall we go?'

Alex's mood doesn't improve much after we leave the shop and stop for petrol – he takes exception to Graeme paying at the pump with his credit card, adamant he's doing it solely to provoke him, to show off that he has a credit card and Alex doesn't. In the end Graeme is forced to give up and apologize before the whole thing escalates.

But later on his frame of mind is more amenable, and he even suggests heading to the pub for supper. It's rare he instigates being sociable, so if he does, we try never to turn him down.

It's busy in here tonight, but on the plus side it's familiar territory for Alex, which helps. I admit I'm sort of relieved when he lopes off to stand near the pool table and watch his friends, observing them for a few minutes as he always does, joining in when he's ready (they're used to this).

We order drinks and food, and Graeme's in the middle of telling me about a pop-up beach on a roof terrace he's been to recently in London when I glance over towards Alex and spot him chatting to a girl. Unfortunately, it's not just any girl. It's his ex-girlfriend, Nicola.

They dated for six years, living together for three of those in Alex's London flat. It ended when Nicola dumped Alex for someone she'd met on a weekend trip home to Norfolk. The new man lasted only a few months.

I know – and I've heard it from other people too – that Alex has always been Nicola's one-that-got-away, the man she always regretted dumping. She wanted to come and visit Alex in hospital after his accident, but it just felt too weird to me, her being his ex. She sent a series of cards instead, which I didn't feel entitled to throw away on Alex's behalf, so they are sitting with all the rest of the well-wishing stuff in a box in our spare room. I resent her for that more than I probably should, for sending things to the house for Alex that I have to hold on to. She sends him Christmas cards too, birthday cards. And the Easter before last a giant chocolate egg was left on our doorstep, no name attached. I knew it was from her.

One thing I really dislike about her is the way she acts as if I don't exist. She'll acknowledge me when she has to, but that's all it is – a begrudging nod to the fact I am alive. Alive, and very much in her way.

It doesn't help of course that she always looks fantastic, whereas I always look like the 'before' picture in a makeover photoshoot. She's a personal trainer, so she carries a year-round glow from all that jogging around the park with a stopwatch. Not a scrap of fat on her, beautifully toned, whitened teeth, designer activewear. She has a lot of wealthy clients, and her job is to look at least as good as they do at all times. She rarely drinks but wafts around the pub with a club soda and lime, networking by touching people's forearms and making them fantasize that they too could look as good as her if they just set down the pint glass, skipped the chips and signed up for press-up lessons at fifty quid a pop.

'. . . yeah, they have deckchairs and stuff, barbecues, music. I mean, it is what it is, but . . .' Graeme trails off. 'Moll? You okay?'

I swallow, look back down at my lemonade. 'Yes, sorry. What were you saying?'

'Just about this urban beach thing. I know the guy who runs it – we could get a day pass if you think Alex might enjoy it?'

I can't resist glancing back over at Nicola. She's leaning against the pool table now and Alex's hand is on her arm. He's laughing at something she's saying, which is enough of a sting in itself. He so rarely laughs at anything I say any more.

It grates on me too that, just like always, she doesn't so much as glance over to check if I'm here. She does the same thing if we run into her in the street, or spot her in the supermarket – she'll raise a hand, smile at Alex, but say as little as she can get away with to me. She doesn't even care if I'm over here getting riled, and it's the inference I'm insignificant that's always wound me up the most.

Graeme follows my gaze, then turns back towards me and clears his throat. 'Just ignore them.' His face and voice have darkened slightly.

'She should know better,' I mutter into my drink.

Graeme, like me, is completely allergic to Nicola. This is partly good, because it means I'm not alone in my disdain for her, but it also makes me worry that I have good reason not to trust her. And though Graeme's advice to ignore them is well-intended, Nicola works hard to make that near-enough impossible for me.

Alex is laughing again now, miming something with his hands, completely animated. She's giggling like a schoolgirl. I see Alex's mate Charlie glance over at me, concerned. I shrug, like this is perfectly normal.

And the horrible part is, this *is* almost normal – turning on the charm around other women is just something Alex does now. Nicola's convinced she's special (she always has been), but there's no way to know if he's doing it because it's her, or if she could be any other girl he happened across. Still, it kills me to see him flatter his ex of all people with his latent ability to be smooth and sparkling, when he so rarely does the same with me.

'Reminds me of you in that shop earlier,' I say to Graeme, trying to make a joke out of it, because if I don't I'm afraid I might start crying.

Graeme, who clearly doesn't think the situation is worthy of humour, frowns. 'God, don't say that. Look, the food'll be here soon. I'm going to go and break up their little powwow.'

'Please don't,' I say. 'I don't want to cause a scene.'

'Well, no, but you're right, Moll. Nicola should know better.'

I watch nervously as Graeme strides over to them. I can never predict how Alex will react to being told off or interrupted, especially in an environment where he's probably overstimulated anyway.

As Graeme arrives at Nicola's side I see her smile wordlessly. He ignores her and speaks to Alex for a few moments, then Alex responds before Graeme turns round and heads back to our table. As he walks away I see Alex roll his eyes and say something else to Nicola – and it must have been funny, because she responds with a laugh, touches his arm again. *Why does she need to keep touching him?*

Our food arrives as Graeme sits back down – vegetable chilli (extra hot) for Alex, fish and chips for Graeme and me.

'What did you say?' I ask him, feeling a mixture of relief and confusion as the waitress deposits our cutlery and vanishes.

'Told him the food had arrived.' He smiles, makes a quick exhale. 'Phew. Perfect timing.'

'What did Alex say to you?'

'That he arranged to meet her here.'

I stare at him. 'What?'

'Yeah, I know. A bit weird.' Graeme glances past me and beckons urgently to Alex, mouthing, *Come on.*

I think back to Alex enthusiastically suggesting we all eat here tonight. 'Do you think he's telling the truth?'

'No way of knowing.'

'Well, what did Nicola say?'

'I wouldn't believe a word that comes out of her mouth,' Graeme says sharply.

Not for the first time, I wonder if Graeme's dislike of Nicola stems wholly from the fact she cheated on his brother then dumped him, or if there's something more to it.

Alex rejoins us then and, without saying anything, sits down and starts eating his chilli as if nothing much has happened.

I can feel Graeme watching me. 'Graeme was saying there's a beach you can go to in London –'

Graeme talks over me. 'Alex, do you think you should be chatting to Nicola while Molly's over here?'

Alex looks up at him but not at me. 'Yeah, why?'

'I mean, Nicola's your ex-girlfriend. Molly might feel a bit upset about that.'

Alex shrugs, so I look down at my chips.

'She asked me to meet her.'

'Why?' Graeme says.

'I don't know.'

'When did she ask you?'

'What? I don't know, Graeme!'

'Just leave it,' I say, meeting Graeme's eye. 'Can we please just talk about this later?'

But Graeme's not finished. 'I don't think that was appropriate, Alex. She kept touching you, flirting with you –'

'So what?'

'Well, you looked like you were enjoying it . . .'

Alex points his fork towards Graeme. 'You never want me to have any fun.'

'No, that's not it. There are just certain people –'

'We do want you to have fun,' I assure him quickly. 'That's *all* we want.'

'So what are you talking about then? You're always saying, *Don't talk to him, don't talk to her* . . . you treat me like a child.'

'Alex, it doesn't matter,' I say, a last-ditch attempt to save the evening.

But it's too late – he puts down his fork, gets up and walks away without saying or eating anything further. On one level it's encouraging that he's heeding the advice he was given in anger management, to remove himself from situations that wind him up. The only problem is, he often forgets to tell us why he's walking away. I've lost count of the number of times I or someone else has been left abandoned and slightly bewildered mid-conversation if we've unknowingly touched on a point that needles him.

'You okay?' Graeme asks as I stab at a chip in frustration.

'Now isn't the time, Graeme. We should have just waited until later.' I tip my head at Alex's picked-at plate of food. 'He won't eat that now.'

Graeme leans towards me. 'Moll, we've talked about this. He needs to know *now* that what he was doing wasn't right – he won't remember later, it won't mean anything to him. You know he needs consistent messaging, or nothing will stick.'

'You tell me this stuff like you think I don't know it.'

'Because you always back down. Because you never want a scene.'

I feel my tears rise quickly. 'Because that's who we *were*, Graeme! Me and Alex were *both* that couple who would never make a scene. You know – we never fought in public, or told people to shut up in cinemas, or complained in restaurants, or argued with the neighbours about fence panels. That was who we *were*. And I know Alex has changed now – I know that more than anyone – but you're asking me to change the essence of who I am too. Do you know how much it broke my heart to see that woman tutting at him in the shop earlier? Do you know how much I wanted to turn round and say to her, *You don't understand, this isn't who he is, he's the gentlest, kindest, most loving . . .*' But I can't finish. The choke in my throat holds back the rest of my words. I have to shut my eyes and lower my head for a moment to steady myself.

'I'm sorry,' Graeme whispers. 'I know all that. Honestly.'

I swallow and breathe out. 'You're the guy who doesn't mind a scene, who isn't self-conscious, who thinks everyone else can generally do one. And that's fine – that's who you are, and I would never criticize you for that – but that isn't who *I* am, and I can't always do everything exactly as I'm supposed to. Sometimes I get it wrong, and I hate myself for that, but this is *hard work* . . .'

'I know that too. I'm sorry, Molly, really.'

We don't say much more for the rest of the meal. Our mood has flattened and Alex doesn't return – he's over at the pool table now, talking to Charlie and taking the occasional shot. Thankfully, Nicola has vanished, but I can't stop thinking about her.

Alex heads upstairs to bed with his water and his meds almost as soon as we get home. Graeme suggests a nightcap but I'm tired too, and I don't want to talk about Alex any more.

'I'm going to bed,' I tell him. 'Do you need anything?'

His back to me, Graeme's looking at a particular photograph on our mantelpiece, the one that sits next to the picture of me and Alex drinking honeymoon cocktails on a Mexican beach. The photo he can't stand is a monochrome shot of Alex and his dad – they're embracing and laughing, and Alex is looking up directly into his eyes. He must be five, six at the most. I think it's a beautiful photo, and I know it's very precious to Alex, but Graeme hates it. He dislikes it so intensely that sometimes I'm tempted to slip it into a box whenever he comes round, but he's so keenly aware of its presence that he'd definitely notice, which would kind of negate the point of doing it in the first place.

'Might just stay down here and get sozzled if it's all the same to you.'

I know why he hates the photo, and as always I am tempted to tell him to let it go, but I don't. I just make a sympathetic face and tell him goodnight.

'Joke,' he calls out to my retreating back as I head upstairs to bed.

Alex is gently snoring when I slide into bed next to him, but a full hour later I'm still wide awake. I can't stop thinking about Nicola. Did she really ask to meet him at the pub, and if so, why?

At first glance, Alex might not appear to be vulnerable, but he is – he takes people at their word and interprets everything literally. Who knows what charms Nicola might be pulling on him with me out at work all day, with Alex living just down the road? I know for a fact that her favourite running route just so happens to take her directly past our front garden.

She was like this before the accident too – and I

assume ever since she decided that ditching him for someone else was a huge mistake – but of course there was a limit to her influence then, because Alex always rejected her. He'd cross the road to avoid her, pull me laughingly behind a building with him if he spotted her, tossed Christmas and birthday cards on to the open fire.

But now . . . I can't shake the thought of her from my mind, or the image of him enjoying how she was flirting with him. Would he have the strength of mind to turn her down if she propositioned him? Would he even know that was the right thing to do?

Tears sting my eyes as I find myself picturing them together. *It's not fair. You got the best of him, and you didn't want it – and now, every day, I'm living with the worst of him.*

But still. I love him. I grip on to the fragments of the old Alex he occasionally throws my way like titbits, and I hold them to my heart.

I look at our texts sometimes, and it's his last-ever text to me before it happened, the one he sent at sixteen minutes past midnight, that always chokes me.

Great night, love you xxx

How much more would he have wanted to say, had he known what was about to unfold?

Downstairs I hear the tell-tale chinking of a glass being removed from the cupboard and, moments later, the suck-pop of a cork being pulled from the neck of a wine bottle. I can't help thinking about Kevin, that this is exactly the sort of thing he would do late at night too when he felt alone, or crap, or like blanking out the world for a while.

I turn to look at my husband sleeping. It's too easy to believe when his eyes are closed that he's the old Alex, returned to me; so lovely to imagine his eyes will blink awake at any moment, that he'll put out a hand, brush the hair from my face and say sleepily, *Hey*.

I reach out, touch his shoulder, run my hand along the line of bicep down to his forearm. It is soft now where it used to be sculpted, but I don't care. I want to lean forward and kiss him in the hope he'll wake up and want to kiss me back, make love to me. But he's in his deepest cycle of sleep now, so crucial for the rest and repair of his newly altered brain. So instead I lift his hand to my lips and peck the back of it, then hold it to my cheek as I slowly fall asleep.

8

Molly – present day

I am heading to London for the weekend, which both thrills me and fills me with trepidation, because I miss living and working there almost as much as I miss the old Alex. It's a sweet form of torture, to look out of the train window and see the trees morph into buildings, the horizon grow high-rises like green shoots in time-lapse. The landscape I used to know and love, my birth-place and stomping ground, the place that made me feel alive and my heart sing. I'm ready for some noise, some energy, the charge of people, a little adrenaline.

Mum is waiting for me at home in Clapham with a pot of freshly brewed tea and a comically oversized plateful of lemon madeleines. She's exactly the sort of mum I always hoped I might one day become – kind, calm, nurturing. She envelops me in one of her hugs, which I've noticed have become a lot tighter since Alex's accident. She always greets me with the level of relief you might see at a military airbase when a plane touches down from a conflict zone.

I sit at the kitchen table and she pours the tea, piles lemon madeleines on to a plate for me. 'How are you? It's so *lovely* to see you.'

I bite into a madeleine, savour that sweet, citrusy tang. God, I miss my mum's baking. I used to dabble but I can't remember when I last had the time or inclination to get out my measuring scales, or come to that, a cookbook. 'I'm fine, Mum. You? How's Dad?'

'Oh, he's fine. He's helping get ready for the church fayre. We're selling lots of Fairtrade, organic things.'

'You should have gone with him, Mum. We can catch up tomorrow before I go.'

'No, no,' she says, waving my insistence to one side. 'It's only setting up the tables and checking the mikes. I leave all that to him. Anyway, I'd far rather be here with *you*.' She pulls up a stool and sits down next to me with her own cup of tea, pats my hand.

I smile. 'Thanks, Mum.'

'You should come along tomorrow, though. I know Peter would love to see you.'

Peter is the vicar at our church. I grew up listening to his sermons each Sunday, and since Dad retired he's been an even bigger part of Mum and Dad's life, as they volunteer at the church several days a week. He married me and Alex, which was important to my parents, and I know he's really keen to talk to me about Alex's accident, something I've been equally as keen to avoid.

It's not that I think he can't help as much as knowing he's convinced he can. I'm not sure I have the energy to discuss the ins and outs of my new life with yet another person whose end goal will be to persuade me that this is exactly what those pesky marriage vows were all about. *In sickness and in health, until death do us part.*

'Maybe, Mum,' I say. 'I'll see how I feel tomorrow.'

She smiles at me, sips from her tea. 'So how's Alex?'

'He's okay,' I tell her, without adding that we didn't part on great terms this morning. As usual, it started over something innocuous – I was nipping to the shop, asked him if he needed deodorant. My wording was careless, and of course he interpreted the question as a suggestion that he needed to *put some deodorant on right now.* Fortunately he'd calmed down by the time Darren arrived to keep him company while I'm away, but I spent most of the train journey feeling disappointed and frustrated. It's hard, adjusting the language you've used all your life when you're with the person you know best in the world. Every little linguistic shortcut we rely on day-to-day – metaphors, half-sentences, nuances and even euphemisms – have had to be stripped back, considered. And as usual it's the unpredictability that's the hardest to deal with – sometimes my careless use of language doesn't even matter; sometimes it can cause the most unbelievable rows.

'And how are you?'

I try a smile across the rim of my teacup. 'I'm all right, Mum. Tired.'

'Is work any better?'

'Nope,' I say. 'But they haven't fired me yet.'

Mum sighs. 'Gosh, I do wish you'd never moved away. You loved your job here so much.'

I frown. 'Come on, Mum. You know that's not help-ful. I can't turn the clock back.'

'But if you were still here . . . we could help you both so much more.'

'You did help.' And they did, hugely – after Alex came out of rehab, they moved to Norfolk for a few months to help us out, staying in a local B&B. They were fully exposed to the gravity of the situation, so they do understand. But I know they're both disap-pointed that life has turned out this way for us, though they try to hide it. I think it's the fact they may have lost their only chance to have grandchildren that probably wounds them the most.

'I hate to think of you doing that horrible job at Spark with that horrible boss.'

I bite into another madeleine and try not to picture Seb railing at me about turnaround times like he did yester-day afternoon. 'What can I do, Mum? We need money.'

'Move back,' she suggests, for the millionth time. 'You and Alex. Me and your dad – we've been thinking.' She whips out her iPad, which always makes me smile – my mum, all her life the most traditional person you could imagine, has now discovered Technology, and you can't keep her away from it. 'We had an architect over, and he drew up some plans for an annexe. There's more than enough room at the bottom of the garden, Molly. You and Alex could move into the annexe, and then we could be here all the time, to help. You could go back to your old job, and you wouldn't have to worry about Alex during the day. Look.' She taps on to a saved file and hands the tablet over to me – the plans are all drawn up for a gorgeous little one-bedroom annexe with a kitchen, living room and bathroom.

The sincerity of her offer, the strange combination of hope and grave concern in her expression, make me want to weep into my cup of tea. 'No, Mum,' I say gently, passing the tablet back to her.

'Please consider it, Molly. You're so isolated in Norfolk all by yourselves.'

'We're not by ourselves,' I remind her. 'We have Eve, and all Alex's friends, and Graeme . . .'

'Graeme lives in London.'

'Yes, but he comes to visit all the time. What I mean is, we're not alone, Mum.'

'But Alex so often tells you he's bored. Wouldn't he have more to do here?'

'Mum,' I say, with a smile, shaking my head. 'It's not that simple any more. When Alex says he's bored . . . it's not the same as when most people say it. He means he's *frustrated*, angry about how much his life has changed. And being in London wouldn't make that better, it would make it worse. He wouldn't cope here.'

It's true – with a shudder I picture him trying to catch the tube, cross the road, negotiate crowds without getting into a fight, cope with all the noise and overstimulation. It's hard not to worry about these things, when it wasn't so long ago he couldn't even remember how to brush his teeth.

'But he was living in London when he met you,' Mum reminds me.

I haven't ever really told her how much Alex hated city life, that he always craved the peace and tranquillity of Norfolk, his childhood home. That for a long time he sacrificed his own needs for mine. 'I know, Mum, but he loves our cottage. He's really attached to it, and all his memories of his parents are tied up in it. I couldn't ask him to leave it, not now. And anyway, he won't do anything he doesn't want to – you know that. I'd never be able to persuade him to move to a city he doesn't even like. He'd take it really badly. He'd think I was trying to control him, baby him.'

'I thought,' she says, after a pause, 'that maybe if we were close by . . . you might feel happier about starting a family.'

'Oh, Mum.' I see the disappointment in her face now, and I feel it whenever I talk to her and she tells me that so-and-so-from-the-church's daughter has had twins, or next-door-but-one has had another little boy. She so desperately wants me and Alex to follow all the social conventions of married life; besides which, she wants me to have everything I ever wanted. She finds it hard to accept the idea that, sometimes, life doesn't really care about your plans.

That was part of the reason she was so devastated when I told her we were moving to Norfolk four years ago, before Alex's accident. She had always imagined being near to her grandchildren – in Mum's world, that's just how things are supposed to be.

I'm always so thankful I never actually told her Alex and I were trying, in the months before the accident

(I knew how much she would get her hopes up, and it would have felt too much like tempting fate). At least now I don't have to add the pain of having had fate against us to the list of daily regrets she has on my behalf.

'It might still happen, Mum,' I reassure her. 'It isn't that we *can't* have children. It's just . . . too soon. You know that. We've talked about this.'

I see her swallow back tears and try a brave smile. 'Yes, I know. Gosh, I'm sorry, darling. I know the last thing you probably need is me putting pressure on you.'

'Offering to build us an annexe so you can look after us is hardly putting pressure on me. Believe me, Mum, if there was a way to do it, I'd love to. But Alex is so sensitive to change now. He's . . . not like he used to be.'

'I understand.' She nods, then blows a breath from between her cheeks. 'Right! More madeleines.'

I smile, shake my head. 'They were enough to last me for the rest of the day. Delicious though.'

'Your dad's request,' she says, smiling back. 'But he knows you like them too.'

Dad lived in France for a while before he met Mum, so she likes to dabble in French *pâtisserie*. It was once a dream of mine too to maybe move out there with Alex, perhaps when our children were still young enough to absorb the language without too much trouble. I had an idealistic dream of living in a village that still had a *boulangerie* and *charcuterie*, of sitting at pavement cafes whiling away hours while our children played in the square, of taking long walks in the countryside, a couple of dogs at our heels. I even had a feeling Mum and Dad might not have objected to an impromptu move across the Channel themselves, Dad being still near-enough fluent in French and obsessed with all things continental.

It's a funny thing, when the future you once dreamed of can never be anywhere but the past.

'You do spoil me,' I say to Mum now.

'Well, that's what you're here for, isn't it?' she says. 'For me to look after you. Now, tell me all about where you're going tonight.'

Where I'm going tonight is a great little fondue place in Balham with Sarah, my line manager from my old agency, and Phoebe. I love it here, and Phoebe's booked our favourite table in the restaurant's cosiest corner. It's awash with candlelight and there's a bottle of red wine waiting for us on the table.

We order a veggie Gruyère fondue to share, along with piles of cornichons and fresh French bread, and get stuck into the red wine. Luckily for my bank account, Phoebe and Sarah have insisted on paying for the whole weekend – train ticket, food, drink – the lot.

I'm keen to ask them both about their lives, because everyone always thinks they have to ask me about mine first. After my emotional conversation with Mum this afternoon, I'm ready to talk about something other than Alex and all my broken dreams.

Phoebe tells me about Craig – he's a rugby player, and she's started going to matches to watch him, and even though she still cheers at all the wrong moments (to the point of occasionally whooping when the opposing team score a try), she's really beginning to enjoy it. She's even started socializing with the other wives and girlfriends.

'Hold on,' I say with a smile. 'You're a bona fide WAG now?'

'Actually, we don't appreciate that term,' Phoebe says mock-snootily, dipping a cornichon into the fondue and nibbling on the end of it.

'Does this mean you're going to start getting papped falling out of posh restaurants?'

'Here,' Sarah says, reaching into her handbag. 'You can borrow my sunglasses.'

I smile and take another sip of wine. This is what I love – catching up with my closest friends, chatting and laughing about simple, normal stuff. Stuff that isn't life or death, catastrophic and consequential. Of course I love Eve, but my friendship with her is different – nine times out of ten the kids are running around our feet, and although I love that too, it's not like this. Here, I can pretend I've simply slipped back into my old life. Here, I can pretend Alex is waiting for me back at the flat, with a nightcap and soft music and a kiss I can sink into.

'I'm so happy for you,' I tell Phoebe. 'Can't wait to meet him. Maybe the next time me and Alex are down, we can.'

'Yeah,' she says – but is there something artificial in the way she widens her eyes and nods several times in quick succession? Can I detect a slight strain to her voice, or am I just imagining it? Is Craig the kind of guy who wouldn't be interested in meeting someone like Alex? But the moment passes quickly, Phoebe takes another sip of wine and Sarah starts talking to me about work.

'So we're recruiting soon,' she says innocuously, swirling a hunk of bread in the melted cheese. 'For the exact job you used to do.'

'Really? Who's leaving?'

'Libby. She's moving to Singapore.'

The agency has a sister operation in Singapore, and occasionally one of the creatives gets the opportunity of a lifetime and a contract for relocation.

'Wow. I'd love to do something like –' But I stop myself, swallowing with some difficulty a little spike of envy as I contemplate again the death of a dream I once had to move abroad with Alex, for us to do something really exciting like that. 'Lucky Libby,' I conclude eventually, a false note of brightness to my voice.

'Or you,' Sarah says, popping the bread into her mouth and looking right at me.

'What?' I say, smiling faintly because I must be missing something.

She pushes her hair back over her shoulder. 'Everyone keeps talking about you, like – is there some way we could get her back? We all miss you so much, Moll.'

'Ha,' I say. 'I'm the one who ate all the free snacks.'

'Exactly. Everyone's put on three stone since you left.'

I smile as the crowd of kids at the table next to us

start roaring with laughter about something. I hear ski slopes mentioned, then hot tubs. The acoustics in here make it sound as if everyone's shouting, but I don't mind. It makes me feel like I'm living, at least.

'I mean, if you wanted it,' Sarah says now, 'Libby's job could be yours.'

I stop crunching mid-cornichon and stare at her. 'How do you mean?'

'Like I say, I'm about to recruit, but . . . I don't have to advertise, if I already have someone I want.'

'But, Sarah, we tried to make it work. The commuting wasn't practical, looking after Alex . . .'

'It's just that I bumped into your mum the other day . . .' Phoebe interjects.

'Ah.' I look down at the table. 'And she told you I might be moving back?'

'Did she show you her plans for the annexe?'

'I mean, hello – an *annexe*,' Sarah says.

I laugh. I can't help it. 'Oh my God. What have we become – thirty-something women sitting around a table getting excited about annexes?'

Phoebe and Sarah both smile, but it's clear they're waiting for a sensible response.

'Guys, I can't.'

'Move back to London? Take the job?'

'Any of it.'

I see Sarah deflate a little. Phoebe shakes her head as she spreads more melted Gruyère over her bread, and I hope it's an expression of disappointment rather than disapproval.

'Alex can't move to London, so I can't take the job.'

'He really can't?' Sarah asks me pleadingly, doe-eyed over our flickering candle.

'He would hate it, absolutely hate it. He didn't exactly love it before the accident.'

'What about commuter belt? Somewhere halfway maybe?'

I sigh. 'Then we'd have no one. At least right now we have friends in Norfolk and family in London. But somewhere completely new – we'd be even more marooned.' I look down at the table. 'And anyway, he loves the cottage too much. It was really important to him. You know – what with his mum, and everything.'

Phoebe and Sarah share a look that tells me my situation has probably been the subject of discussion long before tonight.

'And what about what *you* want?' Sarah says cautiously.

'It's a non-starter,' I reiterate. 'Alex hates change for one thing. He wouldn't go – he'd think I was babying him. It could never happen.'

'That wasn't my question,' Sarah says, her voice softening further.

They're both staring at me in wide-eyed concern, but instead of making me feel comforted it makes me feel more alone than ever, because their incredulity only goes to show they don't truly understand. They think I'm weak, that I've lost my ambition, my drive, my sense of self. And it's true – I *have* lost all those things, but it's not because I'm weak. It's because when I'm trying every day to be strong for Alex, I have no strength left for me.

'What about,' Phoebe says hesitantly, treading carefully, 'all the things you ever wanted, like starting a family?'

Phoebe knows Alex and I were trying, before. I never told Sarah specifically, but she knew how important it was to both of us.

'Seriously, guys,' I say then, 'what is this?' I take a long slug of wine to try and wash away the feeling of being criticized for failing to be the girl they knew before.

'We just don't want you to give up on everything you ever dreamed of, Molly,' Sarah says gently. 'There is another way, and we're here for you. There are so many people here who love you, who could help. We just hate to think of you stranded all the way over there in Norfolk, without help, without support.'

'But don't you understand? If we moved back to London that's exactly how Alex would feel.'

'Graeme's here,' Phoebe reminds me, like she thinks I might have forgotten.

'But Alex's friends are in Norfolk, and Graeme comes to visit all the time. Where we live is quiet, it's relatively safe, there's space for him to breathe. He'd be cooped up in London, terrified to go anywhere.'

'You don't know that,' Sarah says.

'I do know that! I live with him every day!'

Someone from the next table glances over at us and

I think to myself, *God – can I not just have one night out in a restaurant without causing a scene?*

'Sorry, Moll,' Sarah says. 'We're not trying to upset you.'

'We just don't want you to sacrifice all the things you've dreamed of all your life,' Phoebe adds.

I think about what she means, about all the things I once dreamed of, that everyone dreams of. Travelling the world with Alex. Learning a language, perhaps moving abroad. Having children, getting a couple of dogs maybe to complete the picture. Making the cottage our own, a cosy family home.

'You don't get it, do you?' I say then. 'Everything you think I'm going through – what Alex goes through every day is far, far worse. He's the brave one, not me. Imagine waking up one day and everyone else is talking a slightly different language, so you're always two steps removed from everything that's happening. You can't find the right words or think quickly enough to keep up with anything. The whole world feels like noise rushing past your ears, but not just for a moment – it lasts all day. And to make it worse, everyone keeps telling you you've said something wrong or you've done something weird and you're *so different* to how you were before. But you're still you, and *you* feel like you're just the same as you always were – it's everyone else who's different. And every single day you're exhausted and you can't do any of the things you used to or remember anything or tolerate a conversation for any more than about ten seconds

131

and you just can't get a grip on *what's happening* –' I take a breath and shake my head, try to prevent the tears from falling.

'I know,' Sarah whispers, 'I know.'

'The sacrifices I've had to make, the dreams I've given up ... they're nothing compared to what Alex has lost.'

The three of us fall silent, and then we just sit there for a few moments, listening miserably to everybody else chattering, laughing, relaxing, having fun.

'Shit,' I say. 'I didn't want tonight to be about this. I wanted to come here and forget everything.'

'Sorry,' Phoebe whispers.

'No, like – let's stop talking about dreams and disappointments and bloody desperation,' I say. 'Can we just forget it all for one night? Please?'

They stare at me in quiet unease, because of course we live in a world where everything can be fixed, where there is a solution for absolutely everything. And when I first broke the news that there wasn't a solution for what happened to Alex – that this was a problem that couldn't be fixed – their natural reaction was to try and think of other ways, *any* other way, that they could make the situation better. Because they're my friends, and they love me.

I wake the next morning in the sanctuary of my childhood bedroom, staring at the ceiling as my brain stirs to the sound of sparrows twittering through the open window. Mum has hung feeders in her trees and shrubs, nailed a nesting box to the north-facing side of the cherry-tree trunk.

My first instinct is to check my phone for messages from Darren. He texted last night to say he and Alex had spent the entire evening absorbed in football-based online gaming, followed by takeaway pizza – but still, I am always fearful when I go away that the first thing I will see when I open my eyes is a series of urgent text messages declaring disaster in Norfolk. Maybe it's because we were apart on the night of the accident, and I was woken by the landline ringing and my mobile buzzing and the stomach-curdling sound of Graeme's distorted voice saying, *Molly, there's been an accident and it's bad, it's really, really bad*, over and over.

A knock on my bedroom door brings me back to today, and Dad's head sneaks round the side of it. I smile sleepily. 'You're up early.'

'Church fayre,' he says with a beam. 'But I couldn't go without making you pancakes. Your favourite.'

Dad has quite a specific, by which I mean limited, repertoire when it comes to cooking. He's the master of all the toasts – cheese on toast, beans on toast and French toast (he's dabbled in scrambled eggs on toast but always gets overenthusiastic with the whisk and they go all watery). But his pancakes are excellent too – he smothers them with maple syrup and butter for me, just the way that Alex used to.

'You star,' I murmur as he brings a tray over to me. I shuffle upright against the headboard as he places it on my lap and removes a steaming mug of hot chocolate from it (or, as he calls it in his impeccable French accent, *chocolat chaud*), setting it down on the chest of drawers next to the bed.

'Budge up,' he says, and I shift over to make room. He looks smart in a chequered shirt and beige trousers, all ready for the fayre. He smells comforting, of coal tar soap and his favourite herby aftershave.

'So, how's my little girl?'

'Much better for these – thanks, Dad.' I smile, cutting into the delectable mess on my plate and shovelling in a sugary, buttery forkful. Being waited on feels like such a novelty.

'Good night? Phoebe popped round the other day, did Mum tell you?'

'Ha. Phoebe did. Said she bumped into Mum.'

'Well, she stopped by. We had a nice long chat.'

'And devil's food cake?' Phoebe's favourite.

Dad smiles guiltily. 'Well, we thought she might not come otherwise.'

I smile knowingly. 'So you invited her.'

'Mum did.'

'Well, that's nice. I miss her.'

'She was telling us all about her new chap.'

'Mmm-hmm,' I say through another sugary mouthful of pancake.

'Your mother's convinced he'll propose before the year's out, of course.'

I smile. 'You think?'

'Well, who knows. It'll be a big wedding anyway. Might be at the church.'

'Dad! She's only just met the guy.' I slide him a look. 'You just want to marry everyone off.'

'Then children, probably.'

I set down my fork. 'Okay, Dad.'

Bless him, on being rumbled Dad just decides to say all the things on his mental List Of Concerns before I can chuck him out of the room. 'Our architect chap drew up these lovely designs for an annexe and we think it would be perfect for Alex and Phoebe said she could talk to Sarah about getting you your old job back and then you could think about starting the family you always wanted.'

I wait patiently, the pancakes pooling in the syrup and butter on my plate. 'Have you finished?' I ask him gently.

He clears his throat and nods, slightly self-conscious, because my dad by nature is not an emotional outburst kind of a guy. 'Yes.'

'Look, I've already had this conversation with Mum, and with Sarah and Phoebe –'

'So you don't want to have it again with me,' he says apologetically.

'Well, I can tell you what I haven't told them – not in so many words – because I think you can handle it. Can you?'

'I hope so,' he says, looking back at me, unblinking.

'The truth is, Dad, I wanted a family with *my* Alex. Not this new version of Alex that isn't really Alex at all. I'm so terrified that if we had children, I'd always be thinking – *always* – about how it could have been, what a different experience we might have had.'

I see him swallow. He speaks slowly, choosing his words carefully. 'And how do you think it would be, with the new Alex?'

'Well, let's see. He's more selfish now – it would feel like having one more child, so it wouldn't feel shared. I'd have to do most things myself. There'd be question marks over everything – like if the baby was crying, would he just carry on sitting there with the remote control, ignoring it? Would he fall asleep or wander off while he's meant to be looking after them?'

'Well, this was where your mum was coming from, Moll,' he says, covering my hand with his. 'We could be on hand to help . . .'

'Fine, Dad, but if you're not? You can't be there twenty-four-seven. Dad, I don't like to tell you everything because I know you'll worry, but sometimes Alex loses his temper around Isla and George, and he'll complain about them in the car all the way home, that they're a pain, always whining, always wanting what they can't have. And I think to myself, *Is that how you'd be with our children?* And that thought scares me, Dad, because he doesn't love me how he used to and I'd be *wilfully* making him a father to kids he might not . . .' I pause, because I don't want to say Alex wouldn't love our children. I know he would, in his own way, just as he loves me in his own way – but would it be enough?

'I see,' Dad says, scratching his chin, and suddenly I feel guilty because these innermost thoughts of mine are news to him and I don't want to upset him, I really don't. 'Well, look – there must be a medical professional who can advise you on matters like this?'

'They already have,' I tell him. 'And, ultimately, it's our choice, Dad, no one else's. Look, Mum just thinks it's about having someone to help change nappies or blend baby food or babysit once in a while, but it's not really about all that stuff. It's about how I *feel*.'

'And how you feel is . . .'

'Unsure. Since the accident, I feel unsure about everything.'

Sometimes at night when I can't sleep, I catch myself imagining the cries of a small child in the bedroom next to ours; envisaging how life might be today if we *had* fallen pregnant when we were trying, before. How would I be coping, now? Would I be pleased we'd had children when we did, or wished we never had? Was seeing the negative test result so many times in fact a blessing? But as with so many of my *what-if*s these days, there is no way of knowing for sure.

'Anyway, Dad, if I was looking after a baby, how would I earn any money?'

'That's where me and your mum come in – we could look after the little one during the day. Or help Alex do it.'

I look sadly down at my pancakes, cool now in their little puddle of syrup and butter. 'Every day? I could never ask that of you.'

'Well, you don't have to, because we're offering. Besides, maybe Alex will get back to work soon.'

I smile sadly. 'Unlikely, Dad. It's not that easy.'

'Why not?' Dad's a big believer in traditional roles, and Alex not working is hard for him to understand, when on the face of it he very often functions just as he always did.

I shrug. 'Lots of reasons. He's scared of looking stupid, for one.' Not to mention the interview process – I've tried persuading him before to scrub up, even suggested cutting his hair, but he collapsed in hysterics at the idea of me with the clippers (I have no idea what was so funny). He laughed so hard I started laughing too and then neither of us could stop, to the point we forgot why we'd even started laughing in the first place. *Welcome back, Alex.* But then he broke off quite abruptly to ask me why I'd rearranged all the tins in the kitchen cupboard, and I lost him again.

'I suppose what I wanted to say is that there's always a way,' Dad says now. 'You just have to keep looking until you find it.'

'Not always,' I tell him, taking a swig from my hot chocolate.

'Always,' he replies firmly, then pauses. 'Why don't you come to the fayre today? You could talk to Peter . . .'

I remain quiet, because much as I don't think Peter can help me I don't want to offend Dad, who really does turn to God if he ever has a problem.

Through the open window, a summer-scented breeze kisses my skin. As if on cue, I hear children screaming outside, whirling calls of delight as they dash around back gardens.

'Well, please know that your bed is always here,' Dad

says eventually, opting not to press me any more. 'We keep your room just the same. Always will.'

'Don't, Dad,' I mumble. 'It's not as if I've died.'

His forehead crinkles with a faint smile. 'Oh, that reminds me. Mum asked you to have a quick look through your wardrobe before you go. We're putting a collection together for the overseas aid run and she wanted to know if there was anything you wouldn't wear again.'

'Okay.'

'Pop along to the fayre later if you can. I'd best be off.'

'Love you, Dad. Thanks for breakfast.'

'You're always welcome, my darling.'

My wardrobe is still crammed with all the stuff there wasn't space for when I moved into Alex's flat six years ago. I idly slide the hangers across, mentally assigning most of the contents to Dad's aid collection, but when I reach the far end of the rail my heart begins to thump.

Squashed behind a similar coat, the arm hidden so Mum might not even have realized it was in there, is Alex's jacket, the one he lent me on the very first night I met him. The one I jokingly said I'd keep so he'd have to see me again. I bury my face in it, convinced I can still detect his scent, the very faintest traces of his old aftershave on the fabric. It is the smell of possibility, of excitement. Of the future. I picture the smile in his eyes as he told me of course I could keep it, that he'd call me in the morning, to get home safe. And I remember that call in the morning, the one I'd been waiting since the early hours to receive, the sound of his voice and knowing, just *knowing* I'd found the man of my dreams. And now I start to sob, wetting the fabric of the jacket with my tears.

I stay like that for maybe ten or fifteen minutes, mourning everything we've lost afresh, until Mum calls me from downstairs and I am forced to say goodbye to the past once again.

I push back the jacket until it's right out of sight, to keep it safe.

A few hours later I head back to the station to catch my train, having made my excuses to Mum and Dad about the fayre. I think they know I'm not ready to talk to Peter yet, and I'm happy to let them believe I just need some time to come round.

I am staring up at the departures board in the station, trying to see if my platform's been called yet, when my phone buzzes from deep inside my pocket. It's Graeme.

'Hey.'

'Word on the street is you're in London Town.'

Wow — the grapevine's more active here than it is at home. 'Only just. I'm at the station.'

'So am I. Sort of. Well, I'm down the road. Fancy coffee?'

'Um . . .' I waver. 'Not sure. I should get back to Alex.'

'Molly – coffee, not a European mini-break. You can spare half an hour, surely? Get the next one?'

I smile. 'Sorry, yes. Of course I can.'

'Excellent. There's a coffee shop upstairs.'

'I'll get them in.'

'Thanks. I'll pay you back.'

Looking casual in a T-shirt and jeans, Graeme resembles the Alex of old so much I almost double-take. It's a strange sort of torture really, seeing his twin all the time, being constantly reminded of the man I lost.

'Hi,' I say, pushing his coffee towards him as he sits down opposite me.

'Now this is a test of how well you know me.'

'I went for the weirdest one.'

He takes a sip. 'Macchiato. Not bad. If you'd have gone for decaff I'd have been very annoyed.'

'Late night?'

'Interesting night,' he mumbles.

'Is that anything to do with why you're miles away from where you live first thing on a Sunday morning?'

'Perhaps,' he says, poker-faced. 'How was your evening?'

'Not too bad. Considering.'

'Considering what?'

'Considering I don't drink very often these days and it was a late one.'

'Who's with Alex?' he asks, but casually, so it doesn't sound accusatory.

'Darren stayed over last night. Apparently they had a great time.'

Graeme smiles. 'Involving – hold on, I can get this – online gaming and . . .' He looks up at the ceiling for a moment. '. . . extra-hot deep pan with extra jalapeños.'

I laugh. 'Bang on.'

'And we always say he's unpredictable. We should cut him some slack, right?'

I smile. 'Maybe.'

He sips from his coffee. 'How's he been this week?'

'Not bad. Some golf. And he's been trying to help a bit around the house.'

'Yeah?'

'Well, he did some food shopping on Tuesday.' I hesitate.

'Let me guess. Abandoned in the middle of the kitchen floor?'

I smile and nod. 'And he tried to do some washing on Thursday . . .'

'Oh yeah? How is the Dirt-Buster 3000? I've been meaning to ask.'

'Shut up, Graeme! It's not called that.' He took the piss out of me in the electrical shop the other weekend for choosing a model with a *slightly* cheesy name. 'Anyway, I asked Alex to put some washing in the machine while I was out.'

'Ah. He took it literally.'

'Yep. No soap, no turning it on.'

'Never mind,' Graeme says, suddenly becoming more serious. 'It's the thought that counts, right?'

'Yeah,' I say, sipping from my latte, 'it is. We even managed some DIY on Monday night. Stripped some old wallpaper, took off some architraves.' Alex lost interest fairly quickly, but lack of focus has always been a stumbling block for him. For a long time after he came home from hospital I had to remind him to set a timer for things like washing, and brushing his teeth, because he'd do tasks like that only for seconds, not minutes, before forgetting why he was there and wandering off.

'I told you, I've got someone who can do that. I just need to get my guy to call his guy.'

'There's no rush,' I assure him, because there isn't – not in the grand scheme of things.

'So go on,' he says then. 'Give me all the gory details of your heavy night. How bad did it get – sambucas? Karaoke?' His face slackens slightly. 'Don't tell me there were kebabs.'

I am laughing now. 'Shut up, Graeme. All that was years ago. I'm much more refined these days.'

'I don't believe it,' he says. 'I bet there's part of you inside that's screaming for a doner with extra chilli sauce.'

I feel my smile fade slightly. 'You know, last night Sarah offered me my old job back. At the agency.'

'In London?'

'Yep.' I nod, take another sip of latte.

Graeme hesitates. 'Right . . . so how would that work?'

'It wouldn't,' I say. 'Which is why I turned her down.'

'Right . . . but how was she *thinking* it would work? Does she want you to leave Alex?'

I stare at him, the misunderstanding making my pulse race in alarm. 'Leave him?'

'Yeah,' Graeme says. 'I mean, if you're here, and he's in Norfolk –'

'Of course not,' I say quickly. 'Phoebe just had a bit of a powwow with my mum and dad. They came up with this idea of building an annexe in Mum and Dad's back garden. They have this crazy plan that they could keep an eye on Alex while I go out to work . . .'

'An annexe?' Graeme repeats. 'Like, a granny flat?'

'Mmm,' I say, into my coffee.

'Assisted living,' he says, and at this point I'm not sure what he's thinking.

I set down my cup. 'I told them no.'

'Molly, Alex would hate that. Aside from the fact he'd never want to move back to London . . .'

'Graeme, are you listening? I said no.'

'Right.' He gives a small shake of the head. 'You know, I'm still . . . available to move back to Norfolk for a while. To help. If you need me to. We've barely talked about it since I offered.'

'Graeme, don't worry,' I assure him. 'I'm not going to move to London.'

'That's not why I'm bringing it up, Moll. I just wanted to say . . . if you change your mind . . .'

I shake my head apologetically. 'I meant what I said. I don't think it would necessarily be the best thing for Alex.'

'Okay,' he says, looking past me for a moment into the vast cavern of the station's roof space. 'Still, it worries me. That your mum and dad and all your friends are on a crusade to bring you back here.'

I smile, an attempt to reassure him. 'Graeme, it's really not a crusade. It was just . . . you know what my mum and dad are like. They're desperate for me and Alex to . . .' I trail off.

'To what?'

Have a family. Live the life they always dreamed of for us. Experience all the traditional joys of married life.

But I don't say any of that. Whether or not Alex confided in Graeme in the months before his accident that we were trying to get pregnant, I don't know. We've never really spoken about kids. Maybe he assumes I no longer want them. ' . . . just be happy,' I conclude.

We regard one another for a moment, then look away. Beyond the coffee shop, platform announcements reverberate, the echo of them familiar and strangely comforting. A reminder, if I needed it, that life will always carry on – no matter what. It's up to you if you go with it or not.

'So have you heard any more from Nicola?' Graeme asks me then, her name leaving his mouth like the name of a contagious disease.

I frown. 'How do you mean?'

He meets my eye over the rim of his cup. 'I don't know . . . has she been in contact?'

'Not as far as I know. God, don't, Graeme – you'll make me paranoid.'

'You could check his phone if you really wanted to be sure.'

I set my cup down in surprise. 'It sounds as if *you* want to be sure.'

He hesitates. 'Sorry. That was a stupid thing to say. Forget I mentioned it.'

'What is it with you and her anyway? Why do you hate her so much?' I mean, I know why *I* hate her, but Graeme's feelings towards her seem almost as strong.

'I don't . . . *hate* her. I just don't trust her.'

I wait.

'You know – she cheated on him, dumped him, then decided she'd made a huge mistake.'

'How do you know? That she thought it was a mistake?'

He hesitates again. 'I could tell. She's easy to read, Nicola. Plus – you hear things, living in a village. She used to tell her clients that finishing with Alex was the worst thing she ever did. I think she hoped it might get back to him somehow, that he'd take her back.'

Alex always told me he and Nicola had very little contact after they split. And then the thought returns to me – the one that frightens and haunts me most of all. But I can't articulate it, bring it to life.

'Jesus,' Graeme mutters. 'You don't need to hear this.' And then he puts his right hand over my left one, covering my wedding ring. 'I'm sorry, Molly. I should never have said anything. Hungover, foot in mouth. Forget it, honestly.'

'Look, I know Alex has changed, but he hasn't changed like that. He never once gave me reason not to trust him. He was never . . .' I trail off.

A look of faint amusement crosses Graeme's face and he removes his hand from mine. 'Never what?'

'Never mind.'

'You were about to say, *like you*, weren't you?'

My face reddens slightly. 'No, I wasn't. I was going to say, *a ladies' man*, and then I thought you might think I was having a dig.'

'So, in other words – like me. Well, I don't blame you. For having that view of me.'

'I don't have "that view" of you. You're just you.'

'Mmm,' he says. 'A right old Romeo.' He leans forward. 'Look, Moll, I only mention Nicola because I'd hate to think she's taking advantage of him. That's all. She winds me up.'

I look down at my wedding and engagement rings then, and am unexpectedly taken back to the night Alex proposed. He was so nervous he slid the ring on to my right hand instead of my left. I said nothing of course, not wanting to embarrass him, and nor did anyone else (Mum and Dad were there – he proposed in their back garden). But the next morning when I woke, he'd swapped the ring over to my left hand while I slept.

It was always the little things he did that meant the most to me.

I have to ask myself as I'm recalling yet another fond memory – why would Nicola even be interested in Alex? She has a good life: money, a career she loves, the perfect physique and no shortage of male attention (that hopefully doesn't include my husband's). What would she find so appealing about the new Alex, the man with a quick temper, patchy memory, inability to hold down a job or even leave the house most days? What on earth would she find attractive about that?

9

Alex – 5 November 2011

It's been almost a year since I met Molly, and the intensity of my feelings for her is at once sublime and terrifying. She is perfect – *perfect* – and already I struggle to remember exactly how life fitted together before she came into it. It's only now, at the age of twenty-seven, that I have finally understood what everyone meant when they talked about love. *This* is true love – exhilarating, intense, absorbing. I daydream about her at work, I rush home to find her each night, I can't take my eyes off her when we're out in the evening, whether we're with her friends or mine. I can't understand how I've been so lucky when others are so unlucky, how we can be so happy when others are so sodding miserable (case in point – my friend Chris and his girlfriend Diana can't make it through a single day without arguing. They've been together a mere eight months, and already there have been belongings projected from their top-floor flat on to the pavement below, locks changed, phones switched off for days at a time. *Chris*, I want to say to him. *Why do it, mate? Why don't you go out and look for your Molly?* But I don't, of course, because that would make me just about the smuggest git on the planet).

But I *feel* smug. I feel fortunate, and blessed – in fact, I am a walking, talking, clichéd emoticon. But with that smugness, the constant conviction of my own good fortune, comes uneasiness too. I start to worry – obsess, even – about what would have happened if I hadn't talked to Molly outside the toilets in the bar that night. Or what might have happened if Rhiannon hadn't dialled Graeme at that precise moment when *he* was chatting to her. Nothing might ever have happened between us, and then Molly – incredible Molly – would have been lost to me for ever, and I might never have known what true love feels like.

Because I can't imagine anyone measuring up to Molly. She's funny and gorgeous and kind-hearted and hard-working. She's the sort of girl guys are drawn to in bars, at work, on the bus or on the street – she illuminates the world around her, the ground beneath her feet.

And then one night it comes to me: my dad's drinking, the depression, the sadness – it was all because this is *exactly* how he felt about Mum. I mean, obviously Dad was devastated when she died, and he drank to dampen that feeling, blunt the pain. But I've never really known before now what true love felt like. It's a strange revelation to be having a whole twenty years after those tragic events, but at the same time I feel fortunate to finally be making sense of who my dad really is. Because I barely remember him before the accident, before the weeping and the swigging and the strange howling sounds we'd wake to in the middle of the night.

I start becoming a little fixated on the idea of keeping Molly safe – of making sure she doesn't go out alone too late at night, that she gets a taxi whenever she can, that any aspect of her life isn't exposed to unnecessary risk. For the most part I try to keep this behaviour under wraps, because the last thing I want to do is smother her, or drive her away. But the idea of losing her completely terrifies me. If I did, I worry I'd become just like my father – sitting in a bedroom with the curtains shut, watching the racing and drinking cider by the litre.

My best buddy, Charlie, tells me one night that Molly and I are slightly sickening – but he says it fondly, like a joke, like being sickening is a good thing. And with Molly, it really is. Yes, we feed each other morsels of food in restaurants, I cook her pancakes for breakfast at the weekends, we leave each other love notes around the flat and we skip to the gym together on a Saturday morning, but I get giddy from all that stuff. It's all I've ever wanted. Looking back, I've realized that Nicola wasn't really romantic – she had a very practical approach to relationships, involving shared bank accounts, getting on the property ladder, five-year-plans and (whisper it) starting a wedding fund. She had very rigid ideas about how she wanted her life to be, and it was pretty much up to me to fit into that. *Control freak*, Dad said sometimes, which was true – and that extended to every facet of her life. She was paranoid about her body–fat ratio, germs in the flat (I often woke at two in the morning to find her scrubbing surfaces) and achieving exactly the right daily balance of vitamins and minerals.

Molly and I, on the other hand, don't share a bank account, clean the flat when we feel like it and occasionally swap the pancakes for cold pizza on a Sunday morning. Our one concession to discipline is going to the gym, which makes us feel good, but other than that, we've got a pretty relaxed, easy-going approach to life. Moll doesn't worry about me seeing her shaving her legs, or slobbing around the flat in her tracksuit bottoms and hoodie. Where Nicola was militant about food, Molly loves experimenting with new cuisine, and one of our favourite things is to head out into town to discover new restaurants (this month's winner: Cuban).

And just as Nicola was a bit militant about sex too – she had specific days she liked to do it on, and specific things she liked to do, struggling to adapt to any variation in either – I can't imagine Molly and I having a better sex life. We do it whenever and wherever the mood grabs us – which luckily for both of us, is frequently and everywhere. We do it before work, when we get in at the end of the day before we've even removed our coats, in the park, in the toilets at a restaurant, at Graeme's flat, at Molly's mum and dad's house (a risk, and not one I'd necessarily repeat).

'Well, don't ever get married then,' Graeme warns me one night over beers, when he asks me what our sex life is like and I tell him brilliant and nothing else.

I snort. 'That's a myth. You don't just go off sex because you're married.'

'Don't be naive, Alex,' he tells me, like he's taking my sexual wellbeing really seriously.

But anyway, Graeme's advice is misplaced, because yes – I do want to marry Molly. I first started thinking about it only weeks after meeting her.

I know what Graeme would say, the man who careers from girl to girl – not to mention job to job, flat to flat. I'm worried he'll spend the rest of his life aimlessly drifting, that he'll never know true love, commitment. And I know what Molly's parents and friends would say, what *my* friends would say. They'd tell me there's no rush, that marriage is a huge decision, that we're still so young. But I *want* to rush everything, because I don't want to let her slip through my fingers. I can't imagine any deeper thrill than tripping down to the register office hand in hand in our jeans and trainers, declaring our love for one another before heading to the pub for bottles of bubbly, fish and chips. The whole thing would be relaxed, easy – none of the stiff formality that Nicola fantasized about when she talked about our (inevitable, it seemed) wedding. With Molly, I want to jump in feet first, without really thinking too deeply about any of it, because that's exactly the point – my love for her isn't about weighing up pros and cons, or thinking with my head. It's complete and utter instinct.

'Clear a space, then,' Dad instructs. He's in bed again, the curtains shut, but thankfully today the television's off. I've made us both a cup of tea, brought up a packet of digestives.

I move a stack of old railway magazines to one side and perch on the empty side of the bed. 'How are you feeling?'

'Like death,' Dad tells me, his eyes crinkling at the corners. 'How about you?'

'You don't feel like death,' I reprimand him softly.

'No Molly today?'

'She's with friends.'

'Ah.'

Molly's met Dad several times and has declared herself to love him, which is generous of her, since even I can see that my father as he is today is not someone you might instantly describe as loveable. He is miserable and beaten down by life, pessimistic, with skin tinged yellow, his outlook gloomy.

The first time Molly met him, he was having a particularly rough day. I have to say, it was kind of humiliating after being introduced to Molly's mum and dad over three courses with wine at their Clapham townhouse to take her to Dad's ramshackle cottage, step over all the detritus littering the stairs and landing, and introduce them while he was watching the racing with the curtains shut. The bedroom smelt of cigarettes and onions. He was welcoming – of course he was – but the whole experience was enough to make me question myself. Was I just dreaming, that I really had enough to offer this well-to-do girl from Clapham?

'I kind of got the impression he'd prefer you to be living in Norfolk,' Molly said to me afterwards.

Kind of got the impression was a tactful way of putting it:

Dad had basically sat her down, told her cities were dirty and that she'd be much better off with country air in her lungs. He informed her cities were too busy, and – get this – you didn't have to queue for anything in Norfolk. (Molly and I had queued at the village coffee shop only that morning for nearly fifteen minutes while they faffed about finding their latte frother.)

'Actually, Dad,' I say now, 'I've got a few things I wanted to talk to you about.'

Dad shifts uncomfortably. His side of the mattress sags considerably, compared to the side I'm sitting on, bouncy and unused. I told him once he should swap sides, but he looked at me like I'd suggested he try online dating. 'That was your mother's side,' was all he said.

'Well, first off,' I say, 'I wanted to let you know that . . .' I hesitate. I've planned everything out in my head, but now the moment has arrived, I feel unexpectedly awkward, convinced Dad is going to tell me off for being soppy and suggest I help him sort through the post instead.

'Let me know what, son?' Dad says, and the word *son*, the implicit fondness, spurs me on.

'I wanted to let you know that I understand why the past few years have been so hard for you.'

'You mean the past two decades,' he corrects me softly.

'Yes. I mean, I'd never really understood before *why* . . . you know, you felt like you needed to drink, but now, I do.'

Dad eyes me with faint amusement. 'You do?'

'I do.'

'And why is that, Alex?'

'Because of Mum,' I say, and even the word is brave, spoken out loud like this, because we rarely talk about her. Dad has never known how to do it. 'Because of everything you felt for her.'

'Aha,' Dad says. He's not gripping my hand in his or welling up like I imagined he would. 'You've fallen in love.'

I nod. 'So anyway – Dad . . . I just wanted to say, I don't blame you for anything.'

He smiles softly, like I'm missing the point of my own conversation. 'I wouldn't expect you to. I did the best I could for you boys.'

There it is again – the way he says *boys*, like he resents our being twins, that there's two of us, that we come as a package. But I don't want to talk about Graeme today. That's not why I'm here.

'Anyway, Dad – look. I wanted to talk to you about Molly too.'

'Okay,' he nods, his face lifting suddenly in anticipation.

'I'm going to ask her to marry me.'

Finally his eyes well up. 'Marvellous news. Congratulations. I always knew you'd find yourself a nice girl.' He reaches out, grasps my hand. It feels frailer than it looks, the strength of his grip virtually non-existent.

I smile. 'Thanks, Dad. I love her to bits.'

But he doesn't pause to savour the moment. 'So where will you be living? Here with me?'

I hesitate. 'What?'

'Well, you'll be looking to start a family, won't you? Move back to your roots?'

'Er, no, Dad. I mean – yes, we will want to have kids at some point but, at the moment, London is home.'

He snorts. 'You're not a Londoner, Alex. This is your home.'

I laugh lightly, look down at our hands still loosely locked together. 'Dad, you can live somewhere without being from there. The world's a small place these days.'

There is a short silence, during which Dad withdraws his hand. He turns his head away from me to stare at the tiny gap between the drawn curtains, like he's willing it to widen, shed some light on my obstinacy.

'Do you want me to open those?'

'Christ, no. Can't bear the daylight.'

I decide to plough on, ask him what I've been planning to – that my idea is to propose to Molly at her parents' house on Bonfire Night, and that I'd really like him and Graeme to be there too, stay with Molly and me overnight, all have lunch together the following day. 'Anyway, look, Dad –'

'So that's it then? I've lost you to her for good?'

'Don't be ridiculous,' I say. 'You haven't lost me.'

'I haven't got long, Alex. You know that.'

'Come on, Dad. The doctor said –'

'– that I haven't got long.'

'No,' I correct him. 'He said you need to stay off the booze and follow his advice – and if you don't, *then* you haven't got long. There's a difference. He told you that because there's still hope, Dad.'

'Not in here,' Dad says, and although he doesn't move I know he means his mind.

'Dad, I can't move back to Norfolk. You know I can't leave my job.'

'The one you were planning to leave ten months ago?'

I swallow. 'Well, Moll's got the job of *her* dreams, and I can't ask her to give it up.'

'You mean you won't.'

'Look,' I say, to take the focus off Molly, 'I come up as often as I can, and I always will. And you have Graeme . . .'

Dad tuts. 'That useless sod? Oh yes, he's here when he remembers to be.' He shakes his head. 'So I have one son with more important priorities, and one idiotic one.'

It's no wonder, really, that Graeme calls me Golden Boy.

'Graeme's not idiotic, Dad,' I say softly, more compelled to stick up for my twin than for myself, as I so often have been over the years.

'So what do her parents think of you, then? Die-hard Christians, aren't they?'

'They're just Christian, Dad. And anyway, we don't talk about religion. I respect their views, they respect mine. Isn't that what you always said – *respect everyone's differences*?'

'I suppose I did when I was feeling philosophical.'

158

He's speaking stiffly now, full of resentment. I feel it too, heavy in my chest – and straight away, I know that I can't ask him to be there when I propose on Bonfire Night. I can't risk Molly sensing even a hint of disdain from my dad. It wouldn't be fair.

I sigh. 'Shall I do you some lunch? When did you last eat?'

'Oh, please don't. I had enough of that from your brother this morning. Tried to make me eat eggs.'

'Well, you need the protein. Keep your strength up.'

'I always thought it would be Graeme,' he says then.

'What would?'

'The one who would let me down. I never thought it would be you, Alex.'

I have to leave the room then – I can't sit next to him any longer and contain my disappointment, my fury at him for being so cold-hearted, so self-absorbed, when I've just told him I want to marry the girl of my dreams. Halfway down the threadbare staircase I pause, turn my head to the wall and lean on to the banister, heart pounding, tears rising rapidly up my throat.

But I swallow them down, remind myself to stay strong. I can't, I *won't* risk losing Molly over this. Because if I do, I know I'll end up just like my dad, lying motionless in bed, staring at a chink of light, willing it to widen.

After things go so badly wrong with Dad, I don't have much hope for persuading Molly's parents that I'm the right man to make their daughter happy for the rest of her life. But at the same time, I'm determined – I've found her, purely by chance, we've fallen in love and I want to do things properly. I'll do whatever it takes to prove that.

Also playing on my mind is the idle comment Molly made about parenthood one night. We were watching one of those documentaries about women giving birth, and Molly mumbled something about being a young mum in an ideal world. 'Not *too* young,' she clarified quickly while I groped uselessly for the appropriate response. 'Just . . . the right side of thirty, maybe.'

I can see how much she dotes on other people's children and how much she wants to be a mum, and I also know that having a baby out of wedlock is probably the one thing she could do to really disappoint her parents. Plus, at twenty-six, there are a mere four more years before she turns thirty and becomes – in her mind – no longer a 'young mum'. And it's not as if I don't share her dream – in my downtime at work or on the tube I often find myself picturing a close-knit little family, kids of our very own that we'll dote on. They'll have long hair and scruffy clothes, be fans of getting muddy and climbing trees. We'll have crazy, hectic mealtimes and a noisy, messy home. We'll be disorganized and ridiculous but we'll be happy. We'll be everything we're meant to be.

'Thanks for this,' I tell Timothy and Arabella.

Arabella's smiling nervously, Timothy's holding her

hand. They've made a pot of tea and there's a slice of lemon drizzle cake on a plate in front of me.

I know they know what I'm going to say. They must do – why else would I be here alone on a mid-week evening while Molly's out with friends? I'm trying to read their faces, predict what their response will be, and their evident nervousness is throwing me off. Because you're only nervous about stuff you hope won't happen, right?

'Cake,' Arabella reminds me then encouragingly, and not wanting to offend her – she's so gentle, like Molly – I fork off a slice and start to eat, but of course then they're watching me eat cake and it chucks all my usual reflexes out of kilter. I don't think it's ever taken a man so long to swallow a single morsel of sponge as it does me that Wednesday evening.

'Sorry,' I say, trying to smile but feeling a light film of sweat forming across my forehead. Typical that today I opted to wear a pale blue shirt.

'Take your time,' Timothy tells me kindly, like he's a priest sitting next to me in the confessional box and I'm preparing to confess to each and every one of the seven sins.

I clear my throat. 'I wanted to . . . talk to you both. I know the tradition is to just talk to – well, the father, but . . .'

They're both holding their breath. I mean, physically – neither of them is breathing right now, which can't be healthy at their age. I endeavour to hurry it along.

'I would like to ask Molly to marry me.'

Fortunately, they both exhale instantly, and Arabella bursts into tears. 'Oh my goodness!' she gasps.

'My, my,' says Timothy.

'I know,' I continue, determined to say everything I'd intended to, 'that it's quite soon, that we've only been going out a year –'

'Ten months, is it?' Arabella interjects as she's wiping her eyes, but I assume only because she's that sort of person. Likes all the facts, likes everything straight and in order.

'Yes, ten months,' I concur, 'but I love your daughter to bits. I mean, I just *love* her. She means the world to me.'

'Yes,' Timothy says simply, 'Molly's a very special person.'

Too special for me?

'You know how fond we are of you, Alex,' Timothy says now, looking me right in the eyes across the table. 'And we see how much Molly loves you. In fact, we've never seen her like this with anyone before.'

Internally, I exhale. Externally, I am rigid with anticipation.

'So of course – you have our blessing. We'd be delighted to have you as our son-in-law.'

And then Arabella emits an excited squeal, and we're all on our feet and manoeuvring around the kitchen table to hug one another and shed tears and talk excitedly about the future. We sit down and they pour me a glass of wine, and the scene is set: this Bonfire Night, I am asking Molly to marry me.

Molly's parents have requested I agree to just two

things. One, we get married in their church by their vicar and friend, Peter. Two (this was Arabella's), to hurry up and have lots of grandchildren.

I'm happy to say these are both conditions I have absolutely no problem adhering to.

It's perfect Guy Fawkes weather – crisp and cold enough to freeze our breath, a brilliant backdrop for cups of warm cider and sparklers in gloved hands. I have to admit, since Molly recently supplied her parents with the full facts of Dad's addiction (on my request), I've been slightly wary of drinking around them. But I figure tonight is a special occasion.

Arabella has strung lights up between the trees, warmed a vat of cider, baked a parkin, organized sparklers. She's made so much of an occasion of it, in fact, that I might have been concerned Molly would suspect had she not turned to me on the front doorstep when we arrived and said, 'Don't be overwhelmed – Mum always goes a bit mad on special occasions. She's probably made toffee apples and hand-stuffed her own guy.' When I smiled and said I didn't mind, she dipped her chin and said, wide-eyed for emphasis, 'You should *see* what she does at Christmas.'

I really don't mind though, because even if I wasn't planning to propose, making a fuss of special occasions is something Graeme and I always hankered after when we were children. Not that Dad didn't try to do something nice at Christmas, or on our birthday (usually involving supermarket cake and a trip to the nearest pub), but the real effort was put in by pitying neigh-bours and friends. It would be a neighbour's garden we'd stand in on Bonfire Night, a friend who would accompany us trick-or-treating, an acquaintance who might take us to the Christingle service at church, mak-ing sure we had the dolly mixture to stick on our cocktail sticks. More than once I can remember Graeme legging it from whatever event it was with moments to spare, saying he was sick of spending special occasions with people who were only taking pity on us.

While Molly helps her dad with marshmallow skew-ers for the barbecue, I head up to her bedroom to steady myself before our mini firework display kicks off. I stare into the mirror, face-to-face with plain old Alex Frazer, about to ask the girl of his dreams to marry him. I know I should feel so lucky right now, but in fact I'm almost paralysed by nerves.

I think sadly of my dad at home alone. He should be here – the whole situation is so frustrating. I know Timothy and Arabella would welcome him into their home, and despite everything, underneath it all, Dad's a warm, kind person. Life's just not been that kind to him in return.

As I work up to heading back downstairs I end up looking idly through some of Molly's old stuff, and somehow find myself staring at my own jacket in her wardrobe. It's sandwiched between a load of her old clothes – we've simply forgotten to pick it up every time we've been over. But now, I kind of like the fact that it's here, nestled in between her things. It feels like a symbol of something — of being together maybe. I'm worried now that if she gives it back to me, it might be a bad omen. So I'm happy for it to stay here. I can always get another jacket, but I'll never find another Molly.

I'm still touching it when there is a knock at the door and I turn, expecting to see Arabella, but instead my brother is standing in the doorway.

'Hey,' he says, then glances at the jacket in my hand. 'Rifling through her stuff?'

'What are you doing up here?' I say, returning my jacket to its new home in Molly's old wardrobe.

'Don't worry, Arabella knows I'm up here. I'm not sneaking around.'

I force a smile through my nerves. 'It's fine. No one would mind.'

'Nice house,' he says, sitting down on the edge of Molly's bed. 'Her parents must be minted.'

I frown at him. 'I wouldn't know.'

'You *wouldn't know*?'

'Who cares if they are?' I feel irritated suddenly, because in the context of tonight everything he's saying suddenly sounds crass.

'Hey, only joking. What's up — nerves getting to you?' He's leaning back on his hands on the bed, one eyebrow raised.

'Just thinking about Dad. He should be here. You know, I tried to tell him . . . that I understand. About everything that happened after . . .' I hesitate.

'Jesus, Alex — after Mum died. Learn to say it, twenty years later.'

'Anyway, I kind of get where he was coming from. You know, with the drinking and everything. It was meeting Moll that made me realize what it feels like to love someone.' I pause. 'Like Dad loved Mum, I guess.'

'Look, Alex, about Dad . . .'

I look over at him. 'I almost didn't invite you, you know. Tonight.' I was convinced Graeme would behave cruelly like Dad, or worse, pretend he felt indifferent. But aside from a couple of ball-and-chain-style jibes, reminding me we'd only been dating a year, and checking if I was *really* ready, he didn't even attempt to get me to change my mind.

He pauses. 'You thought I'd try and talk you out of it.'

'Maybe,' I admit.

'Well, what do I know, right?' Graeme mutters bitterly. 'Not being a paid-up member of the True Love Club like you and Dad.'

I shake my head. Asking Molly to marry me isn't supposed to be about making other people feel bad, especially my twin brother.

'You know, maybe we're not so different,' he says now, raising his head and meeting my eye. 'Maybe I do want what you have, Alex.'

We hold one another's gaze for just a moment. 'And what's that?'

'The dream, of course! True love. What else?'

'Okay,' I sigh, unsure if he's being as sarcastic as he sounds.

Graeme's voice levels slightly. 'Look, just because I'm excruciatingly bad at holding down a relationship doesn't mean I don't . . . you know. Think about it.'

I nod, say nothing else. My nerves are starting to abate, but that's because I'm in here talking. I should be downstairs, asking Molly to be my wife.

'Sorry,' Graeme says, reading my mind like no one else can. 'Tonight isn't about me.'

'So you're happy for me?' I prompt.

'Yes! Of course. My brother's getting married. Amazing, mate.' He gets to his feet, slings an arm round my shoulders and pulls me into a man hug. I hug him back, and it feels good.

'Alex,' he says then, into my shoulder. 'I should probably tell you –'

'Later,' I say. 'Tell me later. I need to do this now, before I lose my nerve.'

Five minutes later, we're all gathered in the garden, drinks in hand, fireworks prepped. I've got my arm round Molly, who's laughing uproariously at some story Timothy's telling about the vicar playing splat-the-rat at the church fayre. It seems an unlikely game for kindly Christian pensioners to indulge in, but apparently it was all for the kids.

Molly looks beautiful as ever tonight, dressed for the onset of winter in a black down jacket and dove-grey hat, scarf and gloves, long brown hair snaking out from beneath the wool. I can feel the warmth of her breath as she laughs, her intermittent glances up into my eyes

167

a seduction. I picture the boxed engagement ring inside my coat and my heart thuds.

Now. I'm going to do it now.

'Molly,' I whisper, as her dad pauses for breath and I make eye contact with him.

But as she turns to face me, there is a shout from the other end of the garden, next to the house.

'Holy shit,' Graeme mutters, then checks himself. 'Sorry.'

My dad is standing next to Timothy and Arabella's patio doors. Unsteady on his feet, he's shouting my name.

'Alex, is that your dad?' Molly gasps.

Molly's parents have met Dad only once – we went out for Sunday lunch together in April on a rare day when he was feeling well enough to come to London. In the two hours prior to lunch, Molly said she'd never seen me that nervous before – but in the end he was charming and charismatic, and I was intensely grateful to him for not talking only about his problems, for acting to all intents and purposes like a pretty standard dad.

Now, he's being anything but standard.

I drop Molly's hand and make my way across the lawn, Graeme at my back. 'Dad – what the hell are you *doing* here?' I hiss.

'Didn't want to miss it,' he slurs, the scent of alcohol drifting along his breath on to the wintry air. All around us, fireworks are already going off, a reminder that tonight should be about anything other than what it is now.

168

Instantly, I realize, and turn to face Graeme. 'You told him.'

'I'll take you home, Dad,' Graeme says straight away, ignoring me.

Dad shakes Graeme off and moves past me towards the Meadows family who, understandably, seem a little unsure as to what to do, since I bet this doesn't very often happen at the church. Then again, maybe it does – when Molly first told them about Dad's various issues, Arabella generously responded that they got all kinds of people dropping in at the church with a tally of addictions as long as her arm. It didn't bother them one bit, she claimed.

Hmm. I'm afraid we're about to put that claim to the test, Arabella.

'Apologies for the intrusion, folks. But I couldn't not come and raise a glass to my lovely son and his beautiful wife-to-be.'

My stomach hits the floor, and I go with it. I squat down and cover my face with both hands, and it's like someone's hit the pause button on the whole of South London – the sky for a moment goes silent, and nobody says anything. I stay where I am, breathing into my fingers, too afraid to look up and see Molly's face.

'Good one, Dad,' I hear Graeme mutter.

And now, Molly's voice, small and shocked. 'Oh my God. Alex?'

I look up from where I am halfway across the lawn, maybe ten feet away, my dad between us. Timothy has his eyes shut, head tipped up towards the sky; Arabella's got one hand clamped across her mouth. On the barbecue, I can smell the hot dogs slowly charring.

Graeme's somewhere behind me. The whole garden is holding its breath, the sky still on pause.

Finally, I look Molly in the eyes. We have both welled up, so now there's only one thing for me to do. I get to my feet, walk unsteadily over to her, take her quivering hand in mine and drop down again, this time to one knee. I feel in my pocket for the box containing the ring, set it in the middle of my right hand and open it with my left.

Molly's mouth is slightly ajar, her eyes wide and expectant. A single tear drips down her cheek.

'Molly Meadows,' I whisper, 'will you do me the honour of being my wife?'

And then it is like it is in the films. The sky suddenly explodes with a great rush of colour and sound, and someone (my dad, I think) is whooping, and Molly's screaming, 'Yes, yes, *yes*!' and now she's in my arms and my face is in her hair and I'm gasping, 'I love you, I love you, I love you, Moll.' And then I draw away, slip the glove from her hand and slide the ring on to her fourth finger before scooping her into a fierce hug. And then I whisper, 'I'm sorry,' over and over again, because I am sorry — I'm devastated, gutted, that her special moment was just ruined by my idiot dad.

Above our heads, fireworks are squealing and shooting up from neighbouring gardens, brightly coloured streamers throwing explosions of orange and pink up into the blackness.

I don't know how he did it, but by the time we draw back from one another for breath, Graeme has managed to get Dad to do a disappearing act. I'm unsure if that means Graeme missed the moment itself while he was ushering him out of the side gate, but anyway, when I look around angrily for Dad, he is nowhere to be seen – though Graeme has reappeared and is making his way back across the grass towards us.

Arabella and Timothy are, of course, the epitome of grace, sweeping Molly into more hugs and congratulations and distracting her by popping a bottle of champagne they've had hiding under the barbecue in a cool box.

For the briefest of moments as they envelop her, Graeme and I face one another, watching the three of them gasp and exclaim, sharing the most precious of moments as gunpowder crackles above our heads.

'Why the hell did you tell him?' I hiss furiously.

'I didn't. He guessed. I'm so sorry, mate. I tried to tell you, before.'

'Where is he?'

'I packed him off out front. I'll take him back to the flat.'

I say nothing, I'm so furious with both of them.

'Alex.'

'What?'

'I should probably just tell you ...' Graeme nods over at Molly. 'Wrong finger.'

'What?'

'You put it on her right hand. Ring finger's left.'

'Oh *shit*,' I breathe, then hesitate, because Molly's extended her hand so Timothy can admire the rock. Even more excruciating, they're all pretending they haven't noticed. 'What should I do?'

Graeme hesitates. 'What can you do? Style it out.' He pats me gently on the back. 'Sorry again, mate. Better get the old fart home to sleep it off.' Then he heads away from me back towards the side gate and the street. Arabella glances up as he goes, but then I catch her eye and sling her a lop-sided *What can I do?* smile.

I'm just so angry. Already I know that instead of celebrating with Molly tomorrow, I'm going to spend the entire day worrying, in between grovelling and apologizing to her parents on my father's behalf. Even worse, I know Molly will now for ever associate the night I proposed with my idiot drunk of a father. And for that, I will never forgive him.

Much later that night, while Molly sleeps, I swap the ring over to her left finger, so everything will be okay when she wakes up. And then I whisper, 'Sorry,' into her ear, tell her how much I love her, hope that somehow my words arrive to her in a dream.

I try not to worry that the whole mess of it all is an omen, an early indicator of catastrophic errors to come.

Next morning, Dad's sleeping off yesterday's booze bender; Molly's sleeping off the champagne and most likely her disappointment.

So it is Graeme and I who find ourselves alone in the

kitchen the morning after my engagement. He's sitting at the table in jogging bottoms and a T-shirt, like he might be about to head to the park for a run, finishing a cup of black coffee and flicking through the news on his phone. In the background, the radio's humming faintly.

It's chilly in the kitchen; the heating hasn't yet come on. Beyond the window, it's only just getting light.

'You okay?' he asks me.

'Not exactly.'

'Alex, I am sorry. He worked it out when I said I was going to Molly's family Bonfire Night.'

'You shouldn't have even told him that. I asked you not to say anything.'

'He realized pretty quickly it was some sort of occasion, asked me directly. What could I say? Look, it was Dad that got drunk and ruined everything, not me.'

'You didn't think to warn me?'

'I tried. Upstairs in Molly's room. But you were a bit . . . tunnel vision at that point.'

'How the hell did he get all the way to London anyway? He can barely make it downstairs. Or so he claims.' I shake my head, furious and disappointed. I've never once had cause to question the gravity of Dad's symptoms before.

'He took a bloody cab the whole way here,' Graeme tells me.

'God, I'm such an idiot. Everything I was saying about understanding what Dad's gone through, why he drinks . . . maybe he really doesn't care about me.

About us. I mean, look at everything he's ruined over the years with his drinking. Birthday parties, school plays, Christmases . . . and now this. My *engagement*. All he had to do was not cock it up . . .'

'Maybe he thought he was doing a nice thing. Turning up, showing his support. I mean, he's always saying he wants to be closer to you –'

'And turning up pissed at Molly's parents' house is the way to do that, is it?'

'It's the only way he knows to do anything,' Graeme says quietly.

'You accused me before of being embarrassed by Dad,' I say. 'Do you remember? The weekend Molly moved into my flat. Well, maybe you were right. Maybe I am embarrassed by him – and this is why.'

He nods, like that's understandable. 'Well, parents are supposed to be embarrassing, aren't they?'

Molly's aren't. Molly's parents are as normal as it gets. 'Why do you always stand up for him, Gray, give him the benefit of the doubt?'

'Force of habit, I guess.' He smiles faintly. 'Maybe I'm hoping one day he'll thank me for it.'

And then, as he takes another sip from his coffee, glances at his phone again, it strikes me.

'You told him to come last night,' I realize out loud. 'How else would he have known the address?'

Graeme snorts. 'Don't be ridiculous.'

'You did,' I say, slowly becoming convinced of it. 'You told him about last night and you gave him the address because you thought he'd be grateful to you.'

Graeme sets down his coffee cup and leans forward, meets my eye. 'Alex. Don't be crazy. He must have found the address online somehow. Isn't her dad some sort of church official? Open door and all that?'

The floor tiles feel cold beneath my feet. 'Is this some conspiracy between you and Dad – to mess things up with me and Moll because you want me to move home?'

'You really are losing it, Alex, you know that?'

I play my words back in my head and sigh. 'I'm sorry, Gray. I don't know what I'm saying. I'm just gutted about how everything turned out last night, and I'm tired. I don't really believe any of that.' I pull out a chair and slump down opposite my brother at the table.

'I hope you don't,' is all he says.

'I mean, I know you think I'm rushing into things with Moll . . .'

'Alex, you say this so often I'm starting to think maybe *you're* the one who thinks you're rushing into it. Are you . . . absolutely sure you're doing the right thing?'

My arms are coming up in goose pimples. I try to rub them away. 'Of course I've got doubts,' I say, meaning only I'm well aware that according to society in general, a year is a ludicrously short space of time – and that I'd hate nothing more than for people to think I bulldozed Molly into marrying me, or for her parents to think I was too hasty.

But just as I'm about to explain that the only doubts I have are related to what everyone else thinks – that as far as I'm concerned, I've never met anyone like Molly, and never will again – the kitchen door opens like the final twist in a really torturous story, and I turn to see Molly standing behind me.

'You've got doubts,' she repeats flatly.

'Moll,' I gasp, but by the time I've got the word out, she's already fled.

IO

Molly – present day

Two days after I return from London, I am in the kitchen kneading dough for a pizza when I feel Alex standing behind me. 'Hey,' he says, shooting me a rare smile, leaning back against the worktop, just like he used to. I hold the memory in my mind for just a moment, willing time to pause so I can pretend for just a few seconds longer.

But I can't control my mouth, the things that exit from it, new reflexes that come naturally to me now. 'Feeling okay?'

'I like that,' he says, nodding at me.

I glance down at the playsuit I threw on when I got in, the hastily chosen result of having over-sweated on my drive home and having nothing else to hand. It could be argued that, aged thirty-one, I am too old to be wearing a playsuit.

'Oh,' I say uncertainly. 'Thanks.'

'It's sexy.'

I can't help but smile. His flirtation's clumsy when it comes now, but he's still gorgeous, he still flatters me. And anyway, the clumsiness carries sincerity – he means it when he flirts with me, he's trying hard – whereas with all the others, it's more like a practised display of polished, empty motions. But of course it still hurts when it's not directed at me, and now I feel stupidly, girlishly grateful that tonight it *is* me and not some random girl – or Nicola – as the recipient of his charm.

'Let's have a drink,' he says.

I hesitate. Alex isn't really supposed to drink – his altered brain is a lot more sensitive to it now – but on the other hand, I firmly believe that we still have to live. Occasional half-pints are allowed, they've told us that. And of course there's nothing I like better than sharing a drink with him, almost like old times, despite looking into his eyes and wondering if the alcohol might prompt him to return, however fleetingly. I live my life from hope to hope, these days.

'Yes, all right. What do you want?'

'A drink,' he repeats.

I nod. 'What type of drink – beer, wine?'

'Beer.' He moves to the fridge and pulls one out, then hesitates before repeating the action, extending a second bottle to me. 'Here you go.'

Beer it is. He puts his hand round the bottle top and I am about to leap into action – *No, Alex, don't try and twist it!* – when to my relief he pauses. I bite my tongue, try to wait as the process slots into place inside his mind.

'I need a – you know.'

He's forgotten the word; I begin to make a *b* with my mouth but he's already moved past me and so I abandon it, not wanting to say anything he could interpret as patronizing or interfering that might snuff out his good mood. Instead I wait nonchalantly with my dough-stuck fingers wrapped round the beer bottle he's handed me while he recalls where the bottle opener's kept, looks in the wrong drawer first but the right one next, withdraws it, struggles for just a moment and then finally pops the cap off.

'And mine,' I say gently, holding it out.

He does it for me, a tiny act of chivalry I already treasure.

'Cheers,' I say, then clink my bottle against his.

He looks blank; he remembers what this means sometimes, but evidently not tonight.

I take a slug. 'This was a good idea.'

'I like your dress,' he says again, leaning back against the ancient melamine worktop, taking me in.

'It's a –' *Oh, shut up, Molly – it doesn't matter.* 'Thanks.'

'I always liked you, Molly. From the moment I met you. I always felt like we had a connection.' Holding me in his gaze, he takes a swig from his bottle.

'I know,' I say. 'That's why we got married.' I hesitate. 'You remember our wedding day, don't you?' For so long it was my biggest fear – that one day, the memory of it would inexplicably vanish. But so far, he's held on to it.

'Yeah,' he says, like that's kind of a stupid question. Perhaps he's right. 'It rained.'

It didn't rain on our wedding day. It was raining on the night of Alex's accident, so very often he decorates his

179

memories with rain. His psychologist told me this is a quirk of the brain's wiring, a distortion of actual events, muddling truth with imagination.

I smile sadly, fail to correct him. I don't want to say anything to tip the gentle balance we seem to have found tonight.

He swigs from his beer again. 'You're very pretty, Molly,' he says, before lowering the bottle, stepping forward and putting his mouth to mine.

Tears spring to my eyes as I sink into his kiss, his touch. I have missed it so much. It comes so rarely now that when it does arrive I am almost too eager, I virtually climb into it. The kissing we used to enjoy anywhere and everywhere, the tenderness of a grabbed hand, the mind-blowing sex – these are now precious events we only rarely enjoy when one of us isn't too tired, or pissed off. And even when they come, they are still different somehow – Alex is less tender than he used to be, less attentive. More single-minded and self-absorbed. Still, I do enjoy them because how could I not? No matter what the passing of time and the accident have done, he is still gorgeous. He is still my husband, I will always look at him and recall in an instant why I married him. And I still have flashes of the man he was before to hold on to.

Tonight, we only make it as far as the sofa – again a throwback to our former life, when we seized any and every opportunity to rip each other's clothes off. And although it is not very romantic, and there is no candlelight and soft music and clean white linen to sink into, it is still romantic to me, because it reminds me of those early days when we couldn't keep our hands off one another.

Afterwards, we fall into a contented doze, half naked on the cushions, and suddenly, there comes the moment I live for – I feel him absent-mindedly reach out and start to play with my hair, a tiny time-worn gesture that's returned to him like muscle-memory.

I shut my eyes and do everything I can to think not of the past or of the future, but to simply feel him breathing, his touch against me. And all too soon – after ten minutes or so – it is over, as I knew it would be. He clears his throat, removes his hand and gets up without speaking. I find him gruff and bare-chested minutes later in the kitchen, flicking through his phone and swigging from his abandoned beer, but still I am able to sneak up behind him, wrap my arms round his chest, kiss the back of his shoulder and tell him I love him without being shrugged away. Instead, he tells me he loves me too and although his voice is flatter than it ever would have been before, these are the moments I cherish when life gets almost too hard to bear.

We eat pizza much later than planned side by side on the sofa, beers long-since drunk. A repeat documentary comes on the TV, a fly-on-the-wall about women giving birth, and I think sadly back to a conversation I once had with Alex, about wanting to be a young mum. How old was I? It was in our old flat, not long after we met – twenty-six, perhaps?

I sneak a look across at him. He's picking jalapeños straight from a jar, depositing them on top of his pizza. There's no point asking him if he remembers that conversation – even if he does, I doubt he'd grasp its significance now. Because of course I think about having children all the time – about whether we could, how our situation would affect them, whether I even possess the mental, physical and emotional strength to undergo such a huge, life-changing journey with Alex in tow. Because so often I feel as if he *is* in tow – that I want to go at one speed, he another. I am always pulling him along, urging him to do this or that. And Alex, understandably, would like to amble along at his own pace. In many ways, it's like having a child already – so the thought of adding one or more newborns to the mix is fundamentally terrifying.

And yet it's all I've ever wanted, to be a mum – and when other people remind me of that, it's especially heartbreaking, because it's as if they think I've forgotten. They say to me, *Don't forget your dreams.* And what I want to say to them is, *Do you have any idea how ridiculous that is? I haven't forgotten my dreams – I regret the loss of them every day. I grieve the non-existence of mine and Alex's little family with every waking minute, even though it never lived anywhere other than in our imaginations, in the future we were sure we had waiting for us.*

But then I think about Graeme, and about Dave, and about all my friends. And I know there are other ways to be happy, ways that don't involve having a family – I *know* this. There must be new dreams out there waiting for us – it's just down to me to conjure them up. That's my job; my end of the deal. We're always telling Alex not to give up; surely that must be my half of the bargain.

And now comes the most poignant part of the TV documentary – the part when the piano chords are chiming and everyone's tearful and the baby is making its very first, shuddering cry – and I almost hold my breath, a slice of nearly cold pizza halfway to my mouth, because I am willing against all the odds for Alex to say something romantic, to give me some indication that he still thinks about starting a family, that he hasn't forgotten the dreams we once had, the agony we endured in the months leading up to his accident when our crossed fingers were met with so many failed tests. But my hope deflates as he flicks the television on to the sports channel.

'Gross,' is all he says, and just like that, I am reminded once again that the dreams we once had really are dead and buried, possibly for good.

Everything has altered so profoundly. And over three years later I still have no idea how to conjure up new dreams for two, when only one of us is truly on board.

11

Molly – present day

The following day Alex calls my mobile while I'm midway through an interview. I let it ring out, rush through my final questions, pocket my mobile and head casually out of the office as if I'm just popping to the toilet.

I call back as I reach the bottom of the stairwell.

'Alex, it's me. What's wrong?' My voice echoes urgently off the walls.

There is a pause. 'There was a fire.'

'*What?*' Panic shoots through me. 'What happened? Are you okay?'

'Yeah,' he says flatly. 'I was cooking.'

Oh fuck. 'Is the house . . . ?'

He waits for me to finish. Half-sentences no longer work in Alex's world.

'Is the house okay? It's not burned down? Please tell me the house hasn't burned down . . .'

There is an excruciating pause during which I picture him turning to check. 'It's fine,' he says eventually, almost languidly. 'Just caught fire.'

Just caught fire. No biggie.

I am not going to be able to solve this over the phone – I need to be there.

'Alex, are you safe? Call the fire brigade, call 999, do it now.'

'I'm in the garden,' he says. 'Val's here.'

Val is our kindly old neighbour who lives in the cottage across the road. 'Let me speak to her. Pass the phone to Val.'

There is some muffled noise and then Val comes on to the line. 'No need to panic, dear. I saw the smoke. Nothing a bucket of water couldn't sort out.'

Am I the only person left in the world to whom a house fire is actually quite a big deal? 'Okay, just . . . please could you stay with him, Val – for half an hour or so? I'm coming home now.'

'There's really no need,' she says. 'We're drinking bitter lemon in the garden. Lovely.'

This might sound harsh, but with Val in charge it really is a case of the blind leading the blind.

Back upstairs, I head over to Seb's desk. Predictably, he does that thing people do when they're complete arseholes, which is wait until they've finished typing out the entirety of a very long email before deigning to acknowledge you're so much as standing there.

'Yes?' he says snippily, eventually lifting his head.

'I've got to go. I've got . . . there's an emergency at home.'

'An emergency,' he repeats flatly.

'Yes. I'll make the time up, I'll take it as annual leave . . . whatever you need.'

'I don't *think* you have any annual leave left,' he says, like he'd just have to check before being able to confirm that I am, in fact, really starting to take the piss.

'Then unpaid,' I gabble, though even the very word sends a shiver through me. 'I'll take it unpaid, but I have to go. There's been a fire at home.'

Because he doesn't care, Seb doesn't even blink. 'What about your interview? That article needs to be filed *this afternoon*.'

'I can do it, boss,' Dave chips in from behind us. Seb really hates it when Dave calls him 'boss', because he does it with the driest of sarcasm. 'The recording's on the system.'

'God, *thank you*,' I gasp, then turn and flee without looking back.

I discover them in the garden, just as Val said, drinking bitter lemon and stretched out on deckchairs, like day-trippers at the seaside soaking up the sun.

'Are you okay?' I gasp, stumbling twice as I leg it through the long grass towards them.

'No harm done,' Val nods. She's short and slight with grey hair but a determined demeanour that I suspect is related to one or both world wars.

'Thank God. What happened, Alex? What happened to the cooker?'

He shields his eyes against the sun so he can see me, but says nothing. He's probably trying to recall.

'The pan caught fire,' Val supplies.

'Didn't you set the timer?'

He sends a look my way. 'I couldn't find it.' The

186

inflection makes his implication clear – *this was your fault*. One thing I've learned with Alex is that there's always someone else to blame when anything goes wrong, or when he suffers a lapse in concentration.

The sun is hot today; I feel myself starting to wilt. 'But, Alex –'

'You're always nagging me to cook, Molly. You're always telling me I should cook for you.'

I glance at Val, who's watching us steadily. 'Never mind,' I breathe, turning to face her. 'Can you show me?'

Alex stays outside while I follow Val into the relative cool of the kitchen, where the cooker, surrounding countertop and cupboards are black. There's a twisted black lump on the floor with wet towels next to it that I suspect to be the pan. The whole house reeks of smoke, the toxicity of plastic.

I can't prevent a small voice in my head whispering, *How much will this cost to sort out?* even though the important thing, of course, is that everyone is safe and unharmed.

'What happened?' I ask her.

'Well, I saw the smoke. So I came in and we tackled it together.'

'Val, you shouldn't have done that – I'd never have been able to live with myself if . . .' I exhale sharply. 'You should have called the fire brigade.'

'Oh, it wasn't serious,' she informs me matter-of-factly. 'I've worked in pub kitchens since I was sixteen – I've been putting out pan fires all my working life. And I was born in the Blitz, dear.'

I smile. Despite her strict voice, she has such a kind face. 'What was he cooking?'

'Meat, I think – frying it. Seems he walked off half-way through and forgot about it.'

'He doesn't have a sense of smell any more,' I remind her. 'Didn't the smoke alarm go off?'

'I had a look at it. Battery's dead, my dear.'

I lower my head in shame. 'God.'

'You can get them wired in, you know.'

'I know, but . . . the whole house needs rewiring,' I confess. 'I've been putting it off.'

'Bit of a mess, isn't it?'

I survey the blackened wreckage of our kitchen. *Mess* is a tactful way of putting it. 'I'll sort it.'

'No, I meant the cottage in general, dear. Weren't you going to do it up?'

I wonder if she's got sick of looking at our eyesore renovation project from her chocolate-box cottage across the road, at our overgrown plot that looks like a waste ground. 'Well, we were.'

'Are you coping?' she asks me then, which is all it takes to bring the tears to my eyes. I bite into my lip to try and stem the flow but then Val puts her arms round me, so I finally break down because I can't hold it in any longer.

'I'm sorry,' I sniff eventually, pulling away and wiping my eyes. 'I feel so bad you had to sort that fire out.'

'My Don had dementia,' she says softly after a pause.

I nod. I never met her husband, who died many years ago. 'I know. I'm sorry.'

'He was never the same,' she tells me. 'After it came on. It was like living with a stranger.'

'That's exactly what it's like,' I mumble.

'It was very hard work. Every day, just when I thought I was getting used to his new little quirks – that we were making progress – we'd hit another hurdle.'

I smile in sorrowful recognition. 'Yup.'

'Be kind to yourself, dear. But most importantly, don't lose sight of who *you* are. If your Alex is lost, you mustn't get lost as well.'

I swallow. 'How did you get through it?' I ask her, hoping as I sometimes do that someone will be able to offer me that one little pearl of wisdom that will suddenly make everything easy. *This is how you do it. Here's the secret you've been waiting for, Molly.* And then everything will slot into place, my days will get easier, I will feel more hope than I do despair.

She grasps my hands between hers and looks me right in the eyes. 'Love is all you need.'

Now I really do break down. I sink to my knees right there in the middle of the kitchen and cover my face, finally allow myself to have a proper sob, because I know if Alex was me – if the situation was reversed – he'd never give up on me.

Later, back outside, Val says goodbye to Alex. 'Call me if you need anything, young man.'

'Thanks for the lemonade,' Alex says, completely unprompted, which surprises me. I suppose he means he appreciates the sugar hit, since I know he can't taste the lemons.

'You're most welcome.' Val smiles firstly at him and then me. 'My Don used to do the same thing, with coffee.'

I frown. 'Do what?'

She gives me a knowing wink. 'Make it with cold water from the tap.'

I exhale. 'Right. Sorry.'

'No need to apologize. It's an easy enough mistake.'

Is it? Maybe she's right – maybe it's just the sort of thing I'd do myself if I was tired, or stressed, as Alex must have been earlier.

'Anyway, you had some lemons in the fridge. Thought I'd use them before they expired. I hope you don't mind, dear.'

'Of course not.' Inspired by my mum's baking, I had been intending to make lemon madeleines – *intend* being the operative word, as always. 'It was very kind of you.'

Classic wartime mentality: someone makes you a cold coffee, you come right back at them with home-made lemonade.

Val's already heading off. 'See you soon.'

I sit down next to Alex, but I don't know what to say. If I admonish him for forgetting the timer, it'll start a fight. But if I say nothing, he might assume it doesn't matter.

The sun has momentarily dipped behind a cloud, and Alex rubs his bare arms. For some reason this makes me recall his jacket, still buried deep in a London wardrobe.

*

'I'll get new batteries for the smoke alarm,' I say, once we're back in the relative safety of the living room, though I'm not sure what I'm going to do about the smell in here. It makes me shudder, the idea that the whole cottage might have gone up in smoke, this family home that was left to Alex, all its associated memories destroyed by flames.

'Yeah, all right,' he says, then stands up.

'Where are you going?'

'Golf,' he says, like nothing's even happened and a brush with death is pretty standard.

'Oh,' I say. 'Who with?'

He takes a moment to recall. 'Charlie.'

'Okay. Have fun.'

'She reminds me of Mum,' Alex says then, looking down at me with those gorgeous green eyes of his. They still get me, those eyes. They always will.

I swallow. 'Who does?'

'That woman.'

'Val?'

'Yeah. Val.'

'Why does she remind you of your mum?' I can't imagine Alex's mum would have borne much resemblance to Val when she was alive.

He pauses. 'She's kind.'

My heart swells, and I glance at the photograph on the mantelpiece of a laughing Kevin and his happy little boy, the photograph that upsets Graeme so much. I am sure the photographer was Alex's mother, though Kevin never confirmed it. I wonder what she was thinking as she pressed the button on the camera – where they were, what they were doing. Before everything went horribly wrong.

'Don't forget your wallet and mobile,' I say as Alex turns to head off, my autopilot reminder if he goes anywhere or does anything. I'm like a walking, talking smartphone.

He shoots me a look over his shoulder that says, *Don't treat me like a baby.* His eyes can darken suddenly like that – the same eyes that were brimming with love during our wedding vows, now blunt when they regard me. I want to shake him, scream at him, *You do love me – remember our wedding? You do love me!*

But Alex is now a man who would scream back. So just like always, I direct my gaze towards the floor and wait for him to leave.

After he's gone I head back out into the garden to catch my breath, taking a moment to stare out at the woodland topping the hill. The sun has emerged from behind the clouds again; swifts are screeching as they dip up and down, skimming low over the wheat field.

And then I get my phone out, dial Graeme.

'Hello,' he says. There is noise in the background, music, like he's in a shop.

'Hey,' I say.

'Perfect timing, Moll. What do girls like for their birthday? I've got one of those posh parties tonight. You know, the ones where the presents are more like upscale raffle prizes. Helicopter ride for two, that kind of thing.'

Ah, birthdays – another small indulgence of romance I kissed goodbye to after Alex's accident. These days he either forgets, buys me something bizarre like a spatula or a hand towel, or gives me a gift I know for a fact has been purchased on his behalf by Eve or Graeme. Gone are the days of breakfast in bed, red velvet cake from my favourite London patisserie, thoughtful little gifts he's had up his sleeve for months.

'Er . . .' I hesitate. 'Sorry, I'm not really up on what the helicopter set get each other for their birthdays.' The circles Graeme finds himself mixing in never fail to amaze me.

'Well, give me a clue then. Anything. I'm completely lost.'

'In terms of . . . ?'

'You know. Categories.'

'Categories?'

'Of gift,' he attempts and fails to clarify. 'Like – jewellery? Flowers? Food?'

'*Food?*'

'Well, I suppose I mean chocolates. Or something. Biscuits maybe.'

'Is she . . . ?'

'Just a friend,' he says quickly.

With gift ideas like *biscuits maybe*, she's lucky she's only a friend, but I can't bring myself to focus on Graeme's anonymous lady friend's birthday right now. 'Actually, Gray, I was just calling to say . . . just to let you know that there's been a bit of an accident, but Alex is fine. There's nothing to worry about.'

'*What?*'

'A fire, a fire,' I clarify at once, realizing the word *accident* is ill-advised. We all live in fear of a secondary head injury, the looming spectre of Alex becoming incapacitated for life.

'Is he okay?'

'Yes, he's fine,' I say quickly. 'Sorry. Don't panic. He was just . . . cooking and it went a bit wrong, that's all. I just thought I should let you know. You said to call if anything . . .'

'Of course, of course. How wrong did it go?' We all know there are degrees of wrong with Alex.

My head is starting to pound slightly in the heat. 'He walked off halfway through. Luckily Val saw the smoke.'

'What about the smoke alarm?'

I hesitate. 'Out of batteries. Sorry,' I confess.

'No, no,' he says. 'Don't apologize. You can't be expected to think of everything. Where is he now?'

'Gone to play golf with Charlie.' I sigh. 'The cooker's dead. Not that it was particularly great before, but . . .'

'How bad's the damage?'

'Hard to say at the moment. I need to get at it with a scrubbing brush.'

'I'll come up,' he says. 'I'll come and help.'

'No, Graeme,' I say quickly. 'I don't want you to, honestly.'

'But, Moll . . .'

'You've got your party,' I say, and it comes out like I'm bitter but I'm being genuine. The one thing I could actually do with right now is some time to myself. 'That wasn't why I called. I just . . . wanted to let you know.' Aside from anything else, as joint owner of the cottage, I felt like Graeme should be aware, at least.

There's a pause. 'Are you supposed to be at work right now?'

I wince as I recall Seb's face earlier. 'Yep. I panicked and walked out. Dave said he'd pick up my work so I just . . . left.'

'Please let me come up and help, Molly.'

'No,' I say firmly. 'We'll be okay. I'm just making a drama out of a crisis as usual.'

'I'll call someone,' he says. 'I'll pay someone to come in and sort it all out for you.'

I swallow. I'm sure Graeme can't afford that any more than I can, and the whole thing *is* my fault. The least I can do is take the financial hit, though I'm not exactly sure how right now.

'It's my responsibility too,' he says, like he's reading my mind.

Yes, your name is on the title deeds, I think to myself, *but it's not as if you ever get the benefit of that. It's just a piece of paper.* Not for the first time, I wonder if I really should be paying him some rent, but how I'd afford it I still don't know.

'I don't think it's too bad,' I say. 'I'll shout if I need extra help. Promise.'

'I'm glad you phoned, Molly,' he says then. 'You can call me any time.'

'Thanks.'

'I'm always here for you, you know. Whatever time of day or night.'

After I hang up I think to myself, *Why* did *I call Graeme? What exactly did I want from him?*

I wanted to hear his voice, I realize suddenly. Talking to him always makes me feel ... better, somehow. Comforted. The notion is new and startling, because it seems a strange thing to be thinking about my brother-in-law. I push it uncomfortably from my mind.

As I take to the charred kitchen with a scrubbing brush and bucket, I begin catastrophizing, even though I'm always reminding Alex not to do exactly that. What if Val hadn't been in? What if she hadn't spotted the smoke? What if Alex had gone upstairs when he abandoned his cooking, and only worked out what was happening when it was far too late?

And then, as I'm reaching over to the sink to rinse my brush and change the water in the bucket, I see it – balanced on the countertop, a recipe book. The open page is blackened, but I can just make out what it's for. Fillet steak fettucine. The first meal Alex ever cooked for me.

I sink to the floor, collapse back against the kitchen cupboards as I recall our argument of a few weeks ago, when I berated him for not having cooked dinner. *He does remember. He still loves me.*

That he is capable of being romantic and thinking of me, doing something spontaneous to try and make me happy, feels so significant now. It's no longer the sort of gesture I can have the luxury of taking for granted or even expecting. When moments like this come they are gifts to be grasped with both hands, so I do – I sit there on the floor and I savour it like food itself.

I know how much effort it must have taken Alex to cook, or try to. Yes, the house might have nearly burned down in the process, and yes, the meal itself was chronically mistimed – given it was the middle of the day and he already had evening plans – but the fact is, he was making me dinner, following a recipe. And not just any recipe: it's a meal he associates with romance, a plate of food that would have tasted like cardboard to him but the finest of dining to me. And that's why he did it. I wish he was here now so I could kiss him, hug him, thank him. Just so he knows.

After ten minutes or so, maybe longer, there's a buzzing from the countertop above my head. Alex did forget his phone after all.

Unsteadily, I get to my feet and I glance down at the display. It's Nicola.

I swallow hard, attempt to straighten out my voice, before picking up. 'Hello?'

There is a long, awkward pause, during which I picture the usually unflappable Nicola panicking. Breaking into a rare sweat, perhaps. 'Oh, hi!' she says eventually. 'Who's that – Molly Frazer?'

'Hi, Nicola. Were you calling Alex?'

She sends a trill of forced laughter into my ear. 'God, no! Sorry. Wrong Alex.' She makes a noise which I suppose is intended as a kind of verbal grimace. 'Curse of having too many clients, I'm afraid. I have at least four Alexes in my phone.'

But why is my Alex one of them?

There is another uncomfortable pause during which we know we both want to hang up and never speak again, but being frustratingly plagued by that British compulsion to make polite small talk, we stall.

'How are you both, anyway?' she says, at exactly the same time as I manage to say, 'Sorry, Nicola, I'm sort of in the middle of something.'

'Gotcha,' she says, and then I do hang up.

It's a horrible word, *gotcha*. I'm sure she meant it in the context of a wink, pointed finger and clicked tongue, but as I replay it in my head, over and over for the rest of the evening, it takes on a more sinister tone every time.

The catchphrase of bullies, masked men, evil clowns. *Gotcha.*

Speaking of bullies – or come to think of it, clowns – as I'm microwaving our tea later that night and replying to Dave's string of worried texts, I receive an email from Seb.

It appears I'm not even worthy of any body copy or even a subject line, as there is just an attachment that is my final written warning.

I shut my eyes and think desperately back to my fillet steak fettucine discovery of earlier. Because when everything's falling down around your ears, it is the tiny glimmers of light you must hold on to.

12

Alex – 6 November 2011

I am chasing Molly along our street, which is more than a bit embarrassing since I'm wearing only a T-shirt, boxers and my dad's ancient loafers. Molly's wearing her pyjama bottoms and favourite hoodie, softened now by years of wear, and the flip-flops she usually slips on to put the bins out. Neither of us are running – it's more like furious striding, but I have no idea where we're going and I can't catch her up because the loafers are too big.

'Please stop,' I beg, even though she's paused for breath anyway, leaning against some railings surrounding a block of flats. Last night's frost has laced windscreens and dusted tree branches, made all the pavements shimmer slightly.

Molly simply shakes her head, loosening her long hair from the braid she puts it in before bed each night.

'You misheard,' I say then, because I know I need to speak first. But of course it's the wrong thing to say, because it unintentionally and unjustly shifts the blame to her.

She turns to face me, skin pink from the power-walk. Her breath is full of distress, freezing in the frigid air as her words rush out to confront me. 'I misheard that you're having doubts? Less than twelve hours after you propose, and you're already telling Graeme you're not sure?'

'No, I mean . . . I *did* say that, but I just meant . . . I'm worried people will think it's too soon, that after only a year we're rushing things. Moll, *I* don't doubt us for a second. I love you to pieces. Why else would I propose?' I take a step forward and grab her left hand. I squeeze it, feel her engagement ring bite the flesh of my palm like a reprimand.

'You think I shouldn't be upset?' Her eyes are brimming with tears that haven't yet fallen. I so desperately want them not to.

'No,' I say. 'That's not what I meant, Moll. It's just . . . I was trying to second-guess what Graeme was thinking, say it before he did. And I shouldn't have. I shouldn't care so much about what he thinks, I know that.'

'No, you shouldn't,' she breathes, shaking her head at me, hazel eyes still perilously glossy. She withdraws her hand now and pulls it up into the sleeve of her hoodie, maybe for warmth, maybe in defence.

I sigh. 'I don't know. Maybe it's because . . . back in March, that weekend you moved in, he gave me a bit of a lecture about . . .'

'About what?' Molly folds her arms as two runners jog past, double-taking then smiling as they notice Molly's pyjamas and my bare legs (a mildly shocking sight in midsummer, let alone November).

Oh God, we're that couple having a domestic in the

street. I never thought we'd be that couple. Not me and Moll.

'About being there for Dad. Abandoning my plans.'

She stares at me. 'What plans?'

I direct my gaze to the pavement as cars rush by, so desperately wishing we weren't having this conversation in public. I'm starting to feel really cold now, standing here with my bare legs and arms.

'Alex?' Molly prompts me.

I raise my head to meet the challenge in her eyes, her voice. 'When I met you . . . I'd been planning to move back to Norfolk. I'd given notice on the flat and written out my resignation letter for work. I'd . . . got a new job in Norfolk. It was all arranged.'

She emits a small punch of breath. 'What?'

'But then I met you, and . . . everything changed. I didn't want to move any more. I knew . . . you were it, Moll. You *are* it.'

'Why . . . why were you going to move?' Her voice wavers and a single tear drips down her cheek. I reach out to take her hand but her arms remain tight across her chest. She shakes her head. 'Was it to look after your dad?'

I hesitate. I *can't* tell her it was to spend more time with Dad. That would break her. She already feels guilty about any time she takes away from him.

'No, no. I was just sick of the city,' I confess, which is also true.

'Why – God, Alex. Why didn't you *say*?' Her face is all crumpled up, the tears dripping faster now.

'Because I don't care – I don't care where I live, Moll, as long as I'm with you! You make me so happy, I've never met anyone like you before!'

'You gave everything up for me?'

I reject this assessment with a headshake. 'It was hardly a great sacrifice, Moll. I'd do exactly the same again.' Finally, she lets me take her hand. Her skin feels colder now, and I squeeze her fingers between mine, trying to reconnect with her, apologize with my touch.

'And is that still how you feel?' she quivers. 'Do you still want to move back to Norfolk?'

'No,' I say firmly. 'Of course not. Our jobs are here, our life is here. I'm *happy* here.'

Of course if Molly wasn't by my side I'd move out of London in a heartbeat, but that isn't the point, is it? She *is* here, so I'm not going anywhere.

'I never asked you to give anything up for me, Alex,' she says now, 'but I wish you'd been honest with me.'

I try to steady my jaw, stop my teeth from chattering. 'I didn't want to lose you, Molly.' When it comes down to it, it really is as simple as that.

'You shouldn't be so scared of losing me that we don't talk about the important stuff.'

Molly comes from a family that talks about everything. I've seen it first-hand around the dinner table: life choices, career issues, health problems – in the Meadows household, quite literally nothing goes undissected. Everything is analysed, chatted through over cups of tea and Molly's mum's famous carrot cake.

But maybe because so much of my childhood was

based on the unsaid – on latent sadness, hidden resentments and unexplored loss – I am more afraid of talking than I realized.

Still holding Molly's left hand, I reach up and wipe hot tears from her cold cheek. 'I know, and I'm sorry. Ever since Mum . . .' But I stop myself, because I don't want to use my mother's death to guilt-trip Molly into forgiving me.

'You're doing it again,' she says gently. 'Clamming up.'

More cars move past now, exhaust fogging the air, their drivers and passengers staring at us like we're some sort of bizarre billboard advert. For what, I wouldn't like to say.

'Look, Alex. I know you love me, and I love you too so it kills me to say this but if you *do* have any doubts . . .'

Never mind killing her to say it, it kills me to hear it. I pull her into a hug, gripping her harder than I ever have before. 'I don't,' I mumble into her hair. 'Not a single one. I'm so, so sorry, Molly. If I could take back what I said . . .' She shivers in my grasp and I draw reluctantly away. 'You're freezing. Come on, let's go home. I'll make pancakes.'

She lets me keep my arm round her shoulder as we make our way back to the flat, thankfully at a slightly more reasonable pace than we left it.

'Sorry I ran,' she says, her voice a little distorted, like her lips are numb from the cold. 'I just didn't want to be that couple – urgh – arguing in front of your family and pretending not to.'

'I know. That's not us, Moll.'

'It's so crazy today started out like this,' she says. She extends her left hand to admire her ring before glancing up at me and sneaking me a smile. 'I can't believe I'm going to be Mrs Frazer.'

I feel as if someone's finally let the air out on a very tight, uncomfortable balloon in my chest. 'Me too,' I smile. 'I'm so excited.' We walk a few more paces. 'I'm so sorry, Molly, about what my dad did.'

I apologized to her over and over again when we got into bed last night, but she was exhausted by then and a bit drunk from all the cider and champagne. I feel as if I need to say it formally again in the cold light of day.

'It was still magical, Alex, with the fireworks, and you down on one knee, and my mum and dad there. To know that you planned all that . . . I'll never forget it.'

I know I won't either. Whatever the future has in store for us, I'll always treasure that memory of her face as she waited for me to ask the question that would change the course of both our lives.

And so it is that eight months later I am standing at the altar of the Meadows family's church while a sea of expectant faces – some familiar, many not – looks on.

Last night I dreamed that Nicola burst dramatically through the back doors of the church just as Peter asked if anyone knew of any lawful impediment as to why Molly and I should not be married. I'm still irritated about the engagement card she sent us, and the slightly sneery good luck text I received from her only last night (both junked straight away, and the first thing

I'm doing next week is changing my phone number). I'm still half expecting her to try to crash the reception, though admittedly that's a bit far-fetched, and anyway, Graeme's appointed head of security.

Standing in front of me now, Molly looks truly incredible. Her wedding dress — which she and Arabella have been so secretive and excited about for months — is utterly exquisite, sleeveless ivory silk overlaid with lace. Her hair is styled in a loose ponytail that drapes in front of her shoulder, and there's a trio of blush pink roses pinned at the nape of her neck. She's wearing her grandmother's wedding necklace, as well as the pair of drop pearl earrings I gave her before she left for her mum's house last night. She looks classic, beautiful — like a girl who doesn't belong on my arm, that's for sure.

We are nearing the end of our vows. As I repeat Peter's words back to Molly, looking deep into her hazel eyes as her bottom lip trembles and her hands quiver in mine, I don't feel nervous any more. I mean every single word.

'In sickness and in health, to love and to cherish, till death do us part, according to God's holy law. In the presence of God I make this vow.'

And then Peter declares that we are husband and wife, that I may kiss the bride. And once we've signed the register and exited the church beneath a shower of fresh pink and cream rose petals (expertly thrown by Molly's maid of honour, Phoebe, and numerous other bridesmaids), then stopped to pose for some photographs, we head to the reception venue. It's a palatial country house in Berkshire about an hour from the church, and we are driven there in London buses, of course, a nod to Molly's love of her home city.

The stately Georgian home has stunning grounds, panoramic views from virtually every window, and more than enough room to accommodate our huge guest list. There are countless displays of blush pink and cream roses and – always a hit – an oversized chocolate fountain. The whole place is stunning, and it's all been paid for by Timothy and Arabella, who I sense have been itching to blow their daughter's wedding fund on a no-expenses-spared celebration for her since the day she was born. They've even contributed a sizeable chunk of cash towards our honeymoon – the holiday-of-a-lifetime, an all-inclusive fortnight in Mexico. Were it not for the fact it's our honeymoon, this might seem a little indulgent, given we went to America only eight months after we met, and then Prague followed by Barcelona earlier this year. But we both love to travel, and it's something we're planning on doing a lot more of.

The wedding and reception have been far more traditional than I ever imagined. But once it was agreed we were getting married in a church – and it also became apparent we were inviting half of London – it would have seemed a bit strange to head to the pub after the ceremony, not to mention logistically impossible. But Molly happily relayed my preferred choice of lunch to the caterers, so our main course is fish and chips – posh, of course, with triple-cooked chips and some sort of clever batter, and mushy peas served up in jam jars.

This house is absolutely perfect for photographs, and our photographer gets a great shot of Molly and me running away from the camera, hand in hand down a tree-lined path, laughing uncontrollably. I'm relying on our friends and family to capture the more casual moments – like me waving a pint glass around like a loon as I dance, and Molly's younger cousins with faces sweet and sticky from the chocolate fountain.

The day is full of small surprises – Molly having had my wedding band engraved with the date and ceremony time, her rarely seen uncle from New Zealand turning up at the reception just in time for fish and chips, Graeme somehow making it through his best man's speech without calling me Golden Boy, swearing, or even really embarrassing me.

Dad has been insistent on making a speech too, but I admit after what I have come to think of as the proposal fiasco, I've been pretty nervous about letting him near a microphone at all, let alone in front of a room full of people. I've even considered if it would be really unkind to just tell him straight – to come out and say, *Look Dad, I don't want you opening your mouth all day, not after what happened on Bonfire Night. And you know you can't be trusted around a free bar* (a subject, much to my mortification, of extended debate around the Meadows' kitchen table in between wedding-cake testing. Ganache or buttercream? Chocolate or vanilla?

Free bar or paying, so Kevin's less tempted to get hammered?).

In the end, Dad makes his speech without having touched a drop – a testament, perhaps, to how bad he's repeatedly assured me he feels about what happened in November. Sobriety doesn't stop him waffling on, though – he's already told everyone how great Norfolk is, and how he hopes Molly and I will be moving back there soon, because it's my natural home, it's in my blood, blah, blah, blah. Also, because he's not a natural orator he's over-projecting, so it sounds a bit like he's using the mike to tell everyone off. More than once I have to swallow the urge to hiss some guidance along the table to him.

But it's about to get worse, because five minutes in he starts talking about Mum.

'I've never exactly been one for discussing how I feel,' he says. 'So perhaps my darling wife, Julia, passed away without ever really knowing just how much I loved her. I told her, of course, during those last minutes we ever spent together, but I was probably already too late.' He pauses, looks down at the table and shakes his head. I wait, my heart pounding, for him to collect himself. 'She would be very proud, ladies and gents, if she could see the man my son has grown to become today. Can I ask everybody to please raise their glasses to Julia Frazer, who sadly cannot be with us on this glorious occasion.'

As everybody gets to their feet, raises their glasses and calls out, *To Julia Frazer*, I glance over at Graeme, perhaps out of instinct. But he's already taken the opportunity to slip silently into the gloom of the Regency corridor, unseen.

He doesn't make it back for our first dance. The song choice was easy – we heard it in the restaurant where we had our first official date, both remarking at exactly the same time that it was one of those songs everyone proclaims to hate but secretly loves. So it became Our Song – the tune I half sing half laugh to her late at night or ironically at parties. The song we always squeeze hands to when we hear it in pubs or bars, kiss soppily to at other people's weddings. Admittedly the lyrics are about lost love but it's so cheesily romantic we knew we couldn't have any other song. So when the time comes I sweep her on to the dance floor, wrap my arms round her and breathe every last lyric out against her skin.

'I love you, Molly Frazer.'

And then the disco fires up, everybody else piles on to the dance floor, my friends start twerking and that is pretty much that.

We take a break from whirling around the dance floor at about eleven to refuel at the chocolate fountain, where I take the opportunity to apologize to Molly again for Dad's speech. 'I'm really sorry for all that stuff Dad said . . . about Norfolk and everything,' I say. The topic's already one I try to avoid around Moll since our misunderstanding the morning after our engagement.

Molly shrugs good-naturedly, sticks a marshmallow under the stream of chocolate. 'It's okay. I was kind of expecting him to mention it. He goes on about it to me whenever we see him.'

Just then one of Molly's older cousins rounds the other side of the fountain, looking harassed and a bit upset.

'Your brother needs a good talking-to, Alex.' She tries to say it like she isn't pissed off, like she knows that different rules apply at weddings – but the pink spots of heat on her cheeks and the way her mouth is twisting slightly give her away.

I freeze, molten chocolate dripping from the skewer in my hand. 'What's he done?' I ask her, almost afraid to find out.

'He told Doug to eff off in front of the kids, so I suppose you could say he's been teaching my children to swear.' She sends a hot breath upwards into her damp-from-dancing fringe. 'He's taken them off to bed.'

Graeme's one of those people who claims his general lack of tact and self-restraint is simply a version of honesty, and therefore a trait to be admired. Generally I disagree, and I especially disagree tonight. Not long after reappearing from his extended bathroom break, I witnessed him engaging in a heated argument with one of my work colleagues about a champagne bottle he thought was his (it wasn't), and I'm getting a bit annoyed that he seems to think it's okay to behave like this, especially at my wedding.

'I'm so sorry,' I tell Molly's cousin, wiping my mouth with a napkin. 'I'll go and talk to him.'

*

I find him outside sitting on a low stone wall, staring miserably at the spot where only hours earlier Molly's bridesmaids used sparklers to sky-write *LOVE* in the air as dusk sank in around us.

'Hey,' I say, plopping down next to him. It's the first time we've actually had five minutes alone together all day.

Behind us the music thumps on like a heartbeat, the long slope of manicured lawn at our feet falling into blackness where the glow from the dance floor fades. Above our heads, the sky is ablaze with stars.

'I don't know why I did that,' he says eventually. A plastic pint glass dangles from his hand, its contents almost gone. 'Swear in front of the kids, I mean.'

I take a moment to inhale the scent from the roses lining the patio, then look across at my brother. He seems utterly dejected, which I suppose isn't helped by his dishevelled appearance – shirt unbuttoned at the collar, pink tie removed, jacket long gone. Lost, probably. And he looks lost himself – so lost, in fact, that I decide here and now that the odd expletive in front of children at a wedding reception is probably nothing much to worry about in the grand scheme of things.

'Hey, it's all right,' I say. 'You can teach our children to swear, I promise. That can be your number-one job as uncle.'

'Ha,' he says flatly, before downing the last of his pint and crushing the plastic glass in his fist. For a moment I think he's about to project it down the length of the lawn, but then he loosens his grip, looks across at me and tries a smile.

'Great wedding, mate. Like really – top notch.'

'Thanks, Gray.'

'Moll looks beautiful.'

'Yeah, she does. I mean, thanks.'

There follows a pause, so I just come out with it.

'Graeme, what's wrong?' I think I can guess, but I want Graeme to do the talking.

'I think . . .' he says after a pause, 'I'm just sad.'

I nod, let the night breeze float over us. 'About what?'

'Oh, you know,' he says, then trails off.

'Dad?' I prompt.

He turns his head towards me and for a moment our eyes meet before he looks down at his knees and smiles. 'Yeah. I think it must be that, Alex.'

For a moment I think I've got it wrong – that something else is upsetting him – but he carries on talking and I lose my train of thought.

'His speech was a bit much,' Graeme says.

I nod. 'I know. All that stuff about Norfolk, and then Mum . . . I saw you walk off.'

'Couldn't stick it. He was looking right at me as he said it too – did you see?'

I try to recall, and now I come to think of it I do remember staring mostly at the back of Dad's head as he was talking, but I'd just assumed he was addressing the room. 'Of course he wasn't, Gray. He wouldn't do that.'

'He bloody did. Couldn't wait for his opportunity to stick the knife in.'

'I thought you helped him with his speech. Didn't you know he was going to talk about Mum?'

'Nope. He never mentioned it.' Graeme shakes his head. 'You know, nothing I do is ever enough, Alex. Nothing I do will *ever* be enough, I can see that now. He's always going to blame me and I may as well accept it. You're always going to be the golden boy and I'm always going to be the defective son, the one who messed everything up, ruined his life. And yet – I've always tried to stand up for him, help him, compensate for everything that happened. I make excuses for him, give him the benefit of the doubt . . . and this is what he does to me.' Graeme's shoulders heave as he exhales, as if he's getting ready to punch something, and then he looks across at me. 'Do you blame me, Alex? For Mum?'

'No, of course not,' I say, which is what I always say when he asks me this. 'You were seven years old.'

'I'd kind of convinced myself that Dad didn't blame me either. I thought we'd reached a bit of a truce, especially since he got ill. But the way he looked at me while he was saying all the stuff about Mum . . . it was like he was saying, *All this is your fault.* It's like he's started blaming me all over again. Everything I do for him . . .'

'Don't, Gray,' I say softly – but I only mean, *Don't torture yourself.*

Graeme snaps his face towards me, eyes by now glimmering with rage and injustice. 'Oh, here we go. Jesus, Alex, you never want to talk about it.'

I shake my head because he's wrong, but in many

ways he's actually right. I exhale. 'You know what? You're right, Graeme, I *don't* want to talk about it. But only because . . . it's my wedding day. I'm supposed to be having the time of my life with Molly, not sitting down here talking about Mum with –' I stop speaking abruptly, let the end of my sentence drop off into the night.

'With me,' Graeme says, then lets out a loose laugh. 'You're right, Alex. Why on earth would you want to be sitting down here with me on your wedding day?'

'I didn't mean –'

But Graeme's not interested. He nods back towards the house, where our guests are starting to spill out from the dance floor, drinks in hand, wrapped up in cardigans and jackets.

'You're my twin,' I remind him, because in that moment it seems wholly significant – he's my brother, we shared a womb, I will always love him. 'I would never blame you for what happened. Never.'

Graeme looks up at the sky. 'It's time for fireworks.'

13

Molly — present day

It's Friday night, a fortnight or so after I receive my written warning, and I'm meeting Eve for supper at our favourite pizza place in town – a rare treat since money became so tight. The restaurant's packed out, but luckily, they have one small table left next to the steamed-up window.

'God, it's been too long,' Eve says, after the waitress has brought our drinks. 'Sorry I've been so hectic recently.'

I shake my head, brush her apology aside with one hand. 'I want to hear all about Isla's first day.' The kids started back at school this week, and after a comfortable few years at the village primary, Isla's now moved up to the high school in a neighbouring town. Eve's been pretending and failing to be cool about it all summer.

'It was *great*,' she says, sounding so relieved that her words all fall into themselves. 'I had nothing to worry about at all. She just hung out with her normal friends like always, and when she got home she couldn't stop raving about how big the playground is and all this fantastic gymnastics equipment they have. Plus, she was ridiculously excited about getting her own locker.'

'Like mother, like daughter,' I grin, for Eve is the queen of organization.

Eve laughs, sips from her lemonade. 'Stupid, isn't it? I was more nervous than she was. A thirty-five-year-old woman loses the plot, her eleven-year-old holds it coolly together.' She shakes her head. 'Madness.'

'It's understandable,' I say. 'She's your baby.'

'God, tell me about it. She's already started telling me to get off her when I go in for a hug. Tom says I smother them.'

'You don't,' I assure her.

'I don't know,' she says doubtfully. 'I always swore I'd never be *that* kind of mum. My mum was too clingy, too suffocating. Now I'm turning into her, Moll. I mean – look.' She passes me her phone.

I examine the photo of Isla in her new school uniform, standing stiffly in front of the yew tree in Eve's back garden. The expression on Isla's face is hilarious – it's like a cartoon grimace and her whole body is contorted, as if she's physically trying to flee this monstrous woman with the camera.

I laugh. 'She looks gorgeous.'

Eve laughs too. 'Yeah. It's going to be hard to really let go, I can tell you that.'

'You don't ever really though, do you?' I say, thinking how close I am to my own mum.

'I guess not,' she sighs. 'But there's going to come a time when she doesn't need me any more. Can you imagine me then? You'll have to check me into a facility.'

'Ha. See you there,' I say drily.

Eve's face drops a little. 'How are things with you and Alex?' she asks me more sombrely. 'Did you get everything cleared up after the fire?'

Inwardly I cringe, completely aware of how I've just (unintentionally) brought the conversation back round to myself. I hand Eve the phone back, swallowing the pang that always comes with being reminded that I might never experience motherhood, and all its associated highs and lows – everything I crave.

'Yep,' I nod, taking a sip from my ginger beer. 'Graeme sent a guy round. We were worried about toxic fumes.'

'That was good of him. And how's everything at Spark?' she asks me as the waitress arrives with our pizza. Both ravenous, we dig in straight away, tearing hunks of it off with our fingers, steam billowing from the tomato sauce, elastic cheese, shredded yellow peppers. The pizza here is so fresh, so *good*.

'Keeping my head down,' I say. 'Or trying to, anyway. It's pretty hard with Seb watching my every move, trying to trip me up.'

'He shouldn't try too hard,' Eve says, shooting me a look. 'There is such a thing as constructive dismissal, you know. If you feel like he's trying to push you to breaking point – he probably is. That's not legal.'

I smile grimly, despite my delectable mouthful of dough and mozzarella. 'Well, I'm pretty sure Seb knows

I have neither the time nor the inclination to fight him in a court of law. Nor the money, come to that.'

'Has Sarah said any more about that job at your old place? Maybe you should start thinking about having other irons in the fire, just in case.'

Eve and I had lunch a few days after I met Sarah, when I confided to her what Sarah had said. I shake my head. 'I told her no anyway, so . . .'

'But have you thought any more about it?'

I sling her a look. 'You mean Project Annexe?'

'You're not in the least bit tempted?'

For a moment, I stop chewing. 'Should I be?'

Eve shrugs. 'I don't know. Sometimes I think . . .' She hesitates, sets down her pizza slice. 'It's hard to let people help sometimes, isn't it?'

'It's not pride, Eve,' I say, remembering that Graeme said something very similar to me at the start of July. 'It's just that I know Alex, and I know it wouldn't work, moving back to London.'

'But you like the idea in principle?'

'Yes, of course. Who wouldn't? Living with Mum and Dad, my old job back, more money . . . but it's not just about what *I* want, Eve. I have to think of Alex now.'

'But it doesn't ever seem to be about what you want, Molly.'

I stare at her, pizza slice halfway to my mouth. A couple of vegetables slide off the edge, slopping messily back on to the plate. 'Eve, what are you saying exactly?'

'I just think maybe you *should* think about getting out

of Norfolk. Here, it's all about Alex. You'd have more of a balance in London.'

'But Alex would *hate* it,' I remind her. 'You know this, Eve. What are you getting at?'

There is a long pause, during which Eve pretends to finish chewing a mouthful she swallowed long ago. Eventually, to buy more time, she picks up her drink and takes a slug, then finally sets it down and meets my eye.

'Tom saw Alex having lunch with Nicola yesterday.'

'What?' Eve and I have both been on high alert for the reappearance of Nicola since she accidentally-on-purpose dialled Alex a fortnight ago.

'They were at the golf club. Tom was on a corporate day.'

The world seems to grind to a halt, and I stare very hard at the wreckage of the pizza lying between us. The noise in the room seems to dull, like I've suddenly been plunged underwater.

It takes me a few moments to find my voice. 'He's sure it was them?' Alex claimed to have been alone in the cottage all day yesterday, though now I think about it, he did seem unusually tired last night.

'Positive.'

I have to accept this. You could hardly mistake Alex and Nicola – once a couple and both residents of the village since birth – for anyone else.

'I didn't know whether to say anything.'

I swallow. 'No, no, of course you should have done.'

'Tom said . . . they were being very flirty.'

This, from Tom, is bad news. He is not the sort of person who normally even indulges in idle gossip, let alone sticks his oar into other people's business. He must be really worried.

I shut my eyes. 'How flirty is flirty?'

'More flirty than you should be when you're married.'

'Kissing?' I can hardly say the word.

'God, no. I don't think so. But Tom was pissed off enough about it to tell me.'

'Did Tom say anything – to Alex?'

'No, sweetie. I'm sorry. He was with clients, and you know what Alex . . . well, you know what he's like. Tom couldn't risk a scene.'

Oh yes. I know all too well what Alex is like.

And then the subtext comes to me. 'Do you think I should leave Alex? Is that what you're saying?'

Eve reaches over and covers my hand with hers. It feels warm and comforting, like when my mum grasps my hand over her kitchen table as we dig into the last piece of carrot cake together. 'No, Moll. That's not what I'm saying at all. But maybe . . . you should think about bringing the balance back towards you slightly. At the moment, it's all about Alex – and I get that, of course I do. I hope I'd do the same in your situation. But you never even wanted to leave London, not really – and all your support network is there.'

I think about Mum and Dad, about Phoebe, and Sarah, and all my London friends.

'You've been an unbelievable friend to me, Eve.' I have to say it now, because it's true.

She smiles a thank you. 'Look, why don't you come and stay tonight? Tom's taking the kids to a birthday party tomorrow, so I've got most of the morning free.' Bless her, instead of taking time out for herself, Eve's already thinking of ways she can help me out to ease the strain – or the shock.

'Actually,' I tell her, 'I'm going to London tomorrow, staying with Mum and Dad for the night.' I shake my head at the timing of it all. 'A girl in my old agency, Libby – she's moving to Singapore. It's her leaving do.'

Eve's eyes widen. 'And . . . will Sarah be there?'

I nod. 'She's putting my entire weekend through on expenses.'

Eve tries a smile. 'Fortuitous.'

I bite my lip, barely daring to agree. 'Maybe.'

'Do you want me to look in on Alex tomorrow night?'

'Thanks, but Charlie's staying over.' It's not *strictly* necessary any more for someone to be with Alex at all times but, ever since the fire, I've started thinking you really can't be too careful.

'Look, Moll. In case you're worried about Nicola . . . I've been thinking of having a word.'

'No,' I say straight away. 'Don't do that.'

'Well, someone needs to tell her. She's taking the piss, if you don't mind me saying.'

'I don't mind you saying at all. But I need to talk to Alex first.'

'Will he tell you the truth?'

'Maybe not. But then Nicola's hardly likely to either, is

she, if she's already meeting him for clandestine little lunches?'

'Well, that's what I mean. Maybe someone should warn her off.'

I draw back slightly in my chair. '*Threaten* her?'

'No! Of course not. But I'm certainly capable of putting her in her place.'

I don't doubt that, actually. 'No, not yet. I'm going to try and find out what's going on first. If you talk to her she might warn Alex and it could muddy the waters, stop me getting to the truth.'

Like the waters aren't already murky as ditchwater.

It's not long before Eve has to head home to see the kids before they go to bed, so she settles up our bill, insisting on paying for both of us. 'It's my treat,' she assures me. 'I'm really sorry to spoil your night, Moll. I feel terrible about it. Please don't let it ruin your weekend.'

Well that's easier said than done, but I certainly don't blame Eve for any of this mess.

'So, do you think you're going to talk to Sarah? About the job?' she asks me as we hug goodbye on the pavement.

Half an hour ago, I'd have said no. Now, I'm not so sure. Maybe she's got a point about irons in the fire. Because if Alex *is* getting close to Nicola, what's really left for me here? If I lose Alex to Nicola, I lose everything.

I think about it for the entire drive home – about what it would mean to me, to discover that Alex and

Nicola were engaged in something illicit. How would I ever know if it was as a result of his injury, or whether he still would have done it, in another life?

The thought of that brings tears to my eyes, and suddenly, I *do* know. The Alex I knew back then, the old Alex, would *never* have done that to me.

It seems I don't know much any more – but I do know that.

It's been a habit for so long now, to give Alex the benefit of the doubt – to put a bad temper down to his condition, to excuse carelessness, to convince myself he would never have talked to me in a certain way before the accident. But now, as I stand outside the front door to our tumbledown cottage, I am starting to question myself. Maybe he has been getting close with Nicola – clearly he's completely capable of lying to me, as he did when I asked him what he'd got up to yesterday and he told me 'not much'.

I push open the front door and head into the living room, drop my bags, take off my jacket. He should have eaten by now – there was microwaveable curry in the fridge, labelled, a note written for him on the side.

But he's not in the living room, so I head through to the kitchen and peek into the fridge – the curry box is still in there, untouched. On the countertop is a mess of crumbs, a jam jar with the lid off, butter dish uncovered, bread bag wide open with the remaining slices falling out of it like dominoes. Smears of jam and butter decorate the surfaces.

I check the garden, almost expecting to see Alex and Nicola sitting in it, sharing a sundowner and memories of good times. But they are not there.

Pausing at the foot of the staircase I notice Alex's sketchbook on top of a pile of newspapers. Catching my breath, I bend down, flick it open to halfway, to the section of blank pages he gradually fills. Am I about to discover one of Nicola? Is that how I'm going to find out? But there is nothing like that, just a still life of some golf clubs and another sketch of Buddy.

I swallow back disappointment. *If you're drawing things that make you happy, then why am I not there, Alex? Why do I do this, if I don't even make you happy?*

I turn and head upstairs, my heart suddenly pounding in anger and irrational fear – or is it irrational? I don't even know any more. Is Nicola here, with him, now? Am I going to push open the bedroom door and discover them . . . ?

I half anticipate Nicola springing out from behind the door to take me out with some precisely timed karate move as I enter the room.

Gotcha!

Alex is propped up (alone) on the bed, reading a fitness magazine. It's warm up here, but once again, no windows open – just Alex bare-chested against the pillows, looking a little sweaty.

Breathless from the fevered sequence of events in my head, I lean against the doorframe, but say nothing.

'Hi, Molly,' he says, looking mildly interested in my presence, which might mean he's noticed that I'm panting and verging on hysterical. *Well, there's a first time for everything, Alex. Should we call this progress?*

'What are you doing?'

He holds up the magazine but says nothing.

'A *fitness* magazine?' I say, with more curdle to my voice than even I was expecting. 'Why are you reading that? You're not interested in the gym any more.'

'I am,' he says, which is news to me.

I smile, shake my head. As if it has come to this. After all the heartache of the past three years, the struggles, the sacrifices, the heart-wrenching sadness – as if Nicola could just skip into his life again, take him to lunch and transform him once more into the man he was. I've been trying to pique his interest in the gym for *years*. And the closest I've got is golf. *Golf.*

'Did Nicola give you that?'

It occurs to me as I say it that I don't really have a strategy for confronting any of this, which as anyone who knows Alex would say is a Bad Idea. I imagined on the drive home that I'd at least try to handle it delicately, as I do any awkward situation with Alex that's likely to make him fly off the handle. But now it's come down to it, I am just so furious that I don't even care. I'm going to say how I feel, exactly as he always does – I'm going to be rude and furious and impatient and outspoken, and for once – *for once* – he's going to be the one left reeling. Because we haven't come this far to be destroyed by Nicola, Alex – we haven't gone through everything we've gone through just to succumb to her shallow flirtations. That's not how this is going to end.

I won't let it – I *won't*. And if you decide you want to be with her, then that's your call, your catastrophic error – but you're going to hear from me first. I'm going to tell you *exactly* how I feel about it. And, this time, you're going to be the one listening and *I'm* going to be the one ranting and raving.

'Have you eaten? Why is there toast and jam and butter smeared all over the kitchen? It looks like you've been in there and thrown everything around.'

Two questions, subtly different, and a statement close together. I watch his mind trying to catch up with my words, unscramble my sentences.

'And answer the question.' *The third question, the one I asked a few seconds ago, I'm throwing that one into the mix for you too.* 'Did Nicola give you that magazine?'

I allow him a few moments, during which he hesitates – to catch up with what I'm saying, to try and remember, or to invent a lie? 'Nicola? No.'

He's attempting to throw me off, I'm convinced of it. 'You're lying.'

'*What?*'

I'm inviting his rage as I stand here throwing accusations and questions at him, I know that, but I am so furious I cannot stop. 'Do you *know* what it takes for me to do this every day, Alex – and all the time, you're with her? I know you were with Nicola at the golf club yesterday – Tom saw you! But you told me you were here all day.'

Alex stares at me, open-mouthed. He's shocked, I can see that, but I can't work out why – because I'm so angry, because I'm exposing his deception, or because he doesn't follow?

The fury is tumbling out of me now, unfiltered, unedited, in just the same way Alex speaks to me. 'I'm not stupid, Alex, I know what she's capable of! I've been trying to get you to go to the gym for years and now suddenly you're up here reading a fitness magazine! Why are you meeting her? Why? She's your ex-girlfriend, for God's sake! Why would you *do that to me?*'

But my last sentence collides with his reaction, which comes characteristically swiftly. Hurling the magazine against the wall, he gets to his feet. Ordinarily I'd feel unbelievable guilt for riling him up like this while he's relaxing and calm, but tonight I don't care. *Tonight you get to experience a little bit of what you put me through, Alex.*

'What the fuck are you going on about? Shut up, Molly – shut up!'

And then he heads for the door. In an instant he's through it, thundering down the stairs away from me. But I won't be silenced. I won't swallow away my feelings or resist reacting as I'm so practised in doing. I am too angry, and there is too much at stake.

I find him in the kitchen, where he swipes the bread bag, jam jar and butter dish from the worktop in one smooth, effortless motion. I watch them smash on to the concrete, smatter more detritus across the floor, and for once I allow myself to think – *Well, this time, I'm not going to clean that up.*

'I know you were with Nicola yesterday, Alex!'

Finally, he turns towards me, his face clouded over with confusion and rage. 'So what?'

'So I asked you what you did yesterday and you said, nothing!'

'I forgot!'

'You were hiding it from me! Why were you meeting her? *Why*, Alex?'

'It's none of your business!' he shouts, his voice by now a thunder in the confines of the room. 'You're always trying to control me! You can't tell me who I see!'

'You shouldn't be seeing *her*!'

'She understands me!' he shouts then, raising a finger to jab it towards my face. 'She listens to me, she doesn't nag me like you do, Molly!'

'You know, I've been offered a job in London, Alex – I could walk out of here right now and never come back!' I shout, a cruel final attempt to make him care, so desperate for him to feel something.

'Well, go on then! Why don't you? At least then I wouldn't have to listen to you nagging me all the time!'

'How many times have you met her?' I scream at him now, so worked up there is literally saliva bubbling from one corner of my mouth. *'How many times?'*

And it is then that it happens.

I don't feel pain so much as heat and shock, though I do crumple to the floor and gasp for breath. My entire head pounds from the impact, and in an instant all my anger is gone. Instinct takes over, instructs me to stay still, and I curl up like an animal, motionless. I am making myself invisible. Protecting myself.

But though my anger has now ceased, overridden in a second by the instinct for self-preservation, Alex is still going. 'This is *your fault*, Molly,' he snarls at me, from somewhere above my head, and I tense, bracing myself for further impact. My blood is pounding at high speed; I can hear it in my ears, fast and forceful like the heartbeat of an unborn child.

And then, finally, I hear him retreat and the back door slams. I remain frozen where I am in a ball on the floor, talking to myself in my head. *You're okay. You're okay. Breathe. Breathe.*

14

Molly – present day

When I wake the following morning, even I am shocked by the extent of the bruising. It's perhaps partly down to the unforgiving strip lighting in this ghastly bathroom, but I look as if I've been in a car accident.

I contemplated calling Eve last night, but I knew she would be devastated and blame herself – and that Tom would too, come to that – so I decided against it. Besides, I could hardly turn up on their doorstep with a black eye. Whatever would that do to the kids?

So I checked into a budget motel, the cheapest I could find, which meant a dual carriageway for a view, some really impersonal questions and tactless staring from the receptionist and a strange smell emanating from the curtain material. Still, it was a bed for the night, away from Alex.

Not that I imagine, even now, that Alex would probably really register what happened last night. Had I stayed put and waited for him to come back inside, he would probably have done so after a while, nicely cooled off and entirely unwilling to discuss the episode at all. *I'm in a good mood right now*, he'd say. *Why are you always trying to bring me down, Molly?*

My head is banging, and I'm well aware that it might not be only my skin tone that's been damaged. But there is no way I can go to the hospital, face questioning by medical professionals, have to tell them all about Alex and for social services to get involved. Plus there's a large part of me that feels horribly guilty about what happened. I pushed him too far; I was angry. I *wanted* to provoke him, to make him feel some of what I feel. I know he struggles to control his temper, and I know what his triggers are. It's like an adult provoking a child. I should have known better.

Besides, the blow wasn't intentional. He didn't mean to strike *me*. He was aiming for the kitchen whiteboard, the one he hates so much, the one where I write down all the things he routinely ignores. And at just the last minute I turned my face, and caught the force of his punch.

Once my breathing had steadied and I'd found my feet I threw some things into a bag, escaping before he came back inside. I called a taxi from the village and rang Charlie while I was in it, told him I had to go to London a night earlier than expected, asked him if he could please do me a huge favour and look in on Alex. Charlie, who's as laid back as my husband once was, said of course, it was no problem, to leave everything to him. Not for the first time, I sent up a silent prayer of gratitude that Alex has good friends who stuck by him when so many others fell away.

The motel doesn't offer any sort of breakfast, but there is an ancient kettle and some instant coffee sachets, so

I mix up a hot drink, pollute it with UHT and sit back down on the bed. The drink tastes disgusting, but I need the caffeine hit to help me think.

I still want to go to London. I've been looking forward to it, and anyway – I want to see Sarah. I don't know what I think about Alex any more, but last night has clarified one thing in my mind – I at least need to explore if returning to London is even an option. But how will I explain my face – with the truth, or a lie? Will it put Sarah off, remind her my life is inherently unstable, make her think employing me comes with too many question marks?

Not if I leave Alex. Not if it's just me in London, with no one else.

The thought brings a thick glut of tears to my throat.

No, Molly, not now. Not after everything you've been through. Hold on. Hold on.

But I can't go on like this. I think – I think – we've come to the end of the line.

And now I start to weep, for the first time since last night, and once I let them run, the tears come so fast and forcefully I am afraid I might never be able to stop them.

Stop crying. Hold it together.

I can't. I can't hold it together any more.

I lower my head, letting the tears drop on to the knees of my jeans, and just as I do, my phone starts to ring.

It's Graeme.

My first instinct is to ignore it, because I'm really not

ready to talk to anyone. But then I realize that, actually, the one person in the world right now who might have a shot at impartiality is Graeme. Yes, he's Alex's brother, but he's always had my back too. Plus, he gets it – in a way that my parents and friends sometimes fail to.

'Hello?' I manage.

'Moll, are you okay? I just called Alex and he said you'd had a fight.'

What is it about familiar voices that makes you want to break down afresh? I take a couple of moments to respond, my chest heaving heavily with the effort of trying not to cry.

'I'm okay,' I manage eventually, my voice a strange, distorted strangle.

'Oh my God,' he says. 'What happened?'

'It wasn't Alex's fault. He wasn't aiming at me.'

There is a pause. 'What do you mean, he wasn't *aiming* at you?'

I arrive at the London address Graeme has given me and look up at the building. It's in a rundown area where all the houses have been carved up into bedsits and everything's unloved. Graeme's staying with a friend in his basement flat, and as I descend the concrete stairs to the front door I notice a tide of litter strewn around the foot of the building like it's been washed up in some unforgiving storm. On the main road above my head, cars rush past, one after the other, relentless.

He opens the door before I knock. 'Oh Jesus.'

I smile grimly. 'Nice to see you too.'

He doesn't return my smile, just steps aside to let me in. The place is dark and enclosed, with no decor to speak of, just stacks of boxes and bin bags.

'It's . . . a bit different to that Ealing sublet,' I say, remembering the bright, airy flat we stayed in when Alex and I last came to visit Graeme in May. To compliment this place – a grimy, poky, gloomy dungeon of a flat – would be insincere. We both know there's not a lot to love here. 'Do you like it?' I ask him cautiously.

'God, no. But Mike's moving out. That's why it's a bit of a tip.'

'Are you taking over the lease?'

'Nah,' he says offhandedly. 'The landlord's putting the rent up, so . . . thought I'd find somewhere else. Anyway, this area's not the best.'

'Where will you go?'

'Not sure yet,' he says, with what I can tell is forced brightness.

I feel awful about it, really – Graeme owns half a house, for God's sake. He shouldn't be having any concerns about where he's going to live. I think again about his offer to move in, back in July, and am overcome with guilt about how I batted it away.

'Anyway, never mind me,' he's saying. 'Let's take a look at you, Moll.'

He turns me slowly by the shoulders towards the little light there is, examines my face. I swallow, move my gaze past him and focus on the wall behind his left ear like I'm at the optician's.

'Wow. That looks painful.'

'It is,' I say simply.

'Have you been to the doctor?'

'No.'

He nods, understanding I'm sure why involving other people in this is not really an option if I don't want to complicate my life even further.

'I'm so sorry,' he says then.

'It wasn't his fault. I was shouting at him about . . . and he tried to punch the whiteboard.'

'Yeah, you said. But still.'

We are quiet for a moment. 'Cup of tea?' Graeme asks me. 'Coffee?' He pauses. 'Gin?'

I smile. 'Cuppa would be great, thanks.'

We head through to a tiny, windowless kitchen, where Graeme fills a kettle and finds two mismatching mugs in the cupboard.

'So . . . are you getting kicked out of here, Graeme?' I ask him. 'You can be honest with me.'

He shoots me a wry smile. 'Don't worry about me, Moll. I have irons in the fire.'

I smile softly. 'That's what Eve's been telling me to have.'

He leans back against the worktop as we wait for the kettle to boil. It's rattling and whistling, like it's working really hard. 'And do you?'

I swallow, look down at the floor, say nothing.

'Is that why you're here? Is that what meeting Sarah tonight's all about?' Graeme's question is carefully phrased, his tone neutral. I told him about tonight's party on the phone earlier. 'Have you told her what happened?'

'No,' I say quickly, but still I don't meet his eye. 'It's just a leaving do, an old colleague. Sarah just . . . wanted me to come because I worked with her for a long time. She's a good friend.'

The kettle rumbles and shakes as it reaches boiling point, and Graeme turns to fill the cups. 'Builder's, right?'

'Thanks. Two sugars.'

'Don't blame you. Hang on, Mike stashed some biscuits somewhere in here.' He opens and shuts cupboard doors before eventually finding them, tearing open the packet and upending the lot on to a cracked plate, passing it to me. 'Get stuck into those. I'll bring these through – living room's on the right.'

'Thanks,' I say, taking the plate and heading next door into the living room. It's tiny and airless, as dark as the rest of the flat, and the place stinks of fags. My instinct is to open a window, but aware of being a guest, I sit down on the throw-covered sofa instead and inhale a couple of chocolate-chip cookies, appreciating the sugar hit.

Graeme comes through a few moments later and passes me my tea. The tiny sofa's the only place to sit in here, so instead he settles on the floor, his back against the wall opposite, and smiles.

'Thank you,' I say.

'For what?'

'Being here.'

He nods and takes a sip of tea. 'So what are you going to say to the others? About your face? I have to admit, I'm kind of surprised you still want to go.'

'You don't think I should?' I frown.

'No, I didn't mean that. It's just . . . well, they'll jump to a certain conclusion, won't they?'

'I'll tell them it was an accident.'

Graeme laughs lightly. 'You don't have to tell them that, Moll. It wasn't an accident.'

'No, but it wasn't exactly Alex's fault, either.'

'That's up for debate.'

'No, it's not,' I insist.

Graeme pauses. 'So, what were you fighting about?'

I sigh, loath to even say her name. 'Nicola.'

'*Nicola?* What about her?'

'She . . .' I lower my cup, shake my head. 'Tom saw her and Alex having lunch on Thursday. He said they were being *very* flirty. And Tom's not . . .'

' . . . one for drama,' Graeme supplies, for he knows Tom well.

'Exactly. I mean, when it comes from Tom you know it's legit, at least.'

There is a short pause. 'I'm sorry, Moll.'

'You think he's capable of it? Having . . .' I swallow. ' . . . an affair?'

'No, not necessarily. I just meant – you know. It's a hard thing to hear, whatever the context. That your husband's . . .' He trails off, but I don't mind him not finishing the sentence.

'Well, anyway. I was furious, and . . . I thought, after

everything we've been through . . .' I can feel myself starting to get choked up again, but I don't want to cry in front of Graeme. I'm not sure why exactly, but I've always tried to remain strong when I'm around him. Maybe because I want him as my brother-in-law to think I'm capable, that I'm in control, that as long as I'm Alex's wife, he'll always be okay.

'You lost it,' Graeme guesses simply.

'I'm sorry,' I say, scrunching up my face to stem the tears, which sends a shot of pain riveting through my left eye. Involuntarily, I wince, suck in a sharp but silent breath.

'Don't apologize. It's not a criticism. Who wouldn't lose it, in your position?'

'I still don't know what to think. I mean, I've seen them flirting before, and I know she hangs around him all the time, and then I got home and he was reading this *gym* magazine . . .' I shake my head, spitting out the words like I caught him reading porn.

Graeme snorts. 'What, like – bodybuilding?'

'Yeah – one of those "Get a six-pack in your lunch break" jobbies.'

'Ha.'

'I mean, honestly. I thought to myself, how can she have this effect on him that I can't? What is it about her?'

'Nothing,' he says calmly. 'She just tells Alex what he wants to hear. It's classic – he's vulnerable, she's manipulative. It's nothing more than that.'

'But it's my job to protect him, isn't it? From people like that?'

'Yes, but the problem is he's not a child, Moll. He's a strange hybrid now, isn't he? We've said this before. He behaves like a kid a lot of the time, but he's also an adult with free will. It's impossible to protect him from everything. He still has autonomy, and rightly so.'

I snaffle another biscuit from the plate, stuff it into my mouth.

'Look, we've always said we'll do everything we can, try our best, put all the mechanisms and support in place, but at the end of the day . . . he still has to live.'

'But that's just the point, isn't it?' I say miserably. 'I didn't try my best last night. I completely flew off the handle, and what's worse is . . .' I shake my head.

'What's worse is what?' Graeme asks me, and I feel his eyes trained on my face. From beyond the window, the traffic rushes past like rainfall.

'What's worse is, I sort of *wanted* to lose it. I planned it, almost. I was so angry I said to myself – *I want him to feel some of what he puts me through.*' I look over at Graeme. 'That's a horrible thing to confess, isn't it?'

'I think that's a completely human thing to confess, Moll.'

I sigh. 'Well, thank you. You're always too nice to me.'

I hear Graeme swallow from where I'm sitting, but when I look over to him he's staring down into his cup of tea.

It occurs to me then that the room is darkening, that it's getting late. I clear my throat. 'Do you have a bag of peas? I need to try and get this swelling down a bit before I go out.'

He smiles. 'Peas?'

'Don't tell me you've never heard of the frozen-pea thing?'

'No, no, I have. I was just smiling at the idea of you thinking we might be organized enough to have either a functioning freezer or things to put in it. Particularly vegetables.'

I smile back. 'Ah.'

'Sorry. I'm a bit of a useless host, I'm afraid.'

'Not at all,' I say, raising my cup. 'Builder's and biscuits. What more could I want?'

'Oh, I meant to say. You can have my bed tonight. I'll kip in here.'

'On this?' I say, glancing down at the sofa I'm sitting on. 'It's barely long enough for half of you.'

'Well, I wouldn't subject either you or me to Mike's room. He's away for the weekend but it's actually a classified health hazard. Part of the reason we're being kicked out.'

'So you are,' I say gently. 'Being kicked out.'

'Well, Mike is,' he admits. 'I was never really here. Officially speaking.'

'So where are you going to go?'

There is a pause, during which Graeme checks his watch. 'You should get ready, Moll. Don't want you to miss your party.'

'Well, hang on,' I say. 'Why don't you come with me?'

Sarah double-takes when we approach her in the bar. 'Molly, what happened to you?'

'Walked into a door frame,' I lie easily.

Sarah glances at Graeme, hesitates for a moment, then puts a hand to her chest. 'Stupid me. I thought you were Alex, for a moment!'

'The next best thing,' Graeme smiles.

I noticed before we left the flat that he'd applied an aftershave Alex used to love. It completely threw me – taking me instantly back to days gone by as smell so often does. Every now and then I catch the scent of it, and I am forced to remind myself it's not my husband by my side.

'Sarah, you remember Graeme? Alex's twin.' They've met a handful of times on nights out.

'Yes, of course.' She shakes his extended hand. 'But, Moll – seriously, what happened?'

'I was just being clumsy. Didn't look where I was going,' I say, my voice partly dampened by the music.

Sarah's face clouds with doubt, and she looks from Graeme to me and then back to Graeme again, searching our neutral expressions for clues. 'It's true,' Graeme says. 'I saw her do it.'

'Ok-ay,' she says uncertainly.

Feeling horrible lying to Sarah, I look down at my feet.

'Oh, you look gorgeous anyway,' she says, her tone brightening slightly artificially in a way that tells me we'll be revisiting this topic later. 'The only girl I know who can carry off a black eye quite so elegantly.'

'Ha, thanks,' I say, straightening my dress. It's black silk, a little too short, and my heels are the super-high

241

ones that I struggle to walk in, if I'm honest. I left the house in such a rush last night that I wasn't thinking at all when I packed, just threw a handful of clothes, make-up and accessories that I thought might make me look halfway presentable into a bag.

'Right,' Sarah says. 'Drinks?'

'Is that the queue?' Graeme says, nodding over at the packed bar.

'Um, yes,' Sarah says, like Graeme's being a bit rude.

'Sod that. Wait there.'

'Graeme, where are you going?'

'I know a guy. He can get us into VIP. How big's your party?' he asks Sarah.

'Er, fifteen. Twenty, maybe.'

'Graeme, it's Saturday night,' I remind him.

'Yeah, and I know a guy. Wait there, don't queue for drinks. I'll be two seconds.' And then he vanishes.

'God, he's a bit smooth, isn't he?' Sarah says, turning to me, and I'm not sure if she means it as a compliment. 'I'd forgotten.'

'Very different to Alex,' is all I can think of to say. 'You look lovely too, by the way.'

Sarah's showing off her incredible figure in a cream sleeveless dress and the kind of heels I crave to be able to balance in. Her blonde hair is styled into a quiff ponytail, and she has a talent with liquid eyeliner that demands a superhumanly steady hand.

'Thanks, darling. Have you seen Libby yet?'

Libby is my ex-colleague who's swapping London for Singapore. She's getting a relocation, an apartment with a pool and a huge salary hike, and the entire leaving party is consequently rippling with envy. I shake my head. 'I'll say hello when she's finished with Paula.'

'Yep, not much has changed in two years, Moll. She still never pauses for breath.'

Graeme returns then, smiling. 'Head this way, ladies.'

I follow Graeme while Sarah rounds up the group, and we make our way upstairs to the mezzanine VIP area, where four tables are waiting for us.

'How the hell did you pull this off?' I smile at Graeme.

'I told you, I know a guy.'

'Hold on, hold on. There must be minimum spend, or something,' Sarah interjects.

'Relax,' Graeme says. 'It's just the seats and table service. Trust me, you'll have a better time.'

'Well,' Sarah says eventually, a bit awkwardly, 'thank you.'

'You're welcome,' Graeme tells her, before turning to me. 'Just going to mingle for a bit. See you later.'

'You're not leaving . . . ?' I say, feeling inexplicably alarmed.

'No, of course not.' He squeezes my arm. 'Won't be long.'

I sit down with Sarah and two Aperol Spritzes. More of my ex-colleagues gradually find their way upstairs, all making anxious enquiries as to the state of my face and asking concernedly after Alex. They come in waves, but Sarah successfully deflects most of the awkward questions on my behalf, for which I am grateful.

'So,' she finally says, by which time our glasses are almost empty, 'I'll be advertising Libby's job soon. Unless you know of anyone . . . ?'

I clear my throat, set down my drink. Do I dare show even casual interest? Could it start something I can't then stop? 'I might,' I say, my voice quiet against the background music.

But Sarah hears me perfectly clearly, and her whole face lifts. 'Moll, are you serious?'

'Might,' I repeat.

She nods. 'Does this have anything to do with your face?'

I look down at my knees. 'A bit.'

Sarah nods. 'Look – you should talk to your mum about that annexe idea again. Are you staying at theirs tonight?'

'No,' I say quickly. 'I cancelled on her. She can't see me looking like this.' I'd considered asking Phoebe if I could stay with her, but I know she'd worry just as much as Mum, if not more.

'Where are you staying then?' Sarah asks.

'Graeme's putting me up.'

'That's crazy! Come and stay with me, Moll. I insist.'

I hesitate. 'Oh, er . . . no. Thanks. Graeme's been so nice with all this VIP stuff, and . . .'

She nods. 'Fine. But promise me you'll talk to your mum. Shall I put the wheels in motion then? Get them to put together a package, make you an offer?'

This is exactly what I was worried about – things moving too quickly, not being able to put the brakes on. Illogically, I look around for Graeme, but I can't see him.

So I take a deep breath and jump in, feet-first, to this – the biggest decision of my life. 'Yes, all right,' I say, heart pounding with a mixture of fear and exhilaration like I'm inching towards the high point of a rollercoaster ride. 'Ask them to put something together. But I'll have to get back to you, let you know for sure – okay?'

Sarah makes a quick squeal of excitement. 'I can't believe it! One of my best ever team members coming back!' And then she flings her arms round my neck, peppers kisses into my hair. Despite myself, I smile. *This could be good*, I permit myself to think, feeling her arms round me. *This could be really good.*

'What's that?' someone I don't even recognize asks, leaning over the back of their seat towards us, and all of a sudden I worry Sarah's going to stand up, tap the edge of her glass, make an announcement.

I shoot Sarah a pleading look, and she does lift her glass, but only by way of explanation. 'Sorry. Too much of this, I think.' The woman smiles and turns back round, and Sarah grins at me. 'Let's get some more drinks. In fact – sod it. Let's order champagne.'

'Sarah, don't tell anyone yet,' I plead urgently. 'I mean, there's a lot I'd need to sort out. And – you know.' I nod over at Libby. 'I don't want Lib to think I'm jumping in her grave or anything.'

'Fine,' she says. 'But that doesn't mean I'm not allowed to get excited. God, your mum is going to be ecstatic, Moll!'

I don't say anything, because what I haven't told her yet is that if I come back to London, I won't need to live in an annexe in someone else's garden.

I'll need to start flat-hunting.

Because I'll be coming back alone.

15

Alex – 21 March 2013

In the end, it's liver cancer that kills our dad, just eight months after my wedding to Molly. He's diagnosed a few weeks before Christmas, and passes away in March.

On the morning of his funeral, the sun finally breaks through days of persistent low cloud. Graeme has co-ordinated the whole day, having consulted extensively with Dad on what he wanted when it became clear the end was drawing near. He's sorted out the hymns, eulogies, coffin, wake and burial, painstakingly making sure everything was exactly the way Dad would have wanted it.

Despite everything, Graeme's been loyal and steadfast to the last. I, on the other hand, have been a complete wreck – guilt-ridden for not moving back when Dad needed me most, and for never really feeling like we made it up after the disaster of Bonfire Night. I've been waking up in the middle of the night soaked in sweat and sobbing, dreaming about Dad being reunited with Mum in heaven, and the pair of them turning round to ask me why I wasn't there for Dad when it mattered most.

A damn good knees-up was Dad's main stipulation for

the wake, so we head over to the church hall after the service and burial for what is, essentially, a party. Dad asked for the dress code to be vibrant, and consequently the entire congregation looked, from the end of the church nave, like a gently breathing rainbow. Graeme and I went on a bizarre little shopping trip two days ago to purchase identical Hawaiian shirts, since neither of us owned anything that could remotely fit the theme.

I'm sure the vicar privately thinks we're all completely bonkers.

About half an hour into the wake I realize I can't see Graeme anywhere. So reluctantly leaving Molly engaged in repetitive small talk with one of Dad's old drinking buddies, I decide to go and look for him.

Eventually, I discover him in the kitchen. It smells of the sausages roasting for another batch of hot dogs (Dad's favourite), and is thankfully a little warmer than the cavernous main hall which, despite a recent refurbishment the parish has been fundraising for since the dawn of time, is absolutely freezing.

Graeme's leaning over the sink with his head hanging down, and for a moment I think he's being sick. But then he looks up and smiles. 'Sorry,' he whispers.

I don't know why, but my heart almost breaks. 'Hey, don't be.'

'I'm hiding.'

'From anyone in particular?'

He gives this some consideration. 'I know Dad wanted today to be a celebration, but . . .'

I nod, to show him I understand. 'I know. I don't

feel like celebrating either.' Tentatively, I step forward and put my arm round his shoulders. We must look a bit sad, I think to myself, like two small-time comedians backstage at a provincial gig, psyching themselves up for their Hawaiian shirt double-act.

'I never succeeded, Alex,' he says then.

'Succeeded at what?'

'Making Dad love me again, after Mum died.'

I shut my eyes, my heart pounding in a mixture of sympathy and my own regret. 'He always loved you, Gray.'

'Come on, Alex. His will proved exactly the opposite.'

I swallow. There's no denying that Dad delivered a heart-wrenching blow to Graeme in his will. He has left the entire cottage, and all of its contents, solely to me. To Graeme – presumably to stop him contesting anything – he left a few measly stocks and shares, bonds, some savings amounting to a couple of thousand quid.

In so many ways, Graeme was the much better son – yet I'm the one he rewarded at the end. From beyond the grave, Dad's still punishing Graeme for a mistake he made before he even knew what mistakes really were.

The timing, though, is bittersweet – the lease is soon up on mine and Molly's flat, plus the landlord's been maintaining it less and charging more for years. It was already the ideal time to move on and now . . . we have been given an entire house. But never has there been a more emotionally loaded inheritance, and it's paralysing me. How can I possibly move into the cottage, knowing what it represents? Doing so would be almost to collude with Dad's bitterness and blame.

I attempt a clumsy consolation. 'Dad knew Molly and I were getting screwed over on rent, that's all, Graeme. I used to complain about it all the time. But you own your place – I'm sure it's that simple.'

We both know it's not, but it would kill Graeme for me to confirm it.

'No, Alex. He stopped loving me that day. He could barely even look at me after it happened. Leaving the cottage to you was the final way he could say, *I blame you, Graeme.*'

'You weren't to blame,' I say, like I've said a million times. 'And deep down, Dad knew that too. And anyway, look – I've been thinking. You should get a share of the cottage too.'

It's only right – it isn't fair that I'm inheriting a mortgage-free cottage worth three hundred thousand quid, while Graeme's getting only the financial dregs of our dad's estate.

'What do you mean?' He's still turned away from me, staring down into the plughole.

'I mean . . . I'll do what's right. Dad might not have thought he needed to be fair about it, but I do. I'll sell the cottage, and give you half.'

He lets a loose laugh into the sink. 'Don't be insane. I won't let you do that, Alex. Dad's wishes should be carried out.'

'No. Dad left the cottage to me. It's up to me what I do with it.'

There is a short silence. 'You should enjoy it, Alex. You deserve it. Just accept it with good grace.'

'How can I do that, knowing you got cut out?'

'Have you told Molly? That you got the cottage?'

'Not yet.'

'If you sold it,' he says then, looking at me over his shoulder though his body remains firmly turned away, 'I'd be really angry. No matter how I feel about Dad, that place is still our childhood home, Alex – it shouldn't be sold to strangers. That wouldn't be right.'

'But I don't have the cash to square you up . . .'

'Forget it,' he says, far more blithely than I know he feels. 'I've got other plans.'

'What plans?' I ask him, but my question's met by silence, and he looks away.

'I tried to get him to forgive me, you know,' he says eventually. 'On the afternoon he died, just before you arrived. I asked him to say it, and he wouldn't. You know why?'

'Why?' I whisper, rubbing his back, swallowing the tears that are pooling in my throat as I picture Dad as he was that last afternoon.

'Because he *didn't* forgive me. He still blamed me, all the way to the grave.' He starts laughing. 'He just wanted to see his Golden Boy one last time, Alex. He was only interested in you. All he ever wanted was for you to move back to Norfolk, to be with him. Didn't matter to him that I was already there.'

In so many ways it would be easier to hear this if I didn't agree with Graeme – if I thought that he'd simply misinterpreted Dad's attitude towards him. But the worst part is, I don't think he has. I've always felt Dad's resentment towards Graeme as strongly as I've felt his affection towards me. I could sense it, constantly: when he berated only Graeme if we both misbehaved, in the celebration of my achievements and passive acceptance of Graeme's, when he'd switch on the TV while Graeme was mid-sentence. On the surface, all was more or less as it should be, but those bitter undercurrents were always there.

Still, I attempt again to reassure him. 'Did you ever think, Gray, that Dad might have . . . *wanted* someone to blame? He wanted someone to be angry with – and that should have been the driver, but they never caught him. So you were next in line. Things would have been different if they'd caught the guy. He'd have had some-one to direct his anger at.'

I admit that in a very small corner of my heart, I'm relieved I'll no longer have to play peacemaker for Graeme and my dad, mediate for them as I have been doing since the age of seven. It's been a long road.

Our mother, Julia Frazer, was knocked over in a hit-and-run on 3 September 1991, when Graeme and I were seven. Even then we were already chalk and cheese – as different as it was possible for twins to be. Graeme was errant and disobedient, wilful and prone to tantrums. I, on the other hand, admittedly preferred to follow the rules – do my homework, eat what was put in front of me, turn my lights out when instructed. We were living, breathing proof that nature trumps nurture.

On that particular afternoon, Mum was in the kitchen making tea. She'd ordered us to get on with our homework, but Graeme had other ideas – he wanted to go out with his friends, play football at the playing field. Our parents had been having a nightmare few months with him being awkward and headstrong, and they were getting to the end of their tether with it. He was already supposed to be grounded, a concept few parents of seven-year-olds were yet familiar with.

So Graeme climbed out of the living-room window, escaping down the road to the playing field. Too loyal (or was that terrified?) to give him up, I said nothing, and fifteen minutes or so after he'd vanished Mum came through to the living room, spatula in hand. Needless to say, I got a good smack over the back of the legs for my failure to tell on my brother before she stormed out of the house to look for him. It was to be the last interaction I would ever have with her.

She didn't get far, our lovely mum. Dad was out at work in our only car, so she was obliged to follow Graeme on foot. She was mown down on the verge by a hit-and-run driver as she made her way towards the playing field.

The first Graeme knew of it was several hours later when he returned to the house, curious to know why he hadn't been fetched home, whereupon he was greeted by me, hysterical and inconsolable, and the grave face of our next-door neighbour. The police had just left, and Dad had fled to the hospital to hold Mum's hand as she lay dying, to let her know how much he loved her.

Dad changed overnight, of course. For almost two

weeks he could barely look at Graeme, and Graeme himself hardly spoke for nearly six months. What had once been a lively, energetic house (albeit sometimes tense since Graeme discovered free will) was now virtually silent from day to day. There was never any food in the cupboards, never any music on the stereo. Birthdays went uncelebrated, Christmases unmarked. Dad sank into a deep depression and turned to booze. But what could have torn Graeme and me apart ended up pushing us together, because actually, I didn't blame him. I had often been tempted myself to disobey the rules as he did, only I was too scared – and I had always envied his confidence. As Dad shut down, we had to rely on each other, and it bonded us in a way that still surprises me now, when I look back on it. Mum was gone, and Dad was gone too – just in a different way – so we only had each other.

From the main hall now, we hear a cheer go up. I have a momentary yet horrifying vision of Molly's parents being forcibly dragged into a conga by a crowd of Dad's old drinking mates.

'Be sad, Graeme,' I tell him, because I have a sense that he needs someone – anyone – to give him permission to do that. 'Cry if you need to. You never really grieved for Mum, did you? Because you didn't really feel like you had any right to. Don't make the same mistake with Dad. It's okay to be sad.'

'Oh, I grieved for Mum,' he corrects me softly. 'I used to sneak into the bathroom at night, turn the taps on and cry myself to sleep.'

I stare at the laughing parrot on his back. 'You never told me that.'

'There's a lot I never told you.' Finally he straightens up, turns round and leans against the counter, his back to the sink.

'It's gloomy in here,' I say. 'Maybe if you went out and chatted to some people . . .'

'All of those people in there know the story,' he says. 'They know about Mum, and they despise me for it.'

'You didn't kill her, Graeme.' I state the obvious to remind him. 'You weren't to blame. Nobody in their right minds would blame a seven-year-old for what happened.'

'If I could turn the clock back . . .'

'Of course. But life doesn't work like that.'

'You know how I know you're a good person, Alex?'

I smile faintly. 'Because I let you talk me into buying these God-awful shirts?'

He offers a dutiful laugh, though it's slightly muffled by a sudden pick-up in the music next door. 'Well, yeah. But also . . . you never blamed me. You never once raised your voice, or lost your temper, or told me you hated me for what happened. I deprived you of a mum, but you never blamed me.'

'Do you know why?' I say gently.

He shakes his head, because still it won't sink in.

'Because it wasn't your fault.'

A single tear escapes down his cheek now, and he nods. 'Thank you.'

'Come here.' I put my arms round him and pull him into a hug.

'I'm selling my flat, by the way,' he says then into my shoulder. Or, at least, that's what I think he says.

'What?' I draw back from him.

'I said I'm selling the flat.'

'What? Since when?'

He shrugs defiantly in a way I probably haven't seen since we were seven years old. 'Dad's not around to disapprove of me any more. So I'm going to cash in the equity and go travelling.'

'Travelling where?'

Graeme laughs. 'I don't know. Anywhere. Australia, America – who cares?'

I care. 'Gray, just think about this. Today's not the day for making rash decisions. You might feel differently in a couple of weeks.'

'Too late. I've already got a buyer. I put the flat on the market the day after he died. And I quit my job.'

'Jesus, Gray, don't do that – please! I'll give you the money to go, just . . . please don't sell your flat.'

'We both know you don't have any money unless you sell the cottage, and I would never let you do that. And you don't owe me anything, Alex.'

Actually, I do. I owe you the love you never got from Dad.

I stare at him as the timer on the cooker starts to buzz, presumably to inform us the sausages in the oven are cooked. Graeme turns it off.

'Like I said,' I say desperately, 'I'll sort you out, with the cottage. Put your name on the title deeds or something.'

'Screw my name on a piece of paper. It's meaningless.'

'No, it's not!' I am feeling increasingly desperate.

Selfishly, I've sort of been hoping to spend some time with Graeme now that isn't clouded by the spectre of our past, and already he's telling me he's upping and leaving. *Please don't let our family fall apart even more, Graeme. There's only the two of us left now.*

'Who knows,' Graeme says, 'you might never see me again.'

'Shut up,' I tell him. 'Don't say things like that.'

'I'm free,' he whispers. 'I'm finally free.'

16

Molly – present day

Since I haven't stayed out this late in a while, I return to Mike's flat with Graeme when he tells me he's making a move, rather than stay on at the bar. We head back without saying much, silenced mostly by the stares of other people on the tube, passers-by on the street, their curiosity piqued by the state of my face.

When we get in he asks if I fancy a nightcap, but being wary of a crashing headache tomorrow I ask for a cup of tea instead.

I follow him into the kitchen, where I am relieved to finally kick off my shoes.

'That's better,' Graeme says, moving past me to fetch the kettle. 'It was unnerving me, you suddenly being so tall.'

'These heels are stupid,' I admit. 'They pinch my feet, and I can't balance in them.'

'Well, you'd never tell. You have the art of faking poise down to a T.'

'Story of my life.'

He laughs softly, refills the kettle then switches it on to boil.

'I don't get to dress up too often these days,' I confess.

'Makes a nice change?'

'Yes,' I realize. 'And to be in a bar until late, that's a real novelty.'

Graeme nods up at the clock on the wall. Embarrassingly, it's not even midnight yet.

I cover my face with one hand. 'This is late to me, okay?'

He smiles. 'If you say so.'

'So, when was the last time you got in from a big night at midnight?'

'Er . . . last week.'

'Oh,' I say. 'I misjudged you.'

He grins. 'Yeah. Midnight . . . two days later.' Swilling our mugs from earlier under the tap, he dunks a teabag in each. 'So, Moll. About that black eye. I've been meaning to ask . . .'

'No, it's never happened before.'

He exhales. 'Good. Okay.'

'But . . .'

'But what?'

'Yes – his anger scares me sometimes. A lot of the time.'

Graeme shakes his head. 'God, I wish you'd talk to me. You say you're not proud, but –'

'Because I'm not.'

'So why don't you ever tell me how you feel? You always say you're handling everything okay.'

I think about it for a moment. 'Because nothing can change, Graeme.'

'Rubbish. There is *so much* we can do.'

When it comes to Alex, Graeme's one of those no-mountain's-too-high people, which is mostly great, but I know for a fact that some problems simply cannot be solved. There is no easy solution to the riddle of Alex.

'Why don't we ask the doctor about more anger-management classes?'

I shake my head. 'Alex would never go to any more of those classes. You know that.' And it's true – Alex considers himself to be far beyond the assistance of anger management, especially group sessions. I can understand it, in a way – he has made such huge strides since the accident, and he's now in that awkward period of recovery where all the improvements we see are tiny. Marginal gains only from now on. I can see why he thinks he no longer needs to attend classes with people who are at a far earlier point in their recovery than he is.

'Meds, then.'

'I don't think I could go through all that again.' We completely failed to get the balance right before – when Alex wasn't flushing them down the loo behind our backs, the dose would either be so high they'd knock him out completely, or so low they'd have zero effect; and all the while the side effects were taking their toll on him even further.

I think for a moment about Alex's secret sketching, about the latent skill still half buried that he clearly gets something from, and decide on his behalf that I don't want to risk anything that might knock him off-kilter, destroy his ability to be creative.

'A psychologist, then,' Graeme continues. 'Someone new?'

I say nothing.

'Molly, I know he doesn't get funding any more and I hate to be crass, but I'm sure your parents would pay. I know that's incredibly presumptuous of me, but . . .' He trails off, reading my mind. 'Or an occupational therapist, if that's easier for him to accept.'

'Maybe,' I say, for, thinking objectively, this is the only option with any mileage. As I see it, if Alex could just be persuaded to keep one appointment, then it's the therapist's job to get him to stay and listen, convince him they can help.

The kettle boils and Graeme starts making the tea. 'So how often does he lose his temper like that? With you, I mean.'

'Not as often as he used to. But it's worse now when it does happen. You know – he can be fine and then the slightest provocation . . .' Alex's temper ran at more of a steady simmer straight after the accident; now, it goes from nought to a hundred in the space of a second. Less frequently, perhaps, but when it does happen it's always much more sudden and fierce.

'I worry you're not safe.' Graeme fishes out the teabags, sloshes milk into the cups and stirs two sugars into mine.

'He's never threatened my safety,' I say truthfully. 'Not deliberately, anyway. Thank you,' I add, as he hands me a cup.

We head through to the living room as before, only

this time Graeme sits down next to me on the sofa, which is so tiny our knees practically knock together. I pull down my dress hem like a teenager, suddenly conscious of how much shorter it seems in someone else's living room than it does in a bar.

I catch the edge of the scent of Alex's old aftershave again. I breathe in deeply, shut my eyes briefly. He could be sitting right next to me.

'Moll, have you texted Charlie? Just to check . . . sorry.' Graeme shakes his head. 'Maybe you're not too fussed right now.'

'I texted him earlier,' I say, guiltily bringing myself back to reality. 'Alex was already in bed.'

'Right,' he whispers. 'Sorry.'

'I will always care about him, Graeme. You need to know that.'

He nods, and for a moment I think he's going to ask me if I still love his brother. An unwelcome vision of Nicola appears in my mind, and I realize that right now, at this moment, I'm not sure if I do.

'But . . . sometimes I feel angry with him for not being the man I married. I feel as if . . . he didn't uphold his side of the bargain. Stupid, isn't it?'

Graeme doesn't say anything, just shakes his head. He seems unable to speak, suddenly.

'I mean, it's completely illogical because of course it's not his fault, but I think about it late at night, and I think, *You left me. You abandoned me. What am I supposed to do now?*'

It's only when Graeme reaches out and puts a hand

over mine that I realize I am shaking. We sit there like that for a couple of minutes, which all at once feels strange and perfectly natural.

'So, Moll,' he says eventually, gently withdrawing his hand. 'If you could turn the clock back, knowing everything you know now – would you still choose Alex?'

'Choose him as opposed to who?'

The moment skips a beat. 'Anyone.'

'Yes, of course.'

Graeme smiles and shakes his head. 'Sorry. That came out a bit bluntly. It's just that age-old question, isn't it – better to have loved and lost, than never to have loved at all?'

'Better to have loved,' I say firmly, because I truly believe that.

'So if your life could have taken a different path,' Graeme says, turning to face me and slinging one arm along the back of the tiny sofa, 'you wouldn't have taken it? Not even now – knowing everything you know?'

'That's like me asking if you'd rather have been an only child,' I say, aware that conversations like this are dangerous, with too much potential for crossed wires.

'You don't get to choose your family.'

'You don't get to change the past either.'

'True.' He eyes me over the rim of his cup as he sips.

'I miss Alex,' I say now. 'I miss everything we had, so much.'

'Tell me,' he says.

I look down at my knees. 'I miss him being affectionate.

I miss all the jokes that only we shared. You know, I wrote them all down last year, so I'd never forget them, because I know he has. I miss him making me laugh until I literally cry, his cooking, that he was always discovering new bands because I'm *rubbish* at that. I miss going to the gym together. The idea that we might run a marathon one day. I miss trying new restaurants. I miss him smiling at me when I come downstairs before a night out. I miss his optimism.' I smile faintly as my voice cracks then wobbles. 'I miss being close to him. I miss him carrying the heavy stuff. But do you know what I miss most of all? I miss loving *him*, Graeme. *That's* what hurts the most. To know I'll never feel that way again.'

Finally, I look at Graeme, and he is choked-up too. 'I'm so sorry, Molly. If I could swap places with Alex, give you both your life back, I would. In a heartbeat.'

'And now,' I say, 'I don't know what's going on with Nicola, and I think . . . I *know* that nothing will ever be the same again. What we had – it's lost for ever, Graeme.'

'Molly,' he whispers, 'what are you saying?'

I look right into his eyes, take in the scent of him once again. The tears rise in my chest and I have to look away. 'Sorry,' I whisper, my voice catching in my throat. 'I don't know what I'm saying. I barely even know what I think any more.'

'You're thinking of leaving,' he says then, the pieces slotting into place. 'Sarah's offered you a job, and you're thinking of moving back to London. Without Alex.'

I recall our coffee at the station a month or so ago, when he assumed my parents and friends were on a crusade to bring me back to London. And now, I am too afraid to admit it. I can't even tell if he would think it a good idea or a bad one any more.

'Is this more about his temper, or Nicola?' He expels her name like cigarette smoke.

'Both, I suppose. But if Nicola . . . I couldn't bear it, if anything's happened with her,' I say. 'And it made me realize – how will I ever really know now? I can't decipher a lie from an innocent untruth with Alex these days – he forgets so much, gets so confused. And what's left for us, if the trust has gone? What's left for us anyway?' I shake my head. 'You know, my mum wants us to go and live with her because she believes in the sanctity of marriage, of marriage vows, *in sickness and in health*. To her, once you're married, you don't leave, no matter what. But what if it's not a marriage any more? What if your husband isn't who you married? What then?'

Graeme stares at me wordlessly, for of course there are no answers.

'You know, some things you can't ever make better,' I continue. 'We live in this world where there's a solution for everything, where people tell you there's always a way, but the brutal truth is that in some situations . . . there isn't a way. There actually isn't.'

I remember the moment I realized it exactly. I was sitting at traffic lights, two years and two days after Alex's accident, and it suddenly struck me, like a slap:

Alex wasn't getting better. This was our life now. I was never going to see the old Alex again. It was as if in that moment, he'd suddenly died. And then the lights turned green, but I couldn't move. I was paralysed. Cars streamed around me, horns blaring, but I remained motionless, struck still by grief for the next four light changes.

'You know,' Graeme says, 'I think this is the most I've heard you talk. Like, ever.'

'Sorry.'

'No, don't be. It's healthy. I wish you'd done it sooner.'

'What am I going to do?' I ask him, feeling guilty even as I'm saying it, because after all, Graeme is Alex's twin brother. It's not fair to put all this on him.

I suppose what I'm really asking him is, *If I leave, who will look after Alex? How will he feed himself, earn money, make it from day to day? How can I even contemplate abandoning him – what kind of person does that make me? I'm his rock, and rocks aren't supposed to go anywhere.*

But to his credit, Graeme doesn't attempt to answer any of those questions, the same questions that must by now be careering through his head too. 'You're going to sit there and relax while I make some more tea,' is all he says, before calmly taking my cooling cup and disappearing into the kitchen.

I remove my phone from my pocket, press a single button. The lock screen lights up and there we are on our wedding day, running hand in hand. So happy. So blissfully unaware of what the future had in mind for us. Then, like a reflex, I open the text thread between Alex and me. I scroll back – it doesn't take long, he's scant with communication these days – and find the one that tortures and comforts me in equal measure.

Great night, love you xxx

I stare at the screen until my eyes thud, trying and failing to imagine how I would ever begin to contemplate telling him I was leaving.

Maybe, when the time is right, I'll simply slip quietly away like a coward, to spend the rest of my days mourning the love I lost.

Graeme's back, setting down two fresh cups of tea and what's left of the biscuits on an upturned plastic crate, presumably a substitute coffee table. He drags it slowly within reach of the sofa.

'Look, Moll, if Alex's accident has taught me anything it's that all you can do is go with it, take each day as it comes.'

I nod dully, barely able to listen to the coping strategies I outwore ages ago.

'I mean, I get it. I do. One day he loves watching football on TV. The next, he's swearing at me for suggesting we watch it. Or, he'll be manically enthusiastic about going food shopping, then when we get to the shops he won't get out of the car.'

I smile sadly. 'What's your point, Graeme?'

'My point is, I know how much of a rollercoaster it can be, even going from hour to hour.'

'Minute to minute,' I correct him.

'Right. Whatever happened to my passive, reliable brother?'

'It's like you've switched.'

And then I turn to look at him, and it's just as I thought it would be – like staring into the deep-green eyes of my husband once again. He looks the same as Alex used to, he smells the same, and I'm sure if I reached out and touched him, he would feel the same too.

And then for some reason it is suddenly 2010, and I am back in a bar in Soho talking to Graeme. He complimented me on my skills at getting served, paid for my drinks, flirted with me – and for a few short minutes, I found myself charmed. But then he disappeared, and in his place arrived Alex, who advised me in the subtlest of ways that his brother was not really a man I should be hanging at the end of a bar waiting for. And that was the start of the story of me and Alex – and it was a beautiful story, not one I regretted for a moment. And yet here I am tonight with a black eye and a faltering marriage, plagued by a cloud of doubt and mistrust. Tonight, it suddenly seems horribly easy to wonder how my life would have panned out if I had waited a couple more minutes for Graeme to return. Or if I'd simply smiled at Alex outside the toilets and kept on walking.

'I can't keep looking at you like this, Moll,' Graeme says softly then.

'Why not?' I say, my voice small and tight.

'Because Alex is my brother.'

I swallow, hard. My heart is pounding. 'I know.'

'To look at you like this,' he says, reaching out and brushing the hair from my face, his fingertips dancing across the surface of my black eye, 'knowing what he's putting you through . . . it's the hardest thing in the world, believe me.'

'Another couple of minutes,' I breathe, 'and maybe things would have been different.'

'I've told myself the same thing.' He knows exactly what I'm saying. We speak the same sad language these days. 'But that's a really dangerous way to think.'

'Dangerous how?'

He doesn't reply for a long time.

'In just about every way imaginable,' he whispers eventually, but he takes my hand as he says it, and I feel his pulse pounding, like electricity passing from his palm to mine. His other hand is still against my face, and for a moment I imagine he will start to run his fingers through my hair, in just the same way as he used to.

No, wait. That was Alex. Not Graeme. Alex.

On the road beyond the basement window, cars are rushing past, reminding me that we are not alone, that it is not just Graeme and me together in the world. That tomorrow will dawn, and I will return home to Alex, and life must continue. No matter how desperate I'm feeling tonight, no matter how betrayed and sad and low, Graeme and Alex must remain two distinct people.

Graeme is not Alex before his accident, however much he looks, feels and sounds like him. However much I want him to be.

'I think,' I whisper, squeezing Graeme's hand and looking him right in the eyes, 'we should call it a night.'

He smiles sadly. 'You always were a better person than me, Moll.'

'Not better,' I correct him. 'Just different.'

'That's why you were so well suited to Alex,' he says. 'And why I could never have measured up.' And then he gently drops my hand, gets to his feet. 'Help yourself to whatever you need. My bedroom's on the left. I'm just going to . . . get some air.'

'I'm sorry, Graeme,' I tell him.

'For what?' He pauses by the door to the living room, palm against the handle.

'For everything.'

17

Molly – present day

I am nervous when I arrive home on Sunday night, a few hours after leaving London and Graeme. Partly because I am exhausted from a torturous return journey involving weekend engineering works, an extended wait at a train platform somewhere in deepest Essex and a coach ride for the last leg back into Norfolk – which doesn't bode well for my ability to hold a calm and rational conversation with my husband.

But I'm also nervous because I don't know what to say. It's always an impossible balance to strike between letting him know when he's done something wrong, and not destroying whatever delicate equilibrium he may have been able to reach since an altercation. Our fight was on Friday night – it's now a full forty-eight hours later, and already I can anticipate that Alex will have forgotten all about it, wonder why I'm raking over events he can barely remember.

And what about Nicola? Charlie's been with Alex all weekend, so it's not as if I'm worried she will have been hanging around – Charlie's as allergic to her and as loyal to Alex as anyone else – but I still haven't got a clue how to handle the situation, no matter how capable Graeme seems to think I am.

And Graeme, of course. I'm nervous about looking Alex in the eye, all the while knowing that last night I was just a hair's breadth from kissing his twin brother. How can I be outraged about Nicola when last night I was contemplating doing exactly the same to Alex – or arguably, given we're talking about his twin, something far, far worse?

I push open the front door and step tentatively inside. Straight away, I breathe in an unfamiliar odour. It smells like . . . fresh paint.

'Alex?'

Appearing unusually quickly, he leans against the wall. 'Hiya.'

'Hi.' I set down my bag and we regard each other, but neither of us moves.

'Did you have a nice time in London?' he asks me slowly.

'Yes,' I say guiltily, but all the same relieved that he seems to be feeling even-tempered. 'Are you okay? Did you enjoy yourself with Charlie?'

He nods. 'Yeah. I told him about your face. I feel bad about it.'

I swallow. 'Oh.'

'He told me I should say sorry and do something nice.'

I smile faintly. 'Oh. That's . . . that's good.'

'So I got you some flowers and I drew you a picture.'

I pause for a moment, take this in. 'Okay.'

He smiles. 'Yeah, so . . .' Then he shrugs, leans back against the wall like, *job done.*

Well, it's the thought that counts, Alex.

'So, can . . . I see them?' I ask him tentatively.

'Yeah,' he says, like I'm being a bit slow.

So I follow him into the living room, and it is there that I catch my breath. The whole place is clean and tidy, alive with brightness.

'Alex, you painted it!'

He hesitates. 'Oh, yeah. Me and Charlie painted the living room.'

It's a beautiful, fresh off-white, the shade I've dreamed of having in here since we moved in. When I left on Friday, the room was still half covered in Kevin's old wallpaper; Charlie and Alex must have stripped it, cleaned the old paste off, sanded and painted all weekend.

'I can't believe it. Alex, this looks amazing.' My gaze travels the fresh new contours of the room, lands on a vase of flowers. 'Oh, Alex,' I breathe, welling up.

They are cream and blush pink roses – the same ones we had at our wedding reception. I walk over and lower my face to them, breathe in their beautiful scent. Alex hasn't bought me flowers since before the accident.

And next to them, my third surprise – a fine-liner sketch of me, washed over with watercolour. The drawing I've been waiting for, the one I cross my fingers for every time I flick through his sketchbook. My heart pounds with pleasure. I am depicted asleep in bed, looking far more peaceful and content than I ever do during waking hours. His incredible artistic talent blows me away once again, and it takes me a few minutes to compose myself.

I have to believe he drew this with love. I *will* believe it.

'Did you do this from memory, Alex?' I look over towards him.

His face remains blank. 'What?'

I rephrase. 'When did you draw this?'

'Last week,' he says, when he recalls. 'Sometimes I do them when I can't sleep.'

I run my fingers over it, then realize the paper is darker, rougher than the sketchbook I normally sneak a look at. 'You mean, you've done more? Like this one? Of me?'

He nods and shrugs all at once, looks awkward suddenly.

Happiness rushes through me. He must have another sketchbook, upstairs somewhere. He's been drawing me all along. 'Why didn't you tell me?'

He looks momentarily thrown off, like he thinks I might be annoyed. 'Didn't want you to laugh at me.'

'Why would I do that? I don't laugh at you, Alex.' I keep my face open, my expression light, to show him I'm not angry about anything. I don't want to scare him off sketching.

'You do when you think I'm being stupid.'

I step forward, so desperate to take his hand, but at the same time so afraid as always that he'll move away, reject me. 'No. I never think that. I never think you're stupid.' I survey the freshly painted room once more, the flowers, the drawing in my hand. 'I think everything you've done this weekend is incredible.'

274

He breaks into a smile and I return it, knowing the Herculean effort it must have taken him, even with Charlie's help, to stay focused on making it up to me for a full forty-eight hours – to help with all the painting and the flowers, to pick the sketch he thought I'd like best, to remain bright-eyed and upbeat for my return. Not to mention just making it through the days too – eating, sleeping, hydrating, making conversation with Charlie. All the stuff everyone else takes for granted.

I can't forget what happened on Friday night, but this goes some way to helping ease the physical and emotional pain, because this isn't regular from Alex. This is very special.

Incredible.

'What's for tea, Moll?' he says then. 'I'm hungry.'

The next morning as my alarm sounds to mark the start of another week, I smile before I open my eyes, remembering last night and all the things Alex did for me over the weekend, the uncharacteristic tenderness with which he greeted me home.

I sigh; Monday morning again. It seems to have come round so quickly, yet so much has happened since Friday night. Switching off the alarm, I reach down for Alex's hand in the hope of sharing one last moment before the week starts again, but I am already forgotten – his side of the bed is empty, cool. He has vanished downstairs.

Except that . . . he has not. When I reach the living room, the whole place is gloomy and quiet – he is nowhere to be seen – and then I spot the front door, wide open. A shot of panic rivets through me – usually I hide the key somewhere last thing at night, always in a different spot, because I fear him walking off somewhere in the middle of the night and coming to harm. He's not tried yet, but there's no telling when he might decide that would be an interesting thing to do. But last night, I recall now, I forgot.

Has he popped to the shop? His phone and wallet are still sitting on the side, though that's not necessarily an indication of anything, since he frequently fails to remember them when he goes out.

After last night's surprises, the image of Nicola now looming in my mind feels irrational. Still, I can't help but panic – has he gone off to meet her? Did they have something arranged?

I check my watch. I'm already running late for work; I'll have to pre-warn them. Finding Alex could take all morning.

Anxiety-fuelled, I dial Seb. 'Seb, it's Molly.'

On the other end of the line, silence.

'Alex is missing. I need to find him. I'll be there as soon as I can.' It's as much as I can possibly promise.

I hold my breath, praying for Seb to soften slightly, maybe make some suggestions as to what I should do next, offer to help. Instead, he clips coldly, 'Come in when you can then.'

Stupidly, I interpret this as an unspoken agreement to let this one slide.

*

276

'We've been patient long enough, Molly.'

Eventually, having jumped in the car and raced around the village, still in my pyjamas, I'd discovered Alex in the post office.

'Alex,' I breathed at him, 'what are you doing?'

It transpired he'd missed the postman, who'd left a card to say Alex had a parcel to collect, so he went straight to the post office because if he didn't get there on time the parcel would get sent back and then he'd have to call them and they might not have let him have it and he wouldn't be able to explain himself. I gently told him he had to wait twenty-four hours to collect a parcel anyway, that I'd do it with him tomorrow.

I was so relieved that the episode had nothing to do with Nicola that I completely forgot to worry about how late I was for work.

Which is why I am now facing Seb in our CEO's office. And unless it was down to a show of initiative on Seb's part (unlikely, since he has none), in a somewhat cruel twist of fate, our CEO Paul is in the office today too. The man with not only the perma-tan and good-life belly but the power to hire and fire. In general Paul's quite reasonable, but today he has presumably borne witness to Seb bellowing and bitching about me for three straight hours until I finally made it in at eleven o'clock.

But despite Paul's presence today, it's Seb doing all the talking. 'You know the score, Molly,' he says, running a hand over his slicked-back hair like he's posing at a shoot for a low-end fashion brand. 'You've had two verbal warnings and a final written warning.'

'What happened to your face, Molly?' Paul asks me then, and given the context of how much trouble I'm in, I have no idea if the right answer would be the truth, or a lie.

So, for once, I go with the truth. 'Alex and I had an argument. But . . . it was an accident. It wasn't his fault.'

A veneer of distaste temporarily clouds Paul's face. 'Right.' For one crazy moment, I think he might be about to check if I'm okay, if I've seen a doctor, if I need any help.

But Seb is desperate to steer the conversation back round to bollocking me. 'We've reached the end of the road, Molly.'

'You're letting me go?' I say, desperate to take the words out of his mouth, to deprive him of the satisfaction of announcing it.

Seb decides to rephrase it slightly more bluntly. 'Yes, we're sacking you. We have no choice at this stage. You're a disruption to everyone around you.'

I think about my mounting bills, about everything that's happened over the past thirty-six hours, about what's going to happen next. My eyes threaten to well up and I start breathing faster, so I try very hard to focus on Paul's dead pot plant.

'Let's face it, Molly,' Seb continues. 'You never really cared too much about working here, did you? You only took the job because you had no choice.'

I get it, in a way – he's been waiting so long to fire me that he wants to enjoy his moment, now it's finally arrived. Seb's the kind of person who probably practises firing people in front of his bedroom mirror.

Paul clears his throat and shifts from one substantial arse cheek to the other, which I guess is his way of indicating that he might not have put it *quite* like that, were he in charge of this conversation. And I am privately of the opinion that perhaps he should be, given he's the damn CEO.

'Coming from a big London agency like that. Maybe you felt you didn't need to bother with us. Small fry, aren't we?'

'No, it's not like that,' I tell him, because it isn't. 'I *need* this job, Seb. And I always give it my best.'

'Yeah, well,' Seb says, clipping his words, 'your best needed to be a whole lot better, Molly.'

'Well, I'm sorry,' I say, because what else is there to say? But then I catch Paul's eye and he's staring at me intently, and for some reason I feel as if he's impelling me to fight, urging me to stand up for myself because he'd love the opportunity to override Seb if only I'd show him what I'm made of.

I hear Eve's voice in my mind, reminding me that the way Seb behaves is neither fair nor legal. I picture Sarah's delight at my glimmer of interest in going back to work at the agency. I remember all the people who care about me, who love me – and then I remember that I don't need to put up with treatment like this.

So I do show Paul what I'm made of – but perhaps not quite in the way that he was expecting. After all the battling I've done with Alex over the past few years – and on his behalf too – standing up for what I believe in, now they've finally decided to kick me out, feels almost easy.

'Actually, you know – I think you're being a bit hasty here.'

Seb stares at me in disbelief. 'Excuse me?'

I clear my throat. 'I've only ever been late on legitimate, compassionate grounds, and I've almost always made up the time. When I haven't, you've docked my pay. I've worked late and got in early whenever I can. I rarely take a full hour for my lunch.'

Seb snorts, like pointing out why they shouldn't fire me is quibbling over details. 'We've done everything by the book.'

'No, you haven't. Our only meetings have been just me and you – you've never given me the opportunity to have anyone else present, or warned me ahead of time. You emailed me my written warning and never followed it up. You don't even have an HR department.'

'That's not a requirement,' Paul points out, because of course they only do the bare minimum when it comes to staff welfare.

'No, but treating people fairly is.'

'You've been treated exactly as we would treat any other employee,' Seb says, visibly seething that I'm questioning his competence. There's nothing that infuriates him more.

I smile faintly at him. 'Exactly – unfairly.' I get to my feet. 'I've done nothing but try my hardest, nothing but work my arse off since I started here – despite everything – and this is how you repay me. You have responsibilities too, you know.'

'Molly, I suggest you sit down –' Paul begins.

'And *I* suggest you consult your employment law handbook,' I fire back at him, slinging my handbag over one shoulder.

'Where the hell do you think you're going?' Seb barks. 'You can't just *walk out*. We're not finished here!' he adds, a final attempt to intimidate me into complicity.

'Actually, I'm going to consult my solicitor,' I say smoothly, feeling calmer than I have done in weeks. 'Do the same, if you like – that's if you even have one. Because you'll be hearing from me.'

And then I open the door, stride out of Paul's office and straight down the corridor towards the exit, head held high.

18

Alex – 21 March 2013

After we clear everything up from the wake and all the mourners finally depart, we get back to Dad's cottage late. Graeme's gone home to his flat, to give me and Molly time to talk. So then I tell her that we've read the will, that we've inherited the cottage, that this beautiful – if slightly decrepit – old building now belongs to us.

Molly bursts into tears – perhaps from grief on my behalf, perhaps from shock. Or perhaps she's subconsciously relieved, in the way people are when financial pressures suddenly and unexpectedly lift. And then we both stand there in the kitchen, arms locked round one another, allowing all the emotions of the day – which I've just added to massively – to subside.

Some time later she curls up in Dad's old leather armchair, watching me light a fire in the inglenook, an attempt to take the edge off the freezing room. I never did quite get the hang of the ancient oil-fired central heating in this place, but I've been lighting fires here since childhood, Dad teaching me how to concertina the newspaper just so.

The cottage feels weird without him. It's the first

time we've stayed here since he died, and it's hard not to dwell on the fact that the fire was already laid, ready for the next time. Except Dad didn't know that, for him, there wouldn't be a next time.

Molly's already trodden all the rooms again, running her hands along the grains of wood, the bowing walls, the fabric of the house, perhaps seeing the place in a whole new light now that she and I own it. But I'll never see it as anything other than my childhood home, and – if I don't do something about the Graeme situation – a reason to for ever feel horribly guilty.

I need to talk to her.

'Moll, I've been thinking.'

Because it's cold, and we're both tired and emotional, Molly's made us mugs of sugary malted milk from a tub she found in the cupboard, and she curls her hands round hers. Mine's on the hearth next to me, in Dad's favourite mug.

She nods agreeably, waits.

My heart is pounding. 'I was thinking . . . how would you feel about moving in? Here?'

Behind me, the fire flares into life. It's always a magical moment, and we both take it in for a couple of seconds, the flames reflected against our faces as the gloomy room is illuminated.

Molly's eyes widen. 'Here? You mean . . . move to Norfolk?' She didn't ask me earlier what I wanted to do with the cottage. I guess she just assumed I wasn't sure.

I nod, feeling a swell of excitement in my stomach

that I struggle to conceal. I tentatively suggest that now might be the perfect time to start the little family we've always dreamed about. 'Don't get me wrong,' I say quickly. 'I'm not saying you have to give up your career, if that's not what you want. But you always said you'd want to be a stay-at-home mum, like your mum was. And that you wanted to do it sooner rather than later.'

She nods, taking this all in. 'Wow.'

'Good wow? Bad wow?'

'Just . . . *wow* wow.'

'I know you love London,' I continue, 'but we could try something different. And if it doesn't work out – if we decide not to have kids yet, or you want to move back – we could always rent the cottage out and move back to London. But it seems like the perfect opportunity to give it a shot.'

'You were going to move back when I met you,' she recalls now, sadly. 'And you gave it all up, for me. You missed out on that time with Kevin . . .'

Trying and failing to swallow another pang of regret with a mouthful of malted milk, I shake my head. 'Don't agree to this out of guilt. If we're going to do this, it's got to be for the right reasons, Moll.'

She asks me what Graeme thinks.

'I haven't told him yet. I don't think he's expecting us to move back here. But . . . I want to do what's right, Moll. Dad left him nothing.'

'I know.' Her face furrows up with sadness. 'I feel so awful for him.'

'I offered to sell, so he could have his fair share. He turned me down.'

She hesitates. 'Kevin wouldn't want you to sell.'

'No, and it would break my heart to do it. But I don't have enough money to pay Gray the equivalent to his share. I was thinking I could add his name to the title deeds instead, a sort of temporary measure while we work out what to do.' I sigh. 'Not that Dad would want me to do that either, but it's better than nothing.'

'It is,' she says, straight away. 'And it's the right thing to do.'

I go on to tell her about Graeme rashly selling his flat, his plans to travel. 'I'm worried about him, Moll. I'm not sure he's coping that well.'

'Your dad just died,' she reminds me softly. 'Maybe this is what he needs. To go and find himself, make sense of everything.'

She's right, of course. Molly's always right.

We talk for a while by the light of the fire about some renovations we could do to the cottage, to make it child-friendly more than anything else. Dad left me a small amount of money too, which would be enough.

I know Molly's parents would be devastated if we moved away to start a family – they've always had the dream, I think, of living just round the corner from their grandchildren. But there's an outbuilding with planning permission for conversion in the back garden that I've been thinking we could turn into guest accommodation for them so they could stay for extended periods. That way, they could come up as often as they like.

The more I think about it, the more my plan makes sense. We'd never be able to afford to buy in London unless I sold this place, but it's my childhood home. It was never Dad's intention that I should sell it. Far better to start a new life here, bring up our own children in it. *That's* what Dad would have wanted.

'I love you, Molly,' I tell her now, moving over to the armchair and kissing her.

She smiles. 'You know, Alex — doesn't it feel as if Kevin's given us a gift? As in, this could be the start of the rest of our lives?'

19

Molly – present day

A week or so later, Alex and I head to the pub to meet Eve. I have gone to ground since walking out of Paul's office, and am just about ready to face the outside world again.

Phoebe gave me the name of a friend who's an employment lawyer, and we've had a couple of positive telephone calls over the past few days about the possibility of bringing a claim against Spark for unfair dismissal. He's willing to accept the case on a no-win no-fee basis, which I'm guessing means he's fairly confident of winning. The bruising around my eye is slowly fading – easier to hide now with a really good concealer – and I've also had a formal offer from Sarah about taking over Libby's job at the agency. She needs to let them know quickly, so she can start the recruitment process if I turn her down – so all I need to do now is make my decision.

Alex knows I walked out of Spark on Monday morning, but he's not quite got to grips with the details, and of course I haven't yet told him about the job offer from Sarah.

'Sorry, this was a bad idea,' Eve says as we settle down with our drinks.

'Why?'

She gestures to a poster on the wall behind my head. 'Karaoke night.'

I smile. A racket like that is guaranteed to ensure a fast exit from anywhere these days. But it's not started yet; I glance over at Alex, who's standing by the pool table watching his new-found partner rack up. We don't know him – he must simply be a willing stranger.

'How's your eye, Moll?' Eve asks as I sip from my ginger beer and she grabs a fistful of nuts from the packet we're sharing. 'I still feel so awful about it.'

I called her on Monday afternoon after I got home from being fired, filled her in on everything. Needless to say, she blamed herself for my argument with Alex, despite my repeated reassurances.

'I told you before,' I say now, 'I wanted to know about Nicola meeting Alex. I *needed* to know.'

'Have you . . . heard from her since? Seen her?'

I shake my head. 'Have you?'

'Just saw her in the park with some clients on Wednesday. It took every ounce of my willpower not to march up to her and say something, let me tell you. But I resisted on your behalf. Went home and gorged on three jam doughnuts just to make up for my insane display of self-control.'

I smile softly. 'Thank you.'

'Tom got chatting to a colleague this afternoon, though.'

My pulse races. 'About Nicola?'

Eve nods. 'Apparently she trains this guy a couple of

times a week. Anyway, somehow he got talking to Nicola about Alex, and she said something flippant like, she doesn't think he's as bad as everyone makes out. Like every time she's seen him, he's been just as he always was. That she's started to doubt . . .'

'Oh my God,' I say quickly. 'The more I hear about her, the more I despise her.'

'I know. It's such a horrible thing for her to say.'

I throw back some more of my drink. 'Did I invent my black eye, then? Or perhaps give it to myself?'

'Don't take any notice of her. We already know the woman's completely barking.' Eve shakes her head. 'I wasn't sure whether to mention it.'

'I've told you – when it comes to Nicola, I'd always much rather know. Keep your enemy in sight, and all that.'

'Well, Tom's colleague set her straight, apparently.'

'And of course Alex would be like that with her – he tries to flirt with her, charm her! And she does the same! But she's not the one seeing him through every single day, is she? She only ever tells him what he wants to hear. Which is essentially Alex's ideal conversation.'

'I know,' Eve says. 'We all do. Anyone sensible wouldn't so much as dream of passing comment on it, Moll. It's only because you married him, and she didn't. Don't waste any more time thinking about her.' She gives my hand a reassuring squeeze. 'Let's talk about something more positive. Did you get anywhere with the solicitor?'

I nod. 'I had another chat with him on Thursday morning. He thinks I've got a case.'

'Excellent. So what about Sarah – have you decided about the job?'

'You mean about moving to London?'

She nods, sips from her drink.

I swallow. 'No. But I needed to let her know, like . . .'

' . . . yesterday,' she guesses.

'Yep. I keep stalling.' Sarah's emailed me twice since sending her official offer through on Monday evening.

'What's holding you back?'

'I don't know . . . I keep thinking . . .'

Eve leans forward, sets a hand against my forearm. 'What, Moll?'

I make an effort to turf Nicola from my mind. 'Well, when Alex did all that stuff while I was away, with the flowers and the painting and the sketch . . . it meant a lot. They might seem like trivial, insignificant gestures compared to what happened before I left, but for him, doing things like that is a big deal. And I know Charlie helped him, and of course all this stuff with Nicola is still really bugging me, but . . .'

'You don't want to leave,' she says, reading between the lines.

'Don't get me wrong,' I say quickly. 'If anything's going on with Nicola, that changes everything. But . . . I need to talk to her. It's the only way I'm going to know for sure.'

'So you need to talk to Nicola before you let Sarah know about the job,' Eve guesses.

'Well, I know one thing shouldn't necessarily depend upon the other . . .'

' . . . but it sort of does.'

I nod. 'Well, it would change how I think about the future, that's for sure. I need to do it soon.' I sip from my ginger beer, slide her a look. 'Just psyching myself up for it. And if she starts coming out with any crap about Alex not being as bad as we all think – like she's the sodding expert – I won't be responsible for my actions.'

'I will definitely come with you,' Eve says. 'I mean, if you want me to.'

'Thanks,' I say darkly. 'But this is one visit I'm better off making on my own.'

'Just be careful, Moll,' Eve says then, her voice softening. 'Nicola's . . . well, she's pretty manipulative.'

I nod, but I don't make any assurances. Where Nicola's concerned, nothing is guaranteed.

'So, look – if you stay here, what will you do for work, do you think? I mean, I'm assuming going back to Spark won't be an option, even if you're successful with this legal action.'

'I think the word used to describe our working relationship now is *untenable*,' I say. 'So, yeah – I'll need to find something else. And quickly. I know we don't have a mortgage, but we have more than enough bills to send us under if I don't find something soon.'

'We can lend you some money,' Eve offers. 'Tide you over.'

'Thank you,' I tell her. 'But if I get really desperate

I'll ask Mum.' I hate asking Mum for money normally – she only worries – but it's better than incurring late payment charges, final warning letters, or worse, a court order. Our credit situation at the moment is precarious to say the least.

'I wonder if we know anyone who could help,' Eve muses, crunching on some nuts. 'Find you something.'

'I met Dave for lunch on Tuesday – he seems to think I should freelance. But it's not that easy. I've looked into it before. I could never do it from the cottage – our broadband's bonkers, and with Alex around all day I'd never get anything done.'

'Can you rent an office?'

I shake my head. 'Too expensive.'

'Hang on,' Eve says then. 'I'm an idiot.'

I smile. 'What?'

'Do it from ours, Moll – the broadband's super-fast, and the dining room's free. We never use it. You've seen it – piled high with crap. The last time I dusted that table down was for Christmas ten years ago. It's perfect.'

I stare at her. 'Really? I could do that? Tom wouldn't mind?' Not for the first time, I am taken aback by Eve's generosity.

'Of course he wouldn't. It's the perfect solution, Moll. If you decide not to go to London, I mean.'

I nod, let it all sink in for a moment or two. 'Wow, thanks, Eve. That could . . . well, that could work.'

'I should have thought of it sooner. Could have saved you a shedload of hassle having to work for those arseholes.'

'I don't know,' I say. 'I'm not sure I'd have been ready to make the leap before now. I've been so obsessed with stability, not rocking the boat. But . . . it does feel like now could be the right time. What do I have to lose?'

'I'd offer you the spare room,' Eve says then, 'but . . . we might be needing it soon.'

'Oh yeah?'

'Moll, I've been dying to tell you. I'm pregnant,' Eve says.

'*What?*' I squeal so loudly that the woman at the table next to us jumps and flings her drink all over her blouse. Even Alex looks over at us from across the bar, his face clouded by the distraction.

'I'm sorry!' Eve laughs as the woman with the drink all over her top gasps and flails desperately for a napkin. She lowers her voice to a conspiratorial whisper. 'I'm pregnant. I just told her the good news.'

The woman's face breaks into a smile. 'I'll forgive you then,' she says, because that's what people do, isn't it, around pregnant ladies or people with babies? They forgive bizarre behaviour, because babies are so joyful. I wish people would forgive Alex in the same way when he disturbs someone, annoys them, causes a commotion.

'Eve,' I say as she turns back to me, and I pull her into a hug, 'I didn't even know you guys were trying.'

'Well,' she says, brushing a strand of fair hair from her eyes, all flushed and happy. 'We weren't, exactly. But you know – things change.'

Ah yes, they do. Don't I know it.

'So, how far gone are you?' I ask her excitedly, though there's a tiny part of me that is swallowing my own sharp pang of envy, the same way I always do when I see a pregnant woman or find out someone's expecting. Only it's sharper when it's a friend or someone close to me – and laced with guilt too, that I'd be considering my own situation when all I should be concentrating on is feeling happy for them.

'Ten weeks. I shouldn't be telling you yet really – I agreed with Tom that I wouldn't until we're twelve weeks, but . . . well, it's you, Moll. I couldn't *not*, could I?'

'I'm *so* glad you have.'

'And even better – if you are freelancing from ours when the baby comes along, you can see him or her every day.'

My heart swells, and I reach for my drink. 'That is just . . . so perfect. It couldn't be any better timed.'

Eve's face falls a little. 'I'm sorry. I'm being completely insensitive.'

'No! Don't be *ridiculous*, Eve. This is fantastic news. I couldn't be happier for you.'

'With everything going on . . . and I know how much you want a family of your own . . .' She shakes her head. 'I can be so slow sometimes. I'm sorry.'

From across the bar, I notice Alex high-fiving his pool buddy, presumably after potting something. He really is in an extraordinarily good mood tonight.

'Eve, not everything is about me, and not everything is about Alex. I do know that. This is incredible news – there's not a part of you that should feel guilty, or like you can't share it all with me.' I take her hand. 'So when can you find out what you're having?'

'Not yet. Second scan.'

'And are you going to find out?' She did, I think, for both Isla and George.

'Oh, God yes. Couldn't bear the suspense. Tom's easy like always, but I definitely want to know. You know – should we get Isla's old baby clothes out of the loft, or George's?'

'I'd want to know too,' I confide, indulging the fantasy I once dreamed of myself, about the moment Alex and I got to discover the sex of our own baby. We would have gripped hands, stared at the screen, waited to be told, then cried when we heard the words – whatever they were.

'Right,' I say. 'Next round is definitely on me.'

It's only about twenty minutes later that I realize Alex has vanished. 'Where's Alex?'

Eve glances around the pub. 'I don't know. I can't see him. Toilet, maybe?'

I get to my feet, unable to stop the panic that is by now instinct whenever he's disappeared without warning. The karaoke has just started and a small crowd has gathered – maybe he vanished because he couldn't stand the noise.

'Oh, Moll,' Eve says suddenly, her voice heavy with apprehension. 'I see him.'

I follow her gaze, half convinced my eyes are about to land on Alex and Nicola cosied up in a corner somewhere, feeding each other pork scratchings, flirting and giggling.

But I'm not sure if what I actually see is in fact far worse.

Alex is in line for the microphone, biting his lip, looking as serious as if he's waiting in the wings to make his debut on the West End stage. His knuckles have whitened around the water bottle he's gripping.

'Oh no,' I mutter, setting down my drink. 'I'd better get him.'

'No, don't.' Eve grabs my arm, pulls me back down into my seat. 'Why, if he wants to do it?'

And he must *really* want to do it, because as a rule, Alex doesn't wait in a queue for anything.

'I don't want him to humiliate himself.'

'Er, Moll? It's karaoke – humiliating yourself is kind of the point.' She gestures towards the middle-aged woman currently failing to impersonate Kylie Minogue.

'I don't want people laughing at him, if he's not in on the joke. It could all end really badly.'

'It's not a joke, it's a bit of fun. Alex gets that.'

I look doubtfully at Alex's set face. 'I'm not so sure.'

'Fine, it goes wrong – we pull him out.' She nods towards the landlord. 'Chris knows us well enough by now. Just relax.'

I swallow, settle back into my chair, cross my legs (and my fingers). 'Yeah, okay.'

We wait for thirty more excruciating seconds, and then Alex is up. A hush falls over the bar, because most people in here know about Alex, about his accident, that he is usually not disposed to breaking into song. A few people turn to stare at me, to see how I am reacting.

'Oh no,' I whisper to Eve, 'we have to stop him.' The bar will be in stitches. I can feel the humiliation swell up inside me on Alex's behalf.

'No, don't,' Eve whispers, nudging me gently.

But I am quickly struck dumb by the sound of the opening chords. The song is our song, the one we chose for the first dance at our wedding. The song he's always sung to me, despite the fact he's always been tone deaf, the song that's had both of us laughing at his tunelessness in bed late at night. It's the song we squeezed hands to whenever we heard it on sound systems in pubs or bars, the song we kissed soppily to at parties. But it is also a song about lost love, and every lyric has taken on a new poignancy since Alex's accident. My stomach flattens and I freeze in my seat, my heart thumping in time to the music. I am too afraid to move my head or even my eyes in case I start to cry and cannot stop.

And then he pushes his fair hair back from his face and starts to sing. And I am, quite literally, astounded. Not only can he remember every single lyric, but he hits each note with near perfection. He is concentrating so hard, his forehead furrowed, staring out ahead of him like he's reading the notes and words off a blank page in his mind.

The bar is completely silent, and for good reason: he

sounds incredible. This, the man who could struggle to hold a tune on a good day. Who frequently forgets the most basic of words, like *dog* or *car*.

I have heard about cases of people waking up from a coma speaking fluent Mandarin or some such – or people who have had a stroke and lose the capacity to speak but somehow become able to sing. It's almost how I felt when I first discovered his sketchpad, but up a notch – because I would never, ever have expected this of Alex. I've heard him humming occasionally at home, but he's never sung before – at least, not around me.

Eve grips my hand as my husband transforms into a dusky-voiced singer in front of us, suddenly able to captivate an entire room. I am fighting the urge to cry long before he turns his head to look at me; but when he does, a single tear escapes and rolls down my cheek, landing in my lap.

It is another glimmer: he is serenading me in front of an entire room, singing to me about lost love, and I cannot bear how painful it is, how hard it is to hear the lyrics in the context of everything I've been thinking for the past few weeks. He is looking right at me, the old Alex returned, asking me to hang on. Subconsciously, he knows – about the job offer, my doubts, my near-miss with Graeme – everything. So he's surfacing, from everything he's going through, to ask me again to please hold on. *Don't give up on me, Moll.*

Just when I think I have totally lost him, for a few precious moments I always find him again.

I hold his gaze, knowing that I only have a minute or so left – that after that, the spell will be broken. I am determined to see it through, not to miss a single second.

But then, as suddenly as it began, it is over. The bar breaks into fevered, sincere applause, and Alex manages a lopsided smile before abandoning the microphone.

I will him to come over to me, to turn right instead of left, to remember me after the music has stopped. So I don't move – I just keep my eyes on him. *Please don't let it end yet, Alex. I'm still here, waiting for you. Let's enjoy being us for just a few more moments.*

As the applause thunders on, I can feel the eyes of the bar on me, as if it is me who has done the incredible thing, as if they are congratulating *me*.

And now, to my complete surprise and joy, he does come back over to the table, sits down next to me and takes my hand. Eve, bless her, has silently slipped away, to let us have our moment.

'Our song,' he says, kissing me on the cheek, entirely unprompted.

This could be a dream.

I let the tears slide down my cheeks now. 'You were amazing, Alex. It was like dancing our first dance all over again.'

He smiles soppily at me in a way I haven't seen for so long. Since that night, possibly.

'They're all clapping for you,' I say, daring finally to sneak a look around the room. 'This is all for you.'

He leans back in his seat and takes a sip of my drink. Though temporarily happy, he's exhausted by the effort – and slowly, incrementally, my old Alex leaves the room as invisibly as he entered it.

But later that night, I find him again. As he flops down on to the mattress next to me, I don't stop him when I feel his hands move across to me. Tonight I have left the curtains open so we can see the stars from our bed – that dizzying map of constellations imprinted against the inky sky. Little sparks of light to remind me that, however dark the night, brightness can still be found, if you're willing to look for it.

I can't really make out Alex's features, so I picture his face as it was in the pub, staring right into my eyes, sending unexpected electricity shooting through me. It felt like magic, and so does this. And as he moves on top of me I tell him I love him, and tonight feels more intimate than it has any time in the past three years. It feels more like it did when we were trying to get pregnant – never functional, as so many people warned us it would be (one of Phoebe's friends even referred to it as *a chore*) – but exactly how we wanted our children's lives to begin. A starry-eyed start, an act of complete and utter adoration.

Soon it is all over, but even as our bodies gradually withdraw from one another, he reaches out to me, eyes already shut. The muscle memory returns once more – he runs his hands through my hair, lets thick strands of it curl round his fingers. It always used to lull me to sleep, but tonight I am wide awake, shot through with the adrenaline of hope.

As I stare at the ceiling, I wonder what would happen now if we were to throw caution to the wind and fall pregnant? Will I ever have the courage to do that? How would it be? What would our lives become? I picture Eve and her little family of four – soon to be five – and my heart aches once more for what Alex and I have both lost. Because whether he knows what he's lost or not, they were all Alex's dreams too.

'Love is all you need,' I whisper to him against the skin of his cheek as he falls slowly to sleep, squeezing his hand as it starts to slacken in my hair.

And then I feel it. A single squeeze back, to let me know he loves me too.

I finally let the tears fall without trying to stop them as I watch him sleeping, and all at once I know that even while he sleeps he is fighting to keep me, just as I must continue to fight for him. No matter what the future holds, no matter what has already passed, he is struggling to tell me, *I love you, Moll. Don't give up on me now. I'm still trying. I'm still fighting for us.*

I shut my eyes, recall the last time we made love before his accident. It is imprinted on my memory, and I never want to forget it. We had been out for dinner, our favourite Italian, and it was one of those meals where we weren't really concentrating on the food. We ended up leaving before dessert and coffee, catching a cab instead of waiting for the bus, snogging all the way home on the back seat like teenagers. And then we kissed on the front doorstep for what seemed like hours before we finally went inside, but we never even made it upstairs.

Much later, we fell asleep half clothed on the rug in front of our ancient incumbent wood burner as the warmth of the embers inside it slowly died.

20

Molly — present day

The morning after Alex serenaded me at the pub, I return from a quick trip to the corner shop for groceries to see someone rushing out of our front gate. I pause for a moment, initially assuming it to be Darren — he's got some guest passes for his gym and has managed to persuade Alex to join him this morning. But he'd be a couple of hours early, and anyway, it's not Darren — being as he's neither female nor a particular fan of tight-fitting bright purple activewear.

By the time I have managed to wrench open the car door and clamber out of it, Nicola is nearly halfway up the road. It helps, I suppose, that she keeps fit enough to be able to break into a sprint when she needs to. She half turns when she reaches the bend, catches my eye and ploughs on, leaving me standing there helplessly in the street, a carton of milk dangling from one finger, bag of apples balanced precariously in the crook of my elbow.

What the hell is she doing here? Why can't she just leave us alone?

I know I need to go inside. I know I should put away my groceries, make us both a cup of tea, open a packet of biscuits, maybe. And then I should sit down and quietly ask Alex what his ex-girlfriend was doing in our house, and he can feel safe and calm enough to tell me, he can feel as if I'm not attacking him, merely asking.

But I'm not the right girl to do that, Alex. If you need a girl who can do that, I'm not her – and I'm not sure I ever will be. Because despite what you insist every day, it isn't me who has changed – it is you – and feeling good-natured about something reigniting between you and your ex-girlfriend was never going to be part of the deal. So if that's the kind of girl the new you needs, then I'm sorry, but the new you is asking too much.

There's so much I can do, but the rest is up to you.

So instead of going indoors and stowing my groceries like a functional human being and making tea and remembering my breathing exercises and everything else I *should* do when I'm feeling like I'm about to lose it, I decide that – for once – I'm going to do what I *want* to do.

This time, I'm not going to Alex for answers.

Nicola lives in a smart renovated gatehouse on the edge of a country estate. She's only a ten-minute walk from our cottage, and given that she jogs everywhere in trainers, this proximity has always unnerved me somewhat. I'd only really be happy if she was a long-haul flight away or marooned in a castle surrounded by some sort of impenetrable moat system. Being almost within shouting distance of Alex, the love of her life, has always been far too close for comfort.

At first she tries to ignore my frenzied knocking.

I don't blame her, in a way – I probably sound a bit maniacal what with all my urgent shouting too. But I'm not going to let this pass – my marriage and the rest of my life depend on what I can uncover today. After everything Alex and I have been through over the past few years, my future is once again hanging in the balance, and Nicola of all people has a part to play.

Though I suppose that is the very nature of commitment: you put your life and happiness in the hands of another. You relinquish responsibility. You say, *Here is my heart. Do with it what you will – but please just try not to break it.*

Eventually, she opens the door a crack. 'I'm not going to let you in like this, Molly. You need to calm down.'

'You are going to let me in,' I counter breathlessly, 'and we are going to talk.'

She sighs, but it sounds like exhaustion and fear, rather than contempt. And then the door swings open, and before she can change her mind, I am through it.

She looks unkempt and distressed, which is at odds with the cool, calm interior of the gatehouse: it is compact but immaculate, sparse in decor but beautifully presented. There is lots of wood and creamy wallpaper, lights on low and a lingering floral scent. It's the sort of place I could see myself spilling red wine in.

Fortunately for both of us, Nicola doesn't offer me any red wine. She doesn't offer me anything. The most she is willing to offer, apparently, is a short audience in her hallway.

We face one another. I am all at once relieved and disturbed to recall how different we are in appearance. She is blonde, normally well-groomed and perfectly proportioned; I am dark, a little wild-looking and more than a bit gangly. My jeans are baggy and a bit scuffed at the knee; her leggings are skin-tight and she smells overwhelmingly of washing powder.

Was it because I was so different to Nicola that Alex fell in love with me? Is it because Nicola is different to me that he is falling for her now?

'Nicola, what were you doing at our cottage? What's going on? Tom saw you and Alex having lunch at the golf club the other day too. He *saw* you. And you . . . when you're together, you're always flirting . . .' Even as I am gabbling, I know I need to calm down, because the calmer I am, the more likely it is that Nicola will give me what I need, which is the truth. After all, hostage negotiators never got anywhere by screaming, *Just give me the sodding hostage, will you?* My heartbeat starts to slowly ease up. *This doesn't have to be hard. Just stay cool, and she'll give you what you want.*

'I'm sorry,' I say, gritting my teeth, lowering my pitch, even trying a smile. 'I only wanted to talk. Let's . . . let's start again.'

'Come through,' she says eventually, before turning and heading into the living room without saying anything further.

I don't really stop to think about it. So desperate am I for information, I simply follow.

*

'I'd convinced myself Alex wanted me back,' she says coolly. We are sitting opposite one another, me on the sofa, her in a stiff little armchair, drinking tea. It's all ridiculously civilized compared to how she's been behaving towards me since Alex's accident. It seems strange to feel her actually looking at me for once, rather than straight through me.

'Why would you think that? He's married.' *To me, in case you'd forgotten.*

'He's always so flirtatious. He touches my arm, says nice things whenever I see him . . . it's everything I ever dreamed of after . . .'

'After you broke up with him?' I say, partly to remind her it was her decision.

'That was a big mistake. I was too hasty. I finished it and always regretted it. Alex was the love of my life.'

Still? I wonder to myself. *After everything that's happened to Alex, you still see him that way?*

She sighs. 'And when you and he . . . got married, I was heartbroken. Around the time he met you, he was planning to move back to Norfolk from London, and I had this crazy idea that he was partly . . . moving back for me.'

I swallow. It's so strange to hear someone talking about my husband in this way. Nobody else should even be having these thoughts – let alone sharing them with me.

'But he wasn't, and he didn't,' I say sharply. 'So you should have dealt with that. Accepted that we were together and moved on.'

'I've been a complete cow,' she says, looking down at her knees.

I am both surprised and baffled. 'What's going on?' I press. 'What are you trying to tell me?'

She shakes her head, and I brace myself to hear her confirm it. 'For a long time . . . I wanted him back. I'm sorry, Molly, but for a while it was *all* I wanted. Anyway, I ran past your place this morning and he was in the front garden. We chatted a bit, and he said he was having problems with breakfast, so I said . . . I'd give him a hand. He told me you were out.'

I shake my head at her naivety, her ignorance. Alex would have meant I was out at that moment in time – not for long enough to give them privacy.

'He was trying to cook pancakes,' she says, 'and he couldn't find the right type of pan. He seemed to think it should look exactly the same as the picture on the packet.'

Pancakes – they used to be my favourite breakfast. But Alex can't taste anything as bland as pancakes. *He must have been cooking them for me.*

'I tried to kiss him,' she says quietly, head down.

Her words wound me like a sharp puncture, an expertly aimed arrow.

'You did what?' My hands start to shake round the teacup.

'I'm sorry, Molly,' she says blankly, but something in her voice tells me this isn't the climax to her story.

'What did Alex do?' I genuinely need to know, because I cannot even imagine.

'He lost it. Started screaming at me. Like, literally *screaming* at me. He . . . punched the wall next to my head. I was terrified. I judged him all wrong, Molly.'

Did I learn some breathing exercises once? I can barely remember them now.

'I've never seen that side to him before.' To her credit, if she deserves any at all, Nicola seems genuinely embarrassed. 'I didn't realize . . . he was so bad. I thought people were exaggerating what had happened to him. I had this crazy idea that I still knew him best, even after all these years. I convinced myself he was misunderstood.'

'You have no idea,' I say, my voice trembling slightly. 'None. This is a hidden condition, with no cure. All you can do is manage it – and you haven't got a clue what that involves, or how different he is to how he was before. He's not the man you knew – God, he's not even the man *I* knew.'

'I'm sorry,' she whispers. 'I can sort of appreciate that now.'

'Did he hurt you?' I ask her, not because I care as much as I probably should, but because I need to know.

'No. I left straight away. That's when you came home.'

'So that's it?' I demand. 'You wanted him back, and now . . . you don't?'

'It wasn't just about wanting him back,' she says. 'It was about . . . wanting to keep him safe.'

'Safe from what?'

She hesitates. 'It's more about safe from *who*.'

309

I swallow. 'What?'

'His brother. Graeme.'

I feel an uneasy sensation spread through my chest. 'What about him?'

'I assume you've never been told,' she says, 'but Graeme and I had a fling. It was just for a few weeks, at Christmas 2013.'

Three months before Alex's accident.

I have no way to tell if she's lying, but I do know that period was one of the darkest of Graeme's life.

Perhaps if I was more quick-thinking I could call her bluff, say I already knew, but she's moved on. 'And just before Alex's accident, I told Alex about it – about me and Graeme, sleeping together.' She shakes her head. 'I've never regretted doing anything so much in my life.'

'Why?' I whisper, trying to shake off the creeping feeling of dread. It's wrapping me up like a spider's web.

She looks down at her knees. 'I guess . . . I was trying to make Alex jealous. Make him realize how much he still loved me.'

No, I think. *Why did you regret telling him so much? What went wrong, Nicola?* But it's all starting to slot into place – why Graeme hates Nicola, how suspicious he is of her, how allergic to her presence.

Her voice begins to quiver now, and I am afraid she is about to start crying. I can't picture myself sitting and watching while Nicola weeps in front of me. It's not a situation I ever thought I'd need to deal with.

Nicola glances at me over the rim of her cup as a cuckoo clock chimes ten above her head. 'Alex was extremely upset when I told him,' she breathes. 'Much more upset than I'd been expecting, actually.'

I want to scoff, dismiss this out of hand. *Why – because he loved you so much? Give me a break, Nicola.*

'Molly – he was *furious* with Graeme,' she says, and then falls silent, like there's some gap I'm supposed to fill, some piece of the jigsaw I'm meant to be picking up, fitting into place to complete her horrible picture.

'Well,' I am forced to concede, 'if he was, that's because they're twins. It's weird, you and Graeme having a fling.' I shrug, an attempt to negate some of her dramatics, her perceived power over me. 'That's it.'

'But then I heard about Alex's accident.'

Another silence. She's tormenting me with her withheld information now, teasing me with it as if I am a cat. She's dangling it in front of me, goading me to chase it, or get mad and swipe.

She speaks more slowly, more definitely. 'It happened a *week* later, Molly. At Graeme's flat. No witnesses. Just . . . Graeme.'

My stomach makes a clumsy somersault. 'What?' I whisper. 'What are you saying?'

'I think Alex confronted Graeme about me and Graeme sleeping together.'

I want to scream, grab her by the hair, reach down into her throat and *pull* the bloody information out of her. 'What are you *saying*?' I repeat, my voice by now high-pitched and wavering.

'I can't shake the feeling that they had a fight, and Graeme . . . hurt Alex.'

Gotcha.

'Don't say any more!' I get to my feet. 'You don't know what you're talking about! Graeme would *never* hurt Alex – why would you say that? Haven't you tried hard enough to destroy us? What is this – your last-ditch attempt to mess everything up for us?'

'I just need to know Alex isn't in *danger!*' she implores me. 'Please! If I can't ask anything else of you, let me at least ask that. Please, Molly. I know I have no right to love him, but I just need to know he's safe.' Nicola's crying now, apparently genuinely distraught, and it scares me. *She's not lying any more,* I hear a voice say inside my mind. *Look at the state of her. Perfect, put-together Nicola. She's falling apart in front of you. She's not lying, Molly.*

But safe – from Graeme? The idea of him being any sort of threat has never even crossed my mind. It's never had to. And worse, the idea that everything Alex is going through could *possibly* be down to Graeme . . . did he do this to him?

'You're lying,' I say with all the confidence I can summon, which isn't much. 'If you were so worried about his safety, why wait until now to say anything?'

'You keep me at arm's length,' she says, shaking her head. 'You always have done. I knew you'd never believe me. And my entire livelihood depends on my reputation around here, Molly. If I started making accusations like that . . .' She wipes her face, shakes her head in apparent despair. 'And, to be honest, Graeme scares me. I didn't know what he might do to me if I said anything, after Alex . . .' And as she

312

says his name her voice breaks, and she starts to cry again.

I look at her completely losing it in front of me, blowing her nose and sobbing in a way that, frankly, I wouldn't have previously considered possible, and the sight of her distress sends a little chill across my skin. *No, Molly. Fight back. There's no way she's right. Graeme can't possibly be the one who . . .*

'I really don't trust Graeme,' Nicola gasps now through her tears. 'When we were together I saw him in a whole different light, Molly. He used to say such *awful* things about Alex . . . that he'd stolen money from him, that he had no right to the cottage, that he turned Kevin against him . . . I was at Graeme's before Christmas that year and Alex came round. They had a *horrible* fight about money . . .'

Is she right? I cast my mind back. Yes, I remember Alex going to visit Graeme – he wanted to invite him to ours for Christmas – but he never mentioned them fighting about money.

' . . . that's why I've been trying to talk to Alex, ever since the accident. I've been trying to find out the truth!'

'Shut up!' I spit at her suddenly, because I can't take any more. Everything she's saying is sending my mind spinning violently off-axis. 'The only truth is that everyone around Alex loves him! *Including . . .*'

But suddenly, unexpectedly, I can't say his name.

'Please, at least let me come and talk to Alex . . .' Nicola implores as I gasp for air, or words, or both.

'No!' I shout, finally finding my breath. 'Stay away from us, Nicola. *Stay away from us!*'

And now I am fleeing, fleeing this horrible, claustrophobic gatehouse, trying desperately to breathe fresh air but feeling nothing, nothing but blind panic intermingled with a growing sense of foreboding and fear.

21

Alex – 14 December 2013

The period after Dad's death is possibly Graeme's dark-est since hitting adulthood. It was supposed to be a fresh start for him – a chance to see the world, make the most of what he initially saw as his new-found free-dom. It was an opportunity to shake off the shadows of the past and make new, more positive memories. I'd even been hoping that maybe he'd meet a girl – a like-minded thrill seeker perhaps, someone who could help him enjoy life beyond Norfolk and ever-present guilt.

But Graeme never made it to Australia or America. In fact, after rashly accepting a low offer on his flat, he made it as far as London, insisting he was going to spend a few weeks catching up with old friends and acquaintances, and sorting out his itinerary for the months ahead.

Nine months later, he's still there, with considerably less cash in his pocket, a persistent hangover and no imminent plans to get on a plane to anywhere.

As autumn winds down into winter I don't see much of him at all, and as December progresses, he goes off the radar entirely. He's staying north of the river with a friend of a friend, so with Christmas less than two weeks away, I decide to doorstep him, because I'm worried.

It's a nice block of flats on a decent street in Hackney, which reassures me at least that he's not living in some squalid crack den. When I buzz, it takes a long time for anyone to answer, and I'm about to give up, berating myself for coming all this way on the unlikely chance that Graeme would actually be at home on a Saturday, when a gruff voice comes on to the intercom.

'Yep.'

'It's me. Alex.'

A long pause, almost as long as the first one.

'Gray?'

He doesn't reply, but the door buzzes again, so I'm in.

The flat's pretty nice – it's spacious, clean and has the kind of furnishings that make me think Graeme's friend subscribes to interiors magazines. In fact, it's completely at odds with the image I had of him dossing from sofa to sofa, smoking and eating takeaway straight from the carton, empty beer cans at his feet.

If I'm honest, my biggest fear has been that Graeme might slowly be turning into Dad. The pair of us are well aware that the children of alcoholics are sitting ducks for following in their parents' footsteps.

But now I feel guilty – maybe he has it much more together than I've been giving him credit for.

'Tea?' he asks me a little flatly, without even hugging me or asking what I'm doing here.

'No, you're okay,' I say. 'Had a coffee on the way over.'

He nods. 'Take a seat, then.'

I sit down on the olive green pillow-back sofa and dive straight in. 'What's going on, Gray?'

He perches on a striped armchair near the rather grandiose fireplace. It's large and impressive, set in a surround of polished black granite, a backdrop that makes him seem more imposing somehow.

Instead of asking me to clarify, Graeme just waits for me to say what I mean.

'What happened to Australia? America? Seeing the world?'

'We've been through this,' he says, because we have – sort of. We've shared a few snatched exchanges about it over the phone or by text, but we haven't yet had the space and time to really unpick what's going on. And now I'm starting to think that wasn't accidental.

'It's been nearly a year, Gray.'

'So what? There's no rush, is there?'

'But what about the money from your flat?' He bristles suddenly, and it makes me nervous. 'Tell me you've not spent it all.'

'Oh, don't, Alex,' he says sharply. 'Don't come round here and lecture me about money. Mr Moneybags himself.'

I stare at him. 'I'm no better off than you are.'

I realize too late it's an insensitive thing to say; that on paper I am several hundred thousand pounds wealthier than Graeme.

'I mean,' I stammer, 'it's not like I have loads of spare

money washing around. It's all tied up in that cottage.' For his benefit I phrase it to make it sound like the burden we both know it's not.

'Right,' Graeme says wearily.

'So – have you spent it all?'

'Not all of it.'

'Not *all* of it? Well, how much then?' When he sold the flat, Graeme had about sixty grand of equity.

'Why do you care so much, Alex?'

'Because I care about *you*. Because I wanted you to have the opportunity of a lifetime, not piss all that money away dossing around London.'

'Well, maybe London's fun to me! I stayed in Norfolk with Dad to look after him, remember, while you swanned off to London the first chance you got! Maybe this *is* an opportunity – maybe this is all new to me!'

'Fine,' I say quietly. 'Say what you want. But I don't think it's what you intended when you sold the flat.'

'Well, maybe that's what spontaneity's all about. Changing your plans when they don't suit you any more. Maybe I don't want to be Mr Predictable.'

The implication being, of course, that I am.

'So you're not going at all, then? Travelling, I mean?'

He shrugs. 'Maybe, maybe not.'

I hesitate. 'Have you . . . have you met someone?' It's my last-ditch attempt, I guess, to confirm that Graeme might actually be living out the dreams I had on his behalf.

'I meet people all the time, Alex,' he says, leaning

back in his chair and examining the back of his hand like I'm boring him.

'I mean, someone special.'

'Someone special,' he repeats, glancing up at me with a smile.

'Well?' I press. 'Have you?'

'That would make you happy, wouldn't it? Appease your guilt.'

'What guilt?' I say, at a loss.

But he doesn't clarify. 'So, look, mate – I'm not being rude, but I've got a bit on today.'

'What are you doing for work?' I ask him, ignoring his attempt to brush me off.

'Work?' he repeats.

'Yeah, like stuff you do for money?' *Why are you being so obtuse, so deliberately cold?*

'Nothing,' he says flatly. 'I'm living off the flat money.'

'Bloody hell,' I say, more out of frustration than anything else. 'You're really going to waste that money, aren't you? And then what? Then what, Gray? You'll have nothing to show for it except a few mildly interesting stories and a hangover!'

'Well, cheers for stopping over,' Graeme says, getting to his feet. 'I'll see you some time.'

'No,' I say, also standing up. 'I wanted to come over to invite you to ours. For Christmas.'

He smiles again, but it's a hollow smile, slightly scornful, like everything that comes out of my mouth is complete drivel. 'For Christmas?'

'Yeah, at the flat.'

'Hey, why not the cottage? You could hang stockings around the inglenook, pin paper chains to the beams.'

I swallow. 'That's not fair, Graeme.'

He shrugs. 'I'm being serious. I thought you and Moll were moving in.'

'We are. I've been trying to find a job first.'

'Any luck?'

'Yes, actually. You wouldn't know because you've been AWOL, but I actually had an interview last week. I start in the New Year. I handed my notice in at my place yesterday.'

'Well, congratulations.'

'Molly's going to commute until . . .' I pause, unsure for the first time in my life if I should be sharing absolutely everything with Graeme. The doubt is a horrible, unfamiliar sensation, and it throws me off.

'Until what?'

'Until we're settled,' I say, not wanting to divulge our plans to start a family. In fact, we're already trying – to no avail, yet. 'You know, until she's sure Norfolk is what she wants.'

'Careful, Alex,' Graeme says. 'You're starting to make her sound a bit spoilt.'

His needless passive-aggressiveness angers me. 'Do you resent me?' I say suddenly. 'For the cottage? I offered to sell it, Gray, give you half – but you told me not to!'

'I didn't want your pity.'

His words stun me, then quickly anger me. 'Why the hell not? I'm your *brother*! Why not let me do what was right? I'd have sold it in a heartbeat!'

'And have that hanging round my neck as well as everything else?' he spits. 'No thanks.'

'I can still do it,' I say quickly, because it's patently clear the financial windfall he awarded himself by selling his flat hasn't so much worked out as run out. 'I can still sell up.'

For no other reason than lack of time and disorganization, I haven't yet got round to adding his name to the title deeds.

'What – now you and Molly are set to move, now that you've quit your job? You think I'd let you do that?'

'We can find a place for half that money,' I insist. 'It doesn't have to be the cottage.'

'Not everything's about money, Alex,' he replies coldly.

'Then, Gray,' I say, suddenly exhausted, 'please just tell me what would fix things between us. Since Dad died, it's been almost as if you . . .'

'As if I what?'

'As if you can't stand to be around me any more.'

My words stagnate in the air like smoke. I want to blow it away but it clings to the space between us, polluting it. I can *feel* his disdain for me now, I can almost taste it. The brother who got everything, who landed on his feet. But what he doesn't understand is that I don't want it to be that way. I *want* Graeme to be happy, to have everything that I have and more.

'Maybe for the first time in my life I'm discovering who I am,' he says now, and his failure to deny my suspicion breaks my heart.

'Does that mean you have to shut me out?'

'You're overthinking everything as usual.'

'Am I?' I counter. 'So are we going to see you at Christmas?'

'You're not the only person in my life, Alex,' he says then. 'I've got other things I might be doing at Christmas, you know.'

'Like what?'

'Well, maybe I'll spend it on the beach in Australia. Who knows?' he says, and it's like he's taunting me, teasing me for my childish, naive vision of how his future could look. *The rest of us*, he seems to be saying, *didn't get as lucky as you. The rest of us have real-world shit to worry about while you plan your idyllic little escape to the country with your wife.* 'Come on. I've got stuff to do.' He moves away from me now, towards the front door.

I work my jaw, humiliated by his disdain. He's always had that ability – to make me feel a bit idiotic – but he's never before used that power deliberately, taken full advantage of it. And now he has, it hurts more than I expected it to. He's actually asking me to leave.

We pause next to the front door, and I turn to face him. 'Whatever you want me to do to make it better, I'll do it.'

'This is all in your head, Alex,' Graeme says. 'I'm fine.'

'Please come for Christmas,' I implore him again. 'We can wipe the slate clean.'

His mouth is set firm. 'Yeah, maybe.'

And then, because there is seemingly nothing more

to say or do, I turn to head off. But as I do, something catches my eye on the coat rack.

I pause, and Graeme follows my gaze.

It's a black leather coat with a distinctive faux-fur trim, and slung over the top of it, a tan leather handbag I'd recognize anywhere. I turn to face Graeme, but his expression has darkened. 'I'll see you later,' he says, which is his way of telling me in no uncertain terms to say nothing further.

So I obey, turning my back on him and heading back out of the building and down the steps. But my head is whirling from what I've just seen – the coat I know so well, the handbag I'm so familiar with.

And the reason I'm familiar with it is because, once upon a time, that handbag cost me a month's wages. I know it intimately. I painstakingly picked it out and wrapped it up one Christmas many years ago.

That handbag, and the coat, belong to Nicola.

22

Molly – present day

'I need to see you.'

'Is this about what happened at Mike's?' Graeme asks me, like he's relieved. 'God, I've been so desperate to talk to you about it . . .'

'No,' I say, my voice quiet but taut. 'It's not about Mike's.'

'Then what?'

'It's something else. But it's urgent. It can't wait.'

'Moll, you're scaring me now –'

'Alex is fine,' I say, more out of reflex than anything else. Pause. 'Okay. I can get the next train.'

'Alex is out with Darren until mid afternoon. Come to the cottage as soon as you can.'

At first, I couldn't believe what Nicola had said about Graeme. As in, I *wouldn't*. If Nicola had told Alex back then she'd been seeing his brother, as she claimed – he would have come straight home and told *me*, surely? It's not as if it would have particularly upset me – other than Nicola potentially having a shortcut to my husband via Graeme, of course. She'd been trying to get close to him again for years.

It may have made me uneasy, but upset me? No.

But now, I can't shake the thought of her claim that Alex was devastated – and however much of a lying cow I think Nicola has the potential to be, I can imagine her sleeping with Graeme *would* have upset Alex.

What if she's not lying? I think to myself. She's already admitted to realizing Alex isn't the man he used to be – so what would she possibly have to gain from lying to cause a rift between us now? My thoughts begin to gallop, to veer dangerously out of control. Did Alex pick a fight with Graeme that night, and was Graeme only defending himself?

But then comes the thought that really chills me. I think back to Alex's last text to me before the accident.

Great night, love you xxx

Could Graeme have sent me that from Alex's phone, to cover his tracks? To pretend everything was harmonious?

A knock at my front door startles me back to reality. I hesitate for only a moment before heading through the living room into the hallway and opening it.

It's started to drizzle outside. Graeme's got his coat on and looks pink-cheeked, harassed.

'Sodding taxi driver,' he mutters. 'He's got a sat nav and he's asking *me* the way.' He kisses me on the cheek and moves past me into the cottage so quickly I don't even have time to flinch. 'Fancy a cuppa?' he calls over his shoulder from the living room. He's being friendly, which is throwing me off, because in my mind the conversation we're about to have is the most serious of either of our lives. Momentarily I am paralysed where I am in the hallway, unable – or perhaps unwilling – to move.

But finally I mobilize myself and follow him into the living room where he has shed his jacket and is examining, as he so often does, our Mexican honeymoon photo on the mantelpiece. 'What I wouldn't give to be on that beach right now,' he says.

'Graeme . . .'

'I know,' he says quickly. 'We need to talk.'

Does he know why he's here? Has Nicola spoken to him?

'Yes,' I whisper. 'We do.'

'Okay, but at the risk of sounding ungentlemanly, I need to go first. What happened at Mike's –'

'Graeme,' I say quickly, urgently, 'this is nothing to do with what happened at Mike's.' *Or rather, what didn't happen.*

'Oh.' He seems thrown off balance for a moment. 'Okay, what's up?' For a moment, I think he's going to add, *This had better be good, Molly. The sun's shining in London.*

'When Alex had his accident,' I say, 'I need you to tell me exactly how it happened.'

He stares at me then, and it's the kind of stare that says, *How do you know?*

A rush of air escapes from my mouth. It makes a strange sort of sound I've never heard before.

'Why? What . . . what did Alex say?'

I can't take my eyes off him. It's almost as if he's transforming into a stranger before me. The darkness of the clothes he's wearing, his height, the set expression of his face, suddenly begin to look all at once sinister.

'You pushed him,' I say then. 'Didn't you? Alex didn't fall in the middle of the night. You were fighting, and you pushed him.'

There is a long silence, save for the plaintive call of rooks from beyond the kitchen window.

When he finally speaks, his voice sounds hollow and fraught. 'I saw it all unfold in slow motion. I tried to grab him, Molly, I *tried* to stop him falling . . .'

'You pushed him,' I repeat. 'Didn't you?'

The silence that follows seems almost unbreakable.

'Yes,' he says eventually.

My breathing threatens to lurch out of control as my legs begin to give way. I grab on to the top of the armchair next to me for support.

'What . . . what were you fighting about?'

'Lots of things.' He is twisting his hands over and over, the same hands that pushed my husband to his near-death. That destroyed his life for ever. 'Money. Nicola.' He hesitates. 'You.'

'*Me?* What about me?'

He stares at me like to answer this question will break his heart. It's a wordless plea to let him stay silent.

But I won't. 'Tell me.'

'You know, Molly. You must know.'

Please don't say what I think you're going to say. I don't think I can take it.

I let the stillness of the room envelop us, and pray despite myself that it will smother the next words that come out of his mouth. The ones I do, but do not, want to hear.

'I've always loved you,' he breathes. 'That very first night, at the bar, when we got talking . . . I thought you were incredible.'

I stare at him, devastated.

'And then Alex ended up going home with you. I was . . . well, I was gutted.'

Suddenly, my sadness turns to anger. 'Alex put me in a taxi that night. And, Graeme, we talked for – what, *five* minutes at the bar? Then you got on the phone to your ex!'

'No. She called *me*, and straight away I told her I'd met someone. Presumptuous, I know, but . . . I thought you were amazing, Moll. I was . . . excited. I couldn't wait to get back inside, to talk to you some more.'

'All this time,' I breathe. 'All this time you've been pretending to be on my side, to be there for me, there for Alex. And, God, I nearly *kissed* you, at Mike's flat! You let me risk everything! Have you been planning this all along – get Alex out of the way and then swoop in?'

'Don't be *insane*, Moll! What happened to Alex was . . .' But then he trails off and can't finish.

'Go on,' I say sharply. 'What hand did you *really* have in his accident, Graeme?'

'I've always loved you, Moll. You may hate to hear me say it, but it's true. I fell in love with you at arm's length. Loved my brother's wife from afar. And I guess that night . . . I was just so angry with him. You know, I always used to call him Golden Boy. And he was. He got everything: my dad's love and respect, all the sympathy when Mum died – because nobody wanted to hear from the horrible little tearaway who caused it all – Dad's cottage when he died. And he got you.' He shakes his head. 'You know, the only thing I ever had over him was my ability to . . . get the girl.' He laughs. 'And he even managed to take that away from me.'

'Nice,' I say, trying to steady my breathing.

'Yeah, I was being – am – a selfish prat, but I was furious. I *hated* him for all that. I couldn't think clearly, didn't stop to think logically. I was having serious money problems, and he was lecturing me about being responsible. And then he started confronting me about . . . Nicola.' He glances up at me.

'I know about you and her,' is all I say.

'Who told you?'

'She did,' I say simply. 'And she also told me you fed her all sorts of lies when you were seeing her – that Alex had stolen money from you. That he turned Kevin against you . . .'

He shakes his head vehemently. 'She's twisting everything I said. Every time I saw her she'd get me to talk to her about Alex . . . open up to her, so I'd feel as if she gave a shit. But all along she was only using me to get back at Alex. Or get back *with* him. I have no idea.'

'None of that changes what happened between you and Alex that night,' I remind him. 'Keep talking.'

'Well, I just . . . I lost it. I couldn't hold it in any more. I'd just managed to blow sixty grand in less than a year; meanwhile Alex had it all together. And even his bloody ex-girlfriend had dumped me. I felt perpetually humiliated by him. And I just couldn't take it any more.'

'So you thought – what? That you'd destroy his life, kill him – what, Graeme?'

'I didn't think anything.'

'Was it intentional? Did you mean to push him?'

'I don't know,' he admits eventually. 'I could tell you no, Molly – but the truth is, I don't know if I did or didn't.'

'Were you drunk?' The words are tumbling from my mouth now as I try, desperately, to uncover the truth.

'No. You know I wasn't. We were both sober.'

'You're wrong – I don't know anything any more!' I feel the tears rise in my throat. 'I thought he fell down the stairs in the middle of the night, but apparently not. How can I believe you now, Graeme? How can I possibly believe a word you say, ever trust you again? All along you've been making out like you're on my side. You let me . . . oh God!' Furiously, I shake my head, letting loose a few angry tears as inside my rage builds.

'I am on your side,' he says softly. 'I always have been.'

'How can you have kept this from me, all this time?' I

explode now. 'You've been lying to all of us, pretending to be the supportive brother, when all along . . . you've been congratulating yourself for getting away with it!'

'No!' he exclaims, like that's the worst possible accusation anyone could level at him. 'I was going to go to the police, tell them what happened. For a moment I thought he was dead, lying there in his own blood, not moving. But then when we got to the hospital they told us he might make it, that he was in a coma, and I was just waiting for the doctors to say – in two weeks or a month, Alex will wake up. Be back to himself by the end of the summer. Something like that.'

The words sting me deep inside, his recounted thoughts so familiar.

'So I put off turning myself in. I wanted to be by his side. I couldn't have left him like that.'

'Oh, please,' I spit, 'don't tell me you kept quiet for his sake.'

Suddenly the silence of the cottage, the closeness of the room, threatens to overwhelm me. I feel the sudden urge to flee through the front door, jump in my car and drive, drive, drive. Who knows if I did whether I'd ever actually stop?

'But then I started to worry that if I was charged with anything, people might think I hurt him deliberately. And if you thought that, or Alex thought it, or your parents, or our friends . . . I couldn't have lived with that, Molly.'

I wipe a scattering of hot tears from my cheeks. 'But you could live with the lie.'

'Maybe I thought I could.' Then he puts both hands to his face, turns away from me, and there follows a long silence.

I swallow, shut my eyes briefly to try and stop myself from picturing it all, so I don't have to think about the bang to Alex's head that changed our lives for ever.

Finally, he turns to face me. 'Molly . . . just let me talk to Alex. Explain.'

'Alex said nothing about this,' I retort angrily. 'He doesn't remember a thing.'

He looks confused suddenly. 'Then how do you —?'

'That doesn't matter. What matters is that you don't get to choose any more, okay? You don't get to have any say in what happens to Alex from now on! You betrayed him in the worst possible way, put your petty resentments above everything else! I *know* Alex — he would never have been intending to do anything other than help you. He loved you so much — and look how you repaid him! So no — you *don't get to choose what happens now*!'

'I'm sorry, Moll,' he gasps, like my words have winded him.

I release a shot of disbelieving laughter. 'That's it? That's the extent of your apology?'

'As if an apology would mean anything to you now.'

'You're right,' I tell him. 'It would mean absolutely nothing to me.'

'If you tell Alex how it happened,' he says, 'it'll destroy him. He's so angry about the accident. He still can't make sense of it. If he finds out it was me —'

'What time was your fight?' I ask him suddenly, cutting him off. 'You know – that night?'

He doesn't have to think back. 'About half past two,' he says, straight away. 'You know it was. I called you as soon as it happened.'

'You're sure it wasn't earlier?'

Graeme looks thrown. 'Positive. Why – what do you mean?'

'You didn't . . . you didn't send me a text from Alex's phone?'

'What?'

'At sixteen minutes past midnight, you didn't text me, pretending to be him?'

I need to know. I *need* to know that text was sent by Alex. They are the words I cling to, the way they light up the screen illuminating my heart when everything else is so very, very black.

'No, Molly, of course not. Why –?'

'Get out,' I say sharply, cutting him off. 'Go back to London. I don't ever want to see you again. I'm going to try and rebuild my marriage now, salvage something for the future. Whatever you've left us with. And what I decide to tell Alex is up to me.'

'Please, Moll,' he gasps again. 'Please don't tell him. Let me try and do something to sort this all out . . .'

He reaches out and grabs my arm, but furiously I meet his eye and shake him off. I don't want to hear any more. So I simply head into the kitchen and through the back door into the garden, where I stand facing the fields until I hear the front door slam shut.

From around the side of the cottage I can see his dark form pause, at a loss as to what to do next. He looks left and right before crossing the road, and now the darkness of his shape is slowly retreating inch by inch. I turn back towards the fields, to where the sun is starting to peek through the clouds once again, and I strike him from my mind.

The only person who matters now is Alex. My husband. The man who has always loved me.

23

Molly – present day

'You're having a panic attack. You're having an actual, literal panic attack. Breathe. Breathe.'

As soon as I was certain Graeme was no longer anywhere near the cottage I came straight to Eve's house. At least Alex is with Darren, so I don't have to worry about Graeme tracking him down. At least I know that, for the time being, he's safe.

Not that I'm even sure what safe means any more, in the context of Graeme. Safe from his temper? Or safe from his influence, his lies – the sort of thing we all unknowingly soak up from those closest to us on a day-to-day basis?

I don't want to shock Eve – I really don't – as I'm so terrified of doing anything that could harm the blossoming little bump in her belly. But as Eve put it when I first rang and couldn't stop hyperventilating, if no one's died or nobody's due to die imminently, she can handle it.

We are upstairs together in her bedroom; she's lit a pillar candle infused with some sort of calming herb-scented oil and cleared space for us to sit among all the decorative cushions on her bed. Tom, thankfully, is out

335

supervising the kids in their respective Saturday sporting activities.

I've actually started to shake now with the effort of processing everything that's just happened.

'Come on, Moll,' Eve says soothingly, her hand against my back. 'Talk to me.'

I exhale steadily, then tell her everything.

She puts a hand to her mouth. 'Graeme admitted all this?'

I nod. 'Not straight away. Nicola kind of hinted at it. I went to see her, earlier.'

'Graeme,' Eve breathes. 'I can't believe it. He told everyone . . .'

'. . . that Alex fell in the middle of the night.' I shake my head. 'What kind of person would do that?'

'Where's Alex now? Have you told him?'

'No. He's out with Darren. He should be . . .' I swallow. '. . . you know. Safe.'

'From Graeme?'

I stare at her, wide-eyed. 'What am I supposed to think, Eve? Graeme pushed Alex down those stairs. He *did this to him*, and then he lied to us all.'

'You really think he's a threat to Alex?'

'This time yesterday, I would have said no.' I pause, shake my head. 'What do you think?'

'I don't know,' she says, frowning. 'I . . .' But then she trails off.

'What, Eve?' I press her, because I am desperate for someone to tell me what to do if nothing else.

'Well, I've known Graeme all my life, almost, and

he's never struck me as a violent person. I mean, yes –
he's always had a lot of issues, especially after Julia
died, but . . . not violent. Not like that.'

'But he admitted how furious he was with Alex that
night, and when I asked him, he said he wasn't sure if
he meant to push him or not. I mean – what am I supposed to do with that?'

Eve exhales stiffly. 'Well, at least he's trying to be
straight with you now, I suppose. Small comfort, I
know.'

'Three years later.'

She nods. 'God, I know how much you must be
hurting right now, Moll.'

'Am I sensing a *but*?'

'I'm going to stick my neck out,' Eve says, 'and say
I'm sure pushing Alex wouldn't have been premedi-
tated. Were they drunk?'

I inhale the scent from Eve's candle, shake my head.
'He says not. Alex had one beer a bit earlier.'

'Maybe Graeme lied about how it happened because
he was in shock.'

'He said he was afraid of being charged with something. Of losing Alex completely. He said . . .' I shake
my head again. ' . . . he thought he was going to get
better.'

'Yes,' she says, and it's almost an expression of
understanding.

I look at her, and I think about it again, consider the
question that's been buzzing around my brain like a
bee in a bottle since the moment I walked away from

Graeme earlier. 'What do I tell Alex? How can I carry on knowing Graeme was responsible for the way he is now, and not tell him? His life has been completely destroyed, and Graeme's the one responsible.'

'Don't make it about morality,' Eve says, rubbing my back.

'But isn't that exactly what it's about?'

'No. I don't think it is. Morality doesn't stand for much now, does it? Yes, Alex's life has changed, but what good will it do, picking apart how it happened? All that will achieve is Alex possibly getting even angrier with everyone for the lie, blaming all the wrong people, going backwards in his progress, maybe losing people close to him along the way. Wouldn't it be better to ask yourself, how can we continue to rebuild his life, knowing what we know? And yes, it's crap that there is someone to blame for all of this, yet Alex is the one who has to suffer. And yes, it's crap that Graeme lied to us all. But if the last three years have taught us anything, Moll, it's that life isn't perfect and it definitely isn't always fair. You know as well as anyone that life is about playing the hand you're dealt. And how you want to play it, that's up to you – but the one thing you can't do is deal again.'

I get to my feet and move over to the window. Maybe I am expecting to find answers in a calming view, but Eve's bedroom only looks out on to the roofs of other buildings. So I turn my back on them to face her.

'You have some choices to make now,' she says softly.

I nod, say nothing.

'You have a job offer in London, all this new information to process, decisions about your future with Alex . . . look, if you needed to go away for a little while – get some headspace – I'd be more than happy to make sure Alex is okay while you do that.'

I look out of the window once more. 'Thanks, Eve, but . . . I don't think it's me who needs to go away.'

'How do you mean?'

'I mean . . . I think I already know what I'm going to do. About Graeme.'

The expression on Eve's face turns to fear. 'You're going to tell Alex?'

'He has a right to know. A *right*.'

'Molly, please – just think about this.' She looks stricken. 'This could have huge consequences. Once you've said those words, there's no taking them back. Who knows how Alex will react? What if he does something stupid?'

'Why should I protect Graeme? He *destroyed* everything, Eve – he's responsible for everything about the way we live now!'

'Moll, this isn't about protecting Graeme,' Eve says, her final plea. 'It's about protecting Alex.'

'Well, I will be protecting him, won't I? I'll be protecting him from the one person who hurt him the most.'

She shakes her head. 'I didn't mean protecting Alex from Graeme. I meant, protecting him from himself.'

I stare at her, and finally the thoughts rampaging through my mind collapse where they are, exhausted.

'I really think you should give it some more thought,' she says softly. 'Go away somewhere for a few nights, think it through – even if it's just to your mum's. Don't make any rash decisions, you've had a big shock. This is a lot to process . . .'

'No,' I say, quietly but firmly. 'I've already decided. My mind's made up.'

24

Alex – 21 March 2014

And then, just like that, mine and Molly's time in London suddenly becomes a memory, because for the past couple of months I have been able to call Norfolk home once more.

As soon as the idea first leapt flame-like into life in my mind, I felt excited. Who wouldn't – an old cottage with bags of potential and no mortgage, plus enough money to do what was needed to make it ours. A tranquil location, room to breathe. Lower living costs. Fresher air. My old army of friends waiting to welcome me home and the girl of my dreams by my side. And at some point in the future – soon, I hoped – a family to call our own. I couldn't wait.

We started trying just before Christmas, but every month we've been disappointed. It's the sort of thing people tell you not to stress out about – the most counter-productive advice possible. But of course – because falling pregnant is supposed to be so easy – if it doesn't happen straight away you instantly assume you have a problem. I never want to sink a few beers more than on the nights (or mornings) that Molly tells me she's got her period.

And our housing situation is not ideal either, to say the least — we're living out of one bedroom, fighting with highly erratic electrics and spending all our free time trying to move the renovation on.

It's been hard for her, moving here — harder than perhaps I imagined. I guess deep down I know this wouldn't be her first choice of place to call home. She would still probably like to be in London — she loves the sound of traffic and trains, of chatter and music and a flight path above our heads. She was brought up on it; it's in her blood. By contrast, this narrow country lane we now live on and the roomy, neglected cottage we've inherited are silent and calm. Silence and calm are just not part of Molly's DNA.

We've agreed she'll carry on working at the agency until we fall pregnant, at which point she'll take maternity leave, with a view to probably not returning to work. They have an excellent package there, so it would be crazy for Moll not to make the most of it. But it's taking its toll on her — she commutes from home when she has the energy; when she doesn't (late or cancelled trains, big pitches on at work), she stays with her mum and dad, or sometimes with Phoebe. Adding to the stress of her long hours and endless back-and-forthing, of course, is the fact she hasn't fallen pregnant yet. Because only then will we have a light at the end of the tunnel, a date we can look at and say, *This will all end in so many days.*

Every time I go to sleep in an empty bed, my heart aches for her. I miss having her by my side.

And Timothy and Arabella — that's the other issue that's been taking it out of Molly recently. Her mum, understandably, was devastated when we announced we were moving out of London — so much so that she actually started weeping into her Madeira cake. And then Molly started crying too, which left Timothy and me sort of staring at each other awkwardly, and I felt like I had to apologize for upsetting everyone, even though deep down I felt that moving to the country to bring up our kids in a cottage without a mortgage and enjoy a slower pace of life was something that perhaps we should all be celebrating. I knew they were desperate to live out their days just round the corner from their only grandchildren, but surely they could see that this was the opportunity of a lifetime for us? It makes me nervous whenever Molly stays with them for any longer than a couple of nights, because she invariably comes back to the cottage slightly unsettled, and laden with gifts and treats you can 'only get in London', or having been to the theatre or an amazing restaurant — little reminders of the things we're missing out on here.

It exhausts her, I think, to have to keep defending our decision to move to her parents, to keep persuading them that we've made the right choice for our future. It would help, I know, if she could fall pregnant — because then we would be sure of it, unequivocally.

We're ready, now, for the next phase of our lives. We don't want to live in limbo any more.

My new job in Norfolk is pretty good though. The atmosphere is relaxed, the team I work with is great, and we have an interesting range of projects to keep us busy. Better still, I don't have to start every day surrounded by other commuters, battling to defend my personal space. I drive into our company car park, walk into our building and stretch my legs every lunchtime with a stroll around the city centre. It makes me feel so guilty to think of Molly still fighting the commuting battle each day and night, but she's adamant she wants that maternity package, and I know it makes sense too. It would be madness for her to leave without it.

One Friday night, I clock off and head straight down to the little deli at the bottom of the hill near my office. I'm after a decent bottle of red and some cheese for me and Molly (she always comes home on Fridays – Clapham is strictly for weeknights only). She's been staying at her mum and dad's since Tuesday, and I can't wait to see her.

Money's tight at the moment – everything we have is earmarked for the renovation down to the final pound, and the work to date has massively blown our budget – so expensive nights out have come to an end and the long lazy dinners in restaurants we once loved so much are a definite no-no. Plus, we're both persistently knackered.

But tonight I'm determined for us to unwind – added to which, today is the anniversary of Dad's funeral, and I want to quietly toast him. So I pick Molly's favourite wine (though she'll probably only have a sip, so strict is she about her alcohol intake while we're trying to get pregnant), some smoked cheese and garlic olives, plus a loaf of Italian bread, and am just about to make my way back up the hill to my car when I run into Nicola.

'Oh, hi,' she says, like she didn't know she'd be bumping into me at all.

This I'm not convinced of. Nicola's been hanging around a lot recently. I see her everywhere – in the pub, on my lunch break, in the local supermarket. She doesn't always try to make conversation, which sometimes makes me think perhaps I'm imagining it – that she's just going about her business in the town we both live in, and I'm bound to bump into her from time to time. But then I'll glance out of the living-room window and she'll be jogging past our front door; and something about the way she carries herself will remind me how manipulative she could be when we were going out.

Even Molly's noticed that Nicola seems to be cropping up an awful lot. 'There she is *again*,' she'll murmur into my ear, nudging me while we're out and about.

But I always end up telling her that this is just what happens in a small town. You run into people on the street all the time – especially when they live a mere five-minute jog from your front door.

'The house is coming on nicely,' Nicola says to me now. 'I run past, sometimes.'

'Oh, really?' I say breezily, pretending I've never noticed her, even though we both know that on occasion we've actually locked eyes through my living-room window (completely unintentional on my part at least).

'It looks fun,' she says, 'doing a place up like that.'

The truth is that it's not, not really. My end of the deal, since we're living in Norfolk, is that I crack on with renovating the cottage in any moment of downtime I get. Dad neglected the place so completely since Mum's death that there's more to do than we first thought – due to ongoing damp problems, at the very least we need to sort out the roof and lower the ground level outside the house. Then we need to take down trees, rebuild both chimney stacks, rip up the ancient rotten floorings, sandblast some of the stonework, sort out the plumbing, install ventilation . . . the list goes on. Plus the whole place needs rewiring, replastering, new floors, redecorating . . . it's a mountain of a task, and as it turns out, I'm unsurprisingly a complete amateur when it comes to doing up crumbling period cottages. *A lick of paint* has gradually turned into a painstakingly slow and complex process – and though my friends have rallied round to help, everyone has their own lives to lead, and it's tough trying to coordinate voluntary manpower to show up together.

Plus, Molly and I have scant alone time as it is, and I'm loath to use up what little of it we have shepherding processions of people in and out of the cottage.

'It's hard work,' I say.

'I don't see Molly around much,' she remarks.

I sigh, because it's really none of Nicola's business. 'She's still working in London.'

'And how's Graeme?'

I hesitate. Graeme is . . . I don't actually know how

Graeme is at the moment. He never came to stay with us for Christmas, claiming a last-minute trip to the Balearics for the New Year, and I've barely heard from him in the weeks since. He didn't even get in touch on the anniversary of Dad's death. I feel horrible that we've drifted apart so completely – but I have absolutely no idea how to make things better.

Should I sell the cottage and give Graeme half the money, despite him continuing to insist he doesn't want me to? Would that really ease the tension between us? Of course, if I could guarantee it would, I'd do it – Molly and I could buy somewhere small with our share of the money, maybe on one of the new estates fringing the village. But if it doesn't fix things between Graeme and me, I'd regret it for ever – especially as Graeme has demonstrated he'd probably throw all that money away within months of it hitting his bank account. The last time we spoke, he told me his sixty grand was more or less gone, before he asked me for a couple of hundred quid to tide him over. (I promptly transferred it to him the following day, no questions asked, and without telling Molly.) Plus, Molly and I have committed to our future in that cottage, for the short-term at least, and have put our hearts and our money into the renovation. Not to mention all my memories of Dad and my gradually fading memories of Mum being tied up there.

I haven't told Molly that Graeme and I are drifting apart. She thinks he's busy with work in London and I'm busy with the renovation. *Brothers can just pick up where they left off,* I tell her good-naturedly when she remarks that we haven't seen him in a while. *Anyway, he's probably met a girl or something.* I picked a cheap and easy lie, one I knew Molly could believe. I'm also worried that admitting our relationship is starting to falter will make it more real – turn it into a problem that needs fixing, rather than one which may or may not even exist.

'Graeme's fine,' I say lightly.

Nicola looks strangely stricken. 'Oh, really? I heard differently. And I've been so worried about you two. God, if you fall out, then . . . well, you're all the family each other has, aren't you?'

I stare at her. Suddenly the bag in my hand seems strangely heavy. 'What?' *What do you know about it?* 'Have you spoken to Graeme?'

I'm testing her, in a way. Because I saw her bag and her coat at Graeme's place in Hackney before Christmas. I *know* she's had contact with him.

She hesitates, her mouth flapping for a couple of moments, before she closes it and shrugs neatly. 'Don't worry, Alex,' she says, 'I shouldn't have said anything.' She nods down at my shopping bag, the bottle of wine peeking out of the top. 'You should go. You look as if you have a nice night in planned.'

Stupidly, I feel a bit self-conscious about the wine bottle, since Nicola was always on at me about why I would even so much as *consider* drinking when I had an alcoholic for a dad.

My curiosity wins out. 'Nic, wait. You can't just . . .

say that and walk away. What's Gray said? I've been –
I've been really worried about him,' I admit.

She sighs, drawing out the breath like it's painful. 'I
said I wouldn't say anything.'

'To who – Gray?'

She nods reluctantly. I can't tell if she's being sincere
or not. She's so hard to read, Nicola – and that's coming from someone who dated her for six years.

She takes a breath, and I steady myself to hear her
say, *Graeme's been struggling with a serious alcohol problem,
Alex. Just like your dad.*

'Me and him . . . we had a fling. We were together,
for a few weeks.'

I stare at her. 'Are you . . . are you making this up?'
It's the only conclusion my brain can arrive at, because
despite everything – despite the evidence having been
staring me in the face – I wasn't actually expecting her
to say that. Which is far more a measure of my faith in
Graeme's loyalty to me than in Nicola's.

I never even told Molly I'd seen Nicola's stuff there
that day, I wanted to deny it to myself so much. But
now it's all falling into place, and I berate myself for my
stupidity, my naivety. Graeme wasn't cold to me that
morning because he was stressed about money, he was
cold because he felt bad, because he wanted to get me
out of the flat before I realized what was going on.

I haven't asked him, since I spotted her stuff. That's
the sort of conversation I can only have with him face
to face, and anyway, the last thing I want to do right
now is push him away from me even further. Doing or

349

saying anything that might threaten our relationship for good is not an option, and if it involves Nicola, then I'm even more reluctant on principle.

She sighs. 'I wish I was making it up. I feel *horrible* that I did that to you, Alex.'

'Why?' I ask her, feeling anger claw its way up my throat like something rabid from a creepy fairy tale. 'Why the hell would you sleep with Graeme?'

'We just got talking,' she says. 'After your dad died.' She slings me a look. 'I texted you, you know. To say how sorry I was about Kevin. I emailed you, tried to call.'

Yes, I remember all too well. I canned the lot of them. 'What was there for us to say?' I ask her angrily, deliberately failing to acknowledge that today is one year since the funeral. 'We're not together any more, Nicola.'

She works her mouth a little. 'Well, Graeme was pretty devastated, and then you got the cottage, and . . . I think he just felt like it was all getting a bit much. And when he moved to London we stayed in touch, and . . . then I went there for a work thing and we met up. It went from there.'

'Out of all the people in the world,' I say to her, 'you pick my twin brother.'

She puts a hand on my arm. The touch of her fingers feels like burning, even through the thickness of my winter coat. 'I can see you're upset . . .'

Not for the reason you think. I couldn't care less if Nicola slept with every man on earth, apart from one. But now she's been with my twin brother. The man who knows me inside and out, who I've confided in over the years about Molly, who I trust completely – despite everything that's happened over the past twelve months or so. The thought of that is just too much to bear.

'Why the hell would you pick him?' I demand furiously. 'What's wrong with you?'

'I know you're hurting . . .' she says again, clearly interpreting my anger as evidence that I still hold a flame for her – which couldn't be further from the truth.

'You've betrayed me before,' I say sharply. 'I don't care about that. But I do care about Graeme.'

'I shouldn't have said anything!' she cries now. 'Please don't say anything to him, Alex.'

'Is that why he didn't go travelling?' I ask her. 'Because you were hanging around? What did he do, Nicola – treat you to nice restaurants? Expensive jewellery? Blow all his money on indulging you?'

'No,' she says firmly, quietly, 'of course not.'

'So are you still in touch?' I ask her.

'No,' she says simply. 'I finished it because . . .'

'Because what?'

'Because I realized I still have feelings for you, Alex. All these years later. I still –'

'Don't say anything else,' I snap at her.

'Alex,' she says, lowering her voice, 'you're clearly upset. Why don't we go for a drink, talk about this?'

'No, Nicola,' I say firmly. 'From now on, I want nothing more to do with you. Do you understand?

Nothing.' And then I walk away from her and towards whatever's left of my Friday night with Molly, without looking back.

I don't know why I don't tell Molly. Maybe because it's the weekend, and though Molly's exhausted she kisses me and we end up falling into bed and making love almost as soon as she's walked through the door, before she's even taken her coat off, just like old times. And then we open the wine and indulge ourselves once again with talk of baby names. And to bring Nicola up after all of that seems wildly inappropriate to say the least.

Maybe Molly would wonder why I keep bumping into her, or why I would even have a conversation with her, rather than just walking on. Would Molly start thinking there's something going on – that our meeting wasn't accidental? Worse, is that what Nicola wants?

And how can I tell her Nicola's still got feelings for me, that she almost said she still loves me? Molly would quite rightfully wonder how the hell I managed to put myself in a situation where Nicola felt free enough to confess such things to me.

But there's also a small part of me that's embarrassed. First Nicola cheats on me while we're together, then she hooks up with my twin after we've split up. What personal gems did she persuade Graeme to divulge in the passionate afterglow of whatever they had going on? What little nuggets from our childhood has he shared? What stories might he have unwittingly passed on about me – or worse, about Molly? I can't bear to think of it, and I don't want to worry Molly – not while she's working so hard, and we're both so desperate to fall pregnant. So I decide to park it.

I won't tell Molly, but I will talk to Graeme, the very next chance I get.

25

Molly – present day

'Alex, I need to talk to you.'

We're eating supper in the garden a couple of days after Graeme's confession, rolls stuffed with pulled pork and smothered in hot sauce, Alex's new favourite thing. The last warmth of summer is still lingering in the air, though the tell-tale signs of autumn creeping up are all around – dew on the grass, the dusk arriving earlier, a golden tone to all the foliage like it's been washed over in watercolour.

'We need money. We can't carry on as we are.'

'Yeah, I know,' Alex mumbles, mouth full, sauce staining his lips. He looks happy tonight, satisfied, and as always I am wary of rocking the boat, but this is a conversation we need to have. If I'm honest, it's the conversation we needed to have eighteen months ago.

'There are some options,' I tell him, cautious because Alex can get overwhelmed when he needs to decide what to wear in the morning, let alone when he's being presented with huge life decisions. But I have to at least give it a stab.

'All of these are just suggestions,' I say cautiously.

'We could . . . move to London. I've been offered my old job back. Remember Sarah? She said I could go and work back at the agency.'

I really need to let her know today – or at the very least send her some sort of holding communication. I've already missed a couple of calls and swerved several texts from her as I procrastinate.

'And,' I continue, 'my mum and dad have said we could move in with them.'

There is a long pause. Alex carries on chewing as if I've not even spoken, which I actually take to be a good sign. There is no panic, as yet.

'We'd have money,' I say. 'I was earning a good salary at the agency – remember? And my mum and dad would be around . . .'

'And Graeme,' he says then, which pulls me up short, because already it almost sounds as if he's actually not averse to my proposal.

'Well, he might be,' I say nervously – because if I have my way, Graeme will most certainly *not* be around. 'But there'd also be more things for you to do in London, Alex. There might be more opportunities for work. Mum and Dad love spending time with you, and . . . maybe we do need more support. We struggle a bit, don't we?'

He shrugs. 'Sometimes. I get bored here.'

I breathe steadily. *Why have I been tuning that out all this time? He does mean it when he says it. He's bored.* 'So . . . you might be up for it? Moving to London?'

'Maybe,' he mumbles.

'I mean – how about we try it, for a couple of months? We wouldn't have to sell the cottage, and if it didn't work out, we could just come back.'

'I don't want to sell the cottage,' he says, alarmed, picking out the words from my sentence that scare him the most.

'No, and we won't – if we move to London we could stay with Mum and Dad. But if we stay here . . . I don't know. I'm not being paid by Spark any more, remember? So we don't have the money to do this place up. And I'm worried I might not find another job here now.'

He nods, polishes off his roll. 'Yeah.'

'Yeah . . . is that a yes?'

He frowns. 'I don't know. I play golf here. I have friends.'

'You have friends in London too,' I remind him. 'And your Norfolk friends – they could come and stay, all the time,' I assure him. 'There are places you can play golf in London. Dad would love to play with you, Alex. You could go together.'

And we can finally get you away from the poisonous influence of Nicola, I think, but I don't say it.

'Need some crisps,' he tells me, standing up and walking away, back into the house.

I lean back in my chair and take a tentative breath. Okay, so maybe tomorrow he'll change his mind – but this is small progress. It didn't go as disastrously as I was worried it might.

I text Sarah rapidly.

356

Can you hold that job for a couple more days? Still talking to
Alex. This would mean the world to me. Xx

She texts back within minutes.

Yes, of course. Built in some buffer time. But will need to know
for sure by the end of the week. Xx

I'm still sitting in the same spot an hour or so later
when Alex comes back outside, having clearly been
sidetracked by matters other than crisps. It's dark now,
and all the stars are out. My mind has been whirling
with new possibilities and plans for the future, and I'm
feeling almost dizzied by them. It's been a long time
since I've felt hope like this, and even the novelty of
optimism is enough to excite me.

To my amazement, he's brought the blanket off the
back of the sofa with him, which he drapes over my
knees.

From Alex, foresight like this is unprecedented.

'Thank you,' I manage as he sits down next to me
and surprises me all over again by taking my hand.

'It's cold,' is all he says.

'What have you been doing?' I ask him with a smile.
'Your hand's all warm and wrinkly.'

He laughs like I've said something really funny.
'Washing up.'

So we sit there together side by side like the old couple I always hoped we would be, letting the seat of our
jeans go slightly damp as we share the blanket and look
up at the stars. And then suddenly, without warning

like always, he leans over and kisses me, and my romantic, attentive husband momentarily returns.

'Hi,' I say, without meaning to, when we eventually draw apart.

'My dad liked stars,' he says, while I'm gathering myself, heart still pounding from our kiss.

I swallow, remembering Kevin, the amateur astrologer. When the twins were still small, he'd take them up on to the hill behind the cottage and teach them all the constellations. 'Yeah, he did.'

'Sometimes I think he and Mum are up there together, looking at the same ones I am.'

For a moment I am too emotional to speak, but eventually I manage to produce words. 'Yeah. Maybe they're watching out for you now.'

We sit there for a while longer, staring up together at all the stars in our little patch of sky. Then eventually we meander back inside, hand in hand together in the darkness.

And so it is that on Thursday, I find myself sitting in my mum's kitchen eating lemon drizzle cake, while she and my dad look on expectantly from the opposite side of the table.

I glance down as I sometimes do at the lock screen on my phone. Me and Alex on our wedding day, running hand in hand, laughing. That's what I'm fighting for. That day, that moment.

'Alex and I have made a decision.' I take a deep breath. 'We'd love to come and stay with you guys, for a while.'

Mum clasps her hands to her chest. 'You really would? That's wonderful news, Moll!'

Dad rushes round to where I am sitting, throws an arm round my shoulders, pecks me on the head. 'Fantastic, darling. That really is good news.'

'You're sure?' I say a little nervously. 'This will be a big life change for both of you – you know that? You need to be prepared.'

'You're our only child,' Dad says firmly. 'We love you, and we'll do whatever it takes for you and Alex to stay together. That you've been struggling to cope so long on your own is our greatest source of unhappiness, Molly, really.'

'Well, there's more good news. I've been offered my old job back,' I tell them. 'At the agency.'

Mum gives a little gasp of pleasure. 'Oh, darling!'

'So . . . we'll have good money coming in again, I'll be happier, more fulfilled . . .'

'This really is wonderful news,' Dad says.

'Alex seems to think there'll be more for him to do here. You know, he always used to say he was bored stuck out where we are in the middle of nowhere, but I thought I knew better.' I shake my head. 'I was so fixated on the idea that he was unhappy in London before his accident that I never considered . . . that things might have changed.'

'It'll be a big adjustment for him,' Dad says, 'but we'll do everything we can to help.'

'And maybe . . . we could think about that annexe,' I suggest. 'You know – in the longer term.'

'We were considering it anyway, Molly,' Mum says now, topping up my tea from the pot. 'We already had all the plans drawn up and we thought . . . well, why not?'

'I'm really excited,' I tell them both.

'So are we,' Dad says. 'We're excited to finally be able to help both of you, in the way we always wanted to.'

'And who knows,' Mum says, forking up the last crumbs of her cake, 'you might even be able to start thinking about . . .'

I smile and shake my head. 'One step at a time, Mum. One step at a time.'

26

Molly – present day

About a week later, I call Graeme. We've not had any contact since his confession, but from the breathless way he answers the phone, I know he's been waiting for my call.

'I'm not going to tell Alex what happened that night, Graeme.'

He exhales relief down the line, but then there is only silence, which is actually not a bad thing, as it means I can say everything I need to.

'But I want you to do something for me in return.'

'Anything.'

'I want you to leave.'

'Leave . . . ?'

'Leave London. Leave England.'

'Moll, come on . . .'

'I'm being serious, Graeme. When you sold your flat four years ago, you dreamed of travelling the world. I think you've actually been dreaming of doing it since you left school, but you felt too constrained by making your dad happy, didn't you?'

'You want me to go and travel the world?' he says, and I can almost picture his despairing smile.

'Yes,' I assert. 'Go anywhere, Graeme. So long as it's a long-haul plane journey away from here.'

'Moll . . .'

'We've all suffered enough,' I continue emphatically. 'I'm no psychologist but I don't think you've ever got over what happened with your mum, or your dad, come to that. Take yourself off to a beach somewhere far away, heal yourself, recover. Find a new therapist. Learn to surf, learn a language, learn to love yourself. Do whatever it takes, for as long as you need. Can you do that for me?'

There is a long pause.

'No,' he says eventually. 'I'd love to go, Moll, but . . . I can't afford a plane ticket right now.'

'I know. But I found out yesterday I'm getting a pay-out from Spark.'

In response to correspondence from my solicitor setting out my right to make a claim for unfair dismissal – based on Spark's lack of fair processes and the disproportionate penalty they inflicted on me – Paul has agreed to make a small payout. They're running on a shoestring, they don't even have an HR department and they can't afford a legal battle, so they've offered to settle instead of fight me in court. It's not much, but it's enough.

'That's great news, Moll,' Graeme says encouragingly.

'The money's yours,' I tell him. 'It's a few thousand pounds – enough to buy you a plane ticket and get you started.'

'Molly, don't be insane. I can't take that money from you.'

'Yes, you can. I *need* you to do this, Graeme. Take the money, book your plane ticket, come back feeling like a brand-new person and by then . . . I might be able to look you in the eye again.'

He exhales. 'Molly, before his accident, Alex lent me money. I don't know if he ever told you –'

'It doesn't matter,' I say, cutting him off. 'Please just take this, Graeme. I need time to get over this too.'

'But . . . I can't leave you to cope on your own.'

I take a breath, tell him about my new job at the agency – all confirmed in writing this week – and about moving in with Mum and Dad. Yes, it'll be a big change – especially for Alex – and there'll be bumps along the road, but . . . we can do this. I know we can. But if Graeme's living in London at the same time as we are, Alex will want to see him all the time. And I can't do that right now. I need space. And so does Graeme.

Between them, Eve and Val are going to keep an eye on the cottage, until we're in a position to finish the renovations.

I'm not doing any of this for Graeme. I'm doing it for Alex. Because I married Alex, and I love him, and I want to get through this. I *want* to. When I look back at how far we've come over the past three-and-a-bit years, I feel . . . proud. Proud we've made it this far. And I'm not going to let anything derail us now.

'What are you going to tell Alex, when he asks where I've gone?' Graeme says now.

'I'm not,' I say. 'As soon as that money comes through,

you're going to tell him you've decided to go away for a while, and then you're going to tell him whatever you need to, to make him feel okay about that.'

'Okay.' There is a long pause. 'I can do that.'

'So we're agreed.'

He takes a deep breath. 'Molly?'

'Yes?'

'I just wanted to say . . . thank you. For being a better person than me.'

'Not better,' I tell him, like always. 'Just different.'

'Alex was lucky to find you. You know . . . that night at Mike's place, I knew it wasn't me you wanted. I *knew* that, Moll. You were just looking for the Alex you'd lost.'

I shut my eyes, permit a couple of stray tears to fall.

'You're made for each other,' he says. 'I can see that now. How you've dealt with everything . . . there's no other girl for him, Moll. You're the one.'

I manage a smile through my tears. 'Come back feeling better, okay?'

'You know what? I'm just going to follow your lead and refuse to give up. I'm never going to stop believing that things can improve. Starting today.'

After he's hung up, I glance down at my phone, at my new lock screen. It's a selfie of me and Alex that he took the other day then messaged to me, completely unprompted. We weren't out to dinner, or dressed up for a night on the tiles, or anywhere special – we were only in the kitchen, and we both had flour all over our faces after a baking session got out of hand (and, for once, in a good way). It sums us up – mundane yet ridiculous, and occasionally, more able to laugh. We were at home, and we were happy.

Because life is no longer about who we were before. It's about who we are now.

I receive an email a few weeks later, the night before Alex and I move back to Clapham.

Subject: Plans

Hey Molly

Well, as you know, I've told Alex I'm going away, and it went well. So there you have it – I'm going.

The (very) basic itinerary is South East Asia and then Australia – for no other reason than Australia is about as far away from England as I can possibly go, and you said you needed space and time. So with me there, you should have it.

Again, thank you for the money. I'll repay you, of course. I don't know how you found it in your heart to be so generous – materially and emotionally – but like I've always said, you're a better person than me.

When I told you what happened between me and Alex that night, it could have gone any one of a million ways, and instead of doing what you probably would have liked to do, you considered Alex. Which is exactly why I should be pleased you married him in the first place.

I could leave you with some natty little tips about what I think you should do now, and who to call on if you need help, but you've already proved yourself to be streaks ahead of me in the life-competency stakes (not that you've ever needed to prove a thing). So I won't do that. What I will do, though, is wish you both luck with all the love I have. I don't know how long I'll be away for, but I'm going to take your advice and make it as long as I need.

So . . . be good, be okay, email me if I need to know anything. I can be on the first plane out of anywhere if you need me. You know what I mean.

Molly, I need to tell you one more thing. Your name was the last thing Alex said before he shut his eyes that night, just after he fell. You were his first and last thought after it happened. Even though he's not the brother I once knew, he's still Alex – and I know that, deep down, nothing has changed for him.

So there you have it. I won't be in touch again unless you need me, and perhaps this will give us both the space we need to move on to the next (hopefully brighter) phase of our lives.

Lastly, please delete this, and text me when you have. I need to go away knowing this is the start of a clean slate for all of us.

Thank you, from the bottom of my very dysfunctional heart,

G

27

Alex – 28 March 2014

A few days after Nicola tells me about her festive fling with my twin brother, Graeme takes me by surprise and invites me to London for the weekend.

I'm not sure even as I arrive whether I'm intending to bring up the subject of him sleeping with my ex-girlfriend. When I first found out, I thought I might – but as the week has worn on, I've mellowed somewhat. It's almost as if – if I don't think about it too much – I can pretend the whole thing never actually happened.

I mean, how much harm did it do, really? Yes, it was a bit crappy of Graeme – given he's my twin and Nicola and I dated for six years, ending with her cheating on me – but it's over now. It's probably just another fling that Graeme has added to his ever-growing tally. It's already in the past – do I need to rake it up just for the sake of it?

Plus, knowing Nicola, the whole thing was probably instigated by her anyway, and Graeme – whose brain spends a fair amount of time in his trousers – no doubt went along with it in the absence of anything else being on offer at the time. He's been in such a bad place since

Dad died, and we all make weird decisions when we're hurting about something. He wasn't thinking rationally.

No. I'll leave the past in the past, and we'll only talk about Nicola if absolutely necessary. Like if he brings her up, for example. It's been so long since I've spent any quality time with him that I don't want to do anything that might ruin the weekend.

This could be the weekend that we finally turn the corner, I decide, as I raise my finger to the buzzer. This could be the weekend that everything changes for good.

Things are already looking quite positive – Graeme's finally opted to put down roots, of sorts. He's decided to rent rather than sofa-surf, in a ridiculously swanky block out east that I know to be mostly inhabited by stockbrokers.

'This must be costing you a fortune,' I remark as he shows me around. The place is littered with unnecessary gadgets, like an ice maker and a wine fridge and a coffee machine to rival anything you'd find in a high-end deli.

'Did someone a favour,' he says with a shrug.

I pause to examine the toaster, the one that apparently cost more than the price of my first car. 'What?' I laugh. 'You did someone a favour, and they gave you a flat?'

'No, just . . . I get mates' rates on the rent.'

I stare at him. 'Come on.'

'I'm being serious.'

'What kind of favour?'

Graeme just shrugs and moves away. 'There's a gym downstairs,' he throws over his shoulder. 'We should work out before dinner. Just like old times.'

I'm so used to Graeme being bitter about everything that it takes me a moment to realize that he's not being sarcastic.

'Nobody does mates' rates on rent,' I say, unable to drop it because there's something about this arrangement that sounds decidedly shady.

'Yeah they do, Alex,' Graeme sighs, like my life is so pedestrian and boring.

We're hovering dangerously close once more to the topic of mortgages and cottages, so I decide for the moment to back off.

I don't want anything to spoil this weekend.

'Alex. Alex.'

I open my eyes, blink into the darkness. Did I imagine that Graeme just spoke to me? I'm crashed out on his sofa – my bed for the weekend, since this place is a bachelor pad with only one bedroom that occupies the entire (get this) mezzanine floor.

We had a good time last night, working out in the gym and sharing a Thai takeaway with just one beer apiece since we were feeling virtuous (I admit I was slightly relieved when he stopped at one. I've been so worried in recent months that Graeme might be turning into our dad).

I told him that, last week, I added his name to the cottage title deeds – so, effectively, it's now half his. I'd been waiting for the right moment to let him know, having intended it as something of a grand gesture, something to show just how much he means to me, so when my invite to London came, I thought, *Perfect timing*. But when the moment arrived, it felt strangely flat. Perhaps, I reflected afterwards, Graeme simply wished Dad had left him half of the cottage in the first place.

Still, we had a good night – so good, in fact, that it was too late by the time I went to bed to call Molly and wish her goodnight. So I just texted her,

Great night, love you xxx

'What?' I say now, through a clag of sleep haze, half thinking I was imagining Graeme spoke, or that perhaps it was only an echo of the rain that's violently whipping the enormous warehouse-style window next to the staircase.

I blink a couple of times to aid processing, and as my eyes begin to adjust I check my watch. It's just gone two.

'Alex, I need a favour.'

Graeme's voice sounds closer now, so finally I sit up, turn to look at him. He's standing on the wide landing halfway up the staircase that leads to the mezzanine floor, bare-chested in tracksuit bottoms. His face is illuminated by the street lights outside the window, giving him a strange risen-from-the-dead appearance that unnerves me slightly.

'Sure, mate. Whatever you need. What's up?'

'I'm broke.'

I rub my eyes. 'I know.'

'No. I mean, I'm broke . . . and I owe people money.'

I stare at him. 'What people?'

'Does it matter?'

I get up then and walk over to the foot of the stair-case, almost breaking a toe in the half-light on a cast-iron coffee table that's a little too close to the bottom step. '*Ow*. Fuck.'

'Hate that thing.'

I stare up at him. 'Gray, who do you owe money to?'

'Just some people.'

My heart hammers. *Alcohol addiction. A drug habit. Dad's problems passing straight down the gene pool to Graeme.*

'For drugs?' I swallow, then say the word with the connotations I hate. 'Alcohol?'

'Please, mate,' is all he says.

'I've already lent you money, Gray.' And I have – over two grand so far, and all without telling Moll.

But Graeme's silence tells me it wasn't enough.

'Look, I'm not exactly flush myself,' I say.

'You?' he says softly, but like he's wounded, like I've said something really unkind. 'You're like . . . Mr Disposable Income.'

I stare at him, the rain thundering like applause for the new name he's thought up for me. I only realize then, possibly for the first time, how much I hate those names. *Golden Boy. Mr Moneybags. Mr Predictable.*

But I decide not to take issue with it right now. 'But

I *don't* have any disposable income, Gray. Everything's tied up in the cottage and the renovation. I haven't had a meal out with Molly for months. We agreed not to buy each other birthday presents this year. She's been trekking back and forward to London for work . . .' I trail off, because I know that from Graeme's perspective, these probably seem like pretty minor problems. I only just resist the urge to remind him I haven't told Molly about the money I've lent him, that I could have spent that two grand spoiling her rotten.

And then it occurs to me. 'That's why you invited me down this weekend, isn't it? You didn't want to see me, or spend time with me. You wanted money.' I feel so wounded, so idiotic and gullible, I could almost cry.

Graeme doesn't reply.

Suddenly, I feel really furious. 'You know, Gray, you do shitty things and I let them slide because I love you, and now I'm thinking –'

'Shitty things?' he repeats. 'What do I ever do to you, other than let you get on with your perfect life?'

In an instant, I snap. 'How about sleeping with my ex-girlfriend?'

This stops him short, and it takes him a moment or two to recall how to brazen it out, which he does with eventual ease. He even shrugs. 'It was nothing. A fling. You don't even like her. *I* don't even like Nicola, for God's sake! It's over, it meant nothing.'

'Right. But you and me both know that exes are off-limits.'

Instead of looking chastened, Graeme lets slip a

loose laugh and shakes his head. 'Yeah? What about girls your brother really likes?'

I stare up at him. 'What?'

'Yeah. You did a shitty thing to me once too, Alex, and I let it slide because I love you. So you could say we're square.'

I know exactly what he's talking about. We skirted around the issue one night three years ago, when I first told him about me and Molly, but never since.

'You've always thought you were better than me,' he says now.

'You know that's not true.'

'Yeah, it is. Since Mum, you believed what everyone was telling you. That you were the good twin, and I was the bad one.'

'That is complete bollocks,' I insist angrily, 'and you know it. Nobody ever said that to me, and if they had I wouldn't have believed it.'

But it's as if I haven't even spoken. 'Better than me, and entitled.'

'Entitled to what?'

'Molly, for one. You thought *you* deserved Molly, not me. You thought you were better than me, the one-night-stand merchant. That I wasn't even *capable* of falling in love.'

'Gray,' I remind him, 'you went outside to call Rhiannon that night. And you were sleeping around so much back then . . .'

'So you thought you'd swoop in and save her from me? What a gent.'

'No. It wasn't like that. I told you – I bumped into her later. It was just chance.'

'Do you know what I thought, when I saw Molly at the bar that night?'

'No,' I say, because I'm not sure I want to.

'I thought she was incredible. And when I spoke to Rhi, I told her I'd met someone else.'

Slightly premature, I think but don't dare to say.

'Maybe Molly could have been the love of *my* life.'

'You thought that about every girl you met back then.'

'Okay, Alex. You just keep telling yourself that.'

I've stopped feeling cold now. Instead my skin is prickling with uncomfortable warmth. 'I mean, what are you saying – that you still like her?'

'Don't be bloody ridiculous,' he snaps.

'Then why the hell are we even having this conversation? What's the point?'

A pause expands between us like a cat stretching out before going in for the kill.

'You got everything,' he says. 'Dad's love, the cottage, Molly. And what have I got?'

I climb up to reach him then, face him in my boxers, both of us on the wide halfway landing of the staircase.

'Graeme, your name's on the cottage deeds now. We're square. And you *had* money, you had it when you sold your flat. You could be on the other side of the world right now, having the time of your life! But instead you've ended up here and blown it all on drugs and God knows what else, and still you want to blame me! *Still* it's my fault!'

'Well, if the cottage is half mine . . . I want to sell,' he says then.

'What?'

'I didn't want it to come to this, but . . . I want to sell it. I've changed my mind. I need the money now.'

'What? We can't, we can't sell it!'

'Yes, we can. We call an estate agent, and we sell it.'

'And Molly and I . . . we do what? Live where?'

But we both know this isn't about the practicalities of where any of us live. Outside, the rain hammers relentlessly as a ball of thunder rumbles back and forth somewhere high in the sky.

'Do what everyone else does and find somewhere to rent. Or use your half of the money and buy a flat!'

'Graeme, I'm not going to sell the cottage just so you can squander it all. I'm absolutely not going to destroy everything Molly and I have just so you can blow tens of thousands of –'

He interrupts me before I can finish. 'Well, you might not have a choice now, since I own half.'

'You'd do this to me?' I am quite literally stunned. 'I put your name on the deeds last week in good faith, and now you're quite happy to see Molly and me lose our home . . .'

Graeme's voice is dark and cold. 'So you'd put Molly before me?'

I regret the impulsive words that follow before they've even left my mouth. 'In a heartbeat.'

The flat fills with a silence so bitter I can almost taste it.

'I'm sorry,' I gasp, my eyes filling with tears. 'You know I didn't mean that, Gray. You're my brother, I love you . . .'

I take a step forward then, try to put my arms round him, but in reaction he gives me a sharp, bitter shove.

It sends me toppling backwards like a stone kicked from a cliff edge.

In the seconds before I pass out – as I crash-land on the floor below, my head splitting neatly open on the corner of the cast-iron coffee table – I feel two things. First, the sensation of fluid lurching violently inside my brain. I *feel* it, swirling somewhere around the back of my head. And then comes the pain – intense and un-relenting, unfurling like a flower being brutally awoken, dazzled into action by a blast of bright light.

I can't move, so I stay just where I am, helpless as the blood leaves my head, a merciless red river breaking its dam across Graeme's floorboards.

I think, if I was looking down on myself, it might look almost beautiful.

From somewhere high above me, I can hear the rain pounding, pounding against the untouchable roof of this vast apartment.

I hope Graeme helps me. I hope he forgets we've had a fight, because after all, family is family, and that's what matters.

He starts to scream my name, and I can vaguely make out the shape of him squatting down next to me. Which is good, because knowing he's got this means I can finally shut my eyes.

Molly's name is the last thing I say as the blackness swallows me whole.

Then again, I might not have said it at all. The mind can play tricks on you like a true motherfucker.

Epilogue

Molly — eighteen months later

'Sold three,' Alex tells me when I ask, slinging his bag down on the counter.

'Three? That's fantastic!' Mum exclaims. 'Which ones?'

Alex tries to recall. 'Er . . . dunno.'

'It doesn't matter,' I say quickly, from where I am washing up. 'You did incredibly well.'

'He did,' Dad says, coming in behind Alex. 'Chatting away, weren't you? Oh, and what was the best bit?'

Alex looks blank, then shrugs.

'He got another commission!'

'Alex, that's fantastic!' I rush over to him, and even though my hands are soaked and sudsy, throw my arms round him. He stiffens for a moment before reciprocating, after which I hold him for just a little longer before letting him squirm away.

When we first got to London, Alex took to ambling around the local streets and parks with my dad. It was great for both of them — Dad for his overall health and fitness, Alex for clearing his mind. Occasionally he'd take his sketchbook with him, and with Dad's encouragement began to sketch buildings and landscapes, people he saw, street scenes. The two of them head out together pretty much every day around the same time as I leave for work, and it warms my heart to see them setting off side by side, rarely talking but enjoying their quiet companionship. Alex isn't under pressure to speak to anyone or particularly concentrate on anything, but if there's something on his mind, Dad's there. Plus, he likes the routine.

Once he'd built up a modest portfolio of sketches, Dad encouraged him to exhibit at the church. There was a small amount of interest in his work, and a few commissions started trickling in, at first from Dad's friends and acquaintances but eventually from people we'd never met before. Then the pair of them began visiting the occasional craft fair, Alex got some business cards made up, Charlie helped him set up a website, and slowly, incrementally, he began to achieve some small successes. It doesn't bring in much, and it was never about the money, but the difference it has made to his self-esteem, skill development and wellbeing has been immeasurable.

Having Dad by his side for so many of his trips out has negated my fears about him coping in London too. Yes, he finds the traffic and the volume of people challenging, but that's offset by the fact that he has so much to occupy his mind. He and Dad have even joined a gym together, and they potter off there a couple of times a week to go swimming and use the treadmills. As Mum pointed out the other day, they're like an old married couple. It's just so sweet. My dad seems to emit the right kind of energy not to rile Alex up; it happens occasionally, of course, but Dad's a master at dealing with it – primarily because very little fazes him. Every day I feel grateful for the fact he's so mellow.

And if I was worried about Alex being isolated after moving here, I needn't have been. Charlie and Darren visit all the time – any excuse for a trip to the big smoke – and a fortnight ago Eve, Tom, Isla, George and baby Bea came to stay. Only last night Sarah, Phoebe and Craig (now newly engaged) joined us for a big family feast; Alex cooked fajitas (under Mum's expert guidance), which were a huge – if somewhat messy – success. Most weekends, Mum and Dad pop into the annexe for breakfast with us – pancakes, cooked by Alex, drowned in maple syrup and butter. We're all in agreement that they taste even better than they used to. Next on Alex's list of culinary challenges is home-made croissants, just for Dad.

According to Eve, Nicola packed up and left Norfolk for good a few weeks after we did. Rumour has it she's moved to America to try and make it big in celebrity personal training; there was even talk of a contract on a big-budget film set. I can't say I was sorry to hear she'd gone, or even that I wished her well – some things my goodwill just can't stretch to.

Alex and I are still doing up the cottage bit by bit, and we've finally completed enough rooms to enable us to get Kevin's stuff out of storage and back into the house, which has freed up a surprising amount of extra cash for me each month.

Mum and Dad started work on the annexe before we moved back, so in the end we only had to spend a couple of months living on the top floor of the main house while the work was finished. We helped with the decorating, and Alex even suggested a picture he drew of the two of us should take pride of place on the living-room wall.

It's small – just a bedroom, kitchen, living room and bathroom – and it took a while for Alex to get used to it, but we also have a curious sensation of space, since Mum and Dad's garden is so large and well-maintained, and the door to their house is always open. It's somewhere for him (or me) to run to if things get heated, which was one of my main concerns before we moved.

Today, for example, didn't start out too well. We fought fiercely over a glass in the kitchen that Alex smashed last night then neglected to clear up; my feet are still stinging, oozing blood from where I stepped on stray shards. And only last week he grabbed me too hard by the arm, making a purple bruise bloom under the skin. His volatility still scares me, so I have finally, after many months of cajoling, persuaded him to return to a neuropsychologist once a week. His unpredictability remains and always will, but with the psychologist's help I am far more able to roll with it. I'm even managing to pay for it myself, thanks to the money coming in from my new (old) job. And with the help of my new GP, I was able to find my own counsellor, as well as a weekly local carers' group – both a huge support.

Working back at the agency has felt like a dream. I look forward to going, I enjoy being there, and I love the work, people and environment even more than I did before, if that's possible. Our disposable income has rocketed, and I even get to enjoy free lattes while I work. I make the most of every lunch hour, idly trawling the shops, rediscovering London, making small thoughtful purchases for Alex that I know he'll like – a new polo shirt (still an obsession), a new paintbrush, a sketchpad when his is getting full.

One of the best things about working back at the agency is that, against all odds, I still get to work with Dave. Sarah recruited again soon after I joined, and since Dave was dating someone new by this point who fortuitously enough hailed from London, I was able to recommend him. So we now work together once more. He visits Alex and me often, and has taken to trawling garden centres with my mum on Sunday afternoons to stock up on pot plants for his balcony garden, which Alex inexplicably finds to be hilarious.

So for most of the working week I get to pretend that my life is no different to anyone else's, and although evenings and weekends can still be a struggle, I am far better equipped to deal with them now. I have options, room to breathe, hope for the future.

We're even going on holiday in a couple of weeks, the four of us. After an unexpectedly successful long weekend in France earlier this year, Alex read about a place in the Maldives called the Sea of Stars that he's now fixated on visiting. On moonless nights, plankton in the ocean reacts to oxygen, causing biolumines- cence, which makes the water glow. Mum and Dad have holidayed a little closer to home in the years since their retirement, so our long-haul trip is big news among their friends and the church community. It seems like half of Clapham might be turning up at the airport to see us off.

So maybe that long-held dream to start a new life abroad isn't completely dead. We've relocated to London, after all, which may as well have been a foreign country to Alex when we first made the move.

I'll always miss my old Alex, the husband I never got the chance to say goodbye to, but I was wrong to assume I knew what was best for him. Because the point is that I never even really asked, and I'm so glad I finally did. The thing about Alex is, no matter what happens, he always has the capacity to surprise. And whether that's in a good way or a bad, I never really know what's round the corner. Yes, our marriage has been put under the most unbelievable strain since his accident – but it's also been something of an adventure, and that's what I'm determined to look forward to in all the years we have ahead of us.

And Graeme? We've heard hardly anything. Three postcards, and the occasional email to Alex. He steers clear of social media, which is wise, given Alex would probably never be off it if he knew his brother was only a click away. He didn't adapt as well as I'd initially hoped to Graeme taking off, but ultimately, I knew it was best for all of us.

On occasion, when things have been stressful with Alex, I have wavered over emailing Graeme and asking him to jump on the first plane out of wherever he is, but I have always managed to resist, and now I'm glad I have. I was right about needing space: I'm not sure what would have happened to us all, had we not had the opportunity to breathe.

I never told Mum or Dad what Graeme had told me. I never told anyone other than Eve. I knew that if I did, we'd never have the fresh start we all so urgently needed.

'Graeme's back,' Mum says to me one evening about a week before our holiday, when I get home from work.

'What?'

'He's out there, with Alex.' She nods towards the garden. 'Brilliant, isn't it? He's back.'

I dart across to the patio door, and there he is, just like that – sitting at the end of the lawn, head thrown back and eyes shut, drinking in the last of the daylight while Alex chatters away next to him.

On seeing Alex I smile, because he's wearing his jacket again – the one he lent me on the very first night we met. I unearthed it from its hiding place when we moved in, and he's barely had it off his back since.

He remembered, you see. He remembered lending it to me, that I took it home with me in a black cab.

When I handed it back, it was like I was presenting him with a tiny part of his old self.

I leave them to it for the next couple of hours until I see Alex head back inside the annexe, presumably to go to bed. So I make my way cautiously down the length of Mum's lawn to the bottom of the garden.

It is dark now, and all the stars are out. I think about Kevin, about the constellations that he loved, and Alex's theory that he is up there somewhere hand in hand with Julia, looking down on us both.

Graeme only raises his head at the last moment, and when he does, he makes a sharp intake of breath.

'Alex told me,' he says. 'Congratulations.'

I am six months pregnant. So his timing is, in many ways, ideal.

'How are you?' I ask him, smiling.

'I'm . . . I'm pretty great, Moll.' He nods. 'Yeah — pretty great.'

And he looks it too — bronzed, slimmer, healthier. And, crucially, happier.

'Tell me everything,' I say, sitting down next to him on Alex's empty chair.

So he does. He tells me all about his travels (amazing) and his work (selling scuba-diving lessons on the other side of the world). He says he's been in regular therapy for close to six months now, that he feels at peace for possibly the first time in his life.

'So how long are you staying?' I ask as we gaze back up the garden towards the house, so cosy now with all the lights on. It really does look like home.

'Three weeks,' he says. 'Though I understand my timing's terrible. Alex was telling me you're all off on the trip of a lifetime.'

'The Maldives,' I say. 'Did he tell you about the Sea of Stars?'

He smiles. 'Oh yes.'

'We wanted to go before . . . well, you know.' I glance down at the round ball of my belly.

'So I'm really going to be an uncle. That's amazing.'

I look across at him. 'I'd be lying if I said I wasn't nervous, but I feel like with Mum and Dad now . . . there's four of us taking on the world, not two.'

'Soon to be . . .' He hesitates. 'Wait, did it skip a generation?'

I smile. 'Absolutely. Only one little Frazer in here.'

Graeme smiles back. 'That's good. I've heard twins can be trouble.'

We sit companionably for a few minutes more, allowing the darkness to finally enclose us. Then Graeme says, 'Thank you, Moll. For giving me my life back.'

'That's okay,' I tell him. 'I didn't want to lose you both.'

'You know, I've met someone. Katherine. While I was scuba diving. Actually, she was my instructor.'

I turn to him. 'Graeme, that's amazing!'

He nods, sliding a smile my way that looks almost bashful. 'Yeah, it is. *She* is. Anyway, I wanted to tell you in person. I've already told Alex.'

'Tell me what?'

'We're getting married this Christmas. And . . . we've got plans to move back home soon too. Not to London – we're thinking about the south coast, where she's from.'

I smile, genuinely thrilled for him. 'Oh, Graeme. That's fantastic. Congratulations.'

'Thank you. You know, Moll – for the first time in a

long while, I'm really starting to think . . . that everything might be okay.'

We sit there together for a few moments in contented silence, searching the sky for stars. And then I rest both my hands on my belly, the belly that's cradling mine and Alex's baby daughter. We're naming her Julia, after Alex's mum.

'Actually, Graeme, I think it already is.'

Acknowledgements

I would like to thank my wonderful agent, Rebecca Ritchie, for all your help, support and encouragement. Thanks also to my editor Eve Hall, for your never-ending enthusiasm and invaluable creative input. And to Kimberley Atkins, for believing in me and this story from the outset. Many thanks as well to Karen Whitlock, Sophie Elletson, the whole team at Michael Joseph and everybody at Curtis Brown.

I am indebted to the following people and organizations who were kind enough to share their professional and personal experiences with me while I was researching this book. I will be for ever grateful; thank you all for your advice, openness and generosity. In no particular order: Dudley Garner, Linda Atterton, Deb Troops of Headsmatter, Joshua Troops, and Charlotte Fox of Occupational Therapy Norfolk. The charity Headway has also been a hugely helpful source of information; I would especially like to thank Kathy Bullock and the clients of Headway Cambridgeshire for being so open and making me feel so welcome. Any errors, omissions or inaccuracies with regard to medical and related details are entirely my own.

Lastly, thank you to my family, friends and Mark, for everlasting love and support.

Discussion Questions

1. Compromise is a part of marriage. Discuss the sacrifices that Molly and Alex made for each other. Were they equal in this? Are some sacrifices just too large to make?

2. Graeme is incensed that his brother is dating a girl that he spoke to first and Alex is furious when he discovers that Graeme has slept with Nicola. Did they both act badly? Are certain people 'off-limits' and why?

3. Graeme has feelings for his brother's wife. What is the best way forward in this situation? Honesty or secrecy?

4. The man that Molly married has changed into somebody new. Do you think she is obligated to stay with Alex? What would you think of her if she left him?

5. Even before the accident Molly and Alex have different ideas about their future. How important is this in a long-term relationship? Was it a mistake for them to get married so quickly or is love all that matters?

6. Molly tries to cope with Alex alone in their home and understandably runs into difficulties. Do you think that Molly took the best course of action? What other paths could she have taken?

7. Graeme believes that his father partly held him responsible for his mother's death. How guilty should he feel? How much is a child ever to blame when their actions result in tragedy?

8. In their father's will, the cottage was left solely to Alex. What is the best way forward in this situation? Do you think Alex dealt with it correctly?

9. Molly's life doesn't turn out like she expected it to. Do people know what they want in life? How much does the gap between what you think you want and how things end up relate to happiness?

10. Molly comes from a wealthy, loving family and has parents who are always present and willing to help. Alex and Graeme come from a home of tragedy, sadness and alcoholism. How do their backgrounds affect them as people?

11. Friends and family are eager to lend Molly and Alex a hand or listening ear. Do they always do this entirely honourably or does self-interest come into play? Does anyone ever act purely out of a desire to help?

12. Nicola is a constant, and unwelcome, presence in Molly's life. How does this affect her relationship with Alex? Do you think Alex should have acted differently where his ex was concerned?

13. Should Graeme have told Molly the truth about his part in Alex's accident? Should he have told the police? Would this have caused more harm than good?

14. Did you forgive Graeme at the end of the novel? How do you feel about the way Molly acted towards him?

15. The author has chosen to tell this story using both Molly and Alex's voices, each looking at a different time in their relationship. How does this affect how you feel towards the characters? Why hasn't she chosen to include Graeme's voice and how does this change your feelings towards him?

He just wanted a decent book to read ...

Not too much to ask, is it? It was in 1935 when Allen Lane, Managing
Director of Bodley Head Publishers, stood on a platform at Exeter railway
station looking for something good to read on his journey back to London.
His choice was limited to popular magazines and poor-quality paperbacks –
the same choice faced every day by the vast majority of readers, few of
whom could afford hardbacks. Lane's disappointment and subsequent anger
at the range of books generally available led him to found a company – and
change the world.

*'We believed in the existence in this country of a vast reading public for intelligent
books at a low price, and staked everything on it'*
Sir Allen Lane, 1902–1970, founder of Penguin Books

The quality paperback had arrived – and not just in bookshops. Lane was
adamant that his Penguins should appear in chain stores and tobacconists,
and should cost no more than a packet of cigarettes.

Reading habits (and cigarette prices) have changed since 1935, but
Penguin still believes in publishing the best books for everybody to
enjoy. We still believe that good design costs no more than bad design,
and we still believe that quality books published passionately and responsibly
make the world a better place.

So wherever you see the little bird – whether it's on a piece of
prize-winning literary fiction or a celebrity autobiography, political tour
de force or historical masterpiece, a serial-killer thriller, reference book,
world classic or a piece of pure escapism – you can bet that it represents
the very best that the genre has to offer.

Whatever you like to read – trust Penguin.